POVERTY OF THE MIND

My humble beginnings

WINE KELLY

Copyright © 2023 Wine Kelly

ISBN 979-8-98752-221-9 (paperback)
ISBN 979-8-98752-222-6 (hardcover)
ISBN 979-8-9875222-0-2 (ebook)

All rights reserved. No part of this book may be reproduced, stored, or transmitted by any means—whether auditory, graphic, mechanical, or electronic—without written permission of both publisher and author, except in the case of brief excerpts used in critical articles and reviews. Unauthorized reproduction of any part of this work is illegal and is punishable by law.

ACKNOWLEDGMENT

Writing a book Is harder than 1 thought and more rewarding than I could have ever imagined. None of this would have been possible without my best friend, David Hackman and her beloved daughters Ekua and Adjoa Hackman without which I would probably still be trying to figure out how to publish a book, He just saw a friend hungry to learn, hungry to grow, and hungry to succeed in business. He never stopped me; he only encouraged me. That Is true friendship.

I'm eternally grateful to my mom Madam Adel, who took care of me, traded on the scorching sun to put food on the table, taught me discipline, tough love, manners, respect, and so much more that has helped me succeed in life. I truly have no idea where I'd be if she hadn't given me a roof over my head.

To Miss Melinder Tyndall who proofread and encouraged me.

Writing a book about the story of your life is a surreal process. I'm forever indebted to Zoey Kelly For her keen insight, and ongoing support in bringing my stories to life. It is because of her efforts and encouragement that I have a legacy to pass on to my children.

To everyone at Guangzhou, Sasha Static Company, Ltd who enables me to be the CEO of a company that I'm honored to be a part of, thank you for letting me serve, for being a part of our amazing company, and for showing up every day and helping more. Finally, to all those who have been a part of my getting there: JingPing (Apple) the principal of Lingnan kindergarten; China. Dane Angels of

MY HUMBLE BEGINNINGS

Melbourne Australia, Bright Sewor United States, California. Dasha Umnova, Russia. Annie Jiang, Kris Li. Haseeb Khan, Pakistan

I would like to thank God for letting me through all the difficulties.

PROLOGUE

POVERTY OF MIND

When you hear the word poverty, what usually comes to mind are the poor starving orphans of Africa. You think of the child miner in Sierra Leone who must work just to earn a pittance to buy their daily rations. Most people live with limits, most of them self-imposed. They are stuck in a trap, blinded by the possibilities of life. I call this mental poverty: a dearth of willingness, inspiration, and ability to dream, or dare to think. They believe that there is no way to climb the ladder of success. People are conditioned to believe in the negative over the positive, especially when it comes to their circumstances. They are mentally trapped in the childhood environment they were raised in addition to their outer trappings while ignoring their accomplishments.

I would not have gotten here if I believed that a carpenter's trade and a small workshop were the limit of all that I could attain. Working my way out of that maze was a nightmare. Everywhere I turned, there was a wall I had to face. There were school fees and money I gave Mandy and her family. I wanted to lift myself out of the dark, so I decided to raise my personal value. I achieved this by getting an education in the form of a university degree. Most significantly, I leveraged the trust people of those around me. For example, people would give me a job, or they bought what I sold simply because they trusted in me and my products.

The process was insane. I had to devote hours and hours of my personal time and invest my own money before others would risk

MY HUMBLE BEGINNINGS

putting their trust in me. I know from first-hand experience that a university degree was not a secure path to success or wealth. I had seen too many friends who earned a university degree and ended up selling snacks on the roadside out of necessity. Aside from that, I have also hired many folks who had no degree but instead, accumulated the experience and the skills to go far. In the latter case, trust was the deciding factor. This relates to peer revies and previous employer reviews.

In addition to trust, excellence is key. "I repay your trust with excellence." "I work harder than all the other possible candidates combined to help you achieve your goals." That was how I was able to rise to the top. Trust speeds up the level of success you are able to achieve.. Trust *can* lift you up from poverty.

Money will come and money will go. Mandy and Emily both taught me that. Integrity and honour are the best assets you can have. In business, people want to gain a sense of the kind of person you are. This is more important than money. As I accrued "trust" the walls around me started falling away. Money flowed in as a natural consequence of proven competence. I could not have been successful without these basic principles.

CHAPTER ONE

GUANGZHOU

Gated housing estate.

My feet hit the park's jogging track to the rhythm of Eminem's anthem. IN...OUT...IN...OUT. Breathe. Remember to breathe properly. My nightmares still chased me. However, by running, perhaps I could outpace them. In the shrouded silence, I seemed to be the only creature alive. The streetlamps washed the world into a monotone of greys and browns within the gloom of darkness. Up ahead, the willow trees slowly swayed into view. *Breathe.* I forced myself to breathe properly. Breath control was the key to running. *Good, only two more laps.* I picked up my pace, forcing my limbs to move while Eminem spurred me on. The houses were shuttered and dark in the dawning moments. In this hour, only ghosts and fools were awake. *Perhaps I am the fool*, I mused.

As dawn crept up on the world, it brought with it birdsong and life. Lights flicked on in the homes of my hardworking neighbors. I felt like a gremlin was sitting in my head whispering evil thoughts as I looped steadily around the park, counting off the landmarks. There was the dinosaur kids' playground. Patriotic posters announcing the Beijing summer Olympics were plastered all over the place. The breakfast stalls that had been set up in the center were doing brisk trades. I passed the old rice noodle couple, who called out a friendly greeting. I smiled and waved back indicating that I was all set. After the melamine scandal that had broken recently; I figured it paid to be wary of eating food from sources I could not trace.

MY HUMBLE BEGINNINGS

The stand of willow trees hove into view and finally I could stop. *Good, I was getting my life back on track.*

Slowing down into my cool down walk, I flicked my iPod off and put away Eminem. I winced as the whine of a loudspeaker cut through my reverie. Up ahead, a row of spry Aunties were setting up their usual morning calisthenics. I nodded to them politely and kept walking. At least this time, none of them wanted to take my picture. *Good.* They had gotten used to me. Two good omens in one day and it was barely morning. I eased into my cool down, putting my body through its paces properly. Just then, a burst of noise assaulted my ears, cutting through my being. The aunties were blasting an old canto pop song and and transitioned to line dancing. They were a fixture at the park, gathering twice daily to dance and to gossip. This meant that I needed to go, or I would be late.

Twenty minutes later, I was in front of my apartment, fumbling with the keys and juggling a bag of hot food for Anne, my nanny.

The day was going to be a scorcher. It was barely morning and already the air was turning muggy. The keys went into the catchall by the entryway and the food was on the kitchen table.

When I entered, I noticed a crayon drawing was taped to the fridge, and sticky fingerprints marked its surface. I tracked the prints across the kitchen out to the living room. My apartment was pristine before I left for my morning jog. Now, it looked like a toy store suffered a bout of explosive diarrhea. A sticky substance decorated my floors and carpet. As I breathed, I could smell raspberry jam, together with her favourite orange marmalade. Well pixie, that's all the jam you're getting until next month.

Just what had the pixie gotten her grubby mitts upon? I did not keep any sort of paint in the apartment, but every surface below three feet displayed a bright blue handprint of some sort. I zeroed in on the coffee table. All four sides were blocked off with pillows.

***

Ahhh. The Pixie was awake and had escaped confinement. I could feel the beginnings of a tension headache. That gremlin had morphed into a demon.

"Uncle Wine!" The pixie in question stuck her head out. "You're back!" She exclaimed while pushing back her short bangs. She was cute as a button with a killer smile, fair skin, and the promise of beauty. She took after her mother. Her intelligence was something she inherited from both of us. The ability to get in and out of trouble, was definitely something that only came from me, according to Mama.

"Morning child!" I picked my daughter up and gave her a quick hug. Huh, they never tell you that children can function as a keep away charm for stress. Eau de child: one part sweat, one part you, one-part jam. I set my child down. The nanny would soon to get her day started.

"Sasha, where is Anne?" I asked. The place looked like a Jackson Pollock painting in jam. *How much jam can one jar hold?* I massaged my forehead. I wish someone had dumped their dog on me instead. It would have been less work with less mess.

Sasha crawled out from under the table, dragging a jam-stained bear behind her.

"Anne's not here yet. Where did you go Uncle Wine?" My offspring regarded me with guileless eyes. Fair with elegant features, she knew how to use her wiles despite being barely five. I sighed internally, she was my child alright. The apple didn't fall far from this tree.

MY HUMBLE BEGINNINGS

"Jogging in the park, Sasha." I gingerly patted her on the head and informed her with a stern tone, "I need you to clean this up before Anne gets here Sasha. We talked about this. You know the rules. No TV, no sweets until you do. If it's still here when Anne gets here, all these toys are going away. Do not forget to clean the floors." Sasha, the pixie, opened her mouth. Forestalling her, I said "No whining. If I hear a peep, Sasha, I'm throwing them out." She shut her mouth and set to tidying up. Clever child. She had my brains for sure.

The third good omen of the morning: The pixie was being obedient. I left her to it. Anne, the Nanny, would deal with her when she arrived. I needed to get to the office. I followed the trail of pixie-sized handprints down the hallway to my bedroom door with growing unease. It was unlocked.

For my fourth omen: Lord please let my shoe closet be untouched.

Stepping inside, my wishes were granted. I heaved an imperceptible sigh of relief. My room was pristine, save for the twisted bits of metal and wood that was my bedside table and lamp. Night terrors could drive a man to destruction. I shoved the wreckage into the corner of the room - Not today. I needed to get to work.

HUSTLE

CHEWING THE FAT

Bill's restaurant was empty save for a group of businessmen in suits having a three-martini lunch in the corner. I was sitting at the bar enjoying a rare period of quiet after the meeting with Mr. Chen. Bill brought over my namesake: *Tsingtao*; a can of locally brewed beer.

"So Wine, you've found the building yet?" Bill asked as he cracked open his can.

"Yes, renovations begin next week. Nalia is compiling a list of short-listed teacher candidates."

Bill drawled, "Yeah mate, finding qualified teachers can be tough. Many expats come to teach English as it pays better than back home. It can be a face game at times with lots of unqualified folks doing it part-time."

I slugged back a shot. "Uh huh, too many are doing it to collect a paycheck. Not all of them care. Even with a degree, you can't guarantee quality."

Bill raised me a toast "Huh. Yeah, I remember back in the days, the headmaster of the school would just hand us the flashcards and tell us to simply run sing-alongs. Remember when we had to revamp the system? What a headache it was!"

Over in the corner, a group of rowdy businessmen were celebrating, toasting each other in boisterous tones. "YUM BAI!" echoed throughout the room.

I grinned at Bill in a cynical manner. "Yeah, those were the days. We managed by the skin of our teeth! Good times though!"

Bill snorted, "Ha! Long hours, poor working conditions, and red tape everywhere. No regrets though." Bill frowned and snapped his fingers. "Our school. My friend, our potential headmaster, has begun building the curriculum. She says she'll send you a proposal for a list of materials and equipment needs. She has a few friends to recommend for the post of a teacher."

I clapped bills shoulder. "Excellent. Have her forward everything to Nalia. She is looking after the purchasing. I wager the project can be done in six months or so: by Christmas. We can begin accepting students with a January intake."

MY HUMBLE BEGINNINGS

Bill high-fived me with a grin. "I have students lined up already."

He signaled Teddy, who began escorting the gaggle of tipsy businessmen out one by one. Two of them peeled off from the group and sat by the bar next to us.

"Hallo! Ching Dao! I didn't expect to see you here" spoke a ruddy, well-dressed man in a thick Cantonese accent. "How are you? Have you eaten yet?" I noticed he had a pair of generic leather loafers on his feet.

I stood and shook his hand. "Mr. Hong, how curious, didn't see you there. Thank you, thank you. I've eaten already. I just finished up a lunch meeting. Who's your friend?" I turned to Bill.

"Ah, this is Bill Murray, he's my good friend and the owner of the bar."

Mr. Hong smiled and turned to introduce the other gentleman. "Ah, this is Lee Wei. He's the CEO of Phoenix Electronics." This gentleman seemed rather quiet and reserved. He merely nodded and offered a polite how do you do to me. Hong patted Lee Wei on the back.

"This is Ching Dao. He's from Ghana and a good colleague of mine. He helped my cousin secure that contract we needed urgently. He does good work. Finds what you need when it can't be found."

I pretended to blush and joked, "Hong, such high flattery! Even my mother will be embarrassed." I shook Lee Wei's hand. Bowing, I offered him my business card and accepted one in return.

Bill stood up and tactfully excused himself. "Sorry mate, I need to go check up on the kitchens. Nice to meet you Mr. Hong, Mr. Lee." He flagged Teddy, "Can I get you two anything? How about a refill?" With that, he strode away.

With Teddy's unobtrusive presence serving us, I opened with, "What's the lucky occasion Mr. Hong?"

A jubilant Hong leaned in and replied in a confidential manner, "Haha! Ching Dao, we…" he indicated Lee Wei and himself. "…just closed a deal worth a million! I've just signed the S&P agreement on that apartment and bought a new Bentley in cash!"

"Wow! God's blessings on you both! Sounds interesting." I signaled to the waiter to keep our glasses filled. "This round's on me." I offered, to keep the flow of information flowing.

Mr. Lee shook his head slightly at Hong and reached out to tap his shoulder. Teddy chose this exact moment to ask in his discreet manner "Mr. Lee, may I refill your glass? We have a new variety on tap, would you like to try it?"

With Lee Wei prevented from interrupting; Hong whispered in furtive tones, "Oil my friend! Oil! It's very simple, we source from the middlemen from Russia or the Middle East. After all who wants to do business with the cloth heads? Then we find buyers in China. We all have the contacts. He grinned cheekily and tapped his nose. Right now, he looked nothing more than a caricature of a sly fox.

I chuckled "Sounds easy. In practice?" I prompted.

Looking alarmed, Lee Wei prepared to interrupt but Hong simply waved a hand at him. He turned to Lee Wei and spoke in Cantonese.

"This fellow here is very crafty. I've known him for many years now. I've never been cheated in the time I've known him. Many of our mutual acquaintances say so too." Lee Wei sighed and shrugged his thin shoulders. I waited patiently, as Hong spoke softly to Lee Wei. It would never do to hit the grass to startle the snake.

MY HUMBLE BEGINNINGS

We were interrupted by Teddy, our waiter. I mentally increased his tip by 20%, that was perfect timing.

"Mr. Wine, the head chef sends these appetizers over with compliments." Bill was an absolute genius when it came to hiring staff.

Distracted yet again and soothed by Hong's words, Lee Wei relented and spoke for the first time.

"My cousin's sister-in-law is acquainted with a man named Pavel. He's rather famous in this business. We formed a consortium and approached him. I know that the Chen group is looking to buy oil. Do you know them?"

I nodded and replied, "Do you mean, Chen Manufacturing?" Both men nodded in assent.

"Yes, old family clan based in Shanghai. They have factories in this city" Lee Wei added.

My eyes lit up. "Yes, I know the Chens. We became business partners in a few deals. In fact, I've just closed a deal with the youngest son of Old Mr. Chen. Not big, not small: steady money."

Mr. Lee smiled. "Yeah, the youngest son works as the foot soldier of the older brother, I hear he's the second wife's son"

I frowned, "Oh, I'm referring to Chen Song Han. The brother of the COO of Chen group. He's on the board of directors. I heard he was the son of the legal wife?" Concubinage had a long tradition and history in China. It was frowned upon in modern society by the CCP, but the ultra-rich wrote their own rules.

Hong interjected. "Correct, correct! That's the one. I hear he's dating a phoenix these days. The daughter of the Wen hospital director.

Distant cousins of the Chen's secondary branch through marriage I believe. A grandmother and an aunt married."

I froze and then forced my face into a smile. "Shi Wen?" I offered, greatly surprised. My chest felt like it had been stabbed with a knife. Covering for myself, I ate the appetizer without tasting and signaled Teddy for another round.

Lee Wei's face lit up. "Yes, that's the one." Turning garrulous under the influence of alcohol he continued, "Very good match. That's how I secured an introduction to the Chens." He rubbed his forehead and said, "The trick is watching the timing of the oil prices. I hear the Chen group wants oil for a project in China. So, we managed to convince Old Mr. Chen to take the risk, and we talked the Pavel into offering a discount in exchange for a yearlong contract."

Mr. Hong followed up with, "Good, Good! Old Mr. Chen wanted a guarantee from us. So, we needed to also put down some of our money. The oil business these days are very risky and uncertain. The other gentlemen you saw earlier, were minor officials from the trade ministry." Lee Wei nodded and threw this out, "The commission is 5%."

I rejoiced with them. "Gods Blessings! No wonder you two are celebrating."

I had to get in on this industry. Oil deals of this sort usually were lucrative because they were calculated in USD. I had been chasing this type of fish for a year or more. Lady Luck favored me today.

Lee Wei and Hong raised their glasses in good cheer. "Yes, yes" they said happily.

Hong cheered tipsily, "We are swimming in luck!" Lee Wei replied, "Never forget to offer the Monkey God his due! YUUUM BAAIII!" I yelled in unison while thinking furiously.

MY HUMBLE BEGINNINGS

"Fortune's blessings on you both!" I earnestly replied. Close to stone drunk by now, both had a little trouble standing up. They had consumed several pints of beer at the bar, not to mention the heavy drinking with their ministry companions they did all afternoon.

Sensing his cue, Teddy stepped forward to offer each gentleman a wet towel and lemon water.

My phone buzzed. It was Anne, my nanny and housekeeper, acquired at great expense and effort. She informed me that it was time to pick up Sasha, my daughter, from her play date. Both gentlemen were busy sobering themselves up and conducting a hushed conversation in Cantonese.

I stood up and excused myself. "Duty calls," I said waving my phone. "Do continue enjoying yourselves. The bill has been taken care of." I bowed slightly to the both of them.

Lee Wei turned away from Hong to say, "Eh! we're friends, no need to be polite!"

Mr. Hong echoed, "Yes, good friends!" They returned to their discussion.

I stood up and approached the cashier. I put down my credit card and told Teddy quietly, "Don't tell them about your XO or wine. Any beer they drink is on me." Teddy nodded and his eyes became crescent moons. He was jubilant at the ¥100 tip I slipped him. Teddy said, "Mr. Wine, your taxi is waiting downstairs."

INTERLUDE

Later, I sat in a taxi enjoying a quiet ride back to our apartment. It was also a rare chance for me to relax and spend some time with my daughter. The peace did not last long. A quick check of my phone yielded urgent messages, each from a different member of my team.

Then another from Anne, Sasha's governess, confirming that she was free to provide 24hr care next week. Following that was one from my assistant Nalia confirming the trip to Hong Kong.

I looked at my daughter sitting quietly next to me. This itself was unusual, however I think she was tired from her day at school. Her pixie face was scrunched up and her head drooped like a wilted flower. Staring out the window, I watched the world streak by.

It was odd to see how genetics played itself out through the generations. There was something of my sister and father in her.

GHANA

I was born in a one-room cob hut built by my father on a piece of land nobody wanted - next to the rubbish dump. My birth was celebrated, as was the tradition because I was a boy. I was one more mouth to feed in a family of eleven. We lived in the growing town of Ashaiman in the Greater Accra Region south of Ghana, located between the port city of Tema, and Accra, the capital city.

My parents named me Jolie, meaning *a son born on Monday*, joy of life and as my mother said, her "lover." I became the apple of her eye. My father was affectionately known about town, and in our family as "Uncle George." I never found out why. My mother was Madam Adel to everyone else.

Growing up was a joy for us younger children. The moment I began to walk, I'd follow my siblings into the hustle-bustle. In my mind, the rubbish-filled streets and the landfill was a treasure island filled with intriguing trinkets, waiting for our deft fingers to save them from the hands of other dwellers. We would scavenge wood planks from construction sites for our father to use about the house. Bricks were 'cars.' Plastic rubbish that you and I, would throw away today, would be turned into cups, plates, and other useful household goods.

MY HUMBLE BEGINNINGS

Mud was a fact of life. When it rained, the dirt-paved streets turned into rivers with sinkholes that left the unwary, stuck up to the knee in mud. We would wait and watch until the passerby cursing his luck, limped home, shoe-less. We often managed to scavenge Charley Woteys (flip flops) that kept us for a few weeks.

My siblings and I would track mud into the compound of our cob hut. When Uncle George returned home to the mess, he would pursue his lips without a word, line all the children in front of the hut and whip us for creating the mess. Mama would merely watch, stepping in only when she deemed enough is enough. We learned fast. There were two tricks: pouring sand over wet muddy feet or waiting till the mud dries, then using stones to rub it out. We all preferred the latter as it was less painful when scrubbing. The beatings stopped.

Life was simpler back then in Ashaiman and every day was an adventure for us younger ones. We spent our days envisioning countless excursions. Some days, we'd often wander off to Nii Ashai's home, the founder of the village in the 17th century, to climb the famous fruit tree. We loved sitting up in its branches, munching on sour fruit and watching the world go by. Until the elders caught us, and chased us away with a stick. Then we wandered off to the dump to play. Digging through the mountain of other people's trash was a scavenger hunt. We never knew what we would find.

The house built by Nii Ashai looked similar to my family home. His house is now a mini museum, properly gated with brick walls surrounding it, unlike my home. The elders sitting on rickety chairs, watching the traffic go bywould tell stories about how Nii Ashai would extended his cob house, fitting it with more rooms just as he grew accustomed to the lifestyle he had established. He started the village for the sole purpose of farming during the slack between the fishing season. It soon turned into a town when the main road running through the settlement became a main stopover for travelers to unwind.

POVERTY OF THE MIND

With only 4 miles from Tema, and 30 miles from Accra, young people moved to Ashaiman, started families and settled down. We all hoped for a better life. My parents were the same. They met and married each other in this town. Mama was always telling us, "God is watching over us" and "God has his own design for us."

Back then, prosperity was measured in food. If you could afford to eat three meals a day everyday, you were rich. Nobody we knew could. Any meal we ate was God sent. My childhood dreams revolved around food. Our daily meals consisted of gari (cassava shavings) and kakoor (fried plantain), with beans and cooked in palm nut oil. It was monotonous but hunger is the best seasoning. There was never enough to go around, but god willing, between her vegetable garden and her ingenuity, Mama somehow made enough to keep us alive and healthy. When we had more money, we had fish and two meals a day on festival days.

Mama was the breadwinner, yet Uncle George was the head of the family because he was the man, the husband, and our father. His word was law. Mama was our beating heart and the glue that held us together. No matter how tough times were, she was always positive and full of determination. God was her rock, and her shield, after my father of course. Her faith and her prayers kept her and by extension the rest of us going.

I didn't know what mama used to do before she had me, but she told us that she used to pick cocoa until the market crashed. Nobody was buying and the times were tough. We were lucky because Mama found work soon after in a chop bar as a cook. The owner was a relative of a close friend of hers. When I was born, she had to stop. Instead, she started her own businesses, first as a cooked food seller, then as a peddler. She hasn't stopped since.

Uncle George was a carpenter by trade and underpaid by his employer. He eventually became an independent contractor, but the timing was wrong. According to Mama, Ghana's economy deteri-

MY HUMBLE BEGINNINGS

orated when cocoa prices dropped. The economy worsened when President Nkrumah was overthrown by the military. The incoming leader inherited a country on the verge of bankruptcy. From Mama's account of past events, it seemed like Ghana's economy never recovered. Many people left Accra because the military chokehold and corruption was unbearable. People immigrated to cities around the capital, like Ashaiman and made a life here. Between the economic downturn, and the troubles. There was no work to be had, even for the desperate. Still, life was good for us. We learned to make do.

Uncle George was a moderately respected man in our community. In a city like Ashaiman, your business was everybody's business whether you liked it or not. It was near impossible to hide any funny business because sooner or later people would find out. My father was a man of few words, but he had sharp eyes and clever hands. Someone was always asking for his help in one matter or another such as asking him to carve a stool for this elder or that chief. They always went away satisfied. Despite the lack of work, Uncle George always had something each day to contribute to the family pot. I think that was why Mama was so fond of my father. Unlike most of the other uncles I knew, my father wasn't just another mouth to feed.

On days he was free, which was often, Uncle George could be seen puttering around our hut, mending fences, patching the roof, and stocking up on firewood. He claimed that our hut was the "sturdiest and the cleanest." This was quite a funny term to me as the room had a raised earthen floor and no matter how often Mama swept, it would always be sandy. Thus, we were not allowed inside, unless it was bedtime. We never minded anyway, as we cooked, ate, and played outdoors. My father had built us a small shed, and an earthen oven outside for Mama to use as our kitchen. We only went inside to sleep. Thus, we spent most of our time out and about town, finding ways to amuse ourselves and hustling for our next meal.

Our house was the only one in town with a white fence. It marked off our vegetable patch, one Uncle George was proud as a rooster of.

He always said that it reminded him of a picket fence he once saw in a picture. I later learned what a "picket fence" was when I travelled to America.

We shared a compound with a few other families. Between our house and the next, there was a half-built wall of mud bricks. I think Uncle George ran out of steam. Every time Mama came back from peddling, she would always compliment Uncle George on his hard work. I think she did this to raise his spirit.

Mama was usually lenient, except when you crossed her. We always had to be respectful, obedient, hard-working, and honest. There were rules we had to follow, and breaking one meant a scolding first. If we broke them again, we were given a severe beating. There was no third time. None of us wanted to find out, even George Junior, the unruly firstborn.

She told us, "Child, never forget: God watches us. Good or bad, everything you do or say, He will see."

Mama was a big believer in Jesus. Every Sunday before dawn, she would line up all eleven of her children, scrub us, then stuff us in our Sunday best, which was always carefully laundered in the river. We knew better than to protest, because Uncle George would sit on the stoop, savour his tea, and watch us.

It was a rule that Sunday was Mama's day and it had to be perfect. If we ruined it, we would get worse than a beating. So, we kept quiet and stayed obedient. Once we had our breakfast of tea, we would line up two by two behind our parents and began the walk to Church in procession. Each brother had younger child he was responsible for. As for me, I had to pay attention to David. Mama, proud and radiant, led the way. Uncle George's would hold her hand, and chaperone her all the way to church.

MY HUMBLE BEGINNINGS

Mama always kept my sisters close. She would clutch my elder sister, Janet's hand; while Janet held on to Gina, the baby sister. Like chicks after the mother hen. As the sky lightened, and we got closer to the church, we would see more attendees. Mama would be greeted by her church friends, ladies dressed in colourful wraps and bright kente skirts who would stop to compliment Mama on how well behaved her children were, and to catch up on the latest gossip. Uncle George would listen politely, nod and let Mama do the talking. Looking back, I don't think my father enjoyed church. He went because he wanted to make my mother happy.

Church was boring, but the music and the singing were fun. I made sure to pretend to sing by mouthing the words, to keep Mama happy. It was of the utmost importance that on Sunday, Mama stayed happy. What I liked best was watching all the different ladies elbow each other and whisper behind their hands, in between songs while the pastor wasn't looking. When any of us squirmed around too much, Uncle George would look over at the culprit, nothing more. That was enough to make sure that we behaved. I always looked forward to the session after church, where they offered snacks and tea. On feast days like Christmas and the Ashanti harvest festival, they would serve jollof rice, and fried chicken, sponsored by the richer members of the congregation. On those days, I made sure to behave. Fried chicken was worth any discomfort. We couldn't afford it. The closest we got to it were eggs. Eggs were still a birthday treat.

Mama always was happy after church. If Mama was happy, then so was Uncle George. We learned early in life to never make Mama mad. Mama had a stronger arm than Uncle George and he would always back her up. This meant that we got beaten twice, once for misbehaving by Mama and once more for disobeying by Uncle George.

I never knew where the rest of my brothers went after Church. My father would dismiss the whole pack of them with a stern nod and a curt admonition to return in time for Sunday dinner. David, who was just a few years older than me, was often tasked with babysitting us for the rest of the afternoon. He took his duties very seriously. I often earned numerous cuffs on the head as a reminder to behave. I never minded because that meant that my backside was saved a tanning from Uncle George. David never dared hit Gina, the true baby of the family, or Janet, my only other sister. Janet and Gina were a unit, and they protected each other. Janet had sharp elbows and hit back with extreme force when our parents were not looking. Gina was the apple of my mother's eye and could do no wrong. If either of them did not get you now, they got you later - without fail. Us boys learned early to never mess with them. In the words of George Junior "They be evil."

We often saw Mama and Uncle George disappearing into the sleeping area on Sundays even if it was still bright outside. Us younger ones, David, Janet, Gina and me, thought nothing of it and shot off to play. The local chop bar had a TV and a board game set. If we helped out, the owner, Uncle Agyenim, a friend of Uncle George, would feed us the leftovers and let us stay to watch TV or play board games during slow afternoons. If Uncle Agyenim shooed us away, David would lead us to the market, where we would spend the afternoon earning a few cendis running errands for the stall owners and their customers. When no one wanted our help, we would play hide and seek or try to scavenge a few wrinkled vegetables to take home to our mother.

The stall owners knew us on sight as Mama Adel's children, and trusted us as a result. We were taught quite painfully by Mama never to steal, no matter how hungry we were. She would say, "Child, trust is precious and stealing is a sin. We must not stain ourselves or the trust of others with sin. God seea you child." before she sent us off to fetch the switch that she would beat us with. Shaking and crying, we would dawdle over picking the right kind of switch. If we dawdled too long, we would be beaten twice as hard. Once done, Uncle George would scold us with, "No child of mine will be a thief" as he dragged us off to apologize to the person we stole from and offer up our labour in penance, or beat us again if it was refused. What hurt us more than the beatings, were the neighbours and other children assembling to watch the free show - our humiliation. After the first time, we never stole again.

I never needed a beating to learn this, instead, I watched my siblings get beaten. After I grew into short pants, I learned to be a clever child. It was a rare day when I went home empty-handed, and I would be a liar if I said that I never stole. I never got caught. I'm proud to say that those times I had to resort to stealing were less than the fingers on one hand throughout my childhood.

The pain and humiliation our parents inflicted upon us children made us honest. As a result, the traders trusted us and often helped by giving us produce that they could not sell and would not eat. They allowed us the opportunity to earn a few cendis by running errands for them and their customers. Sometimes, if they had any to spare, they fed us alongside their own children from the leftovers at their stalls. We never knew then how lucky we were. We feared the beatings but the lessons learned were priceless.

It served all of us well in later years. Trust is worth more than gold.

WORKING MAN

SINGLE FATHER BLUES

Let me start by saying that I have a great life. It didn't come easy as it wasn't handed to me, not one bit. I was lucky to be at the right place at the right time. Everything I dreamed of having as a child is now my reality. People underestimate the process of bringing your dreams to life. They romanticise the end process, the rags to riches story, and neglect the daily mundane toil it takes to get there. It is boring and oft-times tedious. That's where most people fail. I like to think, given my upbringing. I had mastered that.

POVERTY OF THE MIND

What they don't tell you is that while money looks like a problem solver, it is only leverage or a lubricant. There are some problems that money cannot solve. "Mo' money. Mo' problems" they say. My daughter was one of them. Nothing in my experience equipped me to deal with the logistics of caring for one energetic child. She was an octopus crossed with a cat. She knew how to behave well when asked, but if you turned your back she would be up on something, and into everything all at once. It was a nightmare.

Case in point: Today.

I scanned my living room in dismay. It sported its usual look of a toy genie rave party. There were toys up on the bookcase, which was taller than me. Craft supplies and glitter were all over the place. No amount of chiding of both the child and the Nanny seemed to make a difference. To make matters worse, a prospective client, Mr Han Lui, had moved up his dinner appointment to lunch, citing a last-minute change in flight plans. The cherry on the cake was that our Nanny, Anne, had taken this day off.

Han Lui was well connected with a circle of influence that stretched across the manufacturing industry. I wanted to sign him on as a client because my company dealt in sales and marketing for exports. We did a little bit of everything. If you needed to get the word out and sell your product, we were the ones to call. You could call us a cross between a buyer's agent and an arbitrage firm. What I was really after was his goodwill. The US market had melted down due to the subprime mortgage crisis. It had not yet hit China, but we would be feeling the effects soon.

I had two hours to feed my child, arrange childcare, sort myself out, and head to the meeting. Given the last-minute nature of the appointment, I had yet to arrange a suitable meeting place. I wanted nothing more than to return the Pixie to her mother. Perhaps the hospital would accept returns? Was there a five-year warranty on the Pixie? I sighed loudly and got straight to cleaning up. When I was done, the carpet was clear. I was in no danger of stepping on a stray toys now.

There was a suspicious silence I chose to ignore saturating the apartment. I could not see or hear my daughter. I merely prayed that damage and the mess was repairable. *Breathe!* I told myself. This is nothing more than a complicated logistics problem. I could solve this. I called Bill, my good friend and owner of the secret escape. It was a bar and restaurant, set on the top of some swanky high-rise in downtown Guangzhou, 15 minutes away from the offices I rented. He agreed. My usual terrace room was available. Bill would hold it for me at his usual rates. Network. Never underestimate the value of your network. One down. One more to go: Childcare.

The doorbell rang. *Must be the taobao food delivery.* Kicking a stray doll I missed out of the way, I opened the door to an over-friendly delivery man. *Huh, must be newly from the countryside.* I groused to myself. *They've rarely seen foreigners must less one with coffee coloured skin.*

"Sasha!" I called. "Time to eat. Come into the kitchen. I've ordered your favourite. Kimchi fried rice." Silence answered.

"Sasha! I'm going to eat it all" I scanned the living room and checked her bedroom. No pixie.

There was a scuffling and scraping coming from under the coffee table in the living room. I turned around to see Sasha wearing a ferocious scowl and glaring at me.

"Uncle Wine! You can't!" She told me tones of outrage. She was four and a half, nearing five and as smart as a whip.

"Come along then," I nodded towards the kitchen.

Sasha opened her mouth to protest. I silenced her with a look. It was the same one my father used on all eleven of us.

"Sasha," I explained patiently, "I have to leave for work soon." The pixie frowned and shuffled her feet. I could see the gears grinding in her head. "Would you rather spend this time in a good way or bad way?" I asked.

Sasha sighed and said in a small voice "Good."

I strolled towards the kitchen, "Go wash your hands. We should eat the food while it's hot. The chef worked hard to make this, we cannot waste his efforts." The pixie zoomed past me, sulks forgotten. One thing you could say about this child: she was a good eater. Anne joked that if you held your arm in front of Sasha while she was eating, there was a good chance it would be gone. I was inclined to agree.

Going through the pre-meal ritual of setting the food out and settling down took twice as long as it should. By the time we sat down to eat, an hour had gone by. It was now 11 am. I wanted to strangle my daughter, who by now had forgotten her tantrum and was busy shovelling food into her mouth. Children were the most finicky timewasting creatures.

My phone buzzed. It was James, my head of logistics informing me that the shipment for Mrs Fiona had come in. He wanted to know where to put it? I began to answer when the doorbell rang.

Outside, a middle-aged lady greeted me and introduced herself as "Mrs Luo." I stared at her for a full minute. She was well-groomed, dressed in a plain cotton blouse and tailored slacks. Her shoes were cheap rubber loafers. Practical and sturdy. She kept her composure and explained that she was here to interview for the position of Nanny and was available to work weekends only.

MY HUMBLE BEGINNINGS

"Come on in," I blurted into the awkward silence after her explanation. Mrs Luo smiled graciously at me and nodded, trailing after me into our living room. I cringed as she took in the mess. I only had time to deal with the toys.

Sasha zoomed out of the kitchen, came up to me and announced, "FINISHED!"

"Sasha don't yell." I chided her. The pixie ignored me in favour of scrutinizing the new arrival. "This is Aunty Luo. She will be looking after you today." The imp stuck her tongue out, and zoomed off, shrieking in laughter, to barricade herself in her room. *Ah. I don't have a choice, today Pixie you're stuck with her.*

Mrs Luo was too polite to say anything.

"She's a handful but she's a good child. I'm sorry about that," I explained.

Mrs Luo nodded. "Not a problem. Children are like that."

I shifted a doll out of the way and invited her to sit as I explained her duties. She needed to look after Sasha on the weekends and the nights when I had to be away. Food, and lodging would be provided, She could cook for herself and Sasha. I made a mental note to ask Anne to buy groceries, using the Taobao account I set up for her. I only kept kid-friendly foods in the apartment. Crackers, bread, and fruits. If she didn't want to stay the night, travel would be subsidised. She would have to be on call during the weekday, just in case Anne had an emergency and needed a day off.

The woman nodded. I noticed her curly hair never seemed to move. Her perm was set into place with copious amounts of hairspray.

My phone buzzed again. CRAP! James!

"Can you look after Sasha until 4pm today?" I asked. I was not letting a stranger stay in my apartment, not even one recommended by Nalia, my assistant.

Mrs Luo paused and spoke in shanghai accented Mandarin. "I have an appointment -"

I hastily added, "100 yuan. Food will be provided. I need someone to watch Sasha while I work, and I need to know if you and she will get along."

Mrs Luo pursed her thin lips, then nodded. "I will have to leave by before 5pm. I have an appointment later."

I hoped Sasha would take to her. I liked her stern attitude. The Pixie needed that. I did too. My personal life was a mess.

"We're going out together, I have a meeting to head to. Can you come along? We're heading towards the downtown district." She left to coax Sasha out of her room. She seemed to have the situation well in hand.

I had three new WeChat messages. James sent me a gentle reminder. I fired one back telling him to put it in the warehouse by the docks. He had an operating budget for a reason. We had several arrangements with different warehouse companies. We did have our own leased facility, but I found it easier to not have capital tied up in one asset. Land was expensive and as an "Lao wai" in China, it was difficult and risky to acquire land of this sort. We relied on leasing arrangements and the network of contacts we have built up in the region.

The second message was from Nalia informing belatedly that the Nanny interviews were scheduled for this weekend and the next.

The last was an official notification from the family courts confirming Wong Shi Wen had dissolved our marriage. The divorce was final.

MY HUMBLE BEGINNINGS

Sasha danced into the living room, dressed in a blue sundress and hat.

"Uncle Wine!" She screeched.

"Sasha, we don't yell inside the house. Use your inside voice." I scolded her absently.

"Sorry Uncle Wine!" She sounded contrite as she tugged on my hand. "Where are we going? Are we going to the zoo?"

"Oh… hmm…" I nodded absently. "Yes, the zoo. Later. I have to work first."

She bounced off to go play with her dolls. *I think I better turn the living room into her playroom.*

After a brisk shower, I stood in front of the bathroom mirror, taking deep breaths and trying to calm my nerves. My hands were shaking. Whether from anger or fear - I did not know. It could have been the extra strong cups of coffee I drank earlier. *I need to cut back.* I looked at myself in the eye. *Breath, just breath.* I told myself silently. You've made it, what else is there left to fear? Several slow minutes of deep breathing passed before I my hands stopped shaking. I had too much to do to fall apart now.

It still felt odd, even after a few months, to put on a bathrobe just to cross the hallway to my bedroom to dress. I needed sartorial perfection today. I felt that today was a good day for red. As I got dressed, I admired myself. Coffee coloured skin, broad nose, and almond eyes. I looked good.

GUANXI

POVERTY OF THE MIND

Han Lui smiled at me across the table. We were seated next to eat other. I could see Sasha and Mrs Luo playing a game involving stacking and removing blocks in the background.

"It's a pleasure to finally meet you Mr Wine. I've heard so much about you. Africa is a lovely place. I hope to visit someday." Mr Han said as we shook hands.

"Likewise! I'm happy to be here. What would you like to drink?" The young nubile waitress took our order and sashayed out of the room. I had to bring my child and her Nanny with me. I didn't know Mrs Luo well enough and it paid to be careful. I also had to be patient and allow Mr Han get to the point on his own.

"Mr Wine, I've heard good things about you. I will be blunt. I'm setting up a company in Ghana, I believe it is your hometown. I could use a reliable supplier with a proven supply pipeline. My factories manufacture many things, but not as well the components your company sources." Well, that was straight to the point.

Teddy ushered in a stream of waitresses, who poured tea for us and offered scented hand towels. Bill was a genius when it came to hiring staff. I nodded and waited for him to continue speaking.

Mr Han slid a sheet of paper across to me. "We need. Can you guarantee a steady supply?" I perused the list. We sourced these parts from factories in the province, and provided quality control.

"Yes, all but two" I said as I ran my finger down the list. "I must confess Mr Han, I was hoping to sign you up as a supplier." Han Lui smooth back his hair and took a sip of his tea.

"Good tea," he said.

Our food arrived, borne by a procession of nubile young waitresses with Teddy bringing up the rear. Plate after plate of food was laid out

MY HUMBLE BEGINNINGS

before us. I had ordered Mango salad, steak, and an eight-treasure seafood dish. A small whirlwind rushed past them, setting the procession askew as they fought to balance their trays. A tiny fist hit my thigh, and I looked down to see Sasha. She had escaped from next door.

"Sasha, you need to go back to Mrs Luo. Daddy is busy right now."

The imp kicked me in the shins and screeched, "NO! I DON'T LIKE HER" I could feel a headache coming on.

"Your daughter?" Han Lui asked.

My face burned from embarrassment. "Yes, she is" I replied.

"She looks a lot like you. She's lovely" Han Lui replied, as he made a face at Sasha. The pixie smiled at him with her gap-toothed smile.

I caught her before she could run over and place her sticky hands on my client.

"Could you give me a minute? I'm sorry, our usual Nanny was away" I apologised. I marched Sasha back to Mrs Luo who was just returning from the Toilet. "Mrs Luo, here is your charge," I remarked pointedly. "Please look after her well." Mrs Luo blushed a bright red, and shooed Sasha back to the table. A plate of half-eaten char siew pau and sticky jammy kaya toast sat out, on the low kid's table. Mrs Luo was scolding a petulant Sasha when I left.

When I returned to my client, I was deeply embarrassed.

"I'm sorry, our regular Nanny had to take a day off."

Han Lui patted his chest and remarked, "no matter, children are important. I have a grandson her age. Family is important." Mr Han Lui regarded me for a moment and seemed to come to a decision.

I nervously ate a forkful of mango salad. I slid a brochure across to him.

"This is what we have on hand at the moment. It will take some time to source the rest" I answered honestly.

"That is all right, we're looking for a two year contract. Here's a copy." I looked it over, and it offered fair terms.

"I'll have to check with my assistant, but yes, we ship after receiving payment."

"I do believe that the American Market will not affect my business," I interrupted gently. "China has vast foreign reserves. I do believe we'll be the ones bailing America out.

However, the demand for our imports has fallen. I've sourced alternative markets in Canada and Africa."

Clearly intrigued, Han Lui waited for me to continue. "I have a client who needs these parts your factories manufactures." I drank my tea and called for a refill through the waiter button. "We offer standard rates, do take a look at this." I slid the contract over.

Mr Han Lui perused it and said, "Yes. It seems in order. I do believe I am in need of the services your firm offers."

With my target achieved and a bonus contract secured, I could breathe easier. Truthfully, the manufacturing sector in this province was beginning to take a hit. Many of the smaller firms had folded, without the American demand for cheap imported goods. We spent the rest of lunch enjoying the good food. When Mr Han Lui left, we were fast friends and had found many things in common.

ZOO

MY HUMBLE BEGINNINGS

After we left Bill's bar, I dismissed Mrs Luo, and sent her on her merry way with her wages and a little extra for lunch. I wasn't sure if I would hire her. While I liked her no nonsense manner and thought Sasha could use and older maternal figure in her life as a role model, it was plain that Sasha did not want her around.

I bought the tickets at the concession stand at the entrance and we went inside the Zoo.

We were buffeted by the horde of families and couples out to enjoy the zoo on a Sunday evening. Sasha tugged on my arm, full of excitement, ready to rush off to the first exhibit that caught her eye. Hunkering down to her line of vision, I asked her what she would like to do first.

"Tigers, Uncle Wine!" She exclaimed.

"'Why tigers, my little one?"

"Because they are like my Uncle Wine. Strong!" Little Sasha demonstrated how strong I was by curling her arms while taking a huge bite from her cotton candy. Roaring with laughter at her humorous description of me, I lifted her high into the air and placed her on my shoulder. Shrieking with laughter, she cried out, "To the tigers, Uncle WIne!"

"Let's go princess!" And together, we headed to the tiger enclosure.

***

We spent nearly an hour at the zoo when a sudden announcement was made. The Guangzhou Zoo was celebrating the birth of their two month old baby panda. There was going to be a lucky draw for one potential customer to spend 30 minutes with the baby panda.

Sasha picked up on the Chinese word, "baobei," and uttered, "Baby?"

"Yes, dear. There's a baby panda in the zoo."

"Baby!" she squealed.

Shaking my head at her fascination over babies, "How about we buy tickets for the raffle to see the baby?"

"Can we see baby?" She inquired.

"Well, one person gets to see it. To be that lucky person, we must buy the ticket."

"Okay. Get ticket now, please!" Sasha started tugging at my arms, in the opposite direction of the raffle booth.

"Baby girl, the raffle booth is that way. Come with me."

Looking at the other direction and noticing the large crowd of people, Sasha raised her arms to me, saying, "Uncle Wine, carry, please." Smiling at the determined look on her face, I hoisted her up into my arms, and turned to join the crowd building up in the direction of the raffle booth.

A chance to see the baby panda meant we had to part with 50 renminbi for each ticket. We wanted to increase our chances of seeing the panda, so I got 10 tickets. The winner, as stated on the ticket, would be announced at 3pm.

Since it was lunch time, Sasha and I decided to dine at one of the many eateries in the zoo. After purchasing our boxed meal, we choose a table next to a pond containing koi fish. I had to remind Sasha to finish her chicken rice before feeding the fish with the pellets we bought from one of the attendants. The ever-energetic Sasha quickly finished her meal.

MY HUMBLE BEGINNINGS

Grabbing one of the pellets bags, she ripped it open causing a cascade of pellets to fall into the pond. The koi, sensing the ripple caused by the pellets, sprang into an array of body slamming to get to the pellets. Drawn by the commotion in front of her, Sasha inched closer to the pond, nearly losing her balance in haste. Just in time, I reached my hand out and caught her safely. Chortling, not noticing the danger she was in, she wriggled in my arms thinking I was playing with her.

"Uncle Wine, fish flying!' True enough, the desperation to get to the food forced some of the fish to leap out of the water and over other fish. Laughing at her merriment and close escape, I suggested a walk around the zoo while waiting for the announcement.

Three tall giraffes were being lured through a tall wooden gate by their keeper towards a 10 ft pole placed in the middle of the giraffe stockade. Lumbering over to the pole, the largest of three giraffes wraped its long tongue around a few leaves drawing it to its open mouth. The other two smaller giraffes began to playfully shoving each other. Guiltily, one looked over to check if the older giraffe was watching them. Distracted by the food, the smallest giraffe seized the chance to give one last shove before moving off to join the first giraffe at the makeshift tree, eating their fill.

Within five minutes, the speakers blared with the announcement for raffle holders to head to the panda enclosure to see the winning ticket being picked. Remembering that they would announce it on the PA system, I ignored the statement and continued walking around the zoo with Sasha on my shoulders. After a few minutes, an announcement came, indicating the winner. Unfortunately, our tickets were not selected. Bouncing Sasha on my shoulders as we continued our walk.

Sasha, engrossed with my hair, giggled suddenly. What had she done with my hair? I learned by now, silence coupled with amusement meant mischief was brewing. Reaching up to pat at my head brought a shrill protest.

"Uncle Wine! I was making you pretty!" The pixie groused. I felt around on my head. Sure enough, there were three lumpy braids sticking out on the top of my head. I could not help laughing, Sasha joined in too.

We headed home to eat dinner. I was mis-trustful of outside food and would not eat anything made from ingredients I had not inspected or sourced myself. Anna thoughtfully left a few boxes of Kimchi fried rice in the fridge for me to re-heat. The pixie was mad for them.

It had been a long day, and we were glad to be back. Sasha fell asleep on the way back and was not pleased to be stirred from her nap. I lugged her straight into the bathroom and for a bath. By now, with tutelage from Anne, I had dinner, bathtime, and a bed routine down. It now took me one hour instead of all evening to get through it all.

LAWYERS KIM & KIM

"Yes Mr Kim, I understand. I will call you back in ten minutes." I wanted to chuck my phone out the window. Instead I took a deep breath, straightened my posture, and placed my phone down gently on my high-priced teakwood table. No Ikea modern plywood for me.

I could feel a tension headache building as I stared out of the floor-to-ceiling windows of my personal office in a rented high-rise office suite. It was lunchtime, and a group of enterprising beggars had set up shop by the entrance. I made a mental note to send Nalia to complain to management. At this height, they were nothing more than a series of grimy grey-brown dots.

Nalia coughed politely behind me. I turned slightly startled. I did not hear her come in. I kept an open-door policy in my company, encouraging my employees to come to me with questions, solutions, and problems. It increased morale and allowed me to *cultivate them better*, as the Chinese were so fond of saying. Nalia took one look at my face, set down the documents, then strode out the door. Within moments, she returned with an aspirin and a cup of hot water. Per Chinese custom, water was never cold. Always hot. Cold water, they believed, was bad for your health.

Nalia was my longtime assistant and the first employee I hired. Today, I noted with approval she was wearing a green peasant blouse and a pair of linen slacks with sensible Mary Janes. This did nothing to hide her figure. My gaze travelled up to her chest and then her face. I caught her staring at me with an uncomfortable expression. I accepted the aspirin, and as I did so, Nalia dumped the pile of documents she was holding a little too forcefully on my desk.

"Boss, these are the financial projections you asked for and the sales figures. You need to take a look at these letters and sign them before I can courier them off." She managed to maneuver the desk in between us and now the pile of documents hid most of her enticing figure. Huh, maybe I needed to hit the nightclubs later. I was really getting distracted and needed the release. I nodded at her.

"Thank you Nalia."

In her heart, Nalia was thinking, "*You dirty monkey. You are a good boss except that you're a lecherous wolf.*"

I felt my tension headache dissipate. "I appreciate the aspirin. Could you arrange for a Nanny for Sasha tonight?"

Nalia nodded. "I have an Aunty who works as an Amah. She's retired now, but I think she'll agree to work tonight. My cousin's wedding is coming up."

I hear her loud and clear. "*Pay up you lecherous wolf, pay up.*" I teased Nalia.

"So, when is your lucky day coming? I hear Adam is single." Nalia blushed and hid her face in her left hand while scolding me with a wagging finger.

"Boss, don't say such words. Adam is a colleague and the company policy forbids romantic relationships between employees. We set that policy after the Yin, remember?"

My iPhone buzzed again. Ah it was the Kim Kim firm. I answered and set it to speakerphone. Nalia saw herself out, shutting the door behind her.

"Mr Wine." It was my lawyer. "At present, we are unable to obtain Sasha's passport. There is nothing we can do short of reporting it as a case of theft to relevant authorities to force her mother to surrender it to us. If we take this route, it is likely Sasha will face deportation, given the current climate in China."

A band of tiny imps seemed to have taken up residence in my head. "I understand. Incidentally, how is Kim-nim?"

"Mr Wine, he's suffered a severe heart attack, I will be taking over from him for the foreseeable future." I made a mental note to pen a memo to Nalia to send a fruit basket to old Mr Kim.

"He's recovered well and is recuperating at the Seoul Hospital." Nalia was magic, she was always able to find out who and what without bothering me with the details. The imps had matured to full-grown devils and were currently dancing a conga line through my head. Why wasn't the aspirin working?

MY HUMBLE BEGINNINGS

"About the adoption?" I asked wanting to get this over and done with. The lawyer's voice sounded uncharacteristically tinny at this point.

"We cannot make a case for your right to adopt Sasha, as you are not listed on the birth certificate as the father. According to the courts, you have no legal rights, and cannot sue for any type of custody. We are in the process of negotiating with her mother to have the courts recognise you as Sasha's parent."

I made a non-committal sound. "Understood Mr Kim. Do what you must to fix this. Contact my assistant if you need more funds. She's authorised to release them. I will be travelling for the next week. If there's anything, do keep me updated."

Down below, it was the start of the lunch hour. A steady stream of office workers had begun to trickle from the lobby entrances of each door.

My lawyer continued, "In the future things might change. We will continue to keep you updated. Our assistant will be in touch with yours."

"Thank you Mr Kim, I appreciate it." I hung up, extremely dissatisfied.

I stared out my windows and sighed. Down below, the row of beggars were doing a brisk trade. I never understood why some people didn't just go get a job. Any job was better than begging. Even when we were one minor disaster away from starvation back when I was a child, we never begged for a living. We hustled instead. I never understood why poverty bred laziness and apathy. Mama would whip us good if we slacked off, after that we got another beating from our father. Even then, there was the ever-present threat of starvation and death hanging over all our heads. I shrugged. Somethings are just the way they are. You can bring a horse to the river, but you can't force it to drink.

POVERTY OF THE MIND

*

REBOUND

MOTHER HEN

Five months after the walkout, Uncle George secured a home for the remaining members of our family. The blow of losing almost all his offspring fired up his desire to prove his self-worth. In high spirits, my two sisters and I left the hastily cobbled tarp shelter for a two-room mud hut our parents built a with proper earthen floor. Compared to our previous home, it was a definite step up. With so few of us left, it felt like a mansion. The best feature of our house, in my opinion, was the floor. It was cool in the summer, raised up high so that no water could seep in, and stayed dry during the wet season. It loved it.

Without the rest of my siblings stinking up the place, the hut smelled cleaner. The stench of our playground - the garbage dump - was easily washed off with only three of us and a vigilant Mama on our backs. It was a bittersweet feeling of victory, to be able to afford breakfast AND supper in the evening. Although on most days, it was merely gari (roasted cassava shavings) flavoured with salt- when there was salt to be had. At least nobody went to bed hungry. I learned to cook Hausa Koko (porridge) well.

Sometimes a change could be better, I thought, smiling with joy as I mused. I watched my sisters playing with homemade dolls from rags and hay. Uncle George seemed to have regained his pride. He went all out and built us all extensions to our home, giving us all privacy and space. Two bedrooms, with a kitchen next to a main living area. Sleeping arrangements were no longer a hassle, but sometimes I missed sleeping in a puppy pile. It got cold during the winter (wet) months. My parents took one room, my sisters, the other. I slept in the living room next to the kitchen. I felt proud. My father trusted me enough to protect the family. I was the first line of defence should someone enter. We even had a small courtyard and enough space for a small kitchen garden.

We never knew how Uncle George secured this house for us. I think we never asked because we were afraid that it would vanish into thin air. After all, why look at a gift horse in the mouth? I just felt grateful to have one less worry.

Despite the new beginnings, there was something was amiss about our mud mansion. I felt that there was a somewhat empty and forlorn air about it. I roamed around, mentally comparing the difference between our current house and the previous one. A hollow feeling preempted me from fully enjoying our new circumstances. The house was missing the chatter of my brothers. I didn't miss their bullying, but I missed lively air they brought to the house. The walls here were bare of personal possessions. Gazing at a blank wall, I said a silent prayer to the mighty powers ordain this world. I'm not a religious person, yet thinking of the perils they would face on their own, I felt a cold weight settle in my chest as a mild fear of the future unknown crept over me.

Mama strove harder than before to make life good for us. She continued peddling. As we had just enough to cover our food and nothing else, we could not afford to rent a market stand. She became an itinerant trader and constantly moved around the outskirts of the market in search of new customers. She would sell the little daily necessities of life. Things people needed, such as needles, baskets, shoes, and so on. She also offered on-the-spot mending and alteration services, eventually building a loyal following of satisfied customers. With the extra money she made, she could afford to construct a small folding table that acted as a portable stall. Through it all, Mama never stopped believing. Being a religious person, she would wake up early every day to pray before going out in search of the day's food allowance.

Nothing came easy. Often, she came home tired and disappointed, blank-eyed with weariness. When her empty gaze settled on us, she would slowly come back to life, fire re-lit. She would hug us with renewed determination, and say, "*We will be fine. Our family will not be hungry forever. God has bigger plans for us. God will make all things beautiful in His own time.*" Mama believed wholeheartedly and used her faith to carry on each day. For me, the conviction I got from those outbursts were temporary. It became clear to us young ones that while we had a good start, it would not last. There were so many things we still needed but could not afford.

On a particularly difficult month during the dry season before the harvest, my family didn't have any money for food and were once again close to starvation. What little food we had went to Gina, the baby of the family. Mama and Uncle George were looking gaunter than ever and had no energy to move. Uncle George eventually fainted from food deprivation and heat. Overcome by sorrow, and hunger; and unwilling to see us all starve to death Mama forced herself to swallow her pride to ask our agya yerima (my paternal uncle's wife) for food. I didn't know what it cost her, for she looked broken after. Death was kept at bay for a few more weeks.

The morning after, I walked up to Mama who was then performing her morning prayers. She was beseeching a picture of our Father in Heaven.

As Mama ended her ritual, my voice broke with anguish and I asked, "Where is God?"

Turning to face me, Mama was calm and serene as she replied, "God is in Heaven and He is here. He is watching over us."

I wanted to hug her and make her feel okay, but I didn't want to interrupt. Her prayers were important to her.

Hesitantly, I asked, "Mama, I have never seen God. God is not here. He isn't watching over us. The God you talk about isn't that wicked, right?" I hid my clenched fists behind my back. I didn't want her to see and know that I was angry at God. On top of everything else, it could be the straw that broke the camel's back.

"That's right, my son." nodded Mama, still serene as the picture of the Virgin Mary.

"If right then why are we suffering? Why is our family broken up? Why are we not living together as a family?" I asked bluntly, my secret questions burning from a repressed corner of my heart "Why does He keep watching His children fall apart? Why won't He give us a better life, Mama?" I demanded. Mama sounded wise and wore a sad expression as she gave me a hug and patted my head.

She replied, "Jeremiah 29; 11 said; for I know the plans I have for you, says the Lord. They are plans for good and not for disaster, to give you a future and hope."

"They are plans of good and not a disaster? Our family is a disaster, Mama!" I exclaimed loudly before stomping out of the hut towards the neighbouring farm.

As I played with empty corn husk, I asked myself, *Is poverty a choice or fate? Why are some people rich and my family poor? Is this luck?'* I had never seen or heard of anyone leaving the slums for a better life. Mama was convinced that God had plans for us. I knew God didn't care because my mother and father worked hard to find options to escape the life that poverty set for us all. Yet all their efforts to advance were blocked with an insurmountable wall. Our basic needs were barely being met. There was always some emergency, generated by a short-term fix we made earlier. To me, it felt like a black hole I could never escape from.

I gazed at the setting sun. I had heard stories of the Queens of the markets who started out as we did, and became wealthy enough to afford to eat three times a day and dress well. We worked as hard as they did, if not harder. I did not understand. Then it dawned on me that it was not only hard work, but luck and something more. Maybe a combination of both hard work and luck. If that was true, how could I obtain both? If I ask for work, could I keep a job? What did I need to escape?

People called us lazy and labelled us procrastinators especially when they saw my father sitting at home whittling or tending to the house. I wanted to turn around and punch the person who said it every single time, but I couldn't. I feared my Mama and Uncle George, more than the humiliation of gossip. We were not lazy. My sisters kept house and worked as helpers with the next-door neighbours. I hustled every day to at least earn lunch. My father was trying to restart his carpentry business and Mama worked harder than all of us and kept us together. We worked until our sweat watered the earth.

Maybe everyone was right, that we chose to be poor. Maybe it was true, what people said of us. That we were cursed with bad luck and that we were so lazy that we invited the curse. That couldn't be it, right? I refuse to accept that because it made no sense. Disgusted with myself and the world at large, I tossed the husk away and stood up. I had wasted an evening away in idleness and useless musings.

I walked back towards the hut just as the songs from the crickets began. Living on this side of the world meant you were bound to see more insects than mammals. Out in our courtyard, I sat down on the chair my father built out of scrap wood and storm-broken tree branches in his free time, trying to figure out the rationale behind my parents' poverty and to work out what could be done.

Across the narrow lane, in our neighbours compound, I saw a mother hen encouraging her chicks to peck on the ground. I looked carefully at the hen scratching the ground in search of food for her chicks. From afar, I observed the hen's liveliness. It dawned on me. Just like Mama, the hen had eleven chicks. Just like Mama, this hen had to feed her family too. I thought of my family and felt that we were the same. This was how we could make money. Like how the chicks follow their mother around, we would follow Mama to market.

I immediately went to Mama and shared what I saw along with my idea. Mama agreed instantly, smiling with joy at my initiative. Under her watchful eye all, the three of us remaining would work alongside her with our own baskets, in different corners of the marketplace, to make more money for the family. If a mother hen can take care of all her eleven chicks by having them follow her around, then perhaps I too could be a little chick that trailed behind her. She would vend. I would learn the art of selling by example.

EVICTION

Monday 6 am

I woke up, not by the cock crowing, but by my brother David.

"Na! Why you wake me? D, it's still time to sleep! It's dark outside." I shook off his hand and rolled back into a fried shrimp to try to go back to sleep.

"Hsst! Wake up!" whispered David as he cuffed me lightly on the head to get me to pay attention. It wasn't enough. He dragged me upright. That's when I saw Uncle George, sitting on the stoop. I knew from the shape of his back and the way he hunched, that this was not a good time to provoke him. Silence was needed. I shook off David's grip and sat up.

I hissed. "Brother! What's going on?"

David scowled and motioned for me to get moving. That's when I noticed that I was the last one to wake. David cuffed me yet again before I could fire off another question. He handed me his cup and pointed outside.

"Go wash" was his terse instruction. I didn't know what was going on, but I knew better than to protest, not with Uncle George in that mood.

I washed my face and arms using the communal water tank in our compound's courtyard. I saw that Gina and Janet were already up, and busy with the fire. Of Mama and David, I saw no sign. I heard the clanking of her precious pots and camp stove, mingled with David's whispers coming from inside the hut. My father brooded on the stoop. Gina looked scared, her eyes were large as a baby gazelle. I started to tease her but Janet interrupted me by shoving a cup of hot water into my hands. I accepted and sipped at it to savour the heat it brought to my belly. I turned towards my father. In the gloom and the weak firelight, he was a broken statue staring off into the distance.

I barely noticed the rest of my brothers, who were busy at various tasks around our courtyard. I was hungry, sleepy, and confused. I rose to go find Mama, but Janet shook her head and gave me a stick of firewood and pointed at the fire. Gina huddled against Janet. I understood and busied myself with the work of tending the fire. One by one, each of my brothers came to the fire to be fed. Gina, our resident cook, handed each a plate of gari. It was meagre but at least it was something.

As dawn rose, Uncle George summoned us and told us to assemble in the courtyard. We were told in simple words that we were leaving this house and we needed to pack up. I wanted to go retrieve the picture book I found, but David held me back: there was no time. The plastic sheet we slept on was rolled up and packed away. Our worldly possessions amounted to Mama's pots and pans, her pestle and mortar. The clothes we had on our back, our Sunday best, Uncle George's tools, and the plastic tarp stuffed with whatever we could find was all we would take.

Uncle George motioned for us to line up behind him. I was puzzled, Sunday was yesterday. David pulled at my arm and cuffed me for the third time since waking up, to encourage haste. I stumbled and hurried to get in line. Glaring at him from the corner of my eye, I tried to kick him. This only earned me a sharp elbow to the ribs. David was looking straight ahead, and there was not a peep out from my other brothers. Nobody complained, not even George Junior, my unruly elder brother. I was getting alarmed, but I knew better than to voice any questions I had.

I could see Mama with a large cloth-wrapped bundle tied to her back, silhouetted against the dawn. As usual, Mama had a firm grip on my sisters. It was a sombre procession that my parents led, two by two, out into the morning. I risked a look back. I could see a black cockerel sitting on the fence my father made, heralding our departure.

THE WALKOUT

It was raining like the first flood. The monsoon season had returned. Mama Adel, Uncle George, and everyone else were huddled under the roof of our tent-home. The tarp we used was scavenged from a dumpsite. It came from one of the big charity organisations like Unicef. At least that's what the blue logo read. It was sturdy, but it had several holes from heavy use before we got our hands on it. I was forced to sit under the badly patched leaks next to my older brothers. Only the youngest set was present. Adam, James, Joseph, and David were huddled over something using their bodies to block off the view of what they were doing. Mama Adel had sunk into prayer and was deaf and blind to the rest of the world. Uncle George sipped his mug of hot water and stoically ignored my four younger brothers who were clearly playing poker right next to him. Better they stay home and gamble amongst themselves under his eye, than go out and find trouble.

I was just relieved that I didn't have to put up with Janet's sharp elbows or George Junior's cutting tongue. This year I remember well, for it was the first year that we didn't have to sit in the mud during the monsoon season. Uncle George had managed to get a hold of some wood, and he built us all a platform of sorts that kept us out of the mud and water when our campsite flooded. I was just glad I wasn't forced to sit in the mud again. The leeches were not the worst of it. I was waiting for the thunderstorm to pass, so I could run out to the market to try to scavenge food for my evening meal.

My eldest brother, George Junior, and his cohort had vanished earlier, lured by promises of jobs. We all knew, even our parents, that they had gone to loot. They had caught wind of a rumour which told of a raid on kabule that Johnny's boys were staging in the Ashaiman market. There were good pickings to be had if you knew what you were doing.

Their targets this time were the Market Queens. These were the women traders, who were elected by their peers and were responsible for ensuring that their section ran smoothly. There was one for each type of produce sold. They weren't always rich traders, but were picked mostly for their political ability, then their wealth. You needed funds of your own to draw on in order to perform your duties. One could not be too rich nor too poor as to avoid being swayed by a bribe or the temptation to abuse the power to better oneself.

Uncle George and Mama Adel kept their silence because we needed the spoils my brothers brought back. On most days, they came back with armfuls of fresh produce like tomatoes or eggplants. Once they returned with a bucket full of fresh fish. Mama would accept their gifts silently and cook up a feast with a pained look on her face. Uncle George held his silence and ate along with the rest of us.

I shifted on my haunches, tried to get comfortable, and listened to my brothers James and Joseph bickering amiably. I daydreamed of a future where I was a big market trader. I had a car and a house. I would never have to squat in the mud. Instead, I could have a house girl clean and cook my food. Uncle George's sharp command to my brothers to quiet down jerked me out of my reverie. Looking at the set of his shoulders and the way he sat, my father seemed angry instead of stuck in his usual funk. Hair-trigger. We knew that the next word would mean a beating. It seemed that Uncle George had been this way more often than not over the last year or two. I had rarely heard him being cheerful ever since our eviction from our old house.

"The boys are turning to sin! Do something!" Mama Adel urged. I often heard their soft-whispered arguments in the night when they thought all of us were sleeping.

"At least they're working and bringing back money and food!" Uncle George snapped back. "What do you want me to do?" Even as young as I was, I could hear the resignation in his voice.

"Talk to them. Help them find a job! DO something. DO anything!" Mama Adel hissed.

I never heard the end of their arguments because they always stepped out of the tent at this point to finish it.

In truth, everyone was tired of it. Everyone was doing their best and bearing up as a family unit. My eldest brothers were the ones most likely to throw the towel in. George Junior had his own network of contacts and I suspected he found work of sorts for he often disappeared in the morning and came back at night. I think my Mama was just relieved that he returned to us. The next in seniority were Charles, Alexander, and Moses. I had the feeling that they were merely biding their time. Despite all the casual cruelty and bullying they doled out, they still stuck by us and came back with enough food to keep us going for the week.

I leaned my head back on the brick wall we had pitched our tarp up against and listened to Janet telling Gina the story of Noah's ark. For the hundred time today, I stuffed back my useless wishes and tried to rest. Halfway into the story, George Junior burst into the tent.

"James! Joseph!" He had an armful of tomatoes and eggplants. Alex and Charles stumbled into the tent carrying a large box filled with sacks of flour and sugar. Mama Adel turned white and uttered a prayer. Uncle George's mug of tea fell from his nerveless hands.

"How…?" James and Joseph stammered in unison. "What!?" they asked.

"No, no! Mama! Uncle George! The soldiers were giving these out!" George Junior protested. Color rushed back into my parents' faces. Uncle George looked utterly defeated and sank back into a stony silence. We all knew where the food came from. It was looted, but we needed it. Especially Gina. Any longer and she would waste away.

The tent was barely tall enough for us to sit up straight forcing them all to crawl in and kneel in front of my parents. Attracted by all the commotion, my brothers abandoned their game of cards and came over.

"Come! Come! You need to see this! Johnny's boys are hiring!" Junior announced. "They want good strong men as soldiers" That got their attention. They swarmed Junior, peppering him with questions.

Behind my parents, my sisters exclaimed in delight as Moses stumbled in with yet another cardboard box full of food. He tripped over the low-hanging tent flap, dropping the box on our wooden platform. A corner of the box broke and out spilled a cornucopia of food from sacks of gari to fresh vegetables and dried fish. I was surprised that they managed to drag this much back without getting caught. I cracked open an eyelid and pretended not to be interested as I observed the excitement. My sisters abandoned their game. Gina began to cheerfully list out the dishes she could cook. For once, even

MY HUMBLE BEGINNINGS

sour Janet was happy. Janet was a piranha when it came to food. A full belly meant the world to my sister.

For the last surprise, Junior handed them a brown package concealed in his threadbare shirt. It turned out to be full of spices and table salt that we all desperately needed. Mama looked on in silence. I knew her and it was clear that this ate at her conscience. I stretched like I had just woken up from my nap and scooted over to my sisters to help them sort out the bounty. I had to look down and away as I busied myself with the make work of 'storing' our food away.

My chest burned with jealousy that my brothers, who were for the most part useless good for nothings who caused Mama worry day and night, managed to return as heroes with all this food. While it was true that Johnny's boys staged more raids to hunt down kabule around this time of the year, there was no way that they were giving away all this much food. It was enough to feed all eleven of us for a few weeks. The extra produce would have to be sold or traded for non-perishables before they spoiled. I knew which of our neighbours would gladly trade a sack of gari or some tinned tomatoes for some fresh and good garden eggs. It wasn't fair! They managed to bring all this back to Mama by being thieves. Worse of all, they got away with it. I sighed. God rewarded those who were clever enough to break the rules.

George Junior zipped out of the tent again. He paused long enough to tell Uncle George that he would be back tonight. My father merely grunted. George Junior didn't return that day or the day after. Mama was sick with worry. Two weeks later, he marched into the tent and announced that he had found a job in Nigeria. James and Joseph jumped at the opportunity and went with him. They had their own lives and only returned to sleep with the family when they brought food or needed a place to stay. Mama said a prayer over them and reluctantly gave them her blessing. That day, the food was their going away present. I think they must have known one way or another.

At that time, I was just jealous and sour because I was not the conquering hero. I wanted to leave for Nigeria too, where there was good money to be made. I couldn't because I was too small and too young. I still needed my parents. Back then, I didn't think of it that way. I just saw my brothers abandoning us and hated them for it.

We moved around during those years, as we were kicked out of all the places we stayed. It didn't matter if it was a relative's house or a patch of bare land that nobody wanted. People did not want us around I didn't understand why. They said that we were "cursed by spirits." I hated them and thought that they were jealous of my family. We stood together and we worked together. My father was not one of those useless uncles who sat in front of their houses while their wives and mothers worked. Even in the midst of his funk, he still kept himself busy one way or another. He might not have had a job, but he always had something for us at the end of a long day.

David was the next to leave. We were staying at Uncle Dan's house, our paternal uncle after Uncle George shamed him into it. His wife, our aunt by marriage, took a liking to David and offered him the post of houseboy. Mama and Uncle George agreed immediately. David was guaranteed a future should he impress our aunt and uncle with his diligence.

They hoped that our aunt and uncle would adopt him, as they had three daughters and no sons. David stayed behind when we left. Uncle George pressed his thumb to David's forehead and gave his blessing.

"May your day be bright and your forehead be as strong as a unicorn's," he said in a gruff voice.

We only lasted three months in that house before we were politely asked to leave. It turned out that my brothers had been flirting with our cousins. They were all at the age when girls and boys discovered that there were differences between them. Aunty caught Moses kissing the prettiest one, Mary behind the bushes in her gardens. I suspected Joyce and Ohana were not spared my brother's attention either. They were smarter than their sister and rejected my brothers outright. Aunty was furious. She beat Moses black and blue before demanding that her husband and my father do the same too. She had high hopes for all her daughters and was determined that they all marry well to rich husbands who would take care of them and herself in the style they were accustomed to.

"He who sticks their finger in their mouth and hits their head gets bitten," was Uncle's Dan's summation of the situation.

My parents were embarrassed. It was clear to anyone with two eyes on their head that Uncle George did not have control over his family. Our brothers only stayed with us out of habit. No amount of beatings or scoldings persuaded my brothers to rein themselves in. As time went by, they got worse. I kept my head down, avoided them as best as I could. I don't remember much of those years.

The next place we moved to was somewhere closer to Tema. Our parents found us housing, but we had to split our family up. Mama got a job working for a woman who made and sold gari at the market. Uncle George had to move closer to Accra to his job working for a boat builder by the beach. He took our brothers with him. With their labour, he could earn more. My sisters and I spent my days working alongside Mama. She kept us close and refused to let us leave our sight. We were the only children she had left with her.

When our parents got back together, the rest of my brothers were gone. Uncle George was incensed and spent long evenings staring off into nothing. He exploded frequently, even at Mama Adel who took his temper with stoic dignity. We children were appalled and spent the rest of the year walking on eggshells. It was hard to tell what would set him off. Janet and I kept Gina away from him as much as possible. She was still too young to understand why. We didn't want her to hate our father.

Mama coped by spending more time away from the house working. She had saved enough from her wages to start a small business selling roasted peanuts in the evenings. As for my brothers, we never spoke their names again. They were taboo in our house. From that moment on, they ceased to be kin to me. I would not acknowledge shiftless layabouts who only brought trouble.

*

GRANDMOTHER

The clock read six in the evening, and the kitchen had a warm lived-in feel. On one end, I had the tablet set up facing Sasha and on the other, my work papers took up the rest. My half-eaten dinner lay on the side. I had lost a whole day's productivity and needed to get caught up. There was one person I had not told about Sasha yet: Mama. My family knew, I told Mama after the paternity test, but they had yet to see her.

The call connected, and I nervously waited for my mother to speak.

"Hello, Jolie. What do you need?"

"Mama Adel I'm your son! Why would I need a reason to call you?" I quipped.

"You don't call home unless you need something son." Mama Adel rebutted.

"You have a grand-daughter. Her name is Sasha." I stated bluntly.

"Praise be. That is good news! When is the due date?" My mother asked.

MY HUMBLE BEGINNINGS

"Mama, I'm sorry. It's not mine and Blues. It's one of my ex-girlfriends in the past. I dated her when I was living in Hong Kong" I replied. My fingers felt cold.

"Jolie!" Mama sounded scandalised! "How could you? You know how many times I've told you to be careful! Do you want to be like that Uncle from next door with eleven children from nine different women, and he still lived with his mother?" She scolded.

"Mama!" I said sharply. That was not true. I was responsible "I learned of her a few months ago. Her mother had to leave her with me for reasons I cannot go into" I explained. "I was as shocked as you are now."

"Jolie" My mother sighed. "She's left, has she? No woman would tolerate having their husband's love child intrude…"

"Yes. Blues has." I puffed out my cheeks in a sigh. "She divorced me because of it. I met Sasha's mother long before I met her."

"Child!" Mama Adel scolded me. "Haven't you learned to think by now? You need to apologise to her! Go get her back! She is good for you!"

"Yes Mama, would you like to meet your grand-daughter?" I asked in a desperate attempt to change the subject.

"Quit being a joker and show her to me!" Mama Adel snapped.

"I would like to Mama, but you'll have to come to China to see her" I teased.

"Child! Just bring her over back home" she said. My mother had a bad case of granny lust. Neither of my sisters had married or sired children. The family line depended on me.

"Mama you should come over in summer. Bring Janet and Gina. I'm sure they'll love it here." I suggested.

"You know your sisters. Too busy at work and no time to play. Your sister has jetted off again. To South Africa this time." Mama Adel groused. All the suitors she had arranged for my sisters were utterly rejected.

"Is Gina with you or Janet? Can you get them to turn on the computer and skype?" I asked. I hung up the call. International phone calls were still expensive, but I had gotten to the point where it meant nothing.

My mother, like others of her generation, did not know how to operate a computer. As I waited, I went to retrieve Sasha. We had prepared for this, by exploring the concept of grandmother. Sasha had no contact with her maternal grandparents. I gathered that they barely knew that she existed.

"Halmeoni?" Sasha asked in Korean.

"Yes come meet your grandmother" I replied.

I set up the tablet in the kitchen where the light was better. The kitchen windows faced the morning sun and provided a splendid view of the garden park. I parked Sasha in her booster chair.

"Ooo!" Mama replied in Ewe. "She's precious!"

"Mama she speaks Korean and English" I replied.

"Hello! there precious granddaughter!"

I left my mother and my daughter to get to know each other. I needed to finish up the pitch for my Hong Kong trip. The numbers in the warehouse kept changing. No one on my team could figure out what

MY HUMBLE BEGINNINGS

was going on. We knew it was theft, but we did not know who and how. Both were important things to find out. There was a series of suspicious withdrawals from the Hong Kong account, HSBC. Bill told me that we were working on it.

Petty cash would go missing, including actual merchandise in our warehouse. It was insane. We suspected identity theft but had no traced the leak yet.

Business in China was exceedingly cutthroat.

Over at the kitchen table, across from me, Sasha moved on from eyeing my mother warily to enthusiastically playing a game of pat a cake. Mama had a tongue that could charm the birds out of the trees. It ran in the family. I shuffled through lists of exit and entry logs, trying to track down who did what. It was irritating and I feared corporate sabotage and spying, more than anything else.

Sasha screeched "FINISHED!" and mashed a button on the screen, ending the call. My phone rang again.

"Sasha is as much of a handful as you were when you were her age." Mama remarked. "Can you put her on again and this time. Explain that it's a live person at the other end. Don't just leave her in front of the device!" Mama scolded.

"I've got work to do" I protested.

"Jolie, haven't you learnt by now? It's not work that keeps you going. It's family. You work to keep your family going" Mama reminded me. I was taken back to Uncle George's funeral.

Setting down my papers, I picked up the tablet.

"Uncle Wine" Sasha protested "I am playing with that!"

Hoisting her up, I replied "No, we're going to talk to Halmeoni" as we walked into the living room. Children's argument and logic was circular. I started up the skype again. Mama's face reappeared on the screen. She was lively, with full cheeks and a colourful head scarf wrapped around her head.

"Mama! This is Sasha" I said in ewe.

"I know. Put her on your lap, and explain to her that I am your mother, and her grandmother" Mama instructed. She looked like Uncle George in that moment. I missed my father. I did as Mama instructed.

"Sasha baby, This is my mother, she is your grandmother" I explained carefully.

"Halmeoni?" She asked confused. "Omma said she went to heaven!" I shook my head.

"Everybody has two grandmothers. One from your mother, one from your father." I exchanged a high five with Mama Adel. "Sasha, the reason why you have curly hair, and coffee-coloured skin is because Uncle Wine is from Africa, from a country called Ghana." I touched her hair and her face as I spoke, causing her to squeal in delight.

"Hello again Sasha child!" Mama said with a smile wide enough to crack her face. Mama sang to Sasha a nursery song she sang to me as a boy. I needed to be elsewhere, but as Mama reminded me. This is important. I don't need more money. I work to keep the family going.

"Sasha child" Mama asked, "What games do you like to play?"

"Temple Run!" She cheered enthusiastically.

MY HUMBLE BEGINNINGS

"That's odd. Anne told me that her phone time was strictly limited to once a week. I've told Anne that Sasha was not allowed to use the phone to play any games. All she can do is watch S E A S A M E S T R E E T on Sunday mornings. I spelled out the word." Sasha loved the TV and like all kids would spend hours and hours on them if we let her.

Gently tugging on Sasha's ear, I asked the pixie, "Sasha, do you have something to tell us?"

Mama chimed in sternly, "Gods sees you when you lie child. You may fool us, but not him."

Faced with censure from two grown adults, Sasha hid her face in her hands.

"Oops. Anne told me not to twell." She cheerfully blurted out, after there was no punishment forthcoming "Anne lets me play on her phone when I'm a good girl."

I bought out practically the whole toy store, to avoid her contracting a technology addiction like so many of this young generation. We got into a discussion about games we liked to play. I taught Sasha the skipping game my sisters used to play and we made a bedsheet rope to play skipping with, as Mama watched.

Janet wandered over five minutes into the game. Her voice appeared tiny from the tablet speakers. "This is an early call, Brother. what's the occasion?"

Sasha screeched "I win!"

"Yes you do darling." I sat on the couch and pretended to be winded.

POVERTY OF THE MIND

"You have a niece!" Mama Adel exclaimed triumphantly. "Her name is Sasha. How old are you Sasha, can you tell Aunty Janet?" Mama asked.

"Four and half!" Sasha crowed. "I won!"

"Yes you did baby girl" I crooned to her.

"So, you made a love child and your wife left you?" Janet asked in Ewe. "You didn't tell us that Blues was no longer in the picture." Janet had hit the nail on the head.

"Yes" I replied. "Please drop the subject"

Mama asked, "Janet, you knew?"

Over in Ghana, I saw my sister nod cautiously at Mama Adel.

"Yes I did. Jolie told me he wanted to sort things out before telling you."

Mama Adel's wise eye rest on my face. "I'm glad you did" she said.

STOLEN

I checked the time. It was 3 am. I scrambled for my phone.

Trying not to sound sleepy I asked "Nalia? What happened?" I sat up straight, allowing the covers to fall off me.

"Boss, we've been robbed" she said hesitantly.

"HOW?" I screeched and felt my child start awake across the hallway. I waited for noise, but only silence answered.

MY HUMBLE BEGINNINGS

"We're still finding out. I've called the police and I'm pulling the video camera records."

"Why didn't the security system send an alarm?" I asked. James had it installed last month.

"It was hacked into boss. The thieves knocked it offline long enough for them to clear everything out. We managed to get a grainy picture of the small truck as it drove away on the gate cameras. They're separate from the system."

Rubbing my forehead, I mentally bid goodbye to any sleep I would have for the rest of the night. "Alright, good work Nalia. I'm coming in" I said.

"Boss, we're still gathering evidence and I will have a report for you later."

"Good work. I'll be there as soon as I can. " My day had started whether I liked it or not. The cicadas were singing their hearts out and I heard the croaking of bullfrogs. Beyond that, the neighbourhood lay quiet.

I padded to the kitchen for a glass of water as my head felt packed with cotton wool. My sleep had been plagued with nightmares, despite my early bedtime. With Sasha, curfew for me was 11 pm sharp. Anne had tactfully suggested I come home earlier to spend nights with my child. What she meant was "Comeearlier please, I would like to go home."

I peeked in on Sasha. The pixie was tossing and whimpering fitfully in her sleep. She too was having nightmares. I think she missed her mother. I sat next to her to soothe her back into sleep. It took my mind off my own demons. I called Anne and asked her if she could come in early.

I checked across the street. The lights in her house were still on. *"Yes"* she replied.

I was too worried to eat and left just as Anne came in. She was a treasure. Good help was hard to find.

***

I was on-site by 7 am. The area around me was packed full of warehouses and farmland just beginning to come to life as workers trickled in.

I checked the perimeter. All looked in order. There were no signs of forced entry as far as I could see. *Maybe I need to get some dogs and hire a night watchman to look after them.*

This far out from the city centre, my skin colour attracted staring and pointing by the local bumpkins. This was something I never got used to. I headed into the centre. It looked like nothing was taken, everything was as I left it. My assistant was her usual impeccable self, beckoning me from the office. She was deep in conversation with a uniformed policeman, over a stack of bagged evidence. The policeman's attitude changed when he found out that it was me and not Nalia who owned the lease on the warehouse.

She filled me in. The thieves had only taken the Han Lui shipment. We all suspected corporate sabotage. The entry wasn't forced, and the security alarm system had been disabled. The mystery drove me crazy. We needed more information. The video camera network went offline for thirty minutes around 8 pm, just as our last worker went home. The gate camera was not connected to the network, and we managed to get a picture of a truck driving away. The number plate was obscured. There was not much the police could do.

MY HUMBLE BEGINNINGS

They had long since vanished. The policeman suspected that they were a gang of thieves based in the next province over. There had been a string of robberies in this area.

Nalia beckoned me over "Boss we're still combing the place, I'll keep you updated."

I frowned. To the casual eye everything was as it should be, except for the missing items.

"Nalia, Miss Chen just called, she needs a buyer for <x product >. Do you think we can trust this to Adam?" I asked.

My petite assistant thought for a moment. Her cute face wrinkling up into a frown.

"Yes" she said firmly. "He's outperformed consistently since you promoted him to sales manager."

I nodded firmly at her. "I'll deal with the office. We'll need the entire team in to deal with this."

I headed into the office. There was not much I could do at the present. Nalia was taking care of it. The Hong Kong trip was happening next week. We were submitting tender for one of the smaller supply contracts for a government-backed project in Ghana. This was not a widely known fact. You needed a sponsor to apply. Someone had to recommend you to the board before they would send you a letter of invitation.

I arrived at the office at 10 am with breakfast for my team which I kept small by preference. I didn't believe in hiring too many people. I preferred to invest in training the right people and have them stay with me over the years. It had worked. Ailin, my HR and Legal advisor, poked her head into the pantry just as I set out the breakfast of soya bean milk, you tiao and bean curd.

"Boss! Nalia told me to cover our asses. When we signed the contract there was a strict no-fault contract baked into it. The insurance money will take care of the cost of supplies on our end. Adam is on the phone right now trying to solve the problem of sourcing another batch." She ruffled through a stack of papers. "I've started the insurance claim process. The money should come next month."

I sighed in relief. My team was on it.

"Good work Ailin!" Attracted by breakfast, Bill strode in.

"Hello boss! I heard the bad news" he said. "I've run the numbers. It's cheaper to write this contract off and take the hit rather than trying to replace the stolen material."

I nodded. "Taken under advisement Bill." Bill shambled out again, clutching his cup of soya bean milk.

Ailin watched him leave with a frown and turn ed to me, "There's something else you're after?" I munched on a fried dough stick.

"Yes" I agreed. She took her breakfast to enjoy it at her desk.

I spent the rest of the day buried in paperwork and research. There was a lot to do. Nalia returned after lunch. I ordered in and we had a quick powwow. The only solution we had now was to wait and watch the marketplace. The police, like all police everywhere were doing their jobs, but there was not much they could do.

I might have to hire a P.I. This cutthroat cloak and dagger stuff drove me insane. As far as we could tell, someone had climbed over the fence and up the building wall to cut the mains to the security system. The camera network was hacked shortly after. It was a clean job.

Adam worked a miracle and found someone willing to offload their excess stock in storage for a little above market price. Word got around discreetly, despite it only happening a few hours ago.

I made the difficult call to Mr Han Lui to inform him of the theft. While we weren't the ones who purchased from the vendor, it was our client who did. I prided myself in making sure our company went above and beyond in delivering.

Hong Kong

GRIT

EDUCATION

1981 - Ashaiman

My recollections of how my mother carefully encouraged the three of us to help her vend, brought my thoughts to school. If I studied, maybe I could earn a chance to become a big boss who worked as a civil servant and provide for my family. Most of Mama's rich customers, at the very least, knew how to read and write. All of them went to school.

None of us were educated, but we could speak Ewe, Twi, and read simple words in English. Uncle George, when he had free time, would make us learn the English alphabet using a stick. He drew out the letters on the sandy patch in front of the old mud house. At that time, we hated these drawings, for every time we were out of line, a sharp pain would land on our backs. It was never strong enough for welts to form, in that my father was a maestro. Uncle George was fond of his cane, which he found in the heap after we did away with the one before it. No matter how far we ran, we would somehow face the cane for not being back in time to learn our letters. Thankfully, Uncle George had rudimentary schooling. He knew enough to read at a basic level and passed it on to us. Thus, the amount of time we spent learning quickly came to an end, then we were free to play pirates.

Despite the canings, I was strangely drawn to the idea of attending school, intrigued by the smug looking children in uniform who trailed after their parents during the lunch rush. My days started with getting up at the crack of dawn. I had to complete my morning chores of watering the vegetable patch, starting the morning fire, and helping my older brother collect enough water for our daily use. Only then I was free to play. Every day, I would race with my friends from next door to the dumping grounds. Our laughter and shouts filled the cool morning air as we raced to be the first to arrive on site.

We would linger around the fringes of the dumping site watching out for the two security guards patrolling the site. A short burst of warbling bird calls indicated an all-clear. Then, the race against time was on! My team and I would lunge into the newest heap pile digging in search of "gold" as we called our discoveries. Spending most of my early childhood rummaging around the mountains of rubbish, I found it was common to see a "mountain" coming down and scavengers scrambling for safety. It became equally as common to see our young crew of playmates who scavenged for the thrill of it, turn into full-fledged adult scavengers.

As I pulled out a bucket, I spotted Yao, one of our playmates who held the role of captain in our pirate hunting adventures. He was haggling over something in his bag, tied securely around his waist. I used to share my findings with Yao who promised to keep my treasure safely. One day, I saw him selling my treasure to Kwesi. I asked him why he did it without asking my permission. *"Life isn't always about playing. We need to find money to fill our bellies"* he told me. I realised then, our fun was now his livelihood. Oftentimes, I would notice regret crossing over his face when the younger kids shouted for him to join us in our ventures. Money, I learned, is the key to survival.

MY HUMBLE BEGINNINGS

From my perch at the top of the mountain of discarded trash, I could see the houses of the wealthy and affluent. It dawned on me - most of the rich folks in town attended school. They could read, write, and do math.

Approaching my father one evening after our meal of gari, beans, and kokoor, I cautiously asked if I could attend school. Uncle George, seated on a stool at the doorway of the house with the light of a lamp, was at that time carving a minuscule face into a piece of flat wood, stopped midway lest he do it damage. Placing his carving knife on his right knee and the flat wood on his left, he looked at me clearly pondering on this matter. Head down, my gaze fell upon the flat wood, with its picture bearing close resemblance to Mama. *Is this a gift*, I wondered. I continued looking at my feet as a sigh escaped my father's lips before he spoke.

"Son, do you know why I teach your siblings and you all that I know?" Without waiting for me to respond, he continued, "Schools today are not what it used to be. Education in my time was far better. Since I can't turn back time, I decided to share all that I have learned in school with my children, knowing they are receiving the best education, through me. But maybe what I am doing isn't enough, that's why you seek to go to school?"

My insides grew more knotted up at each word uttered as Uncle George seldom spoke at such great lengths about anything. I felt then that a great wrong had been committed. I remained mute staring intently at a stink bug I noticed, willing it to make a sudden move or better yet, burst into flames.

"Son," my father said again, and I flinched a little instinctively, for I have just spotted the cane next to my father's tools. My father made a sound like amusement in his throat and drew me close to his side. "See this carving? Well, Madam Adel always wanted a picture of herself. Knowing how expensive it is to take a picture, Mama never pursued this idea. Afford it, we can't. But carving, I am skilled at. So, here I am chipping away at this piece of wood for her to remember, even without a picture, she is always worth the effort," said my father as he showed me the partly done picture. "My advice to you is if you really want it, you have to find a way to get it, son."

At six years old, I had no inclination of the hidden meaning in this message, but years later as I recall this conversation, I realized it's a love confession to Mama hidden in a message of encouragement. I shook my head at the irony of the situation for this man, who seldom professed his love, had done so to the person most unlikely to understand it.

As luck would have it, it would take me a few more years before the desire to be schooled overcame me. Around this time, I had already been peddling with Mama for over a year. No longer feeling the need to watch over me, Mama upgraded from her peddling cart to a stall. Yes, business had truly picked up, to a location closer to the main road. Business was booming and my sister's Gina and Janet were roped into helping our parents. Gina with her knack for people, helped Mama by sweet-talking customers into buying more than they needed. My other sister, Janet, was keen on carving. Her sculptures were well-received by buyers and she chose to spend more time with Uncle George in hopes of strengthening her craftsmanship.

"Who knew!" blurted our father once in surprise when he noticed how deft her fingers were. "One of my children did indeed inherit the gift," a ghost of a smile lingering on his lips.

One day, as I stood next to a bread stall shouting and waving my wares for all to see, I saw three boys in school uniforms, heading toward the bread stall. One of the smaller boys was beaming between two of his friends who had their arms over his shoulders. They all seemed to be in a celebratory mood, chatting away merrily. As they approached the stall, I felt myself edging closer to them, trying to listen in on their conversation. I heard one of them ask the smaller

MY HUMBLE BEGINNINGS

boy what bun he wanted to have to buy with the money he got from winning the spelling test.

Surprised, I asked, "Charle, did your school give you that money?" while staring at the bills clutched tightly in his clean and neatly trimmed nails, hands very unlike my bitten nails and grubby hands.

"Yes. Samuel here got the first place in our form's spelling test and our teacher rewarded him with money" one of the boys replied.

"I never knew schools gave money." I said.

"School is fun! Sometimes, I even get delicious food" shared Samuel looking excitedly up at me, taking in my state of worn clothing and trinkets cart. He turned to look back at the buns and choose one that was chocolate filled. "I'll have this," he declared.

It dawned on me that education would be the best way for me to escape poverty. I looked at the retreating backs of the three boys and wondered how I could afford it. To attend school, I would need a uniform, shoes, schoolbag, books, and transportation fees. It was out of the question. Uncle George was in the midst of starting up his own business selling carvings and furniture. Money was tight. We were eating gari and plantain and had run out of salt last week. What more would it cost to educate a child?

The boys disappeared out of my sight to return to their carefree lives. I scowled at God and got back to work. He had never given me anything I needed, much less wanted. I wanted to go to school. The question was did I want it enough? These thoughts consumed me as I continued working into the evening. That night as I sat on our doorstep looking at the stars in the night sky, an idea took root in my mind. I could enroll in school with the money I earn through peddling and if money was short, I would get back to work after school with Mama to raise what I needed to support myself through school. If God wouldn't help me, I would help myself.

After asking the only school near my community about the cost of schooling, it took me two weeks before I could enroll myself. In those times, parents could enroll their child at any time of the year. The school fees weren't high according to the teachers. But for a slum digger like myself, it was not affordable as I also needed money for other necessities. I spoke not of my intentions to study as I felt my siblings would dampen my dreams after hearing the cost.

PALM KERNEL

I wanted to study so badly that I was willing to work the skin off my back for it. The desire, so strong within me, heightened after meeting the boy who won a competition and his two friends. With increased determination, I worked harder and made sure I scraped up better sales to save up for school. Every day, from what profit we made, Mama would subtract 70% of the earnings, most of which went back to restocking while some ended up in house fund. Mama gave me the rest to do as I liked. I usually saved most of it and spent some on lunch the next day. My sisters received a similar treatment and despite getting a smaller amount they were quite pleased with the pocket money they received. Now we were able to purchase some things we needed and furnish our sleeping gears with quality items such as a cotton pillow instead of the rag stuffed gunny sack I had been using for years. We even bought pillowcases. Mama was always fair in dealing with us children. Those who sold more, received more. Hard work always paid off.

I took a holiday from work, one cool, cloudy day and walked the hour and a half journey to school daydreaming how I'd make life better for my family by becoming a learned man. With my learning, I would get a job in the government and we would eat well every day. Many of Mama's customers were wives of government officials. Arriving at the school gate, I paused to pat off the dust gathered on my attire from the long walk, straightened my posture. Faking my confidence, I walked into the gates of the school. Following the signs to the registration counter, I spoke of my desire to be a student with the lady behind the desk only to learn their school fees were astronomically high. Dispirited, I walked away to sit beneath the tall shady Wawa tree. I overheard some of the parents sharing their surprise at how cheap the cost to school a child in a government school as compared to the private sector. I assumed they were rich.

As a child of an out of work carpenter, and a small-time peddler, it was yet another cursed obstacle. I understand now, that to escape poverty you needed money. I didn't have the funds or a way to secure a well-paying job. *God is good, God has plans.* I thought with savage humour. I looked up at the canopy of the Wawa tree and tried not to cry from frustration. I puffed out my cheeks in a loud sigh. It was the only thing I could do. I was a man, and men do not cry. God and luck would never be on my family's side. Another loud sigh escaped me. My sighs caught the attention of a teacher on patrol.

The teacher approached me and sat on the tree root next to me.

"Hello boy, what is your name? Where are your parents? Have you lost them?" she asked. She was dressed well, in a pinafore and caftan. I saw that her name tag read "Miss Araba."

"No, I'm not. I'm just sitting under this tree wondering what I will do with my life now that I can't pay for the admission fees." I replied in glum tones.

Miss Araba quietly took in my patched trousers and my threadbare shirt. She asked, "Have you spoken to anyone in charge of financial aid for poor students?"

Drawing on the ground with a stick, I kept mum. I wondered what I could do to afford the school fees, when the strange word "aid" caught my attention. Hope reared its ugly head. I forced myself to raise my head as I asked, "What is 'aid'?"

POVERTY OF THE MIND

"Aid is a type of payment system. Sometimes the government gives us some money to help the poor and we will make it into a scholarship. In other words, the tuition fees will lower for you, and can be free if you meet our standards" Miss Araba replied.

"Really?" I asked. My hopes rose, for if anything, I was sure I qualified. It was a fact that we are poor. Surely, I am entitled to it, I thought, looking intently at the drawing I made on the ground.

"How about we go and ask, hm?"

Nodding my head, I got off the root I used as a seat. She walked towards an office labelled "Admission" with me trailing behind.

"In here?" I inquired.

"Yes. Let's talk to the lady inside."

Nodding again, I walked in with the teacher, to face a desk piled high with files. In fact, the whole room had stacks of files, leaving little place to maneuver. The teacher shut the door behind me, alerting the occupants of our presence. I spotted movements behind the stack of files. A nappy head of short hair came into view and a lady narrowed her eyes at the sight of us. Reaching for her glasses, she muttered under her breath while her other hand beckoned us closer. A name plate on her desk read "Miss Lahari."

"Miss Araba." She called out in polite greeting. "And who is this boy with you?" she asked of me.

"A young student who wants to register. I think he needs financial aid, Miss Lahari"

"Boy, what do your parents do?" asked Miss Araba.

MY HUMBLE BEGINNINGS

"Ma'am, my father is a carpenter and my mother tailor and a peddler." I answered honestly.

"Where do you live?" Miss Araba asked again.

"In Ashaiman slum." I said. This technically wasn't true, but our new place wasn't really far from the slums, and I felt it was close enough to the truth. I felt like every eye was on my stained and patched shirt.

The two ladies had a small discussion in a language I have heard but never learned, Twi. Clearly, they were trying to determine if what I say had any truth and what to do with me, as I came parentless to register.

"Why aren't your parents here to register you?" asked Miss Lahari.

"I don't think they approve of my decision to attend school." I replied in a small voice.

Miss Lahari looked at me and said, "It is seldom that a child comes to register himself at school. It's usually the parents. But your case is unique. Let me talk to our headmaster. Come with me, boy."

Together with the two female teachers, we walked to the principal's office. There, they sat me on a chair in front of a grey-haired man with a whiskery beard. With his beard, I thought he resembled a cat. He was busy scribbling away at something. The teachers and I waited until he came to a pause in his writing to address the matter. Mrs Lahari, the finance person whom I later came to know, also doubled up as the school's math teacher, explained my predicament. As she ended her speech, I spoke up. "Sir, I request your humble understanding in this matter. I want to study. Please sir, let me study. I want to make a better life for myself and my family."

Peering at me over the rim of his bifocal spectacles, the headmaster spoke with a calm and gentle voice.

"Son I see you as a man and I talk to you like one. I will never deter a child from education. I understand you from experience> We see many cases like yours, and I'd like you to join us. It is students like you, whom we want to welcome. Now the matter of school fees, unfortunately, I cannot grant free education. What we can do instead is to put you on the list for the partial scholarship. You will be entitled to 70% discount on the school fees.

Now, the rest of the money, do you think you can raise it?'

Delight shone across my face. Nodding enthusiastically, I thumped my chest.

"I want to receive education. I will make sure I get the money to pay the rest of the fees. I will work hard, sir and earn it. This will be my way out of poverty." The principal laughed at the sight of me thumping my chest.

"I believe that is true. Education frees people. Now follow Miss . She will register you as a student. You will have to give her the necessary information. Son, I hope to see you when our school starts in 3 weeks."

With that, I was ushered out of the principal's office and to the registration office. I was handed a piece of paper to write my name on. It was the first time I'm writing my name on such an official document. My hand shook and I forever thanked Uncle George and his harsh lessons on the sand. A pencil felt much smaller than a stick. It felt odd to hold such an easily breakable iteminn my hand. Yet, wrote my name. My writing looked squiggly. I prayed they would still register me despite my horrible handwriting.

I was given a piece of paper. Mrs Lahari informed me to bring it on the first day of school in 3 weeks' time along with the school fees. I was elated! I had 3 weeks to raise the necessary funds to be a school student! I knew in my heart of hearts I would make it.

MY HUMBLE BEGINNINGS

Now, I needed to up my game. I spent the walk back home thinking of the ways I could make more money. With how much I currently made, I am was still able to scrape up half the fees. Three weeks might have been too little time. *Maybe it is time to speak to Mama about my intentions,* I thought. *Mama, my angel, often with a word of encouragement, will surely find something for me. I really wanted to do this on my own though,* I thought as disappointment began to darken the bright hope in me.

I was so caught up in my thoughts that I didn't notice the figure standing in front of me, walking right into her, causing her to stumble, and dropping her handbag to the ground. Immediately apologising, I quickly rushed to assist her, observing a unique tattoo, a wooden comb, on her wrist. I recalled Mama once mentioning a lady with a similar tattoo above her wrist, known to the community as Mama Haniah.

Mama Haniah was often seen recruiting in the poorer areas, looking for people to assist her on her plantation. She was known to be fair to those under her care. On weekends, her household would prepare food to be distributed. I remember queuing up at one of the makeshift tents set up to get some Waakye wrapped in Ewe-eran leaves, the traditional leaves used to wrap and hold cooked food. I remembered getting two and devoured them before I came to the tables set out and going back for another to enjoy it with the Gari. It was one of those days when my family had not eaten for days, drinking water only to forget the hunger.

"Mama Haniah?" I ventured timidly. Dusting her skirt, the lady in the headwrap turned around to face me.

"Yes, it is I. Did you bump into me, boy?"

"Yes, Mama Haniah and I apologise again for my clumsiness."

"Boy, your eyes need looking around, not daydreaming with your mind." She chided me.

I bowed my head and apologized. Mama Haniah bent down to pick up a slip of paper.

"This doesn't look like mine. Is it yours?" she asked as she handed it to me. Glancing at it, I quickly grabbed it from her when I noticed it was my admission letter with the bottom portion stamping an approval for the scholarship programme. "You look old enough to be in school for a few years. Do you live here?"

"Yes, Mama Haniah. I live here."

"Ah. That must mean that schooling isn't cheap for your family."

I nodded my head and slowly added, "I am financing my own schooling, Mama Haniah."

"You are, eh? So young already so ambitious, I see. Just like my son." Mutely looking down on the ground, I felt Mama Haniah put a hand on my shoulder. "Are you working, dear?"

"Yes, I am. I help my Mama sell things in the market."

"Is that how you make money to pay your fees?"

"This is my first time to school, Mama Haniah. I didn't know fees were so expensive and the money I make doesn't seem enough." I suddenly blurted, relieved at being able to share my thoughts with an adult.

Patting me on the shoulder again, Mama Haniah asked me to join her as she walked down the street. Since the street was the one leading to my home, I had little hesitation. Mama Haniah was a good listener. I shared with her my inner turmoil growing up poor, and watching my siblings leave. How Mama's heart broke and how I wanted to be a better son to my parents and brother to my sisters.

Chucking, Mama Haniah said "I sense your desire for education." She gave me a word of advice, "Seize every available opportunity and never give up."

Smiling up at her, I promised I wouldn't. She went on to ask me how I knew her. I shared about the time I visited her soup kitchen, and about the time my mother went to her when we hit another snag in life - a period of water diet. I mentioned how we were much better now that all of us children helped Mama vandal while Uncle George worked hard at carving. Money isn't as much as a problem as it was in the past, I shared, as I pointed out my fenced house.

Mama Haniah, quiet as I shared my tales, asked, "Are you a hard worker, Jolie?"

"Yes, Mama Haniah. I am. I work hard and want to be smarter to help my family." I replied with determination.

'You need to help yourself first, Jolie. How can you help your family if you have nothing to give?'

"I don't understand what you mean."

"You will when you are older. Now that we are nearly at your home, let me ask you this. I need someone to work on my plantation for two weeks as it is harvest time for my palm trees. Do you know anyone?"

"I do not, Mama Haniah. Maybe my father is interested."

"No, dear. I need someone young and energetic like yourself."

"Me? How about me, then?" I asked.

POVERTY OF THE MIND

"Yes, you would be quite a good choice. Since I already know you are a hardworking young boy. All we need to do is get your parents to allow you to live on the plantation for two weeks during the harvest time. There will be food and bed for those helping us and of course I believe we pay a fair wage to our helpers. But I haven't asked the most important question. Would you be interested?"

"Oh yes, Mama Haniah! I most certainly would! My house is just there, and I am sure my father is home." I spoke excitedly.

"Let's go talk to him, young Jolie."

As anticipation built up in me, I guided her to our cob house. Observing her surprise and wonder, I felt grateful for Uncle George's insistence on a fence. The extra money we had been earning was put to good use. We now had a few stools out front, one of which I offered to Mama Haniah while I headed to the back where I could hear my father hammering away at something.

"Uncle George! I am home and we have a guest!" I said excitedly.

Taking out the pieces of nails he had pinched between his lips, he mouthed, "Who?"

"It's Mama Haniah. She's here to speak to you about me."

I didn't divulge much about the reason for her visit, wanting my father to hear it from her. Stepping off the stool, I got a view of a beautifully carved wooden three-pegged hook. The detailsof the fauna were expected of Uncle George who was big on nature.

"Is this your new design?"

"Looks good?" Uncle George inquired.

"Very." I replied.

MY HUMBLE BEGINNINGS

"Come. We have a guest." Walking behind him, I took in my father's broad shoulders. Since the move and his new venture, my father slowly regained his leaner build and seemed to shed off the age. Mama would sometimes tease him, saying he looks as young as she feels.

"Madam Haniah, I hear you are looking to speak to me" uttered Uncle George as he stepped out from around the house. He did not offer Mama Haniah's hand, a handshake. I recalled how people would revere someone like Mama Haniah and even touch her feet, seeking blessing. Uncle George would not bow down to anyone, nor did he believe in human saints, but he surely showed her respect.

"Hello. Yes. It is about young Jolie."

"Has he done anything mischievous?" Uncle George asked.

"Quite the contrary. I am thinking of hiring him to work on my plantation for three weeks."

"Madam Haniah. I know you are always helping people. And may God bless you for that. But what can Jolie do? He is of average built compared to his friends. His only known trait – he is quick with his feet."

Mama Haniah laughed, "Well, this young man charmed me. He is passionate about earning money and I need hard workers. I have a spot fit for someone like him, who is quick on his feet and energetic. Moreover, the money is good. Better than what he makes selling his wares."

"I take it he has shared enough of his desire to be rich," said my father throwing a rueful smile at me. I smiled back.

"That he has, Mr George." Mama Haniah said with a smile.

"I cannot say no, for it seems like his mind is made up. What are the arrangements, Madam Haniah?"

"For three weeks of work, he will be paid 210 cedis. Food and board will be provided. Working hours will be long, but with enough rest between for them to regain their energy, from 7am to 6pm."

"Not too bad. but what will he do?" My father asked. Given Mama and Gina's clever way of stretching our money, this could have fed us for half a year or more. As I stood there doing my best impression of an obedient child, I hoped my father would agree.

Mama Haniah folded her hands and replied. "He will be tasked with making sure there is enough firewood to heat the barrels and to turn the wheel of the palm kernel crusher." Here she turned to me and added with a smile, "If you are willing, you can earn more by taking the night shift. A bonus will be given for good, accurate work." She paused and turned back to my father. "All in all, he could earn up to 300 cendis. More if he works well."

My father put his head to the side and pretended to think. In truth, we needed the money. As I would be fed as well, this would be a good deal for us. Three hundred cendis was a fortune. It could buy us a goat, or a flock of chickens.

"Mama Haniah, for it is you who is offering the job and we have heard good news from our friends and neighbours. Therefore, I trust you with my son. When will you be needing Jolie?"

"I thank you for the trust. Jolie will start work in two days." Turning to me, Mama Haniah said, "Jolie, wait at the main gate by the market around noon. A truck will pick you up and take you to the plantation. It is 45 minutes out of town. Just bring a change of clothes and a towel. Everything else will be provided."

"Okay, Mama Haniah." I felt like jumping for joy. All my problems were solved. I restrained myself as my face split into a wide smile.

"Mr George, I promise to take care of Jolie. And thank you again."

Patting me on the shoulder, Mama Haniah turned and walked out of our fenced house. Watching her shrinking silhouette, I sensed movement behind me. Uncle George stood behind me watching her vanish around a corner.

"Jolie, she is a special woman in this community. Working with her would do you good. I do not need to remind you of the importance of respect when in her company." I nodded my head as a thought flitted through my mind.

"Is there a reason why you didn't shake her hands? Respect?"

"That and more, Jolie. Madam Haniah is Muslim. In Islam, it is forbidden for a woman to touch a man who isn't her immediate relation."

My head bobbled in agreement. It didn't matter. I had work, and I would earn the money to cover my school fees. That was all I cared about.

CHAPTER 22

Great Firewall of China 2010 - Guangzhou

When I stepped into my office from the cold, windy Wednesday air, I felt a subtle excitement in the air. I'd barely taken ten steps into the office area when Nalia, with a sprint in her step, walked up to me and handed me a pink memo. It read, "KTV." Nalia, standing eagerly next to me, shifting from one foot to the other, avoided looking at my face as I turned to her.

"When?" I asked taking in her contained eagerness. Excitement poured from this usually quiet woman as she clapped her hands together beaming.

"Boss, you're free today. Nothing's on the schedule. And so far, no pre-arranged deals. How about tonight?"

"Nalia, you know how the business works. We never know when an important call will come in."

"Wo zhi dao. But we all need a break, boss!"

"Do we really? Just 2 days ago we were on a week break. Or is it someone's desire to sing?" I asked jokingly.

Across the hall, a voice shouted in response to my question, "Nalia wants to sing 'Love Story', boss!" A chorus of laughter joined me as Nalia walked to the glass wall separating the rooms, pointing and cursing at Ethan, lead of the legal team and translator.

MY HUMBLE BEGINNINGS

"Okay. Okay," with my hands raised in surrender defusing the situation, "How about dinner and KTV then?" Cheers came back to me. Nalia, beaming, asked if she should book a table at one of my favourite seafood restaurants.

"No. Tonight, let's try that new hot pot place, in the shopping mall."

"Which mall? I can look up the restaurant on Baidu and perhaps look around for a discount."

"Well, there is this new mall down the street. Hang on." Heading to the pantry, Naila and I talked about the hot pot spot I had once noticed while running an errand with Sasha. Unable to recall the name of the restaurant, I remember pinning it on an app. I pulled up my Baidu map app, similar to Google Maps, and searched through my pins.

Robin Li, a man I once met at a private auctioneer's party, shared how he had started Baidu with Eric Xu. With a glass of champagne in hand, Robin, stood on the third stair of a curved stairway, and shared his initial surprise and anger when he discover his patent, which he was the first to file for a method known as RankDex, is utilised by PageRank technology to function Google. This discovery led him to accuse the founders, Larry Page and Sergey Brin for stealing his ideas. Robin swore he would raise sufficient funds to start his own search engine, which he succeeded in raising $1.2 million. He returned home and started Baidu as a search engine on websites like Sina and Sohu in China.

Determined to make Baidu a stand-alone search engine, Robin raised another $25 million over 3 years and turned Baidu into what is now the largest Chinese search engine, able to compete with Google. When he raised his champagne flute, to mark the end of his speech, I applaud with the rest of the exclusive socialite, impressed with this Chinese.

"Right. I think this is the one." Having located the pin, I showed the map to Nalia. "In this mall, and on the same floor with the cinema, there is a popular KTV place.

"Half and half, with one and a half teaspoons of sugar?" she inquired to my preferred coffee option.

"As always, Nalia." I winked as I grabbed an apple from the fridge in the pantry. Walking over to my office, I passed Nalia's desk. Glancing over, I saw a few memos with buyers' names and their wares circled in red. Naila, always a hard worker was trying to secure a potential deal with a client who solely spoke Kejia Hua or Hakka, another native language popular in southern China, one I somehow never managed to wrap my tongue around.

"Here you go, boss. I managed to track down the hot pot restaurant through Baidu andmade an appointment for 6 pm." The strong smell of freshly brewed coffee tickled my senses. Having an open-door policy, an idea I picked up from a business magazine, is pretty unique. My full-time onsite staff, a team of Chinese, were initially tiptoeing around me. Now, they included me in their circle of friends. It is good to have a team I could trust. Smiling, I took the hot mug from the wooden tray Nalia set on my worktable.

"Efficient as ever, Naila. Check with Alan and make sure we have enough cash on the company card for the next 2 weeks. I am meeting potential clients." Nodding, Nalia walked out of my office.

From Alan's room, I heard Nalia passing on my message. Alan was in charge of finances and securing deals. He had been with me since the day I started the business. I met him through our mutual friend, Bill. Shrewd towards financial details, Alan, I noticed even then, was always on the lookout for good deals. True enough, he brought some lucrative deals to our company.

MY HUMBLE BEGINNINGS

Taking another sip from the mug, I turned my desktop on. As it took its time to start, I mentally went through a list of things to do before Sasha got home at 12pm. I pulled out my phone from my new pair of grey Levi's recently acquired from the knockoff street. I dropped Anne a message informing her of my plans to have dinner with the team and asked her if she could stay for an extra hour. While waiting for a reply, I logged into my QQ account to check my emails. After an hour of setting some deals in motion, I sat back in my chair and stretched my arms over my head. I looked over to my now nearly empty coffee mug, contemplating whether to have when a blinking icon on QQ caught my attention. Of late, I noticed newer functions appearing on QQ. Unknown to the world beyond the borders of China, QQ, an application launched by Tencent in 1999, became a wellloved instant messaging software service comparable to Yahoo Messenger.

The Golden Shield or more commonly known as "The Great Firewall of China," enforced by the Chinese government to regulate internet domestically, has blocked access to a number of foreign sites. Turning into a father of a 4-year-old, I understood the desire for constant surveillance and censoring system. I used similar technology on Sasha when she accessed video channels. Certain information or videos are best curtailed. China's political system commanded by the communist stronghold, had seen tremendous advancements in recent years. The rapid development is beyond the capabilities of law, and lawmakers are unable to foresee the possible negative impact on the people. This forced drastic choices to be made. The firewall was initially created to curb China Democracy Party's influence, but later extended to stop the country's secrets being leaked out into the world. It was all done in the name of weeding out disharmony in Chinese society.

Pushing the thoughts out of my head, I pulled up the Baidu website, thinking the last time I used it was when I searched about the copyright lawsuit Baidu won. Thanks to its ability to link users to hundreds of thousands of illegal copies of songs, Baidu became

THE place to download music. However, facilitating mass copyright infringement led to Baidu being brought to court by Universal Music and Warner Bros. Records. Fortunately for the common users like myself, Baidu won. Learning from their rival, Google, Baidu formulated a revenue plan, placing ads in the video logs. Revenue was later split between Baidu and the music labels. *Wise move,* I thought as I typed out a list of songs I would probably sing that night. Plugging in my earphones to the jack, I pressed play, trying to remember the lyrics while I worked on a new target plan for the following month.

SKIN PAIN

We stood at attention in neat rows under the hot afternoon sun out in the assembly yard facing the stage. I hoped it would not take too long, I felt like a roasted yam on the coals.

Teachers patrolled between each line, making sure we were all paying attention. We could see Mr Rex stalking around us, on the lookout for miscreants.

Mr Tano, the head of the English department stood on stage. He held up two books in his hand. Some of the students further away from the stage stretched their necks to see the cover.

"The first-place prize for the spelling competition are these two books, "*Classic Tales*" and

"The Jungle Book" along with a cash voucher of 50 cedis. The second and third place prizes are cash vouchers of 30 cedis each. Just to remind you, the competition will be in one month's time. You will need to sign up with your head teacher by this week. Those who participate are encouraged to work with their respective English teachers in preparation for the competition. Any questions, do ask me or your head teacher. Thank you." Half mustered up an applause obediently as Mr Tano handed the amplifier back to the speaker in charge, a final year student.

MY HUMBLE BEGINNINGS

"Thank you, Mr Tano. And now, everyone, please proceed in an orderly fashion back to your class."

Following the assembly pattern we were taught, my class leader patiently waited for the students in the row next to us to reach stage before beginning our march back. I eagerly tapped the shoulders of the guy in front of me, Kai, asking his and Coujoe's opinion about the spelling test.

"Books!" Coujoe hissed. "Can't they give us something more fun?"

"Like what?" asked Kai, walking backwards to face us.

"How about food for a change?" grumbled Coujoe.

"Nah. If it's me, I'd prefer more money. Books can't feed me," said Kai.

"Are you sure? Not maybe a bag of Milo?" asked Coujoe slyly.

"A bag?" Kai shook his head. "Maybe a month's worth of Milo!" He exclaimed. Kai was a well-known Milo fiend, and could be bribed with a cup of it.

"Hey, come on. Books are good. You get knowledge!" I joined in. "I like books." I grinned at my friends.

Kai and Coujoe looked at each other, then at me.

Kai chuckled and nodded sagely, "We expected that from you, Jolie."

"Yes, Jolie. Bookworm! Lover of Books!" Coujoe quipped as he smacked me on the shoulder.

Kais looked doubtful. "I don't see how books can help you." His expression lit up as he continued "Now, food. Food is king! It's practical." His expression turned wistful. "One day, I'd like to be able to eat three meals a day, and not worry about where my next meal is coming from." We shared a moment of silence. We could each hear our empty bellies rumbling together. None of us had brought lunch to school this week. I had not made enough to afford it this month.

I laughed and shrugged. "Well, you both know I like reading. Reading powers the mind," I said cheerily, tapping the side of my head. "Feed the mind!"

Kai and Coujoe both looked at each other. Kai said in unison, "Remember us, when you're rich and famous!" Coujoe playfully punched my back.

"Hey!" I protested and turned around to see Coujoe skipping away from me with a cheeky smile.

"See you in class, desk mate!" I shouted at him, drawing laughter from Kai. Nevermind, I could always get Coujoe later, we were in the same class.

I turned to Kai and asked, "Honestly tell me, Kai. Do you think I have the chance?"

"Jolie of us three, you are the smartest. But you know I never liked words," replied Kai seriously. "Math is useful." He flashed a victory sign at me. "I had you beat in the test last week!"

"At least you know what you're good at, Kai." Quietly I added, "I think I will join in," just as we reached the entrance of our classroom. Coujoe was already seated, huge smile on his face.

I pretended not to see him and as I walked closer, I pounced and landed a few playful punches on his arm. We got into rough housing until our Mrs Mary, our teacher walked in. We promptly settled down and became model students. Nobody wanted to be sent to see

MY HUMBLE BEGINNINGS

T- Rex. The last class for the day was the English with Mrs Mary. We all liked her as she was patient and kind. At the end of class, I told Mrs Mary of my intention to join the spelling competition. She signed me up then directed me to Mr Tano for more advice.

I walked out my class and followed her to the staff room. Entering was like travelling into a forbidden kingdom, one where large wooden office desks were uniformly laid out with books piled high on them. In one corner stood a lone desk with mugs and a hot water kettle. I stood at the doorway taking in everything, undecided on whether to enter.

"Jolie, come in," I heard my teacher's voice coming from in a room I had earlier saw Mrs Mary vanish into. Eyes down, I put a foot on the floor and tried as best as possible to be seen and not heard. I made my way quietly and discreetly through the maze. I glanced to my left to see Mr Tano standing in the doorway of an office, looking at me. An unexpected flash of guilt ran through me, stopping me in my tracks. He signalled for me to head his way and I followed, eyes kept down to the floor.

"Hi Jolie." greeted Mr Tano the moment I reached his desk.

"Hello, sir." I said, still looking at the ground.

"Jolie, you can ask for Mr Tano's advice in this matter." I nodded my head, keeping my eyes firmly on the chair in front of me.

"I have to go. I wish you all the best," said my head teacher as she walked out the door, shutting it behind her.

I stood in silence for a few minutes, waiting for Mr Tano to say something.

"So, Jolie. Why do I sense your fear?"

"Sir, I have never been in the teacher's room and those who do come in here, are usually here to receive punishment," I said with my eyes on the cracked concrete floor. I could feel Mr Tano was staring at me.

"Sir, please. Tell me more about the competition." I asked. Anything to change the subject.

"Jolie, the competition is in 3 stages. The first 10 people to pass the first round will go to the second round where only half will go through the final round to compete against each other. There are only three prizes available. The words can be found in your assigned reader. I suggest you study the spelling dictionary."

I nodded my head, indicating I understood.

Mr Tano continued "At each stage, the speaker will say a word and the chosen participant will have to spell it out. In each round, the participant has to get 7 words right to proceed to the next round. In the final round, the winner will be determined by the most words spelled in two minutes."

I kept quiet for a while. "Sir, I mean, Mr Tano, I will need to spell 7 words to pass the first two rounds. The final round will be the hardest. Only two minutes to spell as many as I can." I looked at Mr Tano with raised eyebrows.

"Yes. That is exactly right. Now Jolie, you can actually come to see me after school, and we can do some practice."

"Really, Mr Tano? I mean, if its no trouble at all!"

"Not at all, Jolie. See you tomorrow after class."

"Okay, Mr Tano. Thank you!" I replied with joy.

MY HUMBLE BEGINNINGS

As I shut his office door behind me, I felt elation bubble up. I practically skipped out the teacher's room, forgetting my trepidation towards this office. With my eyes no longer on the floor, I noticed something I didn't see earlier. Mr King, our PE teacher sat at his desk with his shirt off. The shirt was in his left hand, with a needle and thread in the other. He was intent on his task and did not notice me. It was clear he was mending his shirt. I slowed down deliberately, and playing it cool, looked over a few more teacher's desks. I noticed a sewing kit of some sort on almost every desk. Some barely had a needle and a thread. While others were store-bought and fully stocked. They even had a thimble and a needle minder. It dawned on me then, the teachers we joked about for looking unkempt, were poor. Like me, they lacked the funds to lead a good life, or even clothe themselves properly. I felt a strong sense of regret remembering the number of times I joined Kai and Coujoe along with our group of friends to gossip about the teachers. Teachers who made sure we have enough notebooks, pencils, and erasers to complete our classwork.

I turned away from the sad sight, thinking our dedicated teachers were willing to go hungry just to make sure their students could make it in life. *Life's blessings to them*, I thought as I made my way to the library, wanting to borrow a dictionary to memorise during my walk home. Normally students weren't allowed to take books home, but Mr Tano made an exception for me.

-

SASHA'S EDUCATION

In time, I noticed, not only were some of my schoolmates poor, teachers were too. It struck me to know people in general, were not rich. Maybe, just maybe, those who were rich held higher ranks in the government. The teachers' dress code showed various level of poorness, in the eyes of their students. Some teachers would always be well dressed, though often come in with the same attire the following week. It was like they only had 6 sets of formal wear. Some teachers would dress shabbily with little care to their clothes. Watching our teachers was like watching a theatre act. Amongst ourselves, we tended to compare and make jokes about the teachers' attire, walking gait, unique quirks. Some of us began to assume and claim that poverty was founded by some of the teachers, who were the true definition of poverty as it literally oozed out of their pores. While all the chatter and jokes were funny, I learned that in life, there will always be someone to compare ourselves to, be it for the better or worse. Yet, comparing isn't important when it comes to self-satisfaction.

Sasha thankfully never has to go through the struggles I faced to be educated. Tough as it is in China to find a suitable kindergarten to accept Sasha, knowing people and through their guangxi – connections with the right people – certain matters are easily solved. My worry never dissipated though. Knowing China and their constant change in policy, Sasha may be getting the education she should be now, but in the near future, homeschooling could be the only option available for her. It's a situation I shuddered to consider, knowing I'm incapable of providing a comprehensive education structure for her.

Diving into the expat pool in Guangzhou to find suitable teachers to start such a programme is another concern knowing how teachers often venture towards higher monetary job offers. The constant change of educators would certainly affect a child's learning ability. Hard to blame the educators though. Expats generally leave their homes in search of travel experience and a salary increase. For an American graduate, teaching in China as a native speaker meant earning nearly triple the amount in America. The draw is too great for many educators to ignore, especially with China being welcoming to the Western world. Of course, there are other English educators in China. Unfortunately, the prevailing preference for the Chinese are white-skinned, blue-eyed teachers.

With a population of over 1 billion people, China, after opening its doors to English educators, started a high demand for white-skinned teachers, a demand the western world is unable to meet. Requests led

MY HUMBLE BEGINNINGS

to numerous people, with no degree in education and little knowledge in this field to enter the country, under the guise of a tourist visa which they use to gain employment. Legal or not, is beyond my judgment, knowing I too crossed over to China with similar circumstances. An opportunity I am thankful for.

The vibration of my phone in my jeans pocket brought me out of revere. Emerging from my thoughts, I looked down at the drafted English contract I was supposed to read through and noticed it was blotched with ink from my fountain pen's tip touching the paper, unmoving. I looked over to the clock next to my now cold coffee. It was 4 o'clock. Shaking my head, I pulled my phone. Mama's picture filled my iPhone 3GS screen, the latest phone on the market. I sighed. *How am I to break the news of losing the case to Mama who has been looking forward to meeting her first granddaughter?*

Touching the green answer icon, I raised the phone to my left ear.

"Hello Mama," I said with a slight smile on my lips.

"Jolly, sweetheart, how come I haven't heard from you for over two weeks?" Mama's voice sounded a bit exasperated. "I really want to hear the results from the courtroom." I could hear the excitement in her voice. Looking up at the circular lights in the ceiling, I noted one fused light bulb needed to be changed.

I exhaled. "Mama..." I said despondently, "Oh Mama... The Korean court decided since I am not listed as Sasha's father on the birth certificate, the document will remain with Sakura." Mama took some time comprehending the court's reasoning.

"Even with DNA evidence, son?" questioned Mama. The lawyers used the DNA analysis obtained in China. But the Korean court prefers the test to be conducted on Korean grounds. My fear was once the test was done, the family court may have a warrant waiting to take Sasha away from me. I shared my distress with my mother who reciprocated my feeling.

"I was really hoping to hug my granddaughter and introduce her to all your favourite food."

"Mama, we must keep praying and have faith."

"Faith, I have, my son. I trust my all in God's plans. If Sasha is meant to be with us in Ghana, God will see it happens."

"Yes, Mama. I know you and Janet spoke to Headmaster Okafor of Chrisdof International School."

"And we even went on a drive down to the school to estimate the distance from home. Mr Okafor had a staff receive us at the gate for a private tour around the school. It is a beautiful school, Jolie."

Smiling faintly, I wrote down the school name for future reference.

"Mama, we can still hope for Sasha to come home one day."

"Talking about Sasha, how is my granddaughter doing? Is she a terror to her teachers, like her father?" laughed Mama.

Joining in her merriment I replied, "Sasha may seem a handful, but no way is she maddening as her father, Mama. I truly feel sorry for the eventful childhood and teenage years you endured with me. But I won't apologize for climbing Nii Ashaiman's favourite tree. At 3 years old, I was too curious to know why the fruitless tree was his favourite."

Laughing louder, "The spanking you got from Uncle George for climbing that tree brought all the neighbours to our door! Why in the name of the Lord did you climb that tree?"

MY HUMBLE BEGINNINGS

"Because Pirate Jim said Ashaiman's gold was hidden in the highest branch of the tree with a special code! Decoding it would make us the richest family in Ashaiman."

"Oh Jolie. You were quite the troublemaker." said Mama.

I chucked. "Mama, you know me best." Looking at the Sasha's picture on my desk, I spoke seriously. "Sasha, is a real talent. The first term report from her kindergarten proves it. Her love for language is astonishing, managing to pick up English and Mandarin in the span of 5 months. Her curiosity is clearly propelling her forward. Mama, I want the best education for her. I am planning to speak to the lawyers again and appeal to a different court. We will keep fighting and searching for a solution."

"As always, Jolie, I have faith in God's plans. We should pray for his guidance and most importantly, never give up." In the background, I could hear my sister Gina calling out to my mum. It was about 8:30 am in Ghana and my sisters normally had breakfast around that time.

Mama and I ended our conversation after I said my hellos to my sister.

After the call, I smiled to myself, once again caught up in the past, clearly envisioning my sister Janet, busy as a bee preparing our usual Hausa Koko with Koose. Hausa Koko, despite its particular taste and colour it is a tasty flowing solution made from ground millet. Koose is another dish of millet paste made into round gooey balls and dropped into hot vegetable oil. These fried balls are Mama's favourite dipping. Gina, on a new diet fad, opted for groundnuts and milk in her Hausa Koko. Janet on the other hand, wasn't a fussy eater. I did miss these Ghanaian treats.

Pushing myself out of my faux leather armchair, I stretched my arms above my head and walked out my office door, into the living room. Ever since Sasha entered my world, my life slowly began revolving around her. I moved my office and home, believing our time together to be precious. *And I have no regrets*, I thought to myself, squatting down, hands outstretched. Sasha saw me coming out of my office, ran from her nanny, and propelled her small body into my arms.

"How was school, little one?" I asked as I carried her to an armchair and sat her on my lap.

"Abeoji, today we went on a nature walk. We sat in a huge garden with so many, many, many flowers and I saw butterflies, and…" Sasha trailed off, making a buzzing sound with her mouth.

"Was it a bee, Sasha? Did it make the sound like bzzz?" I asked, mimicking the sound a bee makes.

"Yes, abeoji! They were all on the flowers! My teacher says, the bees make something yummy. I tried following them but I didn't see the bees make anything yummy," said Sasha a little sad.

Amused, I said, "Sweetheart, bees have a special house called a beehive."

"Really? Can I look inside for the yummy?"

Intrigued by the idea of Sasha putting her head into a beehive, her nanny and I laughed.

"No dear. The bees wouldn't like that very much. But they do make honey which is yummy."

"Oh… How can I eat yummy honey?"

"How about abeoji buy some later today for your breakfast tomorrow? We usually eat honey with bread."

MY HUMBLE BEGINNINGS

Hearing that, Sasha began jumping on my lap and wrapped her arms around me.

"I can't wait to try honey!" exclaimed Sasha who then jumped off my lap to relay everything to her nanny, Anne.

Looking at her holding her nanny's hands and talking rapidly, my tummy rumbled loudly. Surprised by the sound, Sasha and Anne turned curiously to me.

"Sorry ladies, I haven't eaten since breakfast," I apologised. Thinking of Anne's work shift ending soon, I asked, "Anne, would you like to go home a little earlier today?"

"'Why, Mr Wine?"

"It's just that I'd like to take Sasha to Xiaobei to eat some Ghanaian food." Looking at Sasha, I asked her, "Would you like to eat a Ghanaian dinner?" This caused more ruckus as Sasha began shouting her agreement in three different languages around the living room. Laughing again at her antics, I stood up to tidy myself for our little dinner date.

-

I was in a daze on the day they announced the winners. Having never won anything before, the feeling of having one's name announced to the crowd for a reward, felt like being drowned. I remembered Kai and Coujoe pushing me up towards the podium on the stage in the assembly area. It was all a blur of emotions I could barely digest. In a matter of minutes, I found myself clutching an envelope and a gift box wrapped in normal brown paper, tied with an exquisite silk-like polka dot white and black ribbon. Gina would love the ribbon. Immediately after the prize ceremony, our teachers ordered us to march back to our classes.

Curiosity got the cat, and the cat got their tongues. My close friends, Kai and Coujoe, shot curious looks in my direction. They were dying to know what was inside. So was I. I shook my head. We needed to survive the day first. After school, we could unwrap the prizes.

We kept silent during the forced march back our class, for we all feared drawing the attention of the discipline master, Mr Rex, also known as "T-Rex." There was a good reason why he earned that name: he was brutish and dangerous with an unpredictable temper. Everyone, including teachers called him by his given nickname and spoke of him in hushed tones. His god-given name was forgotten. We feared him more than our parents. Mr Rex was rumoured to beat not only students, but also teachers whom he deemed to have stepped out of line. His military training made him into a tough man, and he believed that the only way to enforce compliance was through strict discipline and physical exercise. He expected perfection. In short, to all of us schoolboys, he was the devil incarnate.

Any deviants he caught would suffer the dubious honour of being his whipping boy. If you were lucky, you only had to suffer for one day before another was stupid enough to misbehave. Then, Mr Rex would move on. There was a story of a boy who was punished with detentions for a month. He only lasted a week before he dropped out of school, and disappeared. We never found out what happened to him. Daily, we heard him roaring at some schoolboy in the assembly field, degrading the poor miscreant into submission. He never stopped until you were crying, shaking, and begging for mercy. Nobody stood up to him.

Mr T-Rex's voice is branded into my psyche. To this day, even as a grown man with a business empire, I still tremble in my shoes when I recall his voice. Loud and uncouth voices make my skin crawl.

MY HUMBLE BEGINNINGS

The day I suffered the pleasure of one of his "training sessions," as he called it, is branded into my mind. I was caught littering, truly without intent for the banana peel I was throwing into the bin missed the can by an inch. Yanked by the arm, I felt myself lift partially off the floor by a huge figure. Mr Rex, without a word, dragged me to the assembly field. Numerous attempts at inquiring what caused this hit a brick wall. Letting my arm go, I was pushed to squat, and that's when T-Rex spoke.

"Punishment for littering: 20 minutes in the sun and 30 push-ups."

"Sir, I didn't litter!" I exclaimed my innocence.

"I caught you littering. Your banana peel didn't make it into the bin," said Mr Rex.

"Maybe it missed the bin! I honestly didn't litter!" I repeated.

"You were caught," said Mr Rex. "For that, your punishment is 30 push-ups and 20 minutes under the sun. You're only your last chance Mr Jolie." Mr Rex growled "I suggest you shut up and do as you're told. The next write up means expulsion for you."

I could not afford expulsion. I want to succeed in life. To do so, I knew I needed education. Knowing Mr Rex and his temper, I thought better than to tempt fate and battle him on this. Meekly, I bowed my head in outward acceptance. Inwardly, I was seething. It would be a cold day in hell before I gave this bastard his pleasure.

"Drop and give me 30 now!" barked Mr Rex. "Count them out for me. Miss one and you have to start over." I got down to my hands and stretched my feet straight out.

"One!" I shouted. Push-ups weren't easy. I felt my limbs began to tremble, after number seventeen.

POVERTY OF THE MIND

"Pick up the pace!" shouted Mr Rex.

I lost my temper and snapped. "I"m going as fast as I can...SIR!"

Mr Rex circled my prone body. He practically purred as he told me, "Start over Mr Jolie. You've lost count!"

Rotten lizard! My arms were soft as boiled tomatoes. I had no strength left.

"One!" I growled through gritted teeth. One day, I would come back and buy his damn house, throw him out, and then come back to buy this damn school and fire him. Each push-up took all my concentration and will power. I would throw a feast for the rest of the school and celebrate.

"TWENTY!" I shouted. Mr Rex struck my back with his cane.

"Poor form Mr Jolie. Straighten your back!" He barked. I hoped that I wasn't bleeding. Mama would whup me good for misbehaving at school. None of my school friends or teachers went to the same church as we did, so it was easy to hide this fact from her. She would know for certain if his strike drew blood and stained my shirt. This was my only good shirt. Mama would deduct my earnings if I stained it. I needed to push through the last ten.

"THIRTY!" My arms gave out, and I collapsed to the ground, shivering in exhaustion. I could barely breathe as the ground knocked the wind out of me. I wanted a break, but I knew that Mr Rex was just looking for an excuse to dole out more punishment. We all knew that he lived for it.

"Now stand here for 20 minutes! Arms held straight I will be watching you." Mr Rex headed to the bicycle shed and continued to watch me. Slowly pushing myself up, trying to use my arms as little as possible, I shut my eyes and stood straight facing the school.

MY HUMBLE BEGINNINGS

I slowly opened my eyes at the sound of shuffling shoes and a greasy snigger. It was the school bully, Osei. One of the few boys in school who had a personal chauffeur and a maid who came in every day to serve him a home-cooked lunch of fish, chicken, and rice. Rich bastard. He crossed the assembly square towards the bicycle shed situated opposite the classrooms. Right in Mr Rex's line of sight, he dropped a sweet wrapper. Mr Rex was struck with a queer case of selective blindness because he said not a word. Osei smarmed his trademark leer at me and strolled away. Mr Rex had chosen to ignore Osei. It was clear that he wanted to maintain the fiction that Osei was not here. I understood then that there were two sets of rules. One for the rich, who had all the money and power. There was another set for the rest of us, one that put us firmly under their boot. *The shit-tainted bastard. May the spiders feast on his guts.*

Osei, was spoiled, had no regard for his studies, and could not attend any of the better private schools like the rest of his peers. He flunked out of every school within Accra, Tema, and Ashaiman. It was rumored that he scored abysmally on every entrance test he took.

Being government-funded, our school was obligated to take in all comers and had no entrance exams. Therefore, this was the only choice he left his parents. Osei held himself above everyone, even the teachers, and treated the school as his own private kingdom. His generous parents, grateful for the principal's consideration in allowing Osei to study in our school, often showered the teachers, especially senior management with gifts for bearing their son's quirks. Almost all the school equipment and half the library books came from Osei's devoted parents.

Fuming, I shouted out to Mr Rex, "Osei dropped a wrapper! Why isn't he punished?" Mr Rex chose to ignore Osei and turned to inspect one of the bicycles in the shed.

Mr Rex gloated "Speak again Mr Jolie, and that will be another ten minutes." Osei sniggered and flashed a middle finger at me.

POVERTY OF THE MIND

Crude uncouth bastard. You may have money, but you don' t have class. Clenching my fist, I dug my nails into my palms. I had to endure. One day, I would be richer than Osei and his family.

-

"Jolie, come on, open it already!" Snapping out of my reverie, I shrugged off Mr Rex and Osei the bully. Kai and Coujoe were pestering me to unwrap my prizes. My arms ached from the muscle memory gained from the forty-seven pushups I endured. I set my prizes down on my desk. Starting with the envelope, I ripped it open to have 30 cedis fall onto my lap.

"Wow," I said softly.

Kai urged, "Open the other box!"

Coujoe, the impatient one threatened, "If you don't I will, and then I'll keep it!"

"Charle, hold up. Look at this money. It's a lot!" I said, still looking at the money in my hands.

"Jolie, the gift, hurry, open it before the teacher comes," said Kai.

"Okay, okay!" I replied. I slowly undid the ribbon on the box. The material was slippery and cool between my fingers. *Is this silk?* I wondered. I tucked it in my pocket, for I knew Gina would like it. I tore open the brown wrapping to reveal a book. My heart leaped. *Could it be?* I thought. I turned the book over to read the title, *The Jungle Book*. This would be the first book that I could call my own. It was beautiful and mine. I tucked the book away with great care. Later that night, I took it home to Mama and my sisters to read it to them.

In walked Mr Tano, who was substituting for Mrs Mary this week. She was unwell and was on sick leave. I needed to thank him for all his help. I once asked him why he wanted to help me. His response stunned me, *Because I see the same fire in you.*

Walking up to me, he tapped me on the shoulder twice and congratulated me for doing my best in the competition. Thanking him as he walked towards the blackboard, it never occurred to me how nasty rumours could get. They spread faster than cholera in our small school. They said that the school bought another book for the 2nd place gift at Mr Tano's insistence. I was his special pet. The bell for morning recess rang and my group of friends and I made our way to our favourite Wawa tree.

There was a row planted behind the bicycle shed. I think the principal thought of them as long term investments. The wood was valuable and could be sold for ready cash in a pinch. I knew this because Uncle George often handled Wawa wood. As they stood, their canopies gave us shade and made a natural gathering point for students and teachers alike.

Kai, Coujoe, and I could not afford to eat from the food stalls located under the Wawa trees. When we could, we packed lunch from home instead. Should one of us turn up without food, we would share what we had between us three. As they say, never study on an empty stomach.

"Do you think Mr Tano asked for another book because he knew Jolie wanted it?" asked a voice from one of the groups around us.

I knew that slimey voice. It sounded like Osei. Looking around, I caught I caught the sly glances from his toadies who sat near us. My unease felt like ants crawling up my arms.

"Ignore them, Jolie," Coejoe encouraged. 'They can't do anything, T-Rex is watching."

I stole a glance and sure enough Mr Rex was patrolling the area. This time, it was enough to deter Osei: there were too many eyes watching.

"Let's eat" Kai said with gusto as he dug into his waakanye . Silence reigned as we all chowed down.

"Charle, do you think the same as others," I asked suddenly of my friends.

"We don't know, to be honest." Kai replied.

"All we know is you worked really hard to win." Coujoe added.

I was lucky that day. I had leftover koose for lunch that Mama made for last night's dinner. As I ate, I decided I needed to have a word with Mr Tano. Finishing off my koose, I stuffed my lunch bag into my pants, waved goodbye to my friends, and made my way to the teachers' office.

I found Mr Tano seated in his desk, which piled high with students' books as usual. He was in the midst of grading our work. I coughed politely.

"Sir, may I have a word, please?" I inquired. Without breaking his writing momentum, Mr Tano shot a quick glanced at me.

"Yes, Jolie?"

"Sir, I do not know how to word this well. But I must know something," I whispered. Mr Tano put down his pen, took off his glasses and look at me.

"Tell me."

MY HUMBLE BEGINNINGS

The words felt stuck in my mouth. I swallowed my saliva a few times before raising the much-dreaded question.

"Sir, did you ask the school to buy a book for the 2nd place winner?"

"Yes, I did Jolie. Why do you ask?"

"Was it before or after you knew I was getting the 2nd spot?"

Ushering me to sit opposite him, he waited until I was seated before saying, "The decision to buy another book was made unanimously by all English teachers, not me solely. The title of the book was chosen by the school and I had no say in it."

"But sir, I hear others say you did it for me."

"If you hear differently, it's because people are jealous. Do not let jealousy deter you. Use it to empower you."

Nodding my head, I stood up and thanked my teacher.

"Sir, I shall keep what you say close to my heart. I shall not detour from my path to achieve success and raise my family out of poverty. You help me to make it happen, sir." With that, I put my hand out for a shake, a bold move. Mr Tano grabbed it and pumped my hand.

"You, my lad, are an earth mover, one in a million."

Thanking him again, I walked out of the teachers' room with my head high. My success gave them all skin pain. Yes, they were envious. Imagine their faces when one day, they learn that slum boy made it, and better than they ever could too!

I decided to get myself some shoes. The one thing my parents could never afford to buy for us kids were shoes. I had tough soles that could walk barefoot over all terrain in any weather. My callouses were my "shoes" and my feet were as cracked as the parched river bed. With shoes I would have good looking feet! I would be quite the dapper man when I strutted into school .

Let's make others get red eye at my new shoes.

A FULL MEAL

1982 - Ashaiman

"Mama! I am home!" I shouted as I stepped over the picket fence Uncle George was forever fixing. I sat on the stool to remove my shoes and exchanged them for my slippers. I brushed the dust from the walk from school off my shoes before putting them inside the house, in my sisters' room. I didn't want them to get stolen.

"Jolie, come help," came Mama's voice from the back of the house. Following her voice and other strange sounds, I discovered my mother and two sisters hard at work, stacking bricks to make what I assumed was a brick oven and fire pit. "Jolie, my son, help get the wheelbarrow here."

Walking over to the wheelbarrow, I noticed more bricks along with a large square grill mesh. I lifted the handles of the wheelbarrow and pushed it over to Mama on its wobbly tire.

"Should I take out the bricks, Mama?"

"Yes, Jolie. Put it on the outer side of this fire pit."

"What are we doing with a new fire pit?"

"This is going to be our barbecue oven, brother," said Gina, who was dragging a large gunny sack over to the pit I was working on. "We are going to cook a chicken Uncle George got off a trader nearby Tema Motorway."

MY HUMBLE BEGINNINGS

"Mama, I have news!" I exclaimed.

"Oh? More good news? Today must be a blessed day!"

"I am taking part in another school competition. A debate competition."

"Really?" asked Mama. "That's very good news! Your father will be very proud!"

"Mama, I haven't won anything. Let me finish the competition first."

"It matters not. Just remember to do your best, my son," said Mama, giving me a quick hug. "Remember to tell your father, Jolie."

"What's a debate competition, Mama?" asked Gina. Mama pointed at me, "Well, ask your brother." Gina looked at me, waiting for an answer.

"In the competition, two teams of three will sit opposite of each other. They will then take a side on a matter and fight with the opposition team in words. The team with the most points will win."

"Brother, you are so smart," said Janet with admiration. I could not tell if she was being sarcastic or genuine. My sisters lived to "take me down a peg" as Janet put it.

"No, sister. I think the hard work is paying off. Tonight's dinner of chicken will be even tastier with all the good news I learned today."

"Are there more good news, Mama?"

"I asked Uncle George to take me on as his apprentice" replied Janet. "And he said yes!"

"Really sister? That is such good news!" Janet and I high-fived each other.

"Yes. He finally saw my worth!" Janet declared with pride "and he thinks I have talent!"

"Tonight is a good night for roast chicken then!" Gina interjected, busy chopping the onions, peppers, and tomatoesfor the stew.

I poked my nose into her business, "What are you making Gina?"

Gina replied. "Fish stew. I helped out at the chopbar today. I made enough to buy fish." Gina tossed the vegetables into a bubbling pot beside her. She loved to cook. One day, I hoped to make enough money for her dowry and to allow her to open a chop bar of her own.

"It's a feast day today then!" I yelled and ran around our outdoor kitchen in jubilation "Janet's become an apprentice!!"

My father harrumphed at me. Chastened I ran over to help Uncle George with the fire pit.

Chicken. I thought as I busied myself with the pit. I don't think we have ever had a whole chicken. It ranked up there, right under having enough to eat until we were sated after "getting rich." We rarely had chicken - almost never since we moved to our current house. The only meat we could afford was fish we caught in the large Gbame Drain. But then fish was not really meat. Only on Sunday would we eat fresh fish bought from the fishermen at the docks. We saved up all week to buy that fish. It was part of Mama's Sunday ritual.

Chicken on the other hand was a celebration treat only the guest of honour could eat. The rest of us could only watch with open mouths and hungry eyes. Not a scrap was wasted. The bones were taken away after to be boiled for stock. My mind wandered to the bits of pulled chicken Mama added into her famous tomato red jollof rice. The last we had was in celebration of my older brother David's birthday. I shook away the melancholic memories. They left. I stayed behind. Good riddance!

"Can we really afford it?" I asked.

Mama walked towards the carved wooden table straining under the weight of heavyset pots. Sliding the lid of a medium-size pot back, she nodded at its contents in approval and carried it over to a spot next to Gina who had washed out the family asanka, (a wide bowl-like clay dish with ridges) and tapoli, (an hourglass hand-sized pestle). These were family heirlooms and part of Mama's dowry. They were inherited from her mother who inherited it from her mother, going back many generations. One day they would go to my sisters, in the same way it was passed down to her. Until that day, Mama took great care with them. A well-seasoned tapoli and asanka were an important part of a girl's dowry. She would use it to cook for her children.

As Mama set the pot down, she shushed me. "Hush child, stop asking these questions. Go do the washing, then go fill the fire pit."

I obeyed and hauled the heavy pots over next to our water tank. The next time she had to tell me, I would get hit. I understood that I was being rude.

Mama replied to my earlier question, "Well, Uncle George has good news. Now is a good time to celebrate because business is doing well." I handed the washed wooden pestle to Gina, who finished up with the boiled cassava and yams. Janet crossed her eyes and stuck her tongue out at me. She mouthed "Money crazy" at me causing Gina to snigger. I stoically ignored them both. One day, they would eat those words. As usual neither of our parents noticed.

"Gina. Janet Make sure you both watch your rhythm this time," Mama interjected. The last time my sisters set to pounding the fufu, it wasn't up to Mama's expectations.

My sisters chorused in unison "Yes Mama."

"Mama, Uncle George is doing well, isn't he, since Janet joined him?" I hastily asked.

Smiling, Mama nodded in my direction. "Yes Jolie. Now once you're done, go fill the fire pit and start the fire. I need you to put a layer of firewood at the bottom. Light it up, then heap the coal over it. Let the fire die down. We need long-lasting embers for roasting."

We all turned back in the direction of the music as we heard Uncle George whistling. Anticipation built along with the tune. Janet giggled at the off-beat melody he was carrying. It was a good omen. When our father whistled, it meant things were going well and he was in a jolly mood. Of late, that had been happening with increasing frequency. As his footsteps drew nearer, I heard his bottom settle on his favourite stool at the entrance of the house.

"Mama Adel?" called out Uncle George.

"Coming!" replied Mama, passing the chopping board to Janet. She pointed at the onions and indicated with her thumb and forefinger, the size and length of the chopped onions. Janet scrunched her face at the task and switched over without complaint. Chopping onions was Janet's most hated chore. She always suffered from red itchy eyes for hours after.

Mama hastily wiped her hands on the towel tucked at the waistband of her skirt and sashayed over to Uncle George with pep in her walk. The two put their heads together for a hushed conversation as my father ceremoniously handed the chicken over to her. I heard my father telling Mama the chicken he bought from the trader was one of the biggest.

"It's alive," exclaimed Mama. "I haven't slaughtered a chicken since Janet was born."

As I shovelled firewood and coal into the pit, I kept my head down and my ears perked up, but their voices were too faint for me to hear.

Mama came back to us, and surveyed the now completed fire pit with pride and satisfaction.

"Good job Jolie." Filled with coal and wood as instructed the pit crackled away merrily, awaiting its guest of honor. The last thing we had to do was to slaughter the chicken.

She laid the struggling chicken on the chopping board on the ground. Gina and I joined her as we all stared at the chicken.

I whispered, "I'm hungry." Janet and Gina both shushed me by elbowing me in the ribs. I staggered and nearly fell over. Janet's elbows were lethal! I suspected she learned some secret fighting arts somewhere, like what we saw on TV. My sister was nothing if but resourceful.

"Mama," Gina whispered. She turned to Mama with concern in her eyes. "Who is going to kill it?"

Mama pondered this for a moment, "Not me, but your father should have the honour. We are celebrating his success, and your sister's apprenticeship. His business is good." She called out to Uncle George.

Joining us at the back, Uncle George arched his eyebrows towards Mama who tipped her head at the chicken.

"Well, since it's your day, I think you should do the honours." Mama said, holding out a knife to Uncle George. Uncle George caught us staring at him and winked at us four. In unison, our bellies rumbled. Uncle George gulped down his saliva audibly. With unsteady hands, he took the knife from Mama.

Looking down at the knife in his hand he said, "Well, I think Jolie will help me in this."

"Me?" I croaked, pointing at myself.

"Yes. Us men have to take charge," said my father, clearly more to himself than me. My sisters looked at me and giggled.

I straightened my back and said, "We are men."

"Good! Bring the chicken, Jolie. We will do it near the washing area."

"Okay." I said proudly.

I put my hand on the fluffy bird, feeling its warm body and beating heart beneath my hand. I lifted the chicken gently, both hands beneath it. Sensing my hesitation, the chicken shrieked and clucked loudly, thrashing its wings, trying to get free. As the wing hit me across my face, I held the bird away further from my body, trying to change my grip on the chicken to its legs, like how the chicken sellers at the market would. Fumbling awkwardly, I undid the knot that kept it trussed up by accident. Sensing freedom, the chicken kicked out, and slapped my face with its wings. We wrestled and the chicken won. As it escaped, it scored my arm, gifting me with a set of bloody claw marks.

"Nnooooooo!" I yelled. My sisters shrieked at the sight of the chicken running toward them. "Catch that chicken" I screeched at them "That's our dinner!" My sisters panicked and threw themselves out of its way. They did not want to get scratched by that devil bird. Mama echoed my cry and we gave chase to foul fowl. Bleeding and panting I followed her as we both ran it in circles. Our walking dinner saw the break in our defences and seizing its chance, it rushed past Uncle George, who was heading back to investigate the commotion, and straight out of our gates. Mama and I poured on the speed. No way in hell were we going to let that chicken get away.

The fowl ran around the back, into our neighbour's compound, and ducked into the Aunty Jemina's kitchen with a great big squawk. It's beady eyes darted around, looking for a place to hide. It fled towards a stacked pile of firewood. Seizing its last chance at life, it dove into a gap. In hot pursuit, and past Aunty Jemina's startled daughters, Mama darted forward, swiping at the beast but missed its disappearing body. I ran to the opposite end of the pile and saw the hen trying to wiggle out. Mama attempted to shift the logs.

"Block the other end Jolie!" She called out. Unfortunately, the wood pile collapsed on our chicken, killing it immediately.

The ruckus drew out everyone who boiled out of their houses faster than an unattended pot. Aunty Jemina, and her three daughters, Ohemaa Mercy, Nayaah Sarah, and Efua Joyce were agog with surprise. Their pots bubbled over and the knives and ladles they held stilled. We had no time for them.

"Mama Adel?" Aunty Jemina managed. Her head scarf was askew and her mouth was slack with surprise "W..what's the matter?" she stammered. I thought she looked like a freshly caught fish.

"I think it's dead," Mama Adel said to me. She looked over to Aunty Jemina with an embarrassed smile "Our dinner escaped."

"A chicken, yeah? Good dinner tonight!" Aunty Jemina quipped. That, I thought was our cue to leave. Nayaah Sarah tossed her head in irritation. Stirring the stew, she grumbled, "I don't think it will run anymore, Jolie." Laughter broke through the crowd. I stole a look at her. *Flat as a board, and with a spicy temper. Not my kind of girl.*

POVERTY OF THE MIND

A few of the uncles from next door helped move the pile of wood, enabling me to reach the chicken. Quick as a flash, I retrieved the carcass. Its neck was broken and its head was smashed in making it look strangely flattened. No matter. It was still good. Freshly killed chicken. I raised its limp body for all to see and a cheer broke out amongst the neighbourhood children. These brats were the younger siblings of my friends.

"Give us the feathers!" shouted Ohemaa Mercy in jest, her hands were raised towards the chicken.

I looked over to Mama who replied, "Let us clean it first." Smiling, Mama and I walked back home towards Uncle George who still held the knife in his hand, waiting for the chicken.

That night, it was a feast, our neighbours were not invited, despite their best efforts. Mama presided over our dinner table with pride. There was Jollof rice, fish and vegetable stew, and roasted pepper chicken. We ate to our hearts' content, and for the first time in my life, I understood what it was like to not feel hunger. To this day, the taste of that devil chicken still lingers on my tongue. Sweet, spicy, and flavoured with love.

This feast was the calm before the storm. True enough, what they said of us became true eventually. That we were "cursed with bad luck". Looking back, I can see now that it wasn't my family that trouble dogged, but me. It nipped at my heels like a loyal pet. Even now it follows me. I've mastered it so far, and I like to think that I've got it beat.

THE CALM BEFORE THE STORM

GHANA 1980

The new school year started. Low on funds for some of the things required, I was forced to work harder with Mama in the market.

MY HUMBLE BEGINNINGS

Since I started schooling, I only worked on the weekends. But, having fees to pay, I pushed myself to work every day after school.

Oftentimes, I returned home past 3 am to catch a few hours of sleep before having to wake up at 6 am to start all over again. Over the years, since we moved to our new mud house, conditions slowly improved. Janet's skills at carving were outstanding. She no longer helped Mama at vending. Instead, she had her own stall she worked with Uncle George. Together with their constantly improving skills, Janet and my father expanded their clientele to Tema.

With business going well, they were often called upon by clients who wanted specific carvings like the one my father once did for Mama. Janet also acquired a unique way of carving, bringing life tothem with nature. She demanded higher payments for her services and the money she earned went toward furnishing our little house, making it homelier. The mattresses were her gifts to all of us when she made her first sale. Janet became my father's pride and joy, often discussing her handiworks whenever he met up with his old friends for a drink.

One of the evenings when the sun rays were spreading across Ashaiman market, my sister Janet pulled me aside from my vending spot.

"Brother, it has been about 3 years since you started schooling," she started.

"Yes, Janet. Why? Do you want to start school too?" I asked.

"No, brother. School is not for me unless it is one where I can learn to work with carving tools."

"Perhaps there is. And education is important," I replied.

"Brother, I don't want to talk about me schooling. Instead, I want to help you pay yours."

I kept quiet when I heard this. It's true, the 3rd year is proving difficult for me, what with higher schooling fees. For the last few months, business wasn't as good and I had not been able to save as much as I could have for this school year. I was beginning to feel tired with all the work and studying, with thoughts of taking a break from school, if I couldn't pay.

"Brother Jolie, please accept my help for amongst all of us, you are the only one attending school and I wish to see you completing your education."

"Sister, it is not right for a man to accept money from a woman. This is how father has raised us."

"I know, brother but, we are family and family always look out for each other. Always. Like how you looked out for me when I was harassed in the slums by Osei's gang. Family always stands by each other. That's what you told me when I shouted for you to run from the bigger boys. And boy did you get thoroughly trashed that day for rushing right at them with your little stick. Brother, let me stand by you."

My sister's words moved me. Looking at how grown up this girl had become. No longer a girl, but a young lady in her own rights.

"Sister, you are always close to my heart. I will accept your help and I thank you from the bottom of mine. And thanks to God for gifting me with a wonderful sister." I hugged her. She was elated that I accepted her assistance. Once again, I said a silent prayer to the Lord for gifting me an amazing family. We were not be perfect, but we are always there for one another.

Two days later, I handed over my schooling fees to Mrs Lahari, who as usual had a smile and kind words for me. In addition to her teaching duties, she was in charge of collecting school fees and allocating the budget. Signing off a receipt, she remarked on how I always make my payments on time unlike some students whom the school has to write letters to. I smiled, knowing this was all made possible this time around with the help of my wondrous sister. That day, I aced an entrance exam to enter a new grade. Elated, I walked to the market to share the good news to my sister and Mama.

*

MANDY

It was on this day, a vision beyond compare crossed my path, dimming all the beauty in this world. Dressed in a traditional Kenta dress skirt and a simple deep blue blouse, a young slim girl crossed my path as I walked down the road to the market area. Captivated, I couldn't resist following her from a distance. I observed her talking with other merchants before finally hearing her name from the jewellery merchant, *Mandy*.

It was a name fit for an exquisite young lady such as herself. Her feminine gestures and dainty smile set my heart fluttering. I wanted to introduce myself badly, yet looking down at my worn clothes, I dared not, fearing my appearance would lead to unwarranted circumstances. Determined to pursue her, from a distance, I shadowed her until she stepped toward the more prosperous part of town.

It looked like the sweet girl I'd taken a fancy to, was no ordinary girl. Raising a hand, she waved at a guard seated in the guardhouse of a well-known estate. As he looked back down to his paper, I quietly slipped past the barrier and continued after the tap of her shoes. She eventually disappeared into a humongous house belonging to one of the most prestigious men in our community, General Kontar. Observing from a distance, I felt my heart sink. *She is not in my league.* Social class was more powerful and dangerous than I thought. It effects the way we interact with people, especially those in power. Religions, cultural beliefs, even our sense of morality are marred by social class. I walked back to the market as a hollow feeling spread in my chest.

A few weeks after the first sighting, I saw her again, the girl of my heart. This time, she was dressed in a white blouse and rich yellow floral skirt, just as devastatingly beautiful as the first time I saw her. Ache filled my chest and my eyes stung. I watched her as she strolled around fiddling with the eye-catching trinkets in the market. Sellers shouted their goods, attracting buyers. Sweet Mandy stopped at a stall selling head wraps. Running the cloths between her fingers, her right hand paused over a vivid green wrap. She picked it up with the encouragement of the seller and put it against her skin. The green brought out the wonderful tone of her skin, making my heart ache with a pain I could not ever have perceived to experience.

Close enough for me to catch bits and pieces of conversation, hearing her laugh brought down the walls I had built up since I last saw her. As my guard crumbled, I felt my legs carrying me to her.

Reaching her, I stood beside her and said, "Perfect choice. The colour lights you up, making your eyes even more mesmerising than they already are."

"What he says is true, missus! The colour is perfect! You should get this colour for yourself!" Giggling and flushing from my compliment, Mandy paid for the scarf. Turning away from the stall, she sneaked a peek at me. I flashed my most charming smile. She responded with a sweet, shy smile which brought out a dimple in her cheek, completely owning my heart. Once again, my little game of tailing her began.

Quickly, I stopped at Mama's stand, shouted for my sister, Gina, to watch my makeshift stall for some time and ran off in the direction I saw Mandy disappear. As I caught sight of her, I dug deep for the courage to talk to her. I walked up next to her as she slowly through the market.

MY HUMBLE BEGINNINGS

"I enjoy the colours during this time of the day." Startled by my presence at her side, I heard her suck in a sharp breath.

"I like the things on display. It's always interesting to see what's new on sale."

"Yes, and that too is a lure." I said stopping beside her.

"I am Jolie," I said, thrusting my hand out to her.

"Hello, Jolie. I am Mandy," she said, dropping my hand after a quick shake. I laughed.

"Do you fear my hand is unclean?"

"No! Actually, I am not permitted to touch boys."

"Oh. Is it because you're Muslim," I asked, recalling the time my father met Mama Haniah, not shaking her hand.

"Muslim? What is that?"

"I don't really know. All I know is Uncle George said boys can't touch Muslim women."

"I don't think I am a Muslim. It's just that my parents don't allow me to speak with or touch boys."

The both of us kept quiet at this and continued walking side by side, not near enough to cause suspicion.

"Who is Uncle George?" She asked.

"He is my father. He is very wise." I tapped my temple as I said the last word.

POVERTY OF THE MIND

"Why do you call him uncle, if he is your father?"

"I don't know. Growing up, I remember all my siblings did. Other people do the same too."

"Others call your father Uncle George too?"

"Yes, yes they do. So it felt right to call him like that."

Laughing she said, "Your family sounds interesting!"

I smiled, "Talking about fathers, I know whose yours is.'"

"Then you know talking to me can get you in trouble," replied Mandy.

"I know. But can you blame a heart that won't forget you?" My remark stopped her in her tracks.

"Jolie, do you like me?"

"Yes. I love you Mandy. The sight of you… Your smile melts the coldest of ice and your eyes, are as bright as the stars at night setting my heart a flutter."

"Wow, I never heard that about my eyes before."

"It is all true. Every time I close my eyes, a vision of you appears."

Smiling shyly, "Well, you aren't too bad looking yourself." Thank goodness it was a Sunday and I was in my best suit, knowing I looked quite smart.

"I am but a poor man's son. I can offer nothing but my heart to you," putting my hand to my chest.

With the smile still on her heart shaped lips, lips that I couldn't stop staring at, she said, "I have to go home now. Every two days, I come out to the market. I use a secret path from the settlement's back gate that my father installed to the market. It's a seldom used path. Perhaps we can meet there if you are free in two days' time."

My heart leaped with joy at her words, "Yes! What time?"

"In the evening around this time. Come, let me show you the path." We kept a good distance from each other as she guided me deeper into the market, and finally down a winding path. Turning to face me as I approached her, she said, "Jolie, this is the path. The end stops at the gate. Before that, there is a shady rain tree. We can meet beneath it."

And just like that, she disappeared between the tall grass, once again, taking my heart with her.

THE SECRET PATH

Mandy and I met in secret for months. Both initially very shy, it took her a few weeks before allowing me to hold her delicate hand in my rough dark hands. Every other day, I would meet her on our secret path. Together, we will walk to the rain tree. The trunk of the rain tree was huge. Once, we tried putting our arms around the tree simultaneously and yet, we couldn't touch each other's hands. Often, we would sit beneath the rain tree leaning against the trunk with our line of vision, facing the direction of Mandy's home, keeping an eye open for spies. With our hands entwined, we would share everything our heart desired. As the relationship grew stronger, we grew bold and talked of a possible future together.

Some days when the desire burned hot in me, I would wander over to the rich settlement, observing their daily on goings. Disdain often etched their face when they catch sight of someone like me. No matter how well I dressed, I seem to ooze poverty from my pores. Like a smell too pungent, they'd step away from me in an attempt to keep a distance. In truth, they were the same as us poor folks. We are divided by social class put in place by money, the root of all evil, as the preachers often preached in the middle of the market area. I truly did not comprehend the social divide. I often wondered why the society couldn't allow us to live our lives just the way we wanted without being subjected to the required social norms.

People deemed it right to dictate how certain economic classes acted and lived. My community, I observed, was categorized into two groups: the rich and the poor. According to the society I lived in, the rich were categorized as living in one's own house with two or more bedrooms, or working in the government.

The poor were those either living in the slum or a rented house. Even if you were living in your own single-room house and were uneducated, you were definitely classified as a poor person. Ironically, my family didn't fall into either group. Being both poor and uneducated meant my family was often viewed as a disease in society. People would buy our wares, but tried their best to disassociate themselves from us. We are viewed as a disease-causing organism and any contact beyond business would tarnish people's hard earned social reputations. Sometimes, I would lay awake for hours thinking how I could overcome my family's predicament. Living in Ashaiman, with its growing notoriety, it was depressing to see my family being treated like a calamity. Their misconception truly disheartened me, causing me to eradicate all contacts with such people that is, until I met Mandy. My sweet, charming Mandy.

One particular evening, at our usual spot, Mandy laid her head on my shoulder as I shut my eyes. This must be what happiness is like, I thought. A wave of sadness overcame me, hitting me so hard, I bent double, causing Mandy to lose her support and bump her head against the tree trunk.

MY HUMBLE BEGINNINGS

"Oh my love, I am sorry!" I said, helping her up and slowly touching the sore spot on her head.

"What happened?" she asked.

Apologizing again, I said, "I was feeling how complete life is with you by my side and then the truth hit me. You can't be mine because in your parents eyes, I am not fit enough to be by your side."

"Oh Jolie, do you have to think of that now?" She said sadly.

"I didn't mean to. It just came." I replied.

"Now I feel sad too."

Sitting up, she looked towards her house and sighed. It's hard when my parents expect me to be with someone better.

"Am I not good enough, me do wiase?"[1]

"For the way you love me, you are. But not in the eyes of my parents."

"They want a perfect man."

"'No. No they don't. They just want someone who can do the best for me."

"Mandy! If you can give me time, I can be the best man for you!"

"And how long will that take, Jolie?"

"I don't know, my love. I just know I love you enough to do everything to make you happy."

---

[1] a nickname used on a loved one, meaning the love of my life.

"Sometimes that is not enough," she said as she stood up.

"Come. Walk me to the end of the road. I need to get the vegetables Mama wants."

I bit my cheek to stop myself from saying anything, got up, and put my love's hand on my chest. Looking intently into her eyes, 'I breathe to love you,' and kissed her other hand. Smiling, she kissed my forehead and interlaced our fingers. We stay close to each other when no one is around for the moment we returned to civilization, we went separate ways, pretending we know not of each other's existence.

Merely avoiding her presence was difficult when my eyes were drawn to her radiance. Whenever I caught sight of her in the market area, I couldn't help but follow her figure until it vanished from my field of vision. Ultimately, the market vendors caught up on our rouse. Gossip spread like wildfire. The daughter of the lionized General Kontar was going out with a child of the slum!

Late Friday evening, just as the night creatures began their search for food, I felt eyes watching me from the moment I began clearing up my cart until I wrapped the heavy tarp over and chained it to the baker's shop. Turning around, I found the fruit vendor seated on a chair staring at me. Her husband was behind her fumbling around with the ring of keys in his hand. Unperturbed by her stare, I gave a small smile as I walked past her. A hand shot out quickly, grabbing my hand in a death grip.

"Jolie, you no like be alive, boy?"

"Wh- wh-what do you mean?" I sputtered.

"You kwasea (stupid). No can you think about another girl?"

Mouth agape, I stared at the fruit vendor's angular face. Her huge eyes bore into me. The weak light emanating from the small light bulb under the baker's shop signboard threw ghoulish shadows on her menacing face. Her long red nails dug into my wrist.

"It hurts na!" I yelled and yanked my hand out of her grip. Clutching my hand, I ran down the darkening path quickly.

I heard her angrily shout, "KWASEA!"

The unexpected, furious encounter from someone I had always deemed a compatriot, occasionally watching my stall whenever I had short businesses to attend to, was scary.

CHOICES

We were walking home in high spirits, after a successful day at the market. Janet had secured a fat commission to produce a stool for a wealthy client's wedding. I concentrated on picking my way through the mud and the garbage. I didn't want to get my new Charley Woteys caked in waste. As we turned into the lane that led to our rented compound, a truck full of soldiers roared passed us. Janet was lost in thought, turning over ideas that would hopefully secure her a referral or a repeat client. None of us paid it any mind or thought anything of it.

Mama swung her net bag full of the evening's shopping as we walked. She asked, "What should we have for dinner tomorrow.?"

Gina declared, "We should have chicken to celebrate, like a whole CHICKEN!"

"Feathers and all?" teased Uncle George.

"Yes, if Janet can make a headband for me!" answered Gina cheekily.

POVERTY OF THE MIND

"Your sewing skills are better than mine, dear sister," replied Janet as she jabbed Gina in the ribs. Gina dodged and stuck her tongue out at Janet.

"You're better at it!" Gina shot back.

"Who cares for feathers?" I groused "Can we just decide? I'm hungry!"

Mama said, "Well children, we're going to have okro soup tonight. I've already bought the crabs and the fish." I cheered! Crabs were affordable when they were in season as a celebration treat.

"Ok-kro SO-OUP!" I chanted.

Our house was set off a tiny by-lane cul-de-sac surrounded by four other houses. We all lived in different houses in a shared compound and paid rent to the same landlord. The neighbourhood was deserted and dead quiet. At that time, in the evening, people should have been out and about, making dinner chatting, or getting ready to go to work at the night market.

"We can still get chicken if you …" Mama trailed off, the colour draining from her face. She was the first one to reach the house. "Oh Lord Almighty…" Mama whispered. Bloody words of warning were painted on the walls of our house branding us as cursed trouble makers and thieves. I touched it and smelled my fingers: it was chicken blood. Mama's vegetable patch had been uprooted and destroyed. We would have to go back to eating gari with salt and fried fish on Sundays, I realised with growing dismay.

We walked inside to devastation. In both the bedrooms, the mattresses Janet bought last year, lay on the ground, slashed with murderous intent, exposing the foam and springs inside. We borrowed a cart and made a special trip into accra to buy these. The bed frames that father built for all of us -- chopped up and splintered. The kitchen wasn't spared. Mama's spice rack, lovingly carved by Janet and built by Uncle George -- smashed and charred. All of our food was thrown around and scattered. They took nothing and instead, destroyed or fouled everything. A rank smell of urine permeated the entire kitchen. Mama's tipoli and assante lay smashed to bits. These would have gone to my sisters when they got married.

Mama crouched down and picked up the broken bits of her heritage.

I saw my name on the wall painted across the walls, "Jolie. Die." This was a warning. All eyes turned to look at me. Without a word, Mama and Uncle George began clearing up the mess with sluggish movements. I wanted to apologise but I did nothing wrong! I did not force Mandy, she agreed. We were in this together! It wasn't her fault and it wasn't my fault! It was Kobe, her father's fault! Society was cruel to the powerless. I had to apologise though, my actions caused this. Paralysed by guilt and indecision, I stood there like a lump of wood in the middle of the kitchen.

"I'm sorry." I managed, finally. My parents refused to look at me as they sorted through the wreckage for salvageable possessions. My family worked around me treating me like a statue.

It was my sister Gina who took me aside, "We all knew you were seeing Mandy. We said nothing. This," she indicated with her left hand, "was expected. We knew you wouldn't listen to us when we told you not to do it. I hope you learn from this."

Uncle George burst out in anger, "Compared to themselves, they see us as less than dirt!"

That night, dinner was a sombre affair of Hausa Koko. It was the only thing they missed in the destruction of our house. We ate in grim silence. The deal was done.

REALITY

POVERTY OF THE MIND

Early 1986 - Ashaiman

"Meet me behind the kente seller's shop. I'll be waiting. Same time." I stared at the note which had some money tucked in it. The young child who handed the paper to me tugged at my sleeve, hand out. I gave him the money and he immediately ran off. My heartbeat quickened. *Could it be? But how?* I wondered.

I recalled the fruit seller's comments a few days after the warning from the soldiers. She informed my mother, loud enough for other peddlers to hear, "Mama Adel, did you hear? General Kontar has his daughter under house arrest for going out with some peddler's son. Poor child. No more freedom."

This woman was well known for having a slimy okra mouth and delighting in spicy gossip. My mother just shrugged her shoulders when she came to pass me some small change.

The fruit seller continued, "Mama Adel, someone just told me that your house has been trashed. Did you find the culprit?" She looked closely at my mother, watching for a reaction. I opened my mouth to reply, only to have Mama Adel rest her hand on my arm.

"We are thankful to God we weren't home when they came and not having anything valuable, not much damage was done." Mama smiled at the fruit seller's wife. Huffing at Mama's reply, we were let go to carry on with our work. I tucked the note into my pocket and waited for the mid-afternoon sun.

I closed up and stole off to the waiting spot. Going around the kente shop, I spotted Mandy immediately. Overwhelmed at finally seeing her after months, I hugged and kissed her. I took Mandy's hand and kissed her open palm, enjoying the feel of her hand in mine. As I was about to ask how she got away, Mandy gave a cheeky smile and shared she did exactly the same with the bodyguards as the kid. As we quietly snuck off to our favourite tree, I kept glancing back, taking in the beauty of this sweet girl who's willing to risk her father's wrath to see me. I squeezed her hand, making sure she wouldn't vanish.

"I chose you. And you will continue to be the most loved guy in my life over and over and over without a pause, without a doubt in my heartbeat I will keep choosing you," said Mandy, holding my face in her hands. She kissed me on my nose then lips.

I am a fool, I thought to myself, *A fool in love.*

"Mandy," I spoke softly returning her kisses, "you are a poet, my love."

"Our love has turned me into a poet dear," she breathed, turning away from my lips, trailing kisses from my brow to jaw. Trembling, I pushed her away gently.

"We can't, my love."

Pulling her hands out of mine aggressively, Mandy pouted, "Are my kisses that bad? I know I am not as good as girls your age."

"Your soft, alluring lips, my sweetheart, are intoxicating. Too much of them can make a man lose his mind. I fear myself for when I can think naught but to be like this all the time."

"Oh Jolie. If only this would last forever."

"Who say it can't?"

Mandy leaned into me, hiding her face in my shoulder, drawing concern.

"Dear, what's the matter?" I asked.

"Why does loving someone bring so much joy and pain?"

POVERTY OF THE MIND

"Love is like war, my sweet Mandy. And we are on opposing teams."

A muffled inaudible whisper came out of her. The words I caught, frightened me. Heart hammering and hands shaking I forced her to face me.

"Say it again…" Mandy raised her head, took a shaky breath, and repeated herself.

"Jolie, Mama… Mama, she has chosen someone for me."

"What do you mean *chosen someone*"? I bristled.

"My parents have decided to plan my life for me. I am to wed someone of their choice."

"Nooo! Mandy, talk to them. I can be like Tom Ewusi. He made it big. So will I! I am already making it in school and I work hard. I can work harder to be with you!"

"That is a story, Jolie. In this day, that is impossible!"

"Everything is possible, my love. Believe me. We hear stories of rags to riches and I will be there one day. Give me the chance, my heart!" I pleaded.

Mandy took my hand in hers, kissed my fingers, and without looking at me said, "Marrying you is impossible. Loving you is a gift. I shall keep this memory because…"

"Mandy, please!" I interjected urgently.

"No, Jolie, hear me out. This will be the sweetest memory for me. I have to do what my Mama wants. I cannot disappoint my family and we know you are too poor to care for me." she ended in a whisper.

MY HUMBLE BEGINNINGS

"I can make it happen, Mandy, in time. Give me a chance!"

"Our time is up, Jolie. What we have is sweet. But it will take you 20 years to be where Kobe is, Jolie. Maybe more! Kobe can provide a comfortable life for me right now if I marry him tomorrow. With you, I will be but the wife of a poor man and jeered for leaving all the luxuries in life behind for you." she said harshly.

"Kobe? Kobe is a scoundrel! Is money all you think about?" I demanded, pulling my hands out of her grip.

"I look at the big picture, Jolie and what I see is true. Us, together will hurt me, and my family. The shame will kill my parents. I cannot do that to them. I'm sorry, Jolie." She pushed me away aggressively and ran down the dusty road towards the housing settlement.

"Mandy!" I called out to her as I gave chase. Reaching her, I grabbed her arm, and turned her towards me. Her tears streamed down her cheeks, as sobs broke through. "Dear, we can run away! Start a new life in a place where no one knows us."

"Are you crazy, Jolie? Runaway with you? Leave everyone and everything I love behind?

Think it through! How far can we go? How will we survive? What about your education?" she launched at me, aggressively hitting at my shoulder, pushing me away. Her final mocking remark thrown carelessly over her shoulder as she walked away, "At this stage, to be with you is suicidal!" Her words deadened me. Was this truly the woman I was willing to give it all up for? Or was it just her situation forcing her hand?

I watched the sea of grass, lost in the rhythmic swaying and bending. I stayed seated as the sun slowly bowed down to the coming night. A large flock of birds joined the group of quietly squawking one in the rain tree, increasing the noise in the silent evening. I shook myself out of the tsunami of emotions. Turning to face the dark path, I took one last look toward the lights flickering in the distance and began my walk home.

SNAKE

I sat in the corner of the family home, staring at the marking on the wall. I looked around the room, noting the new cupboard. Through my haze of despair, it dawned on me no matter what we did to fill the space in our home, we would remain poor. A sob escaped me as a new wave of emotions hit me. "*Mandy*," I croaked. Hearing me weep, Janet just stepping in, forcefully shook my shoulders and her hand landed hard across my face. Mama looked in from the back, drawn by the loud clap sound.

"Snap out of it! You acting like this is giving Mama pain!"

The sting on my cheek brought me back to reality. I caught the sadness etched on Mama's face and just as she turned away from me, I saw a tear roll down her cheek.

"Mama,..." I uttered helplessly.

Gina peaked in the door, glaring at me angrily. She guided Mama away to the back where we usually cooked. I heard a thud as things were moved around outside. More loud rattling sounds followed by shouts came from the back. Janet rushed out. I was close behind. Mama was standing on a stool in a corner while Gina used a stick, hitting at the ground.

"Stand back!" Gina barked.

"What is it?" Janet and I demanded.

Gina pointed at the thing in front of her. A dancing head emerged from metal bowl she lifted with the edge of the stick. Janet stood

MY HUMBLE BEGINNINGS

rooted to the ground. I rushed to the front remembering the sacks Janet used to store her wood shaving. Pulling out an empty one, I ran back to see Janet join Gina reluctantly trying to kill the snake.

"Here!" I shouted. "Get it into the sack!" The huge sack was laid on the floor. Janet stepped back, handing me the stick which I used to coax the snake into the gaping mouth of darkness. Gina stepped back as well. Mama reached a trembling hand out to Gina for support, just as the snake decide to end the drama by slithering into the gunny sack. Janet ran over and used a piece of discarded string to tie the opening. We looked at each other, then at Mama and Gina.

Pointing at Mama, "Mama hop, skip and jumped onto the chair ." Three pair of eyebrows raised, including Mama's.

"Am I that agile?" she inquired. We all burst out laughing.

***

Things were all back to normal. I was attending school and in the evenings went back to my usual spot, hawking goods. I had a new product, Janet's miniature African figurine carvings and the community was taking well to them. Demands poured in for her carvings and Janet was busier than ever making the most of her time. Her profit margin was the highest amongst us and she was not shy to share her newfound wealth. I smiled thinking of her talk of one day buying a house for Mama while being envious at the same time as I too wanted Mama and Uncle George to talk about me with pride.

News travelled through the market grapevine of General Kontar's arranging his only daughter's marriage with Kobe Biobaku. The Biobaku family owned hectares of a palm oil plantation. Rumours had it, they own shares in the local banks. A couple of weeks after I heard of their news, Kobe paid me a visit at home. I was in our only room having just returned from school, reading a book I borrowed from the school library when I heard someone shouting my name. I walked out to the door and came face to face with a man I had seen a few times in the marketplace. When his debtors failed to make timely payments, his goons will threaten them and even trash their business.

Kobe. He didn't come alone. Two gorillas flanked each side.

"You! Come here!" he bellowed. *For such a skinny man, he sure has a loud high-pitched voice,* I thought. I walked up to the edge of the fence. "I heard of you entertaining thoughts of courting my woman."

"May I ask, who is your woman?" I ventured.

"Mandy, General Kontar's daughter."

I was quiet. *The rumours are true,* I thought, my heart swelling with unwanted emotions, as my carefully built wall shattered.

"Stay away from her or I'll send you to the grave." he snarled at me. One of his goons cracked his knuckles in a menacing manner. In a one-on-one fight, he would lose. With three fighters, my chances of winning were slim. Eventually he would win, being rich and powerful. *Girls will always flock around him like bees to honey.*

I hung my head low, "I no longer see her," I said quietly.

Unsatisfied with verbal threat, Kobe grabbed a fistful of my shirt as he raised his right hand to strike me. He thought against it, letting me go, "I don't want to dirty my hands by touching filth like you. Surely rumours of you seeing Mandy were just that, rumours."

He turned away from me and snapped his fingers. The bigger of the two men, swiped at my legs, dropping me to the ground and kicked me in the side a few times. I cried out in pain, clutching my side.

"That's just a small taste of what you will get if I see you with Mandy," warned Kobe.

I slowly picked myself up when I noticed they were no longer in sight. Hobbling to the back of the hut, I felt my determination returning. *I will not chase Mandy. She will chase me.* I vowed.

*

CELEBRITY

FAMILY

Late 1986, Ashaiman

"Jolie, we are sorry to say the terms of the scholarship has changed, said Mr Kplom, the new headmaster for my school. The last headmaster was suddenly replaced.

"Changed, sir?" I inquired.

"According to the new requirements, to be liable for the scholarship, you need to continuously get A's in all your subjects."

"Sir, this was never told to me."

"This is the decision made by the education committee. Now, your last exam grades, you got a couple of Bs'. That is unacceptable. With the drop of grades, we are unable to offer you the scholarship next term."

"I know I slacked. I'm sorry. I really need this scholarship, sir. Please, can you give me a chance?

"I don't think that's possible, Jolie."

POVERTY OF THE MIND

"Sir, please…Can I retake those subjects?"

"I will bring your request to the board but in the meantime, I'd advise you to prepare for the worst."

"Sir, please! The school fees are high! I am but a poor boy!" I pleaded, hands clasped together in prayer.

"From what I understand," said the headmaster putting down his pen, "you have family members who work. Try to raise funds for the next term fees."

"Time is too short, sir!" I exclaimed. "And we aren't rich! The money we make is just enough."

"I'm sorry, Jolie. Those are the rules and I am only here to enforce them," said Mr Kplom shaking his head apologetically.

I walked out of his office dejectedly, wondering how I would make payment when what I had was enough to cover the arrears only. In class, I could barely wrap my head around my situation. First, I lost Mandy, then my scholarship. In the midst of it, I got trashed by Kobe's thugs. Did our family's bad luck strike again? Was it all related? I questioned myself as an exasperated sigh escaped my lips.

"Jolie!" Mrs Lahari, our math teacher, reprimanded me. I pulled myself out of my thoughts. I sighed again.

"Sorry, madam," I replied trying to concentrate.

Pacing in the length of the room that evening, I gritted my teeth, heart full of anger and revenge. Being furious and unable to vent my feelings to anyone, I launched a series of punches on the mud wall of the room, leaving bloodied stains behind after a few punches. As my arms hung by my side and my breath shorted, I wanted to pay everyone back for all the names my family and I had been called. I wanted to prove to the community that the fallen they threaded on had more chances to pick themselves up and move forward. Our bad times will not remain forever. *But, how?*

I wrapped my bloodied fist in the old rags that once served as my face cloth and towel. I felt the small room slowly suffocating me, forcing me to throw down my rags and run. I took to the streets, scaring mothers and children who were loitering out gossiping or playing games. I kept running, going towards the old cob house we once lived in. Arriving there, I saw my father's proud fencing gone, only the base remained. A woman was in the compound preparing okra stew for dinner. She finally looked up when I walked into her compound.

"Who you look for?"

Panting from the run, I cleared my throat a few times. "Madam, how long have you lived here?"

"My husband naa, he got this 3 months ago."

"Did you buy it?"

"Buy?" she exclaimed harshly. "This place, boy, all this house, no one can buy!"

"Why not?" I asked. "None are for sale?"

"This place all own by Mr Biobaku. No buy here. Just pay."

I stared at her in disbelief. Biobaku. Kobe's family. How this name is ruining my life. "All these?" I waved my hands at the surrounding area.

"These until the main road. All Biobaku's naaa."

POVERTY OF THE MIND

I stared at the houses around me, finally understanding the men always looking for Mama or Uncle George during our time here. They were rent collectors.

"Can someone buy a house here?"

"Buy? This land Belongs to government."

"Then you're squatters. No need to pay."

She laughed at my answer. "Boy, you young. Innocent! I teach you lesson. Nothing is free in this world. Go with your questions. I mus cook naa." she ended, shooing me with a wave of her ladle.

Taking another long look at the house, I left the lady behind, walking down the path I once used to frequent with my siblings. As I neared the slum, the overpowering smell of stench, decay, and food, enveloped me, causing me to gag. *How*, I wondered, *how did I find the joy in running to this place, playing games in that pile of heap*, as I finally came to the edge of the slum.

A rat ran bravely across my foot, causing me to leap aside. Unperturbed, I continued walking around the edge of the slum. A boy with a jaunty looking hat raced past me, roaring, followed closely by his friends, all dressed in rags. They sprinted between scrap pickers and scrambled to reach the top of heap piles, claiming it as theirs. I stood to watch as the boy in the oversized dirty red shirt made it to the top. Immediately, the others stopped. He barked out commands in pidgin. The scramble begin. The one who got the best-looking item would get to stay at the top with the leader and be his first mate. I turned away smiling. I knoew the game well enough. I played it with my friends as a child too.

I quickened my pace, walking around the area I once called home. A few people recognised me and inquired about my parents. One was a friend of my mother's brother, Uncle Danso.

MY HUMBLE BEGINNINGS

"Jolie? It's you?"

"Yes, uncle. How are you?"

"By God's grace. How are your parents?"

"They are good, uncle."

"Good good. And your Uncle Danso?"

"Who?"

"He is your mother's brother. I heard he is now in Tema?"

"Oh. My Uncle Dan. Mama sometimes speaks of him. I hear he is well."

"Good then. Tell your father one day I come visit."

"You're welcome."

I took the path passing the market area where my family vended. People were packing up their things, some pushing their carts down the dirt road. I continued walking down the road, watching the night activity beginning. One thought kept repeating itself in my head, *my Uncle Danso who is doing well in Tema. Perhaps this is the way.*

I finally reached our family compound, walked around to the back, and stood next to the open fire where the cooking pot was boiling water. I looked at Mama who was bent over the chopping board, cutting up some tomatoes. I spoke quietly to her.

"I lost the scholarship."

Mama stopped what she was doing and slowly turned to facet me before saying, "How can you lose a scholarship?"

"They changed the rules, and I didn't qualify anymore. I am told to be prepared to pay for the next term fees."

"How are we to do that when we can only now manage to put better food on the table?" Mama asked, looking at the array of ingredient in front of her. Rich man's food, she once called it, to eat chicken. Since we weren't rich enough, we all settled for fish.

I squatted down next to Mama, took a knife, and helped her clean out the fish gut and scales. Mama resumed cutting the tomatoes and onions. *She's preparing fresh pepper to go with the fish*, I thought.

As the knife scrapped the back of the fish, with scales flying around, I said without looking at Mama, "I've been thinking about it, Mama. Perhaps Uncle Danso can help me with fees. Because I really want to study."

Her hands stilled at hearing her brother's name. Mama looked at my direction and saw my determinedly clenched jaw. She pondered upon the available options before finally agreeing, "Maybe you can talk to your uncle and ask him for assistance." She turned away with a sad look on her face.

"Mama, don't be sad, please." She ignored my remark and pointed at the fish. I continued cleaning the other side.

The next day, Mama spoke to her close childhood friend, Madam Kuki. Madam Kuki walked into our compound, chatting loudly to Mama. She sashayed around our yard in her green and white kente cloth with a golden headdress. As Mama was speaking to her, I noticed how shabby and tired Mama looked in the dreary house clothes she had on. Her white blouse was yellowish and stained from repeated use. The skirt that was once bright purple was now a faded version of its old self. Her hair, once ebony black was tinged with white hair.

MY HUMBLE BEGINNINGS

Mama, who was years younger to Madam Kuki, looked older. The years had not been kind to her. As the two ladies spoke, Mama gestured to me. She spoke of my ambition to continue schooling and the bus fare needed for the journey to see my uncle. Madam Kuki chuckled, tapped Mama on her forearm, and agreed to fund my trip as long as I remembered her when I made it in life. Mama said nothing as she smiled sadly.

She offered a sweet drink to Madam Kuki and they sat around chatting for hours about the good old days when they both worked in the cocoa plantation. Mama chatted how she moved rank within the cocoa community, from picker to assistant manager.

"With the fall of the cocoa industry though, life has been difficult," she lamented as they both fell quiet.

Early the next morning, I woke up, folded my rag, and placed it in the corner of the room. I went to the wash basin, looking at the broken mirror on the wall, willing myself to sound convincing enough for my uncle to assist me. I filled the basin with what little water we had in the bucket and quickly scrubbed my face and arms clean with a hard soap and a towel. I put on my best shirt, one I used for church on days Mama dragged us there. I went up to my mum, hugged her and started the one-mile walk to the bus stand.

The bus made hourly trips between my community and other communities. It linked villagers to other smaller communities between Ashaiman and Tema. It is one of the cheapest commodities around and was usually full. The short distance to Tema which is only an hour away, could take up to 3 hours. The bus arrived about 15 minutes after I got to the stand which was barely a bus stand, with just a pole sticking out of the ground and a metal board at the end, depicting a bus. I joined the gathering crowd either standing or squatting under the scorching sun. The barren land around the bus stand did not allow trees to grow. Only the occasional shrub survived the harsh land and sun.

POVERTY OF THE MIND

From a distance, I saw the rickety bus approaching, its engine noise-deafening as it got closer. The bus was a small, dusty yellow, 30-seater with a few broken windows. There was no air conditioning so the windows were open all the time for ventilation. On days like this, it could get very humid.

Everyone slowly queued up while waiting for the bus to arrive. As it approached us, I saw the driver, a burly, pot-bellied man, with a heavy moustache wearing a stained singlet, sweating profusely. He pulled a lever to stop the bus and pressed a button on the dashboard, opening the doors to those queuing up.

As we slowly boarded the bus, the driver asked us for our intended destination and quoted prices. Those who paid received a ticket stub and walked further into the bus to find a seat. I climbed up the worn steps, paid for my destination, and walked onto the bus. I found my seat the moment the bus driver shut the doors and pulled on the lever, jerking the bus forward. I was launched into my seat.

Apologising to the person I bumped, I straightened myself in my seat and prepared for the long journey to Tema.

***

"Tema Terminal!" shouted the bus driver, arm raised to pull the lever for the door opener. I looked at the pencilled map Mama handed me along with the bus fare. "He still lives there, as far as I know," she said as she hugged me. I followed the map and eventually arrived at a milky yellow brick house that fit the description Mama mentioned.

"Hello!" I greeted as I knocked the worn wooden door. "Uncle Danso?"

I waited for some time. Hearing nothing, my hand was poised to knock again when the door opened abruptly, revealing a woman wearing a black and white knee length dress. The lady was ready to step out of the house, not expecting to find me standing at her door.

"Oh Jesus!" she exclaimed. Hand resting on her chest, she looked at me, "How long have you been here?"

Not sure who the woman was, I politely stated my name and why I was there. She stared at me before finally nodding.

"Dan is my husband. And you say you are Adel's son? The Adel married to George?"

I nodded.

"Come in. My husband will be back soon. He went to the store to get Nido."

Inviting me in to sit on their sofa, she asked me what I wanted to drink. "A cold drink please, in law."

Danso's wife had just served me a cold sobolo. I took a few sips, savoring the sweet floral tones in the drink. We chatted about our families while waiting for Danso. As I was finishing my drink, I heard the door open and my uncle walk in. I recognised the strong square jawline from Mama's side of the family. Standing up with my in-law, I waited for an introduction. Handing his shopping to his wife, Danso took a good look at me and hugged me tight.

"Jolie! I was there when you were born. How well you sat in my hands!"

"Uncle, thank you for receiving me."

"Come! Sit! Have more sobolo?"

"Yes, please. It's tasty."

POVERTY OF THE MIND

After my in-law filled my glass and handed another to Danso, we shared news about our families.

Eventually, I faced him, looking at his drink, with sweaty palms, ready to state my reason there.

"Uncle, I am here for a reason. For a few years, I started studying with a scholarship. Some changes were made and I no longer qualify." Danso said nothing waiting for me to go on. "I came here, hoping to seek your help in paying my school fees. I have been doing well, Uncle. If you help me this once, I can be better prepared for the next payment."

Danso put his finger into his cup and pulled out a stray hibiscus leaf. "Education is like a teabag. You never know how strong it is until it's in hot water." Putting the leaf down, Danso looked at me, "Jolie, I am glad you are studying well. But money, money is a problem. My business still isn't picking up."

I heard a baby crying somewhere in the house. *There is a newborn*, I though.

"Uncle, is there no way you can help me?"

"Unfortunately, I am stretched thin now, Jolie." I kept quiet, nodding my head.

I can't push him, if he can't help. Dejected, I asked if it was okay I finished my tea before I head on home. Danso insisted I take a bag of hibiscus leaves for my family as a parting gift, which I accepted dejectedly from my in-law, smiling at the wide eyed infant in her arms.

"Jolie, anoma anntu a, obua da. If a bird does not fly, it goes to bed hungry. In this case, you need to make your own move."

I thanked him for his hospitality and wise words walking away, shoulders bowed in defeat. I left the house with so many unanswered questions in my mind, *Are they really siblings? Why he isn't helping his sister's son? He is rich and our family is poor. He should be more willing to help his own sister, shouldn't he? How does he eat his food knowing his sister's financial status, knowing his sister sleeps in a slum? What does he need all these money for?*

I got back home disappointed, knowing very well that my uncle was rich but refused to help. After talking to Mama, and while enjoying the hibiscus tea, I understood that my Uncle was scared of his wife's sharp tongue and he dared not help any member of his family without prior concern of his wife. *His money is only for him and his immediate family.* Any extended members of my Uncle's family would not get a dime. I shook my head. *I can't rely on extended family.* With a heavy heart, I realize my hands were tied.

A STAR

1987, Ashaiman

Making my way to the artist centre, I decided to listen and talk to as many people as I could for information about who were the wannabes like me and who were the recruiters. For an hour, I stood near a group of people, discussing agents in the square. One of them began to describe a recruiter he had just met who chose his girlfriend for a small part in a show. I bent down and pretended to dust sand off my trousers when one of the listeners looked my way asthe man continued to describe the agent's appearance. Gathering enough information, I took a walk around the square, scanning the crowd for a man known to sing and was about 5 foot 5.

On my left, I heard music and a group of men singing. Trying my luck, I headed that way, hoping one of the singers would be the agent. I pushed myself through the gathering crowd as the group was playing a popular song yet none of the singers seemed to fit the description I heard. I was about to head off in the opposite direction when the glint of a gold watch caught my eyes. *Gold watch with diamonds?* I wondered as I took a closer look at the man playing the harmonica. *Yes, it's him.* I waited until the band ended their song before approaching Nii. Greeting him, I asked if he was by chance looking for a strong hardworking young man.

"Hardworking in the acting world, abrantie, is not enough." Nii said as he took in my appearance. "Hmm. Not a rich kid."

"No, adwumawura (working man). I am poor butI am a good worker. I think I can have good luck in acting." I said, faking confidence.

"Talent is necessary. I do see something in you, abrantie."

"Adwumawura I will work hard. I always do my best in everything."

"Is that so?" Nii asked.

"Yes."

"Well then, let's play a game. Go to the market and act like a deranged beggar. Convince people to give their money to you."

Taking off my shoes and placing them in the plastic bag I kept tucked in a corner of my waistband, I messed my neatly combed hair and rubbed some sand over my feet. I walked over to a beggar I had seen sleeping in the many narrow alleyways near the marketplace, lifted a dirty coat from his pile of clothes, and put it over my shoulders. Nii watched me as I made my way to the centre of the marketplace, arranging my shoes together and sat on them. I began slowly chanting, raising my voice higher until I was waving my hands at the sky, sharing my grief and anger towards the Gods' unjust ways with the crowd, spinning a tale of how my loved ones were taken away from me by the landslide outside the town.

MY HUMBLE BEGINNINGS

Some stopped to listen and those who did threw coins into my outstretched hands. I managed to collect 2 Ghana cedi in 30 minutes.

Nii, impressed at my performance, took me over to a spot where two plastic chairs and a foldable table lay. He pulled out a feather pen with a flourish, grinned at my astonished face, and asked me for my details. As I wrote my information down, he walked over to a payphone not too far from the little setup and called up someone he addressed as "Ser". As he spoke excitedly, I stood up and took a look around the centre, observing the general populace around me. Two wannabes like me, strolled into the square. Dressed in flashy shiny clothes, their intent was clearly to draw the attention of recruiters with their swagger. Laughing at their colourful gear, I looked down at my clothes, thinking how shabby they were compared to theirs. *Nii didn't choose me for my attire*. I heard Nii saying my name to someone on the phone. He looked over to me and beckoned. I ran over to him as he hung up the payphone and discreetly pulled a string with a coin attached to one end out of the coin slot. He winked cheekily at raised eyebrows, raising a finger to his lips. A secret.

"Abrantie, will you be able to do this job? Work on a show?"

"A show? Like a TV show?"

"Yes. And if all goes well, maybe you will have a role in one of our upcoming series. What say you?"

"I'd like that very much, adwumawura!"

Jubilant, Nii hailed a lady carrying a large calabash pot on her head. Nodding at Nii, she headed in our direction while shouting out her wares to those around her.

"Asana with milk, no milk," I heard her. Stopping in front of us, she inquired, "Asana?"

"Yes. Abrantie is too young to drink." replied Nii thumping my chest.

Turning her gaze towards me, she asked, "Milk no milk?"

"Milk, please," I responded, grinning from ear to ear. I have always loved Asana. It's not an expensive drink, but to truly appreciate it with either biscuits or bread would cost more than the money I generally carried in my pocket. To celebrate the special occasion, Nii ordered two bowls of asana and 3 pieces of bread, passing two to me. He also ordered another bag of asana with milk for me to take home for dinner.

The next day, Nii met me at the corner newspaper stand as agreed. Despite his insistence to pick me from my home, I insisted we meet at the corner. I didn't want him to see my home, fearful I would lose the job if he chanced upon the squalor surrounding my family. He brought me to the TV station in a stunning pine green Mercedes Benz 280SL car. I sat stiff in the car, fearing I would somehow damage the leather of the two-seat convertible. Keeping a lively conversation going throughout the journey, Nii took my silence for nerves. He shared details about the wonderful engine under the hood and the safety features of the car nicknamed "Pagoda," a name inspired by the concave styled hardtop of the car. We came to a gated parking lot with security guard who stopped Nii.

"Purpose?" he asked.

Nii pulled out a white laminated card from his breast pocket and handed it to the guard. Inspecting the card in his hand, he squinted at Nii then pointed at me.

"And him?"

"He is here to audition."

MY HUMBLE BEGINNINGS

He continued, gesturing to another guard who came out with a clipboard, "He will need to register before entering. Name and car number," he said pointing to the board.

Nii scribbled away furiously while muttering, "This is some new procedure, eh?" Nii handed the clipboard to the guard in exchange for a visitor's pass.

"Wear this while you are in there." The barrier raised and the green Mercedes drove in search of a parking lot.

The audition turned out to be a hit despite being a long and gruelling seven hour wait. Even after being chosen for call backs, I was told to wait around for a few more hours to sign a contract of confidentiality. My initial excitement wore down by the impatience of others and led me to a corner of the room where I sat on a brown rattan sofa with flowery cushions. I started to solve a crossword puzzle I nicked from a book in the waiting room.

Finally, my name was called, contract signed and a takeaway, dinner I presume, handed to me. Nii came over and shook my hand.

"You did great, adwumawura. Let's get you home."

By the time I reached home, my body was beginning to ache from the long day and my throat was sore from repeating lines.

It was two weeks before I heard a neighbour call my name at the market. She spoke of a man driving a green Mercedes Pagoda, looking for me. *Could it be*, I wondered as I dashed to my mother's stall and instructed my sister to look after my cart. Running over to where the neighbour had last seen the car, a dozen thoughts crossed my mind as I prayed. Reaching the three-lane street, I immediately spotted the Pagoda parked on my left. Walking up to is, I scanned the crowd for Nii.

POVERTY OF THE MIND

"Jolie!" I heard coming from a shop nearby me. I scanned the shops ahead and saw a man waving, gold watch glinting. Grinning, I hurried over to him.

"Hello, abrantie."

"Adwumawura, why you so hard to find? I had to ask so many people!"

"Sorry, abrantie, but I am here now."

"Sit, sit. I have good news for you." I sat opposite him, my heart racing, waiting for him to finish his jollof rice and chicken. As he licked his thumb, "Who knew along this street, there is a small piece of heaven?" he said smiling at the shopkeeper who came to clear away the plate.

"Abrantie, are they doing a call back anytime soon?" I inquired.

"No, no call back. Even better. You got selected to play a character in the tv series "Thursday Theatre.'"

"Really, abrantie? You no mess with me?"

"Adwumawura, this is money talk and I don't mess with money talk! If they like you playing this character, they will prolong the life of the character or use you again. So, when we meet them, play your cards right!" said Nii with a stern finger pointed at me.

"I promise to do my best!"

"Good, good. Now, the first filming is this weekend. I will pick you up at the same place as last week, at 7am."

"I will be there, abrantie."

MY HUMBLE BEGINNINGS

"Dress casual for they ask you to change into clothes suitable for the character."

"Okay." I nodded.

"Now that that is done, I am off to meet my next appointment," said Nii as he stood up, shook my hand, and walked off to his car, leaving 5 cedis behind for the bill.

***

On the day of the filming, I aced the scene in two takes and proved to be a success with both the director and assistant director taking a liking to me. They pulled up a list of episodes and got the co-editors to include my name on more roles. Some that paid more than what my family earned in a month. In the end, Nii came in, coerced and sweet talked them into writing me in for a few more episodes. I finally signed a contract with 12 episodes to my name, playing 5 different roles. Going through the contract, I scanned through until I reached the finance column. Even after deducting Nii's salary, the amount was enough for me to pay off the following year's school fees and more!

Per the contract, I kept mum aboutthe production and filming. My family, ever curious over my weekend excursions finally penned it down to teenhood. My few parts took only six visits to film. But I was required to be on site at certain times should impromptu changes occur. Nii, now my manager, did all the chauffeuring. For about three months, I spent my weekends in the studio while my cart gathered dust. I worried about not making enough money from my daily evening sales but the thought of Mandy's eyes glimmering with pride and love sustained me. Eventually, the day came when all the cast gathered for a big meal, signalling the end of shooting. The Director, who I came to call (name of respect) raised his hands and thanked us, giving a long speech about the small family onset.

When he finished, amidst the clapping, I heard some actors cheeky asking if they could eat drawing laughter and a booming "Of course, NOT!" before saying, "Got you! Let's eat!'"

The editing team took another two weeks to get everything in order before the show aired in November. Nii invited me to his house to watch my first onscreen appearance. Excited, I dressed in my second Sunday best and made my way to our usual pick up point.

Greeting me as I walked towards his Mercedes, today with the hood down, he asked, "Excited?"

"Very!" I let out.

"You look good today, adwumawura. Today, you will meet my wife and sons."

Seated comfortably, I looked quizzically at Nii, "Abrantie, I never knew you were married."

"Not many know this. I keep my personal life private. Like you." He winked at me as he drove past a large privately owned courtyard. Drawn by the size of the houses, I smiled. *To date, he still doesn't know where I live nor do I intend on sharing.* Leaning back into the seat, I sighed, loving the feel of the leather seat beneath my hands.

"My wife will like you Jolie. She enjoys meeting dedicated people and cooking. Combining the two keeps her happy for days and a happy wife means a happy home. Remember that Jolie." Nodding, I thanked him again for having me.

The evening was perfect. Nii's gorgeous wife, Madam Delasi, insisted I call her "Aunty D." She was surprised at how young I was. She gave me two pecks on my cheek and told me how I reminded her of her late brother. Tall and gangly he was, she said. Nii gave her shoulders a squeeze and asked her to get the drinks for us. When she left,

MY HUMBLE BEGINNINGS

he whispered she lost her brother to a road accident. He was about nineteen then. I didn't know what to say, so I kept quiet until Nii's young sons emerged from their rooms. Excited to see a star, the boys insisted on showing me their rooms. With one pulling at each hand, I followed them to their room, admiring the width, comparing it to my home and the softness of a mattress. I was saved from jumping onto it like the boys by Nii's voice, asking them to show me around their home. They chatted on and on about meeting movie stars and the latest films, but I barely heard them as I took in the gloriously spacious house. Everything had a place and its perfection highlighted how poor I was.

Nii beckoned me over to the sofa. As I settled in, he handed me a glass and clinked it with his.

"To our cooperation."

I drank to that, enjoying the sweet taste of hibiscus.

"It's about to start. Wife!" Called out Nii. She hurried into the living room with her white apron. Taking it off, she sat down next in the armchair next to Nii's. Their two sons joined me on the sofa. We laughed in the right places and the boys gushed over my appearance. I felt a growing sense of pride in my acting abilities.

When the show came to an end, Aunty D invited us to the dining room, seating me on her right with her young sons opposite me. She then began to lay the table with dishes I only dreamed of and never tasted. I felt myself salivating as I took in the sight of akple, light okra stew with chicken: tatale, ripe plantain crushed and mixed with flour chili, onion, ginger, and spices then fried; abunuabunu nkwan, green leafy soup with bush meat, and of course, bowls of pepper - a must-have.

"I hope you don't mind grasscutter. My father is a famous bush hunter back home and when he visits us, he often passes on his catch to us."

"I haven't tried much meat, Mama. Forgive me if I do not eat it right."

"Oh! Xoó asi, is Jolie no eat meat?"

Nii looked at me bewildered. "Jolie? Is this true?"

"No, no abrantie. I eat meat. Just not often. I can't wait to sample the bushmeat, Aunty D!"

Glad to hear my response, Aunty D placed an akple and a bowl of okra stew in front of me.

"Akple is the same as banku. Take a piece and dip it in this. Go on, try!" she urged as I watched Nii put Akple into his mouth.

I pulled off a small piece between my thumb and two fingers and dipped it into the steaming stew. With the slippery okra sliding off the akple, I popped it quickly into my mouth and swallowed. Looking up at Aunty D's face, I smiled broadly, "Delicious! I like this very much!"

Thrilled at my response, Aunty D filled my plate with all the dishes laid out before serving her husband and her sons.

"Let's say grace," she said after seating herself, holding her hand out to me and her oldest son. I clasped my hand in hers, for the first time, feeling thankful for the good food in front of me.

FAME

Two days after it was aired, on our usual meeting day, Mandy came directly to my stall, congratulating me on my TV appearance.

"Looks like you're famous now, Jolie," she said. "Is this the reason why I seldom see you manning your stall over the past few weekends?"

MY HUMBLE BEGINNINGS

"Have you been looking for me, Mandy?"

"No, but I passed by your spot and noticed it was vacant a few times."

"Well, you guessed right. I was busy with the tv show."

"How does it feel like mingling with all those celebrities?"

I knew she meant the lead actors, as others were asking about them too. "They are just like us, perhaps more demanding at times."

Mandy laughed. "Tell me more about them, please!" she begged.

I smiled at her eagerness. "And what would Kobe think?"

"What has Kobe to do with this?"

"You are clearly his girlfriend," I said, pointing at the beaded bracelet she wore with his name.

"Kobe and I are just friends," she declared, taking off the bracelet and tossing it into the trash can. I raised my eyebrows at her actions and shrugged.

"I'm not free to chat now, Mandy. Maybe tomorrow."

Surprised at my change in behaviour, she asked, "Do you not love me anymore?"

"I loved a girl who was mine and then she wore the name of another." Stunned, Mandy lowered her gaze, turned and walked away slowly. I looked at her retreating back, my heart breaking again, thinking my chances of getting her back were gone now that I allowed my ego to talk.

POVERTY OF THE MIND

In the following weeks, as more scenes with me acting aired, I became a local celebrity. Mandy's mother used to turn her nose up every time she passed by my cart, but started to take closer looks at me, clearly curious. I have not seen Mandy since, but I began to receive packed cakes and even a bracelet with my name on it from her. I knew she was trying to work her way back into my heart.

Kobe must have gotten a wing of the change in Mandy's behaviour for one day I got a visit from 5 of his goons. Surrounding me as I began to close shop for the night, one of them grabbed the bag I was holding and threw it on the floor, stomping on it. Two shoved me out of the way as the three of them got busy working at dissembling my cart. I struggled to free myself from the two holding me down. Rage took over me when I saw them pocketing my daily earning, lashing out with unexpected strength. I kneed one man in the balls, hit the other in the face, breaking his nose. I rushed over to my cart, pulled at one of them and elbowed the other across the face. I spun and kicked the man I elbowed in the back, grabbed my stool and broke it over the head of another, sending him to the ground. The last man tried to flee but tripped over the broken stool. I walked over to him, punched him in his side, and turned him over.

"Why my cart?"

"Kobe!" He managed to utter between gritted teeth.

"What!" I growled as I raised my fist.

"No, please! It's Kobe! Kobe who sent us!"

Shaking him aggressively, "Why!" I shouted again, both my hands on his collar.

"Warning," he gasped out. "Don't see Mandy anymore!"

MY HUMBLE BEGINNINGS

"Listen to me, you dog. Tell your master, Mandy can choose me if she wants. Now leave before I break your arm."

I stepped aside, grabbing the leg of a stool, should they try anything. The young man on the ground pushed himself up and ambled over to help two of his friends up. Together, propping each other up, they hobbled off into the night, tails tucked between their legs. I heard not from Kobe's goons again.

I arrived at my designated spot the next day to see a set of new stools, a bow on each stool. The last one had a card.

"It's your admirer," scoffed the same old lady who called me "kwasea," not too long ago. I ignored her taut. A ghost of a smile lingering on my lips. I looked up and down the street. Just as I suspected, Mandy was hiding behind a shop wall watching me. Her rich pink head wrap complimented her bronze skin, giving her away. I set my cart down and walked towards her hiding spot. The pink head wrap vanished from sight. I quickened my pace. Approaching her hiding spot, I found her crouching behind some oversized rattan baskets.

"Mandy?" I asked, looking down at her. Lifting her head from her folded arms, Mandy looked up at me.

"I was hoping you wouldn't find me." Mandy grabbed my outstretched hand and raised herself from her crouched position.

"You have to stop gifting me things."

"I heard about the fight." she muttered.

"Oh? And who told you?"

"Kobe came to brag about sending five young strong men to beat you up. My parents were concerned about how his actions would affect us. Mama asked around and found out the outcome from the fruit seller."

"I see."

"I am sorry Kobe did that to you. It's all my fault. Had I not mentioned your name in his presence, he wouldn't have hurt me or you."

"He hurt you? How?"

"He hit my arm when he found out I came to see you."

"Sorry."

"Jolie, can't you see? I clearly love you still," she said as tears began to trickle down her face.

"You said your parents hate me, Mandy. You said we can never be together."

"But now that you are famous, they are more open to saying your name around the house. Please, Jolie, be my lover again. I miss you."

"I have to think about it." I wiped her tears and walked back to my stall. I didn't know if fame was enough to bring me to Mandy's house. Through gritted teeth, I muttered, "*Wealth and money to get the woman I love.*"

I began the tedious task of unloading my cart, thoughts still on Mandy's tear-stained face.

FAMILY PRESSURE

1987 - Ashaiman

MY HUMBLE BEGINNINGS

On a lovely, sunny Friday morning, as I was conversing with a customer, I saw Mama heading down my way in a long white lace floral motive dress. I smiled. The extra money I made from acting helped improve everyone's wardrobe. Noticing a distressed look on her face, I walked around my stall to face her.

"Mama? What's the matter?"

"Jolie, General Kontar's wife just came by. She asked me and you to dinner."

"She did? Isn't that a good sign?" I asked as I felt fireworks go off inside of me chest.

"I don't know, my son. And I am not comfortable naaa."

"Mama, let's go and see what they have to say." Worry still clouded her eyes even though Mama nodded.

That evening, I admire myself in front of the mirror. The blue baggy denim jeans gave my legs a longer look. Paired with the floral sleeveless beach shirt, I turned to Mama. She smiled, saying I looked good. After putting on my karate dark blue shoes, Mama, still in her lace dress, took my arm as we walked out of our home. Gina came from around the house and was surprised by the way we dressed.

"Where are you going, Mama?" she asked.

"Dinner outside, dear," replied Mama briefly. Gina waved us off.

I spotted a tall beefy man standing outside the chop shop. Stepping past him, Mama and I noticed it was strangely deserted of clients. Worry lines began to show on Mama's face. Seated at the centre table facing the door, Mandy immediately spotted us, excited to see me. A look of concern crossed her face quickly faded as she laid eyes on

Mama. Her mother waited until we were at the table giving us a cursory smile.

"Madam Adel, how are you? I have heard much about you." asked Mandy.

"I am well dear. And yourself?"

"I am too. This is my mother, Madam Kontar."

"Madam, it's a pleasure," said Mama smiling.

"It is good to finally meet Jolie and his Mama. All the way here, Mandy can't stop talking about you, Jolie."

"Really?" I looked over to Mandy who kept her head down, playing with her tissue.

Mandy looked up, smiling shyly at me. She was fiddling with something, undecided. Finally, she handed it to me. A comb. Taking it, I arched my eyebrows questioningly.

"You missed a spot," Mandy whispered, as Madam Komtar handed Mama a menu.

Impulsively touching my hair, I excused myself to the washbasin where a mirror hung. Mama and Madam Komtar were looking over a menu, trying to decide what to order. Using the comb Mandy handed to me, I briskly combed my hair, making sure I looked neat.

Returning to my seat, I discreetly handed back the comb, winking a thank you to Mandy.

Throughout dinner of jollof rice and fried chicken, not a word was uttered. Cold sweat began to roll down the back of my spine. As the shop owner cleared the table, Madam Kontar addressed me imperiously.

"Jolie, Mandy here is a beautiful and good daughter. She is a good catch." I kept quiet, knowing where this was heading. "Mandy's father, General Kontar is a respectable man. He is preparing to move up ranks. We need to have good and strong people around us. Efie biara mmaninsɛm wɔ mu . And in my house, I want no trouble." Madam Kontar intoned firmly.

"Jolie here, is a good son and has done no wrong. All he did was fall in love with your daughter."

"Their love is young and foolish. Mandy has come to realize that what her family wants is more important." At Madam Kontar's words, I turned to look at Mandy. Again her head hung low, avoiding my eyes. My heart broke.

"Mama Adel. Mandy and I, along with her brothers, will be returning to my hometown, to allow General Kontar time to concentrate on his work. When we return, Mandy shall wed Kobe and in that time, Jolie shall forget Mandy," ended Madam Kontar.

She stood up and together with Mandy, who took not one look at me, walked out, down the road where a car was parked waiting for them.

"Gina! Quietly go and call the priest." I heard Mama whisper. Light feet pattered past my bed and vanished out the door. I pried open my heavy eyelids and moaned at the strength required to even move my head. Mama came back to sit beside my mattress, changing the wet cloth on my head. The burning heat on my head reduced.

THE AMERICAN DREAM

RED EYE

POVERTY OF THE MIND

1989 - Ashaiman

I once saw a pair of red leather shoes at the stall of the shoe vendor who sold me my first pair. I casually asked if I could try them.

She took a cloth and gave the red shoes another buff before handing them to me, "These are my best pair. They will make any man wearing them walk taller."

"I feel taller just looking at them," I said with a smile. Sliding my right foot in, I stood up and admired the shoe. The red wine colour made it feel exquisite. "How much?"

"They're worth ten times your last pair." Sighing, I reluctantly took them off and thanked her. The feeling of loss then defeated the raging emotions in me. I returned home after speaking to Nii who told me my chances of acting again were slim as I appeared too often on screen. I would have to pay to keep him as my manager to continuously look for auditions. *Pay him with what money?* I wondered, recalling how most of my earnings had been used to pay my school fees and dining with Mandy.

Like the red pair of shoes, I learned that the money I had wasn't enough to make Mandy mine. Despite my achievements, her parents still hated me. They tolerated my presence during the dinner because their young sons were clearly awestruck. I realised it was all a facade when General Kontar walked me to his house gate.

"Jolie, forget my daughter. Fame is fleeting. You can barely afford to feed your family, how can you even afford to marry a girl of your class? I will never give my daughter to a beggar. Today is your first and last time in my house. You will regret the second time you try coming close to my family." With that, he summoned two gorilla goons to frog march me out of the house.

MY HUMBLE BEGINNINGS

I walked back to my home, fuming and kicking the sand. I was disgusted by General Komtar and his actions. Everything he did or said, was a facade, a lie. He disregarded me as a person. I was an obstacle, a thing to be "fixed." I loved Mandy with all my heart. Everything I did since I saw her was with the goal of making her an honest woman.

I was grumpy and taciturn at dinner, choosing to wolf it down and retreat to my study corner. Pulling out my notebook, I jabbed at an empty page, as I went through the options. Janet and Gina put their heads together to whisper at me. I ignored them. Mama was concerned and tried to draw me out of my shell, but I ignored her too. Uncle George shook his head at me and retired to smoke his pipe out on the verandah.

For days, my family observed me pacing around aimlessly, sometimes talking to myself or shouting into the air. Uncle George and Mama tried to get me to go to school, but I knew, I couldn't give my best. I tried vending, but in my mindless state, wares went missing and I incurred losses. Mama stopped me, sending Gina to man my stand instead. That week, I earned nothing. I slumped further into my gloom.

One day, I overheard the fishmonger telling the fruit seller of a trader who left his hometown, went to Accra, and made it. He was away for years. One fine evening, said the fishmonger, he turned up in front of his parent's home, like the prodigal son. He brought along gifts and enough wealth for his parents to retire, earning him the respect of his whole village. Hearing that, I realised what I needed to do.

I approached Mama who was bent over the washbasin, doing some laundry.

"Mama," I called.

She looked at me and smiled, "Are you better, Jolie? I see you washed your uniform. Going to school next week?"

I glanced up at my school uniform that I had washed earlier in the river, before bathing, a puddle of water pooling on the dirt as it dripped.

"I washed it because it was dirty," I said matter of fact.

"Oh?"

"Mama, I have decided on something."

"What is it, my son?"

"I want to work abroad, Mama. Ashaiman and Ghana has nothing to offer me. I am certain life has something to offer me and I have to chase it."

Mama stopped her washing and sat up. A long sigh escaped her lips.

"What madness has consumed you now?"

"Mama, listen to me. I know this for a fact that I can make it if I try. There is a life out there, not here in Ghana, out there, where I can make it big! I want to go, Mama."

"Traveling abroad doesn't guarantee success son. You can make it here too."

"Mama, this place has nothing else to offer me. It has taken more than it can offer to me."

"Jolie, my son, listen. Those people who travel abroad have money. Money we don't have!" implored Mama.

"Do I look like someone whose son can sit on an airplane? You must cut your coat according to your size," added Mama.

MY HUMBLE BEGINNINGS

"Mama, the people sitting in an airplane aren't different from me. They too want to try their luck abroad."

"They are different, the difference is they are rich. They have people abroad to help them with a place. Tell me, son, who do you know that has a home abroad?"

"Mama, your bible reading this morning had a line from Proverbs 14:23, 'all hard works brings profit, but mere talk leads only to poverty,'" I reminded Mama of her daily reading. "Maybe we are merely talking Mama. We aren't doing much to get ourselves out of poverty. We have to make a decision. Every accomplishment great or small starts with a decision," I said determinedly to Mama.

"We don't have enough food on our table, or a permanent roof over our head and my son is here talking about boarding an airplane," lamented a distressed Mama.

"There are more rich people than ever before, over 100 billionaires my teacher Mr Tano once told me. They are getting plenty of pleasure. Why aren't they worried about the poor? Why can't advancement be on merit and open to everyone, regardless of class, race, religion, or sex? Why are opportunities not genuinely equal? Why can't the government improve public education and open opportunities to all?" I burst out in anger.

Mama stared at me. Shocked at me ranting.

"The government talks about poverty alleviation but I don't think enough is being done to truly eradicate poverty. It seems to me that no one cares, it's all to win political points," I thought as I stared down at the article on the table.

Why can't they reduce visa requirements, especially for poor countries with people who want to travel for a better education and better life? Why do they shut their doors to the poor ones and only the rich can travel for a better education and better life? Yet they talk about poverty eradication. How can you eradicate poverty if you don't give opportunities to the poor to come out of poverty?

Helping the poor is truly a much worthier goal than narrowing inequalities. If the poor had a chance to get richer it will be a benefit to the whole country. It's a great disadvantage to be grow up in extreme poverty.

I was always thinking of the best way to get out of poverty. I refused to be poor in Jesus' name.

"Mama, I will find someone who can lend us some money to travel abroad." I said happily. *I will travel and come for my Mandy I will take her back from Kobe*, I said to myself.

Mama wasn't talking. She had a sad-looking face.

"Mama aren't you happy your son will travel to give you a better life. I will sit in an airplane. Soon I will be rich. I will come back to for my Mandy. I will drink coke and eat chocolates and ice cream anytime. *I won't have to wait till Christmas to drink coke and eat rice with chicken stew*, I said to myself.

I will become a fully grown man. I will have money and I will prove to everyone that my parents' poverty has nothing to do with the future of my life. I can bring the change, the economic prosperity that my family lacks.

Uncle George told me that a man never breaks his word. I was a man. I would find a way. Mama Adel thought I had forgotten about America in the manner of the young: flame up to fizzle out.

MY HUMBLE BEGINNINGS

I was thinking. I had all this extra energy previous consumed by my studies with no avenue to put it into. I threw it all into work.

***

It was an election year and hope was in the air. Everywhere I walked on the dusty streets, groups of elders stood conversing in hushed, urgent tones. "Vote for a better Ghana" they argued. People saw hope, I saw money. Voters needed food and drink. I talked to Gina who agreed to help. She wanted something of her own, but did not have the capital. My youngest sister was terrible at managing her money while on the other hand, I was good at it, but had no other skills from the art of trading.

Gina was an excellent cook and was well-known for it in our community. In fact, she had had many suitors who sent their elders to ask for her hand in marriage. There was one man who offered us fifteen cows. Mama Adel was against it and so was Gina. Uncle George regretfully turned him down. He was old enough to be our grandfather many times over.

So, Gina and I set up a small roadside eatery near the church in our neighbourhood under a shady Wawa tree. We sold snacks like bamfo bisi, Dzowoe (spicy peanut balls), and Ghanaian Chi chin. We also offered cooling drinks like coconut water, tea, and coffee. To attract customers, I would read the newspapers aloud to help them keep up with the election. We attracted quite a crowd of regulars. Many came to eat Gina's food and bought a drink so that they could stay to listen to the newspapers being read.

To raise capital, I subletted my spot in the Ashaiman market to another woman trader and put in a portion of my savings. We made good money and could afford to replace some of the things that General Komtar smashed up. Gina was ecstatic. For the first time in her life, she called the shots.

Gina was a spendthrift. She spent money as fast as she made it, usually on stocking the kitchen with spices and ingredients. We struck a bargain. She would pay me to manage the backend while she concentrated on cooking good food. We made a perfect team despite our arguments. Gina had a temper greater than both of our parents combined, and twice their tact and empathy too. Only Gina could talk a snake out of its teeth and venom, then convince it that its quality of life was better.

A few months in, disaster struck. The trader whom I sublet my stall to, wanted to give up the lease as it wasn't doing well. My customers preferred me and didn't want to do business with anyone else. I needed to go back to man my stall or it would be given to someone else. I had worked too hard to give it up. I didn't want to lease it out again because it would be difficult to find another person at favourable terms last minute. So, I talked to the trader and one thing led to the next. I hired her to take my place at Gina's eatery. This freed me up to return to running my own stall. I still was responsible for buying the food supplies at the market and keeping track of the earnings. Gina raised hell if even ten cents were missing.

Mama and Uncle George were happy to see me hard at work. Our family was doing well despite the social unrest and the ongoing food shortages. I wasn't satisfied. It wasn't enough. I was earning a small interest from the loan I gave Gina, in addition to my own work of running my own stall. I wanted to have many businesses that generated enough money to win over Mandy's family. One part share in a small eatery wasn't enough.

I needed millions of cedis, not thousands. I had to do something and fast. Mandy would get married to Kobe in the next few years. I had no chance after that. Mandy was right. That lucky bastard had everything I wanted. I would have to work twenty years just to get to Kobe's starting point.

MY HUMBLE BEGINNINGS

One day, as I was walking home to get lunch, we lived not far from the market, I spotted white foreigners having lunch at a stall. They looked like newly arrived important officials being chaperoned around on their "slum" visit. When it came time to pay the bill they used their own currency, with the admonishment to "keep the change," to the envy of the watching crowd. In our terms it was equivalent to a month's wages. Tourism. I needed to get a job in an establishment where they catered to white foreign wealthy visitors.

I hired someone to watch over my stall two days out of the week. I hit the road and headed to Accra. I tried Nii first. He was sympathetic, but insanely busy and had no time for me. He didn't have any jobs for me either. General Komtar's influence at work again. I didn't waste time in bitterness. It was the way of the world.

No other director had the time of day. They turned me away politely saying that I was "over exposed." "The public was tired of seeing you on the screen. Come back next year." they all said.

I didn't give up. I made friends, did favours, and shook my network of friends to see what fell out. I did small shows where I entertained people as a stand-up comic in some of the more popular bars for peanuts. I didn't mind.

I was after bigger fish. I got lucky one night, when an actor friend told me about a bar manager at a hotel who needed someone to fill a slot on weekdays. The manager's name was "Jacob Dumelo." Mr Dumelo was a fan of Thursday Theatre, and he was ecstatic to have one of the actors in his bar. My luck turned and I was hired. I was set to entertain guests for two nights a week until the regular gigging band recovered.

We got to know each other well, and once my gig ended. He offered me a job as a bar back meaning I was an apprentice bartender. Done. it had only taken me three or four months, but I had done it. My foot was in the door.

POVERTY OF THE MIND

Election season was over. I had quit my stall and subletted my lease and my business to another trader. I missed school, and I missed Kai and Coujoe, but I had other things on my mind.

If my scholarship had not been revoked, if I had made the grade, I would be moving on to high school. Maybe I could have earned a degree and worked in an air-conditioned office like Mama always said. Wishing didn't fill the pot.

I had Mandy to think of. Madam Komtar told me that they moved back to the countryside but I heard from the grapevine that she was studying her matriculation course at a girls college in South Africa. I worked hard, kept my ears open, and saved. I never forgot my dream of going abroad. If I secured a job there, I could come back in a few years, with everything I needed to marry my Mandy and take her away from that awful Kobe.

I moved away from home and paid something like twenty cedis for a in a shared room to sleep in during the day. I didn't stop vending. I sold roasted peanuts and snacks to movie goers on my days off.

Gina forced me to learn how to cook. When I told her I would have a wife for that, she talked me into learning anyway.

I loved my job. I learned to make cocktails, pull beer, and deal with sodden drunks. I loved the tips I collected and started setting it aside for my plane ticket to America. I even made enough to open a bank account and was the first person in our family to do so. TAKE THAT JANET! HA!

It still wasn't enough. I learned from my co-workers that there was an agency that helped with the necessary documents and guaranteed a job upon arrival in America. With my acting money, I had two thirds of the amount needed. I couldn't wait. Mandy would be engaged this year, and married three years after that once Kobe graduated. I didn't have time.

MY HUMBLE BEGINNINGS

CROCODILE

"JOLIE! ICE NOW!" I waved a hand to indicate that I heard over the music and the noise. It was Friday night and we were slammed, as well as shorthanded. One of our bartenders had called in sick so it was up to me, Elolo, and Abraham to pick up the slack. I hurtled through the kitchen doors narrowly missing Budune, one of the line cooks, on his way out.

"Jolie! here!" Stopping on a dime, I narrowly missed face planting, arse over teakettle on the grimy tiles.

I didn't like Budune. He was my elder, and rich enough to afford the food needed to be obese. Reluctance held in my stiff shoulders as I turned around to acknowledge him. The wattles on his face were shaded by the flashing strobe lights that came from the swinging metal doors.

"Yes, Mr Budune?" I answered aggressively, chin outthrust, with my back straight.

"Here" he said, offering me a sack of ice.

Outside I heard frantic yelling and clashing. Elolo was getting impatient. Grabbing the dripping ice, I turn tail and fled. I could feel his gaze resting on my posterior. Bloody disgusting. I wasn't a woman nor was I for sale. Greasy arse bandit.

I rushed back out, just as Elolo was about to storm into the kitchen to haul me out by my ear. I still got a stern look, which meant that I would be on shit duty for the rest of this week.

Crap. I loved my job, but not to the point where I loved cleaning the toilets drunken patrons violated. Used condoms were the least of it. Strike three for Mr Budune. I wished I could tell him to take a fucking hike, but he was my elder by a generation and more importantly, well respected at the bar, despite the unsavoury things lurking in his reputation.

I raced around, cleaning, washing, and wiping at top speed. This earned Elolo's approval for I was given permission to pull pints of beer for thirsty patrons. Most folks there were a mix of foreigners on holiday or officials from the big aid charities. It was a wealthy crowd and if I was pulling pints, I was able to earn extra tips. I needed every dollar I could get for my plane ticket out of the country. I didn't know where I would go, but Ghana had no avenue for me. I would live and die in poverty. Mandy would never be mine. Never.

Abraham, the senior bartender called me over and set me to making cocktails under his supervision. I was the bar back, and not normally allowed to mix drinks, but today was an. exception: we were just that busy and needed all hands on deck. I forgot my hunger and weariness as I was riding on an adrenaline high as I raced around top speed, mixing, pouring, and stirring exactly as I was told to. I didn't want to mess things up. A promotion meant a significant pay raise and cut of the tips, instead of the dollar notes I had been palming. My colleagues treated me well, but the beating when they found out would wipe out everything I collected in doctors' fees .

An older woman. caught me by the wrist as I was rushing by to fetch the limes.

"Oy, booyyrr…wherrsh my Long Island Iced tea?" she slurred drunkenly.

I pasted on a smile for the wrinkly old tomato and replied in my best in English, "Coming Ma'am." Her face made me want to throw up. Again, I wasn't for sale. I kept my smile on, even as I wrenched my arm away from her. Ah, the perils of being good-looking.

Our bar had a regular stable of boys and girls who came in and left on the arms of our wealthy patrons, both black and white. They weren't employed by the management, but we had an understanding. If they brought patrons in and encouraged them to buy bottles, we would give them a small percentage, as well let them use the place as a pick-up point. I kept well away from them. Half hated me, while the other half wanted me to join them. I had heard how that ended - I wasn't born yesterday. The whole arrangement made my skin crawl.

Abraham saved me and sent me to clean the toilets. For once, I was grateful. It was better than being a hunk of meat on display at the bar. Grabbing my mop and bucket, I cautiously stuck my head in the boy's toilet. It was empty save for the vomit and the human waste splattered all over the place. Being an upscale bar in the wealthy districts of Accra meant that we had flush toilets and running water. While it made things easier on me, it also meant that most of the time on busy nights, there was some boy or girl servicing a John in the cubicles. Cleaning took me an hour, and by the time I was done the toilets were spotless but I smelled terrible and I wanted to throw up. I couldn't wait till the next hire came along, then I could pass the duty off to them.

Mr Dumelo came to check in on the toilets. He caught me as I was finishing up. Taking pity on me, he sent me to my break to get cleaned up and eat something.

I loved my job to bits, my bosses were as grumpy as my explosive Uncle George, but we looked after our own. I was fed and given access to the showers and washing machine, despite being a lowly bar back. After a quick shower and change, I headed into the kitchen for something to eat. Usually, I got a bowl of hausa porridge, or leftovers from the customers' plates. Once I was lucky enough to get an order that was sent back: fish and chips with coleslaw. It was my first experience with foreign food. Bland but filling. I wanted my fufu.

The kitchen was largely deserted at this point. All the line cooks were in the break room, packing up and clearing up. The kitchen closed at midnight, and the bar carried on until dawn. Standing by the entry way, where he would catch me, Mr Budune was there, wearing a crocodile's smile - all teeth and predatory intent - his arms were scaled with tattoos and his wobbling jowls spoke of being a successful hunter. He was morbidly obese in a land where two-thirds of our daily income went to food and people still starved. He had my food held out in his hands, my eyes were drawn to it involuntarily: steak and fries with brown onion gravy. Meat. I hadn't had that for a more than a year.

"Here Jolie, I saved this for you."

"This man is bad juju," my brain told me.

I took a hesitant step forward, lured by food. Budune's beady eyes tracked my progress. I craved the meat, drooling. Outside, I could feel the thumping and grinding of the pulsating music. Hunger won out. I full intended to grab the food and flee but Budune blocked off all routes of escape. I was forced to eat where he could see me.

He smiled his toothsome smile, muttering things like "Good, good! You need more meat on your bones" or "This fellow is a handsome fellow" all in Ashanti Twi, which I understood but could not speak.

Wolfing down the food, I ate without tasting. As he spoke, he could not stop touching me all over my shaved skull and my arms. Funny enough, I could not stop eating nor could I voice out a refusal. As I swallowed the last bite, I wrenched away from him and fled to the safety of the bar, where Abraham and Elolo were. I didn't care that I had half an hour left on my break, or that I wouldn't be paid to go back early. Both of colleagues were glad to see me hard at work. Shame made me keep my mouth shut. *What kind of man lets himself be fondled like a woman for food?*

I was promoted to bartender after that, and properly taught to make drinks. Budune the crocodile was a constant presence on the edge of my life. He was always one to bring me my food and watch me eat.

MY HUMBLE BEGINNINGS

I spoke to John Dumelo, our manager and he put a stop to that. He believed in a strict division between the bar and the kitchen staff. Neither should mix. I had to change my address three times, sneaking out and telling no one where I would go when I knew he would be at his shift. I had to give up vending snacks outside the theatre for my food money. Thankfully, the pay raise I got covered my costs. I loved money, but I couldn't spend it if I was dead. I went back to performing as a stand-up comic on my days off, drawing on my fame from Thursday Theatre. Budune couldn't afford to spend all his days off in the establishments I was hired to perform in. People still remembered me, even though I was semi-retired from acting. It wasn't by choice, it was a question of money: Nii's fees and the cost of auditions, transport, and photographs were out of reach for the likes of me.

My colleagues looked after me as my much they could. Jacob Dumelo assigned him to the morning shifts that had him arriving just as I was leaving. They didn't believe me when I said he was a disgusting arse bandit but took notice when they saw how he was constantly sizing me up like a fattened calf up for market. They couldn't fire him because he was here as a favour from the owner to one of his relatives.

It all came to a head one day when he showed up outside the movie theatre. I was selling snacks on my day off. I was squatting next to my makeshift cart as usual, waiting for the next movie to start. Budune was busy stuffing his greasy face with my snacks and chugging down glasses of tea at the stall located across from the theatre.

I would have seen and remembered him if he had shown up at my snack stall and bought from me. I had enough of his sly stalking and insinuations. I wasn't a woman. I wasn't for sale. I couldn't take it anymore. I need to fix the bastard if it was the last thing I did.

Marching up to Budune with my heart in my stomach, I had my trusty, metal iron ladle ready to rain hell on him. Budune peaceably sipped tea and watched me approach. I wanted nothing more than to beat him up, but too many people were watching. I couldn't very well say "he's been stalking me." No one would believe it.

"What the hell do you want?" I smacked my iron ladle down into the plastic table, adding yet another crack to the weathered surface. The stall owner came running out, shaking his fist at the damage, but took two steps back and did an about face when he saw who I was talking to.

Budune smiled placidly, showing me all his pearly white teeth.

"Stall owner, give this young man a glass of chai" he called over his shoulders. "Sit down, young Jolie."

I bristled and raised my ladle ready to wack him a good one.

"I've got a business opportunity for you" Budune continued "I know you need money." He slid a piece of paper over to me. It was a brochure advertising for workers. I sat down and laid my ladle on the table. This sounded too good to be true. The stall owner bustled over with the tea and retreated to a safe distance. My instincts screamed at me to run, but I needed the money. *Mandy.* It wouldn't hurt to hear him out.

The street was dead quiet. Quieter than it should have been during a post-lunch siesta period. The tea stall owner had holed up behind his stand, pretending to be invisible.

Resisting the urge to scratch my arms, I answered "I don't want your business opportunity. Stay away from me"

Budune drank his tea and replied, "I can get you what you need."

Ants ran up my arms at his words.

MY HUMBLE BEGINNINGS

"What do you think I need?" I asked, ready to rabbit away if need be. *Men are brave,* I thought. We do not run.

"You need to earn money, if you want to marry your sweetheart." Budune did not quite sneer, by the curl of his upper lip, I knew what he thought of me and my efforts. I bristled and got ready to stand up. "Jolie, my friend is in need of your skills. You're a good salesman, and you can read and write well. He'll pay you in USD"

That got my attention.

Budune stood up. "Call the number or come and talk to me at work." Budune strolled away leaving these words behind.

I never intended to call that number, but two things pushed me into it. First was Mandy's engagement. I heard it through the grapevine and read it in the newspapers. The Komtar's threw a party for their daughter that was the talk of the town. The second was I caught a glimpse of Mandy and her friends celebrating at one of the bars on the opposite street. She didn't see me. I spent the rest of the night fighting off a wave of sadness and anger. That night when I finished work, I made an appointment as soon as the sun came up. I would come in on my day off next week. Life was not fair. I had no choice.

Their offices were set near a wealthy housing estate. I would later come to find out that it was actually a subdivided mansion turned into a flat. It was well appointed and looked like it was straight out of a Dr Who sitcom drama. There was no receptionist, only a lady who introduced herself as "Aunt Pearl." I couldn't tell if she was Ga or Ashanti. By the way she dressed and carried herself, I assumed Ashanti. There wasn't much furniture in the room. It had a couch, coffee table, and a messy office desk.

"So boy, Budune tells me that you are in need of money eh?" Aunt Pearl asked, once we sat down.

I nodded, fiddling with the starched edge of my cuffs. She gave me a dispassionate look once over that left me feeling like a side of beef hanging on a butcher's stall. It was worse than the looks I got working at the bar. At least they acknowledged I was human.

I was given a questionnaire to fill out. It was a simple one, asking about my height, weight, interests and talents. For the first time, I was grateful I had invested in my education. I could read and write well. Aunt Pearl waited until I was done.

"Good, good boy. I recognise you from Thursday Theatre. I think you'll do well here. If you please your customers, you'll be rolling in money in no time."

I noticed she had the same crocodile smile as Budune. I'd bet my last cedi that they were related. I could not help but feel pride at that.

She paused and asked me, "You understand that you're going to be having sex with the customers and that we're an escort agency?"

I was in shock. I expected many things, but sex work was the last thing I thought of. At the end, she asked me to strip down to my skin.

"I need to inspect you boy."

"I haa...uh...I Have n.." I stammered.

She gave a genuine smile. "I see boy," she beamed at me kindly "No need to worry about that. You'll be paid well. I hear that you want to move abroad?" She asked.

I froze. How did she know? Unease crept into my chest. Aunt Pearl flashed her brilliant, even white teeth at me.

MY HUMBLE BEGINNINGS

"I can help you boy, but you must listen to me and do as I say. I can even find you a job where ever you want to immigrate to" Hope, that insidious beast flared up.

"You can?" she nodded. I hesitated but I did ask she asked. I didn't quit my job at the bar.

When I got home, I burnt the thing. There was no way in hell or heaven I would do such a filthy thing.

PURE LUCK

I was curled in the fetal position under a heavy, coarse camel blanket, fending off the cold I felt coming from the change in season and autumn rain. I had a mug of beer to warm me up on the inside. Sleepy and clinging on to Anne, Sasha strolled into my bedroom and gave me a wet kiss on cheek, immediately tucking her head back under the green school hoodie. I waved them both off from my comfortable bedroom.

Hoping to catch a few more winks as the thunder rolled in the rainy sky, I was pulled out of my slumber by a buzzing sound emanating from my phone. In a blurry state, I peeked at the bright picture on my phone with one eye. A fair skinned man in a blue/black jumper holding a twenty pound snakehead by the gills grinned insanely back at me. I concentrated on the name above the picture, Mr Hong – Oil dealer. I met Mr Hong in a noisy Hakka specialty restaurant in Qingdao. At the time, he was speaking animatedly in Russian to Pavel Smirnov, a person I had also met.

"Killing two birds with one stone, I see." I said as he stood up to hug me.

With a twinkle of cheekiness in his eyes, he replied, "Can't help it, eh?" and introduced me to Mr Hong.

That night, the deal Mr Hong tried to seal didn't go through. The Pavel instead, after sharing a beer with me, took me to a corner and advised that I keep on good terms with Mr Hong.

"Who knows. He may come with a too good to be true deal. Good money, my friend." said Pavel. Following his advice, Mr Hong and I remained in contact with the occasional business transactions.

Tapping on the green icon, I heard a deep voice.

"Hello. Wine, I know it is early, but are you up?"

"Hello, Mr Hong. I am up, but barely. How are you?" I asked propping myself up against the bed headrest, pulling the blanket closer around me.

"I am good, Wine. Wine, listen carefully."

Sensing the urgency in his voice, I turned on the lamp on my bedside table and pulled the drawer out to reveal my notebook and pen. I flipped to a blank page amongst my nightly scribblings.

"I am listening."

"I have a vessel docked in Qingdao Port. The buyer who initially brokered the deal with me screwed up and now I am stuck."

"Okay. And how can I help?" I felt the excitement building up as I made some notes.

"I have to leave this port in a week's time as I have no clearance to be docked here for long. I am not allowed to leave this port empty handed according to my bosses. Wine, I need a buyer urgently."

"Mr Hong, I know a few who are interested, and I will start calling now."

MY HUMBLE BEGINNINGS

Ending the call, I threw off my blanket and jumped out of bed, heading straight towards the kitchen to make me a cup of instant coffee. While waiting for the kettle to boil, I dialled my assistant's number, putting it on loudspeaker as I slathered some jam onto a slice of bread. It took two rings before I heard Nalia's groggy voice answering my call.

"Ni hao," I greeted pouring the hot water into the cup with the three in one mix "Nalia," I said while sipping at the boiling hot cup of coffee I made in haste, burning my tongue. "It's Wine." I heard rustling sounds in the background. "Sorry to wake you up. We have a big deal in our court."

"Big deal, boss?"

"Yes. Crude oil. Round up the team and call the first three companies on the list we made."

Sensing my urgency, she replied "I will get right on it, boss."

I hastened my morning routine, taking twenty minutes instead of the usual thirty. I was about to step out when Nalia called.

"Boss, only one buyer responded positively."

"The Chen family?" I asked before she could continue.

"Yes, boss. He said he trusts you for in the previous dealings, your insight paid off."

"Thanks, Nalia. I have his private number. I will take it from here. Is the team ready?"

"They will arrive by 7am, boss."

"Tell them breakfast is on me and if we close this deal and we will all get a week off."

"Got it."

Ending the call, I heard the ding of the lift. The doors slid open to reveal Sasha's nanny carrying a red backpack.

"Anne, I will probably be home late. Can you stay here until I get back?"

"Sure, Mr Wine. But until 10pm."

"Got that. Thanks, Anne," I said, getting into the lift, pressing the close button. As I walked out of my residential area, I dialled the number to a private line.

"Mr Wine. I have been expecting your call since Nalia contacted my assistant."

"Miss Chen, I hope you are well and as always, beautiful."

"My my, still quite the charmer, Mr Wine. I heard you have found your long-lost daughter."

"Indeed. She is quite the charming little one, like her father."

"I wouldn't be surprised, Mr Wine. Now, tell me about this vessel."

"Miss Chen, the vessel is currently docked at a port. The last deal did not go as planned. The seller, a man I know, has contacted me. Miss Chen, I know you are interested. What I want to know is how much are you willing to part with."

A long moment of silence followed as my heart raced. Her voice came back.

MY HUMBLE BEGINNINGS

"I will come to see you at 10 am in your office. I will send you a list of details I need to see."

"And I will be prepared with your favourite cup of zheng zhu nai cha."

Laughter broke through the phone. "Mr Wine, I should not have divulged my secret indulgence to you. I hope you remember the particular show I like?"

"Yes, Miss Chen. I will see you at 10."

"See you then."

Galvanized, I pumped my fist into the air right in the middle of the street on Guangzhou as people began leaving their homes to take the metro, drawing stares from those around me. Ignoring them, I quickened my pace to the office to meet up with my team.

The meeting with Miss Chen went well. We had managed to convince her to speak with her board of directors about the sale. The Chen family keeps business in the family, keeping only family members on the board of directors. Miss Chen worked closely with her father, the chairman of the company.

"I will speak to the Chairman soon. Only matter is, the COO is currently away. He will be back in two days," said Miss Chen as she stepped out the front door. Her chauffeur, upon seeing her, rushed out to open the back passenger door for her.

Smiling at him, she got into the car and gave me a nod of goodbye. Walking back in, I saw my team of five looking at me expectantly.

"What did she say, boss?" asked Nalia.

I held up two fingers and said, "Two days. Now, we wait."

POVERTY OF THE MIND

A day after the meeting with Mr Chen, brother of the Chairman, I got a call from his office. Accepting the request to speak to me, I cleared my throat and tried to rearrange my thoughts in Chinese for Chairman Chen, a highly educated individual, who insisted on speaking to me in his native language, despite being able to speak fluent English.

"Good morning, Chairman Chen." I answered cheerfully.

"Wine, are you well?"

"Never better, Chairman."

"I have always perceived you to be a smart man Wine. But this. Hm…" Apprehension built up as the hesitation dragged on. "Wine, this is too good of a deal to skip out on."

Relief washed over me. Smiling, I replied, "Chairman, it's a one in a lifetime deal. So, are we good?"

"Very good! You have met all our demands. Now, we will secure the bank instrument. But do we have enough time?"

"Leave that to me, Chairman. I will pull all the strings I can to get it done by today."

"And so I shall."

"Thank you, Chairman."

I immediately made the important call to Mr Hong, the seller and to the bank that handled all my deals. They agreed to organise everything, readying it by late afternoon.

By the end of the day, the transfer went as planned. My team watched me in bated breaths, pacing the floors of the office, occasionally staring at my mobile phone. The sudden ring I received startled me. Rushing to it, I fumbled as I pressed the answer button.

"Wine!" shouted a clearly delighted Mr Hong. "How did it go?"

"Very well! Without a glitch, even." I sank into my chair, I continued "'Mr Hong, thank you. You don't know how nerve-wracking this whole week has been."

Mr Hong's laughter boomed from my mobile phone. As I held the phone away from my ear, I directed my gaze to my team giving them a thumb's up. Cheers and shouts of happiness vibrated through the office as they jumped and hugged each other.

"That's loud!" remarked Mr Hong.

"It's just my team being overjoyed. Mr Hong, it's been a pleasure doing business with you."

"Thank, Wine. You owe me a beer!"

Ending the call, I spotted a message from the bank informing me of the successful transaction. Smiling, I got up to join my team remembering to tell them the next week would be a holiday.

AMERICA

When my plane landed at the famous JFK airport, I was so excited that I started sweating. I had my passport and breezed through the immigration check with no problems. I felt like I made it. Here, the streets were paved with gold. Back home, people could live well on three US dollars a day. Here, you can earn that in one hour. With the job I was promised, I would make well over that. I could not wait to return home with my newfound riches, buy a plot of land, and marry Mandy.

When I walked out to the arrivals hall, no one was waiting for me. I went to the pay phone as instructed and tried to dial the number I was given. It was disconnected. I tried contacting the agent who sent me. No one picked up. There was no job waiting for me.

I felt rich because I had made it to America. Compared to back home, life was easier here. If you knew where to look and how to ask, you could get a meal and a place to stay for the night FOR FREE. I slept out on the streets for the first month and relied on soup kitchens to get by. Once you adapt to the culture and social customs, life was much the same as back home.

The Americans respected a good hustle but thought of me as a criminal in the making. I didn't mind, it was no worse than the scorn I earned at home for being a gravedigger's son. I was robbed within the first week. They took my suitcase while I was missing. It was a huge blow, as it contained my return tickets, and passport. Despite applying and taking any job I could get, it was tough to find good employment. The people who could hire me, often didn't need my labour or couldn't afford it. The people who could, did not want me. Still, I worked many jobs: from cooking, to construction to cleaning often for half the pay an American would make. I fell back on selling food and cheap sunglasses. I worked near the tourist traps and stayed around the Bronx or Harlem.

My days passed one by one. I would wake up, clean the front step of Mrs Janice's shop. She reminded me of Mama. Then I'd go buy a coffee at the coffee shop and use their bathroom to wash my face and freshen up. After that, it was off to my part time job at the hair salon, to help Mrs Janice open up. She paid me ten dollars per week, one each day, and three extra as a bonus. She also fed me brunch. It was usually a sandwich, or leftovers from her dinner. It was enough for me to afford one meal per day. The church was good for free meals but that meant staying and listen to the service first. I was indebted to Mrs Janice. I don't think I would have survived without her help. She reminded me of Uncle George, in the way she talked to people.

MY HUMBLE BEGINNINGS

The morning rush hour found me on the street corner, selling newspapers. Cops there were more expensive to bribe. I learned to recognise who to avoid and who would look the other way. Late afternoon between the lunch and dinner rush, was my downtime. I used it to nap, catch up with the friends I made, and drink a beer or two. It took the edge off my day. Of course, when I had the time, I dreamt of Mandy. At night, I worked as a bouncer or took bar work when I could get it. I averaged thirty dollars per day over the course of one month. On a good day, I would make fifty. There were a few times I had to dust of my acting skills and beg or panhandle as they called it. I hated every minute of it. No man should have to beg when he is capable of work. It was a tough adjustment, and I was scammed more than a few times before I learned better. I slept out on the streets. At the start it was because I had no where to go and no one to call on.

I found my feet eventually and discovered that I liked America. It brought its own set of hardships and rewards. America is diverse. I met many Ghanaians like me who travelled to the states in search of a better life. Not only that, it was fascinating to see what they brought with them. I met and befriended many other immigrants from all around the world. To this day, I still keep in contact with them.

As time went on, I started making a name for myself by being useful. Like my father, people in my community started to come to me with their problems, and I would try my best to help them.

Americans called this the "hard luck life" but I thought I had struck it rich. Things were much easier compared to back home. In America, being poor still meant that you ate meat, had clothes on your back, and access to electricity and running water. There was help available in the form of government programs that provide money for food and shelter, if you qualified. Back home, this would be an unattainable luxury.

I took part-time jobs, doing anything and everything to survive. This consisted of mostly cleaning, construction, and restaurant work. I was always looking to make the next dollar because I had Mandy waiting for me at home, and debts to pay.

Eventually, I got lucky, and managed to score a job teaching English to newly arrived immigrants at the Church I went to for its soup kitchen meals. My students loved me, and I made extra money by giving out tuition. By American standards, it wasn't much, but I was counting in Cedis. My family could live very well on three USD a day.

When my visa expired six months in, I learned to hide from the cops. I fell in with a crew of "ghetto niggas" who lived in Harlem. They spent their nights partying. By day, not many had jobs as far as I could see, but always managed to have money to spend. Mama would call them "bad seeds." Despite all that, they were good people. I ran "errands" and "interference" for them and they paid me well for the work I did. They taught me how to drive a car and party. In return, I didn't look too closely to what they were doing, and did as they asked.

I had a good life, despite the danger. Sleeping rough could be risky at times. There was a lot of violence, drugs, and addicts floating around. There was a subset of people who preyed on the vulnerable, and for a while, I looked like fresh meat. I made myself useful, to those in charge, and stopped looking like prey.

The temperature at night was cooler than back home. People told me that I had to start preparing for winter early, because winters in New York could be very rough. The homeless regularly froze to death during a cold snap. They would fall asleep and never wake again. Only in spring when the snow thawed would their bodies be found. Those who could afford it, rented a place to stay or moved down south for milder weather. I wanted to save the extra cash so I preferred to sleep out on the streets.

MY HUMBLE BEGINNINGS

Despite all my hard work, in-between letters, calls and gifts to Mandy, my living expenses, and partying, my savings were scant. I barely broke even at the end of every month. I did have a rainy-day cushion, hunger had taught me that, but it was nowhere near enough to pay off my debt and fulfill the expectations of my relatives and family waiting for me back home.

I hopped on freight trains, going from north to south. I worked on construction sites, farms, and orchards, all in return for a meal, a roof, and some extra cash. I saw most of America that way. It was a beautiful country, with rolling mountains, wide rivers, and nature.

I missed fufu. It was hard to cook Mama's food, but the experience was worth it. The abundance I found in America more than made up for the lack of home cooking. Meat was so cheap! If I found a job, I only had to work for two or three hours to afford chicken. I could buy a burger with meat and cheese inside for only a dollar or two. People ate meat almost every week, and not just at celebration times. It took a while for me to wrap my mind around the concept. The Americans were fond of excess, from choices to portions. It was insane.

My life in American came to an end all too soon. My visa expired, and the police caught me on a raid in the factory I was working in. When I look back, I see the anxiety, the hard times and the danger. In the end: my heart holds only fondness for my time in America .

AMERICA

THUG LYFE

"JOE! Ey! Pizza's here!" Mira yelled from the living room. I heard the door shut and the sound of the pizza man driving away. I put Mario on pause to go join Mira.

"My name is Jolie" I corrected her politely. "Not Joe." I said as I helped myself to a slice of pizza. Mira put her hands on her hips and cocked an eyebrow at me.

"Boy! What kind of boy's name is Jo-lee anyway?" She scoffed, "Sounds like a girls name, you a man or what?" She smacked my hand away from the food.

"HEY! My Mama gave-"

Big Red blew in through the front door, with a bag of groceries and a six pack of Budweiser in the other, breaking up the impending altercation. Insult me, and I'll live. Insult my family and I'll kill you.

"Hey baby!" Big Red's meaty hands closed in on Mira's slender shoulders "Missed me?" he teased.

Mira scowled. "Hey you big lug, let me go!" Coughing politely to remind them that I was still here, I clattered the cupboards as loudly as I could while I put the groceries away. Big Joe and Mira broke apart, both flushed and panting.

I cackled "Eey, chale! Free show na?" I liked Mira, but she had spicy temper. Mira scowled and snapped

"Shut your mouth nigga!"

I cackled louder, ripped a beer loose from the six-pack, and cracked it open.

Big Leo patted my back driving me forward. He was an honest-to-goodness giant of a man, almost seven-foot - 6 ft 11" to be exact.

Big Red exclaimed, "Thanks buddy! Good job on that driving! We would never gotten away if it weren't for you, driving all smooooth-

MY HUMBLE BEGINNINGS

like" I grinned, pleased at the praise. We clinked beer cans like they were wine glasses. "Maaan, the way you slid us away from those cops, that was some mad driving skills" Big Red exclaimed in admiration.

"That ain't nothin'" I said modestly. "I didn't wanna get caught and deported that's all." I explained.

Mira leaned over and cuffed me on the head, "Boy, you best keep your humble bragging to the down-lo. I ain't gonna tolerate no swelled head in my house!"

Big Red shrugged his massive shoulders and said in a placating tone, "Better listen to what she say, she run dis house."

Mira interjected from her perch on Big Leo's lap, "Ahnd don'tcha forget that!" She waggled her finger at me.

"Okay! Okay" I said, well and truly chastised. "So, you got any more of them jobs for me?" I asked "I could use the money. I need to send money back home."

"Awww babes! Anchovies and onion? You know I hate onion!" Big Leo complained as he bit into a slice. Mira who was on her fourth slice herself smacked him on the shoulder.

"Shush! eat your food!" she said. Red ignored her to reply.

"Jobs? I don't know Jolie, The police are onto us. We gotta wait til the heat die down before we pull another one. It's too hot right now, you know what I mean?"

"Alright Red" I agreed, pausing as a thought struck me. "What about the construction site you work at? Are they hiring? I'm a good worker."

"Boys, if your asses needs the toilet, you better get in there now. This Mama needs her me- time in the bath!" Mira announced. We shook our heads. "Alright, the bathroom is no-go zone for the next thirty minutes" she declared as she strolled away for a shower.

When Mira left, I tried not to look disappointed. American food was strange. All this meat, cheese, and grease was sitting a little too heavily in my stomach. I had polished off half a pizza and beer wasn't helping. I felt myself relax into a food coma. This meal was second after that devil chicken, even if it tasted strange to me.

Big Red flicked on the TV and cranked up the volume. "Look Lil' Joe. I like you. I really do. I can't give you no jobs no more. It ain't right to bring you into this. You gotta leave town, I heard from my cousin that the cops are looking for us." I felt my stomach sink into my shoes, and all that food wanted to come out.

"You're kicking me out?"

Red spread his hands, "No. no. Me and Mira, we're moving out next week. Our landlord hiked up the rent and we can't afford it." Rubbing his chin ruefully, he chuckled "Mira, you know her, told me that we could afford it, we'll make it. That Mira, she a stubborn city girl. We're moving back to Tennessee, to my Mama's trailer park. We've got enough from this job to buy a double-wide with a small room for the kids."

I schooled my face and asked earnestly, "Red, where am I supposed to live?"

Panic began to claw at my insides. I had just gotten back on my feet and thought I could relax. In fact, I had sent back most of my earnings from this job and spent the rest on groceries and a present for Mandy. We were eating pizza I paid for. I did not have funds to relocate or find another apartment.

MY HUMBLE BEGINNINGS

Big Red gave me his puppy dog eyes. "I'm really sorry Lil'Joe. Best I can offer you is a ride down south. You have to leave before you end up in the slammer. It should be alright to come back next year."

I wanted to strangle the stupid bastard. *So you string me along, use me up and then discard me!* I kept my mouth shut because he was twice my size. That was one of the reasons why Mira was with him.

"Red, you know I can't leave. Miz Mable just gave me a job at her hair salon."

Just then, breaking news flashed across the television screen.

"Special report in the news today. The bank on Higgs and Weston was robbed. Police are looking for these men, one of which was described as a 'giant,'" the TV announcer said.

Big Red pointed a thick finger at the screen. "Did you just hear the man?" I scowled and wiped grease off my face.

"You told me I wouldn't be recognised!" My voice rose in anger. "That it would a clean and quiet job! How did it turn into this mess?"

Big Red glanced at the bathroom door nervously, "Shhhhst! Keep your voice down, Mira doesn't know! She thinks I've been saving for years." I gaped at him in awe and disbelief. The balls on this man!

"Red. I. Don't. Care." I enunciated my words very carefully. "I want the rent I paid for next month back. You told me that you were staying until the end of the year" I put the countertop between us, and carefully stayed out of reach.

Red frowned. "Lil' Joe, I was straight with you at the beginning, I told you things might change. You can't just listen to the good and forget the bad. Clean up this mess. Dis my roof you're living under nigga!" He stormed off in the direction of the bedroom.

I glared a hole into the melamine kitchen countertop. Regretfully, while my gaze was pure acid, it had no effect on its clean white surface. This meant that I was back to sleeping on the streets next week.

I vowed I wasn't going to let him run off with my rent money to live out his life in wedded bliss. My share of the rent amounted to three hundred dollars. That would have stretched the entire month. I scrubbed and washed the kitchen out of habit and anger. Gina and Mama had beaten the habit of cleaning into me thoroughly. When Mira was done and out of the bathroom, the apartment was sparkling clean.

"Eh, Lil' Joe!" Mira called out cheerfully, "Why you so grumpy?" She ruffled my afro hair affectionately, taking in the spotless apartment "Wow! You did a real good job there!" I grunted an assent. "Bathroom's free if you want to use it," Mira called over her shoulder breezily. The bedroom door shut, and Mira's laughter mingled with Red's.

I wrenched open the fridge to stare at all the food they bought with *my* money. Then at the spotless apartment.

Fuck' em.

REALITY BITES

HOME AGAIN

I was dumped at the Accra International airport without ceremony. A dispirited immigration official waved me through the arrivals gate. I only had the clothes on my back. Everything else was confiscated by the American border control before my deportation. I thought of calling Uncle Danso to come pick me up, but I was too ashamed to. We had mortgaged his property to gain a loan for me to go to America.

MY HUMBLE BEGINNINGS

It took some finesse to earn my way bus fare back home. I hitched a ride from kinds souls from the airport to the Accra market, persuading the stock boys to let me in as a coolie at the Accra market yards. By the time I slunk home two days later, it was early evening. My house no longer felt warm and comfortable, to my eyes, it was too small and dank. I found Mama Adel in the kitchen chopping onions. She said nothing and motioned for me to help. Mama knew I had come home with nothing.

This close to dinner time, industrious mothers all across our neighbourhood were busy cooking and scolding daughters who pounded the night's fufu, or kenkay. The familiar blend of manure and raw sewage, mixed with frying spices and onions hit me hard. The last forty-eight hours came crashing down. I had been banned from America. I had come home. I was lost. I was alone. How could I confess my failure to my family?

Janet and Uncle George clattered into the kitchen, hungry as lions, chattering animatedly about a new commission they just finished. I saw Uncle George with new eyes. He seemed to have shrunk and he looked his age. Once the moment passed, he was my father again, tall and strong.

Like a stupid child, Uncle George gaped in surprise and said "Jolie! You're back early!"

I had put on height and weight during my time away. Janet's sharp eyes took in my American clothes and the hunched set of my shoulders as I squatted on the ground. She heard Mama Adel's placid silence and understood. News travelled fast in our community.

Uncle George's weathered face cracked open in a warm smile. "Come son, let me look at you!"

I was supposed to be in America for another six months. My sister shooed me off, to take over my chores for me.

POVERTY OF THE MIND

Standing up, I pulled on my best smile and turned to face Uncle George. "I'm back, I came back early," I repeated. My father patted me on the back, oblivious to the strained silence emanating from Janet and Mama Adel.

"Come, come!" Uncle George drew me into our living room. Despite my ignominious return, my father was happy to see me home. He sat on the living room bench, while I stood before him. "How was it boy? Did you work well?" Uncle George asked.

Petrified with terror, my throat closed up on me. Forcing my words out I stammered

"Th.ther...there was nnnno..." I began in a whisper.

My father snapped "Speak up boy!" I had to lie.

"I..I ..found work over there. I worked in a hotel." It was partially true. I had secured temp work at a hotel as a bus boy and had earned good money, but I blew most of it on Mandy and parties. Faced with Uncle George's imperious frown, I had to lie. Clearing my throat I spoke. "It was good work. Boss man liked me. He said I worked well."

Outside our window, the neighbourhood brats ran around in play. They chanted "Nanuma wyee ay. Nanuma."

Steeling my conscience I said, "I was working when the police came to arrest all of us. They locked me up with no food or water. They said my visa expired, and that I was an illegal person. So, they took all my money and sent me back. I had to come home." My expression downcast, I finished and waited for my father's reaction.

Uncle George seemed to understand. His mouth tightened, and his shoulders hunched. I flinched, any moment now, I would be beaten and chased out of the house. Sighing heavily, my father patted me on the back "All young men need to go on a journey." He stood up and limped away to the kitchen. No mention of my debt was made. I wasn't stupid -- the axe would fall later.

That night, my sleep was plagued with nightmares, as it had been since I arrived back home. I chased after Mandy, while demons and spirits tried to drag me down. Close to dawn, I managed to fall asleep only to be dragged awake for what felt like thirty seconds later by Mama Adel. It was mid-morning and Mama wanted me up to watch her stall while she did a house call for a client. All I wanted to do was roll over and go back to sleep. Mama Adel was having none of it.

"Get up boy! Your sister is working in Tema" she told me.

The guilt that pricked me, had me up and ready within ten minutes, according to my America-tuned sense of time.

I spent the rest of the day at the market taking down orders and selling smaller finished pieces. The ladies loved me and bought anything I sold. I had added height and weight during my time in America. Food was easier to come by there. The hardest part was answering and deflecting all the questions about my time in America. I gave them heavily sanitised and edited versions. Much of what I did, was not for public consumption. I didn't manage to catch a glimpse of Mandy, much less see her. I heard that she was doing well and had finished school in the year I was gone. She was studying for her A-levels and would marry Kobe once he graduated. Mama Adel returned after lunch with a satisfied air and a fat new commission. Before I could make my escape, she corralled me and sent me out to deliver finished orders. As I set out, I could see the span of days stretching out, one by one. I would work for Mama until I died. This was as good as it got for me. The thought was terrifying .

At dinner, Mama Adel was full of praise for my sales skills as she talked me up to Uncle George. It took all of my strength to keep my back straight and a smile on my face. Janet was the only one who noticed. She knew me too well. Us children ate in grim silence and retired early. I stretched out on the couch, wrapped myself in a blanket and tried to get to sleep.

Again, my sleep was plagued with nightmares. This time, I lived out my life in the slums. In my dream, as I grew older, life sapped my strength from me. Mandy married Kobe and had beautiful babies. She forgot about me. As I hit my thirties, I gave up and turned to drinking and sleeping around. I never married, nor did I take responsibility for any children I sired. I was one of the jobless Uncles I saw who were full of excuses and who had to rely on their wives to survive. I died alone in my own vomit. People came and took me away to make what was left of me into black magic. I woke up from this one screaming in terror. It roused my whole family who came out fighting, under the impression that we were under attack. Janet, my uncaring sister, checked me over for harm, made me hot chai, and told me to go back to sleep. Then, promptly did the same. Night terrors were of no concern to my pragmatic sister. She had to work in a few hours. So did Uncle George. Mama sat up with me and prayed over me until I fell back to sleep.

This time, my family let me sleep in. I woke up late in the morning hungry and muzzy headed. Feeling restless, with a bad case of itchy feet, I set to cleaning the house after a hasty breakfast of toast and tea. When I was done, the house was spotless, and all our laundry done. I found my school homework tucked away in a forgotten corner of the living room. Nostalgia hit me hard, as I dug them out to look at them. Times were simpler back then. I only had schoolboy problems to deal with. Despite all the hustling I had to do, I still had time to play chaskele with Kai and Coujoe at recess. I wondered where they were now. Sending up a silent prayer for them, I hoped they were doing well. They needed to make it - I hadn't.

Mama found me on the floor, slumped over my schoolbooks, bawling my eyes out, with my fists stuffed into my mouth to stifle the noise. I wasn't aware that I was crying. Between the crippling pain seated in my heart, and the white noise that was felt more than heard -- I had tried and I had failed through no fault of my own. God was good, he had plans. There was no way out. Mama Adel took one look at me and understood. This was something she faced, day after day after day, for most of her life. Hugging me in sympathy, we cried together. She cried for me. I cried for a future lost. I don't know how long we sat like that together.

Too soon too early, Mama Adel commanded me pull myself together and help her get dinner started. I was into much heart pain to pay attention to her. SLAP! The force of her hit brought me back to reality. Mama had a strong arm on her. I had forgotten but was brutally reminded as I lay sprawled on the ground on fire.

Mama Adel retracted her hand and sternly pointed towards the kitchen. "Jolie Child, ENOUGH." she pulled me upright, giving me no room to protest. "Go wash your face" she said in kinder tones. Her scowl, and her posture with hers arms akimbo spoke of danger. Muscle memory and ingrained obedience had me moving. I no longer feared my mother's beatings- I had survived worse. This was for my own good, Mama always had my best interests at heart.

When I came back into the kitchen, Mama Adel had hot tea for me to drink. She sat me down at the kitchen table and fed me toast. As I ate, my tears stopped flowing. Never one to be idle, Mama Adel got started on dinner. She began to speak as she deftly chopped onions.

"Son, do you remember when you a very small child?" She asked. Humouring her, I sipped my tea and held my peace. She held up her hand at her waist and continued "and you asked for schooling. We had to tell you 'no.' It broke our hearts son." I sighed. I didn't see the point of this story. I knew what happened next. I tried. I failed. I lost my scholarship because I didn't make the grade. "You worked for it son. You found a way to go to. At the market all your teachers always spoke well of you, especially Mr Tano."

I shook my head, I wasn't the best student at school, the only subjects I managed to ace easily was English. I loved reading.

"Uncle George did not say it at the time, but we were so proud of you. You were the first in our family to go to school." My chest heated from pride. Mama Adel continued as she moved on to the garden eggs. "Don't be too hard on yourself Jolie. You're a clever child, God sends tribulations to test us. Work hard, He will provide."

From then on, I was left to my own devices. Gina's chores were my chores. Janet and Uncle George were exempt, they had to earn us our way out of my debt.

Janet caught me outside in the backyard, weeding the vegetable garden after dinner. The sun hadn't set yet and I needed to stay busy. What better way than to get started on tomorrows chores. My sister stood over me, arms folded, and wearing a ferocious scowl.

"Jolie, what's going on?" She demanded. Desperate to deflect her line of questioning, I said the first thing that popped into my mind.

"Why is Gina working in Tema?" Janet's blunt reply confirmed my suspicion.

"We need the money." Rudely shoving her foot into my field of vision, Janet demanded, "And?"

I deflated under Janet's flat gaze. Janet had all of our parents' toughness and temper, but had inherited none of Mama's empathy or Uncle's George's tact.

"I got caught and deported." Shame at my wild spendthrift ways caught up with me, I pretended to be industriously weeding. Janet puffed her cheeks out in a sigh.

MY HUMBLE BEGINNINGS

"You sent enough back to cover two thirds of it. I can pay down the rest with the new commissions we're getting, to prevent them from getting too eager, and Uncle Danso's land." Janet hauled me up by my ear in a vise-like grip, forcing me to crouch down to accommodate her short stature. Guilt stayed my hand, my sister was strong, but I was stronger. Janet's asserted her dominance over me as I crouched under her leopard gaze. She stated "I can pay the rest off for you. I don't care how, you need to come up with 100 USD every month. If you work hard

, and put your clever brain to it brother..." she shook me like a dog, "... together, we will pay it off in less than a year."

Dumb with terror, I barely manged to stammer "Uncle George doesn't know?"

She let me go as she said "No. he doesn't."

Our parent's love had firm limits. They would not risk their livelihood over me. They had Janet.

"God save me, God save us" was all that I could say.

Nightmares kept me up. Around midnight, I gave up and sat awake thinking. As dawn broke, my mind settled. I was clear-headed if exhausted. I had a plan. I needed to head into Accra to look for Nii, and Jacob Dumelo, my manager at my old job. Janet gave me no chance. With Uncle George's approval, she hauled me off to her workshop and put me to work. The both of them gave me no quarter as they ran me ragged all day. I was the lowest and newest worker, and they made sure everyone knew it. I spent the day fetching, carrying, and sweeping, while wearing a film of sawdust. Mama must have found time to have a word with Uncle George, for my entire family conspired to keep me under their eye at all times. If I wasn't at the workshop, I was at church with the family or at home doing my chores under Mama Adel's watchful eye. Each night, my nightmares were chased away by physical exhaustion. I crashed into a dreamless sleep and woke gripped by feelings of unease. My days blended into a routine: awaken, chores, eat, work, eat, home, chores, eat, sleep. Repeat.

I had the illusion of choice: two to be precise. I could work with Mama Adel at her market stall or work in the carpentry workshop with Janet, and Uncle George. My father was adamant I pick up the basics of carpentry, even if I had no talent for the finer details. He told me, *"Book learning and dreams won't feed you son."* Reality had proven him right. Common sense had me buckling down to the grindstone. The first task my father set me to was to sanding and polishing finished items. It was stupid mindless work that left me free to think. I didn't regret my time in American, nor the burden it placed on my family. What stung me most was a sense of failure. I wasn't clever enough, and I got caught. I had to rely on my family to bail me out. My dreams of wealth were as distant as the moon.

While it was true that I had no talent for carving, putting together a simple piece of furniture was easy enough if you were meticulous and paid attention. Over time, I learned to like the work, finding it rewarding and taking increasing pride in my growing competence. Under Uncle George's tutelage, I learned how to make quality furniture that would last for generations.

Between my father and sister force feeding me knowledge, I learned everything there was to know about the type, storage, and handling of wood. If I made a mistake, I lost my lunch, giving everyone else a slightly bigger share. Naturally, everyone else tried to make sure I got things wrong. I won in the end both my lunch and their respect.

Janet taught me style. How to take simple serviceable pieces and turn them into elegant works of art for wealthy clients. I learned our traditional motifs and those of several other tribes. I learned how to have a good eye for good artwork. It would prove invaluable in later years.

MY HUMBLE BEGINNINGS

My sister and father gave me their knowledge, and I gladly soaked it up. My time in America taught me the value of possessing a set of marketable skills. It would pay better than unskilled labour where I was lucky to earn three dollars an hour. Being a carpenter was not something I strived for, that was Janet's dream, but a skilled trade was not worthless. I would not become a millionaire by being a carpenter, nor was it a guarantee of a steady livelihood. Uncle George had spent more than half my life unemployed and puttering around the house. Looking back, I am forever indebted to my stubborn sister for teaching me. I could not have gotten far without it. Biding my time, I stayed obedient and busy because it was the sensible thing to do.

The workshop ran like a dream. We had several apprentices that did the fetching and carrying, and two full-fledged carpenters who had graduated but had yet to serve out their bond. Apprenticeships in Janet's workshop were in sought after, despite the high costs and long hours.

My family was relentless in the pursuit of perfection in all facets of the business. Our workshop produced excellent carpenters with trustworthy work ethics and were always in demand. My sister had built a thriving business with a solid reputation while I was busy failing and chasing after Mandy.

Janet handled the day-to-day management while Uncle George oversaw production and controlled the direction. My father was quietly grooming my sister to inherit. He was proud of Janet and saw her as his "son" and heir. We weren't Ashanti, but Ewe. In our culture, inheritance of wealth flowed down the male line, not the female line. Women did not inherit; men did.

Janet was true to her word. Every month she gave me a report on how much my work earned her in US dollars. Her delivery was in a tone that matched my performance for the month in a sanctimonious manner. Did she have to rub my failure in my face all the time?

I averaged 10 dollars per month. Once, I hit 50, due to a lucrative commission I snagged from a bar owner. Still, I received no wages for my work, save for the lunch. I still had to earn that. I was under strict watch and worked to the bone with no freedom. I was in a constant state of semi-exhaustion. As much as I wanted to see Mandy, on most days I had no spare energy to think of her.

Six months passed before my parents trusted me enough to shift their attention to other matters. Inflation continued at a rapid pace, but the government's experiment with free-market economy brought massive amounts of foreign currency into Ghana. We were able to request payment for large orders in US dollars.

I calculated that half of our gross revenue was funnelled into paying down my debt. It was the interest that was killing us. After deducting our payroll and suppliers, there was just enough to save and put food on the table. I understood why Janet was frustrated with me, even as I remained unrepentant. I would pay her thrice of what I owed once I made it. All I needed was time and the right opportunity.

Foolishness

SO HELP ME GOD!

I spent the month recuperating. My creditors did not come looking for me. In that time, I could not do much but brood and watch my savings dwindle. I played my father's last words over and over in my head. *"A crab does not give birth to a bird. Settle down boy before you end up dead."* I had nothing to do but stare up at the ceiling of the thatched hut and think. I hated this. I would not and could not live life as my father had. An entire life spent in poverty and hard toil with nothing to show for it. I often wondered what would have happened to him, and the rest of us if my brothers had not walked out or if Janet's talents for woodworking were dismissed. What if she had been married off at thirteen to the first suitor. We would have starved to death. All of us.

MY HUMBLE BEGINNINGS

The noon heat baked into my bones, drying me out from the inside out. I had the room to myself today. All my roommates were out working. Moving was difficult, and as much as I wanted to punch something, it was impossible. I settled for flinging my corn husk pillow at the bare walls. It slid off and landed on the dirt with an unsatisfying thump. I thought back to the good times I had with Mandy and my heart melted. I was doing this for her. Her parents had made the difference between them and me clear. I hated being powerless. I had to do this for me too.

I levered myself up to sit stiff-legged on the room's only stool: an upturned plastic bucket used to mix the evening's gari before cooking. My options were bleak. I had a month or two to start paying down the debt and I didn't have Janet to help me this time around. Janet was largely responsible for my broken bones.

Obadiah was the first to return. His peculiar stench preceded him, making me miss my old job as a bartender in Osu badly. I had gotten used to taking a shower there every day and having clean clothes. Poverty was an unending series of bad choices. Do I eat today or do I buy soap to wash my clothes?

"Jolie! Na! don't be so grumpy! The doctors said that the cast will come off next week!" he said, as he tossed a package of waakanye at me. In that moment, I wanted nothing more than to punch his cheerful mug. I caught my food one handed.

"Thanks Charley!" I managed. Bloody Obadiah did not leave me in peace. Instead, he sat down next to me and started eating.

"So you see na, today boss was good to usso we got extra food. Did you know that there was …" The idiot would not stop his cheerful prattle, "So you see, Jolle, if I hadn't kept working today, I wouldn't have gotten this food!"

I managed a grunt and a nod then indicated I needed to go outside to pee. Obadiah, the kind cheerful soul he was, helped me move outside to relieve myself.

I could not wait till the cast came off. I was being driven insane.

Once the hospital sawed my casts off I put my plan into action the next day. I sold off all my luxury goods and managed to recoup almost all the money I spent. During my time at Madam's Pearl's stable, I had come to realise how things worked. People paid vast amounts of money to human traffickers to smuggle them into Spain where they would head to the UK or the Netherlands to find work.

The exchange rate worked in our favour. A paperboy in the UK could live like a king over in Ghana. I had to play to my strengths. I did one thing very well, and that was to hustle.

I had three weeks left until the creditors came knocking. I went to see Nii who was pleased to see me despite my recent exploits. I remembered him and Aunty D with fondness. Nii was doing well. He had his own media company. The receptionist was a spicy little number with curly hair and a bodacious figure. She ushered me into the swankiest corner office I had seen in a long while. I bet the suits on wall street did not have one as fancy as this one. I paid it proper homage by standing there with my mouth open in awe like a buffoon, forcing myself to shut my mouth and straighten up. Nii strode in, greeting me with good cheer.

"Jolie! You've been good na?" Nii's face wrinkled up into his professional smile. I returned it with genuine fondness. I liked him despite his fake-actor manners. He treated me well.

"I've been good. Look Nii, I'm not here to ask for a job as an actor." I began. Nii raised an eyebrow. He leaned back on his leather swivel chair.

MY HUMBLE BEGINNINGS

"You're here because?" he asked.

"I'm here because I need your help to run a recruitment campaign," I answered. He leaned forward, with interest in his eyes. "I need your help in creating a media campaign." I slid a piece of paper forward. "This is what I require, I'm willing to pay." I slid over another check. Nii's eyes widened at the amount. It was most of what I had. "Can you help me?"

Nii rubbed his hands together with glee. "I believe I can," he said and we shook on it. The next three weeks were the busiest I had ever been in my entire life.

My time in America taught me the value of not looking too closely at things in case I found something that I didn't want to see. It had taken everything I had to deliver on my promises to Aunt Pearl. I paid off my debt to the loan sharks and had money left over for plane tickets and visas to Europe as planned. I didn't like dealing with Aunt Pearl. I had no doubt that the day I stopped being useful to her was the day I found myself up on the butcher's block.

ASIA

*

PRODIGAL SON

HOMECOMING FEAST

As the car pulled up in front of the gate I marvelled. The house was magnificent and bore the hallmarks of Janet's whimsy. The window lintels and door were decorated in whimsical designs. The black and gold wrought iron gate stood wide open to welcome me back home. As our Jeep slowed to a stop up the gravel driveway, the crowd of relatives and neighbours let out an enthusiastic cheer. Mama stood at the head of the welcome committee next to my sisters.

POVERTY OF THE MIND

We barely had time to unpack ourselves and my luggage from the Jeep before we were swarmed by our friends and family. Everybody wanted a piece of my good luck as they welcomed me back. My cousins, and Aunty Grace's daughters were delighted to see me.

Mama was the first to reach me. She shooed everyone else off with loud cries of "Jolie! my son!" as she pulled me into a back-breaking hug. It was good to be home.

"Mama, I have presents for you, but you have to let me go" I teased. In the background, Uncle Dan and my father stood by, supervising the unloading of the luggage. "Gently, gently!" I cautioned. "There are breakables in there!"

Crying from joy, Mama Adel said "Jolie, m'boy. I'm so proud of you." She kissed both my cheeks and let me go. With a flourish, I produced a velvet box from my coat pocket and presented it to her. I could see Aunty Grace looking on with avarice. One hand was clutching her pearl necklace.

As one, the crowd gasped in delight as a string of the pearls of the first water, with matching earrings were revealed. Aunty Grace had to help Mama Adel put them on. It was a delight. Mama's pearls outdid hers by a mile. Janet and I shared a sardonic grin over Mama's head. HA! served that old miser right. Where was she when we needed help?

I looked around for Gina, but she had disappeared. I spotted her hurrying around the side of the house to the kitchen yard followed by an unfamiliar old woman. Three men, dressed in shirtsleeves and tailored slacks, chivvied by Uncle Dan, carried the last of my luggage into the house. Small, unfamiliar children darted about, screeching in laughter. The whole front courtyard had a festive air as it was bedecked with paper ribbons and lanterns. I could see the customary white fence Uncle George had erected around our vegetable garden.

MY HUMBLE BEGINNINGS

Janet was next. We looked each other up and down before breaking out into identical grins. I had missed Janet, in my years away. "I've got a present for you too" I said with glee. Janet's present was a fabulous gold wire bracelet inset with diamonds. It was a simple thing, but I knew Janet would appreciate the craftsmanship. Janet put it on with a squeal of delight.

"Good taste! Thank you, it's beautiful." Led by her nose in the air, Aunty Grace grasped Janet's hand to admire it. Her other hand went to the diamond bracelet on her wrist.

"It's beautiful." She managed. Turning to me she said, "You've done well Jolie, you're a big man now." Her smile by this point was a grimace. I did have a present for her in fact: an ugly expensive gold brooch that I knew she would love.

Mary, the prettiest cousin - the one my brothers were caught kissing - appeared by her mother's side.

"Welcome back" She said to me. Turning to Grace, she whispered something in her ear, and they both bustled off. I liked Mary. She was a sweet and generous soul. When they bustled off, Janet and I exchanged a discreet high-five.

Janet fanned herself and remarked, "That Mary, she did well, not like her Mama." Arm in hand, Janet I had sought refuge from the late afternoon sun in the house.

Standing at the entrance, I couldn't resist imitating Aunty Grace. I jibed, "What a beautiful bracelet! It should help your horse face catch a husband."

Janet's elbow caught me in the ribs and I doubled over in pain. It was hard to laugh properly when your ribs were stinging. Janet was the eternal spinster by choice and had never shown an interest in the numerous suitors who chased after her.

POVERTY OF THE MIND

"When are *you* getting married brother?" She asked acerbically. We both knew that while General Komtar had set a bride price to be paid to him, he hadn't broken the engagement between Kobe and Mandy.

"This month!" I sang cheerfully, sticking my tongue out at her.

Janet's face soured. "I wish you wouldn't" she muttered under her breath. I kept my peace, for I knew that the conversation wasn't over. Just then, Mama Adel came inside ahead of the crowd and swept us all off to the dining room, declaring that it was time to eat.

The inside of the house was an ode to wood. The parquetry on the floors was herringbone over concrete. I knew for a fact that Uncle George did most of the work himself. He did not trust other carpenters. Every single bit of furniture was carved. I pointed to a monkey dancing on the banister on the stairs.

"Is that supposed to be me?" I asked.

"Sharp eyes you have there Jolie" my sister smirked.

Rolling my eyes, I complained, "I'm hungry."

The dining room table and the sideboards were groaning under the weight of all the food on offer. We had everything from Jollof rice, to okra stew. There was enough to satiate any glutton. Resplendent in a kente wrap dress, Gina stood over the buffet, directing a stream of smartly dressed kitchen maids. I goggled at her and turned to Janet to ask a question, but she had vanished on me. *Both my sisters are magicians*, I thought grumpily. *Always disappearing*. I approached Gina to give her a present. Waving me away, she shoved plates of food into my hands.

The house was packed and full my parents friends. I spotted Uncle George holding court in the dining room surrounded by a gaggle of his old drinking buddies. I recognized a few of them we visited every

Sunday when I was a child. The others were new faces. I had been away from home for too long.

I hastily beat a retreat to the parlour before my father could catch me and show me off me to all his friends. I was famished. I hadn't eaten since my pre-dawn flight from Indonesia.

The verandah doors leading to the side garden were thrown open, creating an airy open space. Groups of Aunties and Uncles stood around talking and drinking fruit punch. Mama had thriftily planted an orchard instead of flowers. They were young yet. In a few more years, they would bear fruit and give shade.

Tables and chairs were set under white canopies. My family had spared no expense to celebrate my homecoming. I spotted Aunty Grace having a furious argument with Uncle Dan. Picking the table furthest away from them, I sat down to eat.

The food was delicious. I hadn't eaten like that for nearly half a decade. Fufu and gari were impossible to find in Indonesia. When one did, it was expensive and of such poor quality that it would normally be fed to the livestock. I was in seventh heaven as I dug in. The spiciness of the fish head curry was different from the Indonesian style curries I had become accustomed to eating. Our spice blends were vastly different from theirs. Delicious!

Small children blew past my knees as they chased each other around the orchard in play. When Cousin Mary picked up a screaming boy who had fallen over to sooth him, and scolded the culprit, his brother, I knew who they belonged to. Looking at my cousins and their brood, it looked like Aunt got her wish. All the men my cousins married were dressed well in suits and expensive watches. I spotted a Rolex on the wrist of Joyce's husband. They sported the effortlessly healthy look of those who exercised at the gym and had expensive salads for breakfast. Aunty Grace and Uncle Dan's argument had culminated in him storming off, while she flounced off in the opposite direction. I was just glad she hadn't spotted me. I preferred not to ruin the taste of Gina's food.

Gina had given me a lavish portion of Jollof rice to go along with my pepeh soup. Normally, I loved Jollof rice, but not after my long stint in Indonesia where I ate rice for lunch, breakfast, and dinner. I was sick of rice but I ate it all anyway. It went against the grain to waste any food. Discreetly unbuttoning my pants, to make way for my bulging belly, I closed my eyes and laid back, listening to the drone of insects and the buzz of happy people enjoying good food.

"Cousin Jolie," a soft voice called. Started awake, I sat up straight and looked around for the source. It was Cousin Joyce. The last time I saw her was when we left David with them. "Mama Adel is calling for you," she said. Straightening my clothes, I followed her and her gauzy hat through the throng into the parlour. My arrival caused a susurration of whispers from a gaggle of women surrounding Mama Adel. I spotted a few beauties in the crowd but had no time to admire them. Cousin Joyce was pulling me along too quickly.

"Jolie!" Mama Adel cried cheerfully. "My Jolie, do you remember Madam Kiku?" I wasn't given a chance to reply as she kissed both of my cheeks and presented me to a woman who was almost as broad as she was tall. On her head sat a fantastical concoction of feathers and flowers that I believed to be a hat. I smiled and we shook hands politely. I remembered this lady. She lent me the bus fare to go to Accra.

"Turn around boy!" Madam Kiku demanded. At the end of her inspection, she declared with satisfaction "You grow so tall!" As one, the crowd craned their heads upwards to take in my height. I had shot up like a weed, in my late teens. I spotted a few calculating looks on the faces of a few aunties. So, this is what a cow feels like before it's led into the slaughterhouse. Old women were meddlesome and terrifying.

MY HUMBLE BEGINNINGS

Addressing the crowd, the incorrigible old woman said, "The last time I see this child…" she held her hand up to her shoulder "…he was this tall and he wanted to go to Accra! So, I say, 'why?' You know what his Mama told me 'Give Jolie a chance, he is a clever child.' Mama Adel fairly exploded from pride as her chest inflated. "Look at him now!" Madam Kiku declared.

Mama Adel chimed in, "My Jolie, my good luck charm! He built all of this." She indicated the house and the ground around us. Her eyes were crescent slits from smiling.

I happened to I spotted a woman standing by the corner who was by far the best looking of the bunch. She had curly hair, sloe eyes, and a good figure - soft and curvy in all the right places.

Madam Kuki caught me looking. She elbowed me in the ribs knowingly and dragged me over to her. Silence fell as the throng gave way. This was too good of a show to miss.

"This is Lorraine." Madam Kuki's jab to her ribs made the young woman step forward to offer her hand. We shook in an awkward fashion. It was hard to keep my eyes on her face as the urge to run and hide was too strong. Thankfully, she was a beautiful woman. I had to fight to keep my eyes off my chest. Her dress was a fantastic mermaid tail gown in umber with exquisite embroidery. It looked like a couture piece from the fashion houses of Paris.

Madam Kiku gestured at Lorraine with pride, "She's my niece. She's just graduated from Africa University with a degree in business. I hope you two can get along well." The electric fan placed in the parlour did nothing to disperse the stifling head. My smile froze into a pleasant grimace as the aunties around us broke out into a rash of knowing chuckles and sly grins. I nodded a "how-do-you-do" as politely as possible.

Before I could escape, Mama grabbed my hand and pulled me aside. I stumbled as she grabbed my ear to whisper, "She's a nice girl and you need to settle down. You're not getting any younger Jolie. When are you going to give me grandchildren?" Her grip on my arm tightened.

"But..Mama! Man-" My protests were cut off as Mama gave me a stern look. I knew that one. She might not beat me anymore but she could have a word with Uncle George. I still needed his help. Mama Adel sighed and patted my chest.

"Just talk to her Jolie." Utterly defeated, I straightened my back.

"Yes Mama" I muttered. Mama Adel released her grip on my arm, forcing me to stumble back. Looking across the room, Lorraine seemed to be having a similar conversation with her aunt. At the same time, both our elders gave us a not-so-subtle push of encouragement.

By unspoken agreement, we drifted off into the vegetable garden, away from the party. Once out of sight, laughter overtook us.

I leaned against the rough bark of the Wawa tree as I gasped for breath, "I'm sorry about that. I couldn't refuse." Folding her arms across her chest, Lorraine let her annoyance show.

"Me too, Aunty Kiku can be very pushy. I love her to bits, but-" she shook her skirts outs, dusting off imaginary bits of dirt. "I'm actually seeing someone..." she said in delicate tones. I sighed in relief.

"Me too, I came back home to start the marriage arrangements."

She asked, "So, what do you do for a living?" she questioned frankly. "Aunty has high standards for me, she would never introduce someone who didn't make the cut."

MY HUMBLE BEGINNINGS

I tried not to boast as I replied modestly "I run an import-export business based in Indonesia. We deal mostly in furniture." I smoothed down my ecru jacket and asked, "What about you?"

She folded her arms and replied, "I'm looking for a full-time job, but right now I help make ends meet by reselling luxury bags to auntie's friends. It's good business, I haven't had to rely on anyone for my expenses."

"It's a good way to earn spending money." I agreed. Lorraine glanced across the garden to the dining room windows.

"You think it's been long enough?" she asked.

"Probably" I hedged. A thought struck me. "I've got some good stock, freshly brought in if you're interested. I'm flexible, I could work on commission, or you could buy them outright."

Lorraine replied, "I'm interested. Why don't you take down my contact number? I'm in Accra until the end of this month. I'm staying with my Aunty right now." We swapped phone numbers and business cards.

"Why don't we do lunch two days from now, I'll be heading into Accra with Uncle George, then."

Feeling pleased, I escorted her back into the house and left her in the care of her aunty - Madam Kuki. Before Madam Kuki could pounce, I pled an urgent desire for the lavatory and I made my escape. The house was still packed with various groups socializing and eating but the group in the dining room had petered out. There were only a few sleepy old uncles left, snoozing or talking on the settee next to a tray of sweating drinks. I stuck my head in the parlour where the cuckoo clock struck four, and hastily retreated before a gaggle of Aunties could seize me and present their daughters to me. Saying "no" would be damn near impossible.

Most folks were out in the orchard, dozing away on picnic blankets or chatting in the parlour. The upstairs was packed with Aunty Grace and her clan. Cousin Mercy waved me a hello andpassed with her lacy white hat as she went into the guest bedroom. I checked the rooms for Mama or Uncle George and found Mama dealing with a sick child with Cousin Sarah. She shooed me off and told me to go find Gina if I wanted my luggage.

Gina wasn't in the kitchen, Janet was. She was chatting animatedly with the kitchen maids. Dinner was being prepared. A fat cook laid battered pieces of chicken into hot oil. My stomach rumbled despite the feast I gorged myself on earlier. One young woman was pounding fufu, causing her bosom to sway in a delicious fashion. As usual, Janet was the first to spot me - she caught me staring.

"Brother!" she hissed, "Your eyes are like a fish, wide and bulging."

I had no words to say. I confess I was exhausted, suffering from jetlag and stressed with my upcoming wedding arrangements. I had yet to obtain the most crucial component: General Komtar's permission.

"Let me help you push them back in before they fall out." She slapped me hard. The kitchen maids all gaped in shock. The old woman I saw earlier, tsk'd and wagged her finger at me. She said something in Twi. The entire kitchen reverberated with laughter. I didn't need to understand the words to know that it wasn't complimentary. Heat rushed to my cheeks as I directed my anger at Janet.

"What did you do THAT FOR?" I complained. She merely balled her fists up and gave me a level stare. We both knew that I was at fault. We locked gazes, neither one of us was willing to concede, much to the consternation of the kitchen maids watching. As one, we realised how silly this was and burst out into laughter. The knives and ladles had fallen into idle hands, as everyone stopped to watch us two siblings. It was a good show. I was saved by that old woman who barked out a sharp command. Everyone hastened to get back to work with flaming ears and red cheeks. Like I said, old women were terrifying forces of nature, you crossed one at your own risk.

To recover, I had to sit down on a handy kitchen chair, upsetting an auntie who was chopping vegetables next to me. Janet shooed the lady off with a polite request and sat next to me.

Wiping tears of laughter from her eyes, she said "I'm glad you're back brother" Janet stated.

"So am I" I agreed. "It's good to be back home. So Janet, where's Gina?" I asked with puzzlement. I had not seen my youngest sister all day.

Janet sighed and replied, "She went back to her chop bar." In the background, silence reigned. That meant that people were busy eavesdropping. Shaking my head, I pointed to the kitchen verandah.

"Outside," I said. Janet nodded.

"Looking at you, you need strong coffee."

I perked up. "Dear god, I do!" I exclaimed. "I've got some good Indonesian coffee you'll like but it's in my luggage. Do you know where it is?"

"Upstairs in Mama's bedroom. Uncle George locked it in."

A kitchen maid, the same young woman I was admiring brought a tray of iced coffee and snacks out to the verandah and set up a folding table and two chairs. Despite eating earlier, my stomach rumbled. She scurried past keeping well out of arm's reach. I snorted. Women! I wasn't a beast. I appreciated them and never grabbed at what I could not touch.

Janet snorted said "No need, save it for tomorrow. We've already got coffee." She pointed out the window where our snacks and glasses of iced coffee sat sweating in the summer head. It was good to have servants and money. In the old days, Janet would have chivied me into making and serving coffee.

It was a relief to relax with Janet on the kitchen verandah away from the crush of people. I could hear the party petering out as it got closer to dinner time. Out in the entranceway, Mama was cheerfully sending people off. The faint roar of cars trundling down the driveway indicated the party was coming to a close. We weren't about to put on two feasts for our guests. It wasn't my wedding yet.

Mama Adel could get loud when she was happy. I could still hear Aunty Grace and Uncle Dan, arguing upstairs. I mentally shrugged. God's blessings on that old prune. I hope she and Uncle Dan made up. We sat in silence for a while listening to the party wind down and our relatives bicker. I hoped that they weren't staying for dinner.

Janet broke the silence, "So brother, did you know" she said brightly, "Gina's opening a new branch in Acrra?" I shook my head. Janet threw a gingersnap biscuit at me, which I caught in my mouth like a performing seal.

"Really? I'm proud of her, does she need any help? or money?"

Janet snorted in laughter and commented acerbically, "Gina would ban you from her kitchen and refuse to feed you if you did."

Frowning in confusion I said, "That makes no sense, I'm trying to help," and ate a cookie. Mhmmm...delicious, I adored Gina's gingersnaps.

Janet jibed "Jolie, I'm not sure you've noticed, but our baby sister isn't a baby anymore. She hasn't been for the last two decades." I opened my mouth to protest but Janet stuffed a crispy bamfo bisi into it.

MY HUMBLE BEGINNINGS

I spat it out in protest. "HEY!" I bit down on the corn snack savagely. "Can you stop the abuse and explain yourself properly?"

Janet smirked at me. "Jolie, Gina has pride enough to match yours. She's just much more tactful about it."

I nodded slowly. "So... she doesn't want my help?" Janet chuckled ruefully and shook her head.

"Not in the way you plan to offer." She leaned over and jabbed me in the ribs. "She's come into her own Jolie. She's got a chop bar that's packed every day for lunch and dinner and it's so successful that she bought her own property a few years back. She's independently wealthy. Gina footed the bill for all the food in this party. It made Mama happy."

I gasped in surprise, raising my hands to fend off Janet before she could stuff another bamfo bisi in my mouth.

"What about you" I hesitantly asked. "You all know how I've been doing" I paused to take a sip of sweet, watery iced coffee. Janet gave me a cheeky grin.

"Me? Business is good, I've been holding small exhibitions around Accra. Uncle George is getting on in age, his body can't take it much longer. I've been trying to persuade our father to take it easy but he refuses to slow down."

Commiserating with her, I said, "The day Uncle George and Mama slow down, that would be the day we have to start worrying,"

To distract Janet I chucked a cookie at her. It bounced off her head and landed in her lap, causing her to scowl at me. My grin was unrepentant. "So do you think I could get Gina to cater my wedding?"

"When is it happening?"

"This month, as soon as I get General Komtar to agree" I replied. "Mandy had sent me a list of things she wants." I took out a much folded and battered piece of paper. "She wants a church wedding and a lavish reception," I complained to Janet.

Janet remarked dryly "Let's see what she wants."

I handed it over "Be careful, that's the only copy I have."

"Let's see: Church wedding, orchids, two receptions. That's reasonable, if expensive." Janet scowled. "The bride price is ridiculous." She tossed the paper at me. "This woman's family believes we're made of money?"

I spread my hands. "Well, they needed a way to sooth the pride of the Biakou family."

I could feel her stink eye burning into the side of my head. "Look Janet, I'm sorry but she's my heart! I have to marry her." I waved a hand at the house and its compound. "We wouldn't have gotten all this, if the thought of Mandy wasn't there to motivate me!"

Janet snorted and rolled her eyes. "You're not thinking properly. I want to support you Jolie, I really do." Janet's face was coal black from anger as she ranted on "I think no good will come of this. She's not a good person Jolie, she's caused you to do so many stupid things."

"Janet!" I hissed mindful of the extra ears working in the kitchen behind us. "She'll be family soon!"

"Mama and Uncle George don't need the trouble she'll bring us." She stood up, brushing cookie crumbs off her dress. "I'm done here, bring in the tray and things into the kitchen when you're finished. The kitchen maids will wash it. Don't flirt with them. Aunt Nkrumbah has her eye on you. If Gina hears of it, you can kiss your chances of her catering your wedding goodbye, as these are her staff."

The screen door slamming behind her summed up our feelings precisely. Why was she so stubborn? Mandy was a sweet girl, and a sweet woman. It wasn't her fault she had an awful family. Janet just needed to give her a chance. I polished off the rest of the biscuits, and left the tray behind, stalking through the kitchen in high dudgeon. I didn't feel sleepy anymore, I was ready to spit fire.

BRIDE PRICE

"Pass the coffee Jolie." The silver pitcher, Mama's pride and joy, was a heavy, unwieldy thing to manage. As Aunt Grace held out her coffee cup, her pinky finger stuck out. "Here, thank you!" She said in a perfunctory manner. A large ugly brooch sat high up on her collar, where no one would miss it. I had to stifle a smirk as I went around filling up everyone's cups. Aunty Grace had the taste of a magpie. My gift was a success.

"Mhmm pass the koose Gina" Janet said.

"Hey!" I protested. Janet smirked and deliberately ate the last one. Glowering at her, I settled on a stack of toast and strong coffee.

Mama Adel and Gina were busy comparing recipe notes. I helped myself to a small serving of leftover fish curry. Uncle George was absently sprinkling sugar and condensed milk over his rice water.

"Kobe Biaboku jailed for attempted assault," Uncle Danso read.

Janet sniffed "Hmphf."

Uncle George shook his head in disapproval. "That boy had it coming."

POVERTY OF THE MIND

"At noon yesterday, the golden son of the Biaboku family accepted a plea bargain sentencing him to five years in prison." Uncle Danso continued. Uncle George listened intently, so did I.

"Sister Grace, you should come and visit again sometime" Cooed Mama Adel. I caught sight of Gina rolling her eyes, a very Janet-ish thing to do, and raised my eyebrows at her.

"Predicted to be out on good behavior in three years."

Gina hid her face in her coffee, slyly indicating with her chin, Mama Adel's posture: pride.

"Thank you Sister Adel, your house is lovely. Why don't you and your family come down to our place for Christmas, I think you'll love it. We've just put in a swimming pool." Aunty Grace replied in an offhand manner. Janet and I rolled our eyes. The old crow hated to be upstaged.

Gina interjected. "Aunty Grace, gingersnaps?" she asked sweetly.

Mama Adel boasted "Gina is the best chef in Ashaiman. Her restaurant earned five stars in the <famous magazine>"

Although Aunty Grace daughter's had married well to wealthy men, none of them had found as much success any of us.

The impending argument caught Uncle George's attention causing him to step in hastily to agree "That sounds lovely Sister Grace"

"I hear the presiding judge is Kobe's uncle by marriage --" he broke off as my father nudged him, sending him a subtle signal for help.

"Oh.. mh? Oh yes, look at the time! It's almost 8 am!" Uncle George and I took the escape route offered.

MY HUMBLE BEGINNINGS

"Oh yes. We are, we need to be at the church by 10 am." Aunty Grace brightened up. Clasping her pearls and her brooch she added, "Yes, we must not be late."

Gina tactfully began clearing the remains of breakfast. Janet stood up to help her.

Breakfast broke up. I was too nervous to eat much. Mama stood up as well, getting ready to see us off.

"Husband?" Aunty Grace asked, "Do you have my good hat?"

I retrieved it from the hat stand in our entranceway, wordlessly handing it to her.

"Jolie! Everything's here." Uncle George called out. We got the Jeep started and Aunty Grace loaded into the car without further trouble. I volunteered to drive for an excuse to keep quiet. I was too keyed up and nervous to endure an hours worth of small talk. We were going to see Mandy.

A COW FOR A DAUGHTER

The pastor ushered me into the reception room. He was sweating profusely, more than the heat and humidity would account for. The air was chillier than Satan's frozen heart, with the air conditioner at full blast. Aunty Grace was uncharacteristically silent for once. General and Madam Komtar were arrayed opposite us, across the conference room table. Behind them stood the pastor and a nun. There was no sign of Mandy. I set my hard-earned marriage gifts down on the carpet between us.

"We are here..." Aunty Grace began, her fair skin turning red. General Komtar remained impassive. I could have cut the tension with a knife as I presented the knocking gifts, the bottles of schnapps and peach brandy, spreading them across the table before Madam Komtar. I had only seen her twice. She resembled my Mandy to a startling degree. She did not acknowledge me.

"We are here to ask for your daughter Mandy's <full name> Komtar's hand in marriage." Aunty Grace began again. Uncle Danso and Uncle George were statues, with smiles that started to show signs of wear. An unfamiliar woman, stood up at a nod from Madam Komtar.

"We see that she is a suitable match for our Jolie, who is kind, who is brave, who will..." Aunty Grace began reciting a list of my virtues. She did not introduce herself.

The pastor, who was trying very hard to fade into the background spoke. "This woman is sister Madeline. She is standing in for Madam's Komtar's sister who cannot make it today."

The silence was broken up by Aunty Grace's proud recital.

"...provide for your daughter well. We see he is a good man, who works hard..." The woman, dressed in a simple's nun habit, went around the various bits of luggage counting off against a list. We would not be bringing these home. These were gifts to the Komtar family, for the privildge of marrying their daughter. I knew the last and most important present had not been received yet.

There was no introduction from either of Mandy's parents. Madam Komtar's expression was strained, despite her polite smile and dry eyes. The pastor never introduced himself.

Dressed in a flashy white suit, ruined by a pair of awful crocodile loafers, he looked like he was about to step up to the stage for an afternoon of charismatic fundraising. He would not have looked out of place in a rap video.

"God's blessings on this union" he stated as he smiled at my family and me. Sister Madelaine nodded, setting her white headscarf askew.

She spoke in a melodious string of accented Twi, which I did not understand.

The pastor translated. "Everything on the list is accounted for." Aunty Grace finally fell silent sat back down in a self-satisfied huff of rustling skirts.

General Komtar spoke for the first time. "Good." He looked at his wife. She spoke to Sister Madeline.

"Bring out my daughter." Madeline strode away to do her bidding. I stood, rather awkwardly, behind Uncle George and Uncle Danso. Both of them looked at me with pity in their eyes. I sat up straight, refusing to be cowed. All the same, I was glad Mama Adel had chosen not to come.

When Mandy entered the room, all eyes fell on her. She strode in head held high, as if the carpet was a catwalk. Her mouth twisted into a grim line, as she took in the scene that flashed into a radiant smile when she spotted me. My beautiful bride. She strode to me and we met in the middle between her family and mine. Snapping her phone shut, Madam Komtar leaned in to whisper to her husband. General Komtar turned to me, his thick eyebrows furrowed.

"Good, the wire transfer had just come through." Motioning at the pastor with the crocodile shoes, he demanded in crisp tones, "Proceed."

We clasped hands. I looked upon my Mandy. No matter, we would have the wedding of her dreams later. Mandy gripped my hands, her eyes full of unshed tears. The pastor began sweated buckets, despite the overworked air conditioning unit. Placing our hands on the bible, he said, "Repeat after me."

We began in unison, having long memorised the words by heart. Oppressive silence reigned. The Komtars strangled any hope for joy in the room. Even Aunty Grace confined herself to a single pointed sniff, and a not quite glower directed at the Komtars. The menfolk of our family bore up well under the oppressive tension with gravitas and dignity.

The pastor began the marriage vows. "Do you take …"

"I <Jolie full name > take thee Mandy Komtar to be my wife, in sickness and in health till

death do us part." I repeated. Mandy had her hair pinned up under a befeathered hat, with a lacy black veil. I had to suppress the urge to take it off her, and watch her long hair fall down her back.

"I Mandy Komtar take thee Jolie <fullname > to be my husband, in sickness and in health

till death do us part." She offered me a sympathetic squeeze of my hand.

Together we repeated "And before God and these witnesses I promise to be a faithful."

"Wife to Mandy <fullname> Komtar" I said. My heart nearly burst out of my chest with pride

and love. I had done it. Against all the odds.

"Husband to Jolie <fullname>" Mandy whispered. Yes, our hearts whispered. It was done. She was mine. A weight fell off my shoulders. Now we would live happily ever after.

The crocodile-footed pastor intoned with a wide smile, "I now pronounce you man and wife." He turned to all of us to bestow his congratulations upon each family.

MY HUMBLE BEGINNINGS

The door opened and the proceedings were interrupted by yet another personage, who strode into the room, apologising profusely for his lateness. In short order he introduced himself as Mr Joseph Kwambe and the lawyer for the Komtar's. Motioning me forward, He presented us with two documents.

"Please sign this." I looked it over, it was a marriage license. Pre-approved, save for the relevant signatures. I signed as indicated. Mandy did too.

General Komtar spoke to his daughter for the first time. "You've made your bed. Lie in it." Madam Komtar flinched. Mandy stood proud before me. I could not see her expression as she was looking down. Rubbing her back to sooth her, I weighed up General Komtar in my turn. For most of my life, he was the bogeyman, standing in the way of our love. Time had not been kind to him. He had shrunk and lost most of his hair.

He regarded me properly as he said, "Well done." Pride put steel in my spine at these simple words. It was the first time he acknowledged me a person worthy of notice. "You will not be getting anything else." With that, he cut off me off and dismissed me. I did not ask or look for handouts.

Madam Komtar's gaze remained locked on my wife who matched her stare for stare. Mr Joseph handed the both of us copies of a document. My heart hurt for my Mandy as she stood there bleeding without blood. It effectively disowned Mandy, and any children that came of our union, unto perpetuity. The document stated she was no daughter of the family and never was. Her name had been stricken from the family bible. Uncle George received a copy and turned to Uncle Danso for help in deciphering it. All of us signed it where indicated by the lawyer.

Drawing Mandy to me, I hugged her as she remained stiff in my arms.

Madam Komtar spoke up, the feathers on her church hat were trembling. "It is done." She leaned heavily on her husband for support. I shrugged mentally, she was Mandy's mother. It was natural for her to feel upset at giving her daughter away. The Komtars filed out of the room, with Sister Madeline leading the way, leaving Mandy behind. From start to end, none of them acknowledged my father or my Aunt and Uncle, forcing them to be silent bystanders at what should have been a joyous celebration. I barely got a mention, only because I had paid to marry their daughter.

Those of us who were left, were free to stretch and smile.

"Wife." I said to Mandy at their exit.

"Husband." Mandy gave me a smile. .

"Married." I agreed. I cupped her cheek tenderly. Uncle George coughed, breaking up our tender moment. We left the gifts behind: they werethe bride price I had to pay to her family. No matter, Mama Adel and my sisters had prepared everything she would need at home.

Uncle Danso sighed. "Well boy, as they say, It is done."

Aunty Grace smiled at Mandy. "Welcome to the family." She said kindly. "I'm Mama Adel's sister-in-law." Drawing Mandy to her she asked, "Will the rest of your things be coming later?" Uncle Danso frantically shook his head at his wife over Mandy's head to no avail.

In clear tones Mandy replied, "No, it's just me."

"It's time to go Grace dear." Uncle Danso hurried his wife away. We couples walked hand-in-hand back to the Jeep. We dropped our relatives back home, with an invitation to the wedding set in two weeks. The drive home was subdued.

A WEDDING

MY HUMBLE BEGINNINGS

"Now we welcome the blushing bride." Uncle George announced with a cheeky grin. I did not know my father had that in him.

The wedding march played and the ground lit up as Mandy walked down under a long faerie tale trellis Janet made. My father, who was my best man, had to elbow me in the ribs to bring me back to my senses. The lanterns lit up, when we stepped under the wedding trellis to say our vows in front of God and our family.

"I swear to be faithful. I swear to be loyal, to listen…" I declared.

"To love." She responded.

"Let God unite us in sickness and in health." I continued.

"Till death do us part." We said in unison.

Mama Adel was crying in the front pew when the pastor announced, "I now pronounce you man and wife. You may now kiss the bride!" to the jubilant cheers of the crowd. Our kiss was chaste, as per Mandy's request, to the teasing jeers of the crowd. The father-daughter Waltz was next. Uncle George stood in for Mandy's father. Then, it was our turn. It was the first dance we had together as a married couple. The crowd coo'd and aaahhed. My sisters, remarked loudly that we would make very pretty babies causing Mandy to blush and our guests to break into raucous laughter.

After that, the wedding party broke up into the reception where food was served. My wife did all the mingling and socialising. I was on holiday and didn't want to work. Common sense told me that this was a good time to make connections with the moneyed elite of Ghana. *That could wait*, I thought. Mandy flitted from table to table greeting guests, accepting compliments, and so on. People stood talking in groups to better enjoy the food. I liked to keep celebrations simple. Food, drink, family, and friends. I didn't know any of the guests save for my own relatives. Most of them were friends of the bride who were in Ghana to attend the wedding on short notice. My sisters were having a field day promoting their businesses. Judging from Janet's cheerful whistling and Gina's walk both had just secured lucrative commissions.

I wandered away to find a comfortable spot to nap. Janet decorated the fruit orchard, setting up benches under trees and iron trellises. Mama planned to train beans and other useful fruiting vines to climb all over them. It was peaceful.re. I didn't have to pay attention to people. I could let my guard down for a while.

Uncle George found me dozing on a bench Janet had set up in the fruit orchid.

"Jolie, we must talk," he said. The bench creaked under his weight as he shifted to favour his knee. I sighed. I had an inkling this conversation was coming. I wasn't blind. None of my family was for this marriage but Mandy was a sweet girl. I was confident that she would win them over with time. I saw my father as he was for the first time. He was spry as ever, but seemed to have shrunk. I sat up straight and faced him man to man.

"Uncle George..." I began cautiously.

"Jolie. Son. What blood sacrifice did you make to get all this?" Uncle George asked bluntly. To make himself clear, he pointed at the house and its grounds, most of all, to Mandy. My wife was dancing with Janet of all people, down on the dance floor. The band we hired, was playing a popular hit by the City Boys.

"Uncle George, Mandy is a goo-" What he said had taken some time to process. My next instinct was to come out fighting. I stood up and took two steps back. I could not hit my father. "....Juju. Jolie. This is bad juju..." Past the orchard on the lawn, Mandy was sitting down to eat instead of dancing with Janet. It felt odd, like my brain had skipped forward in time.

MY HUMBLE BEGINNINGS

"MANDY IS MY WIFE! I WORKED HARD!..." I wasn't conscious of the fact that I was angry and yelling at my father. Uncle George's lips pursed, a sure sign of his temper. Attracted by the commotion, Mama Adel and Janet came over in a rustle of skirts and irritation. "MAGIC? YOU'RE INSANE! I MADE MY OWN LUCK YOU CRAZY OLD MAN!"

Standing up he slapped me hard. I didn't feel it.

"WHAT DID YOU DO ALL MY LIFE? NOTH---" Someone, Janet I think, had my head wrapped in a chokehold with a muffling hand over my mouth. There was absolute silence before the background noise started again. The band played louder, to cover sounds of scandal brewing. The various guests reacted with pity and disgust but most of them were titillated to watch such a scandal unfold.

"You STUPID BOY! HOW--" My father berated me. I lunged at him, only to find myself being dragged away by the combined efforts of Janet and Mama Adel. That useless old man. Where was he when we were hungry, when I needed school fees? I earned this! Why didn't he get a job or hustle harder? We all did! HA!

I felt Mandy near me. She pressed her ice-cold fingers against my forehead, while muttering something. Mama Adel was praying softly over my father, trying to sooth him. I think I fainted, for when I came to, I was installed in the little room off the kitchen we used as a pantry. Mandy was sponging my brow down with ice cold water and saying something in a low chant. My heart eased at the sight of her sweet face. There was silence outside. I didn't know how much time had passed but it was clear that our wedding party was over.

My sweet wife was so good to me.

"What happened?" I asked. I had the mother of all headaches. All I wanted to do was to crawl into bed and sleep after downing two aspirin. Mandy shook her head and took me by the hand to lead me upstairs like a little lamb to our bedroom. She pointed to the bed. I got in and crashed straight into sleep.

BONFIRE

As I passed Janet in the stairway, she grabbed my shoulder forcing me to pivot to meet her gaze. She growled, "Fix it!" and shook her head in disgust, storming off in the opposite direction towards Gina's room. I heard her comforting Gina who was sobbing uncontrollably. I sighed loudly and headed towards the kitchen to check on Mama.

Mama was in the kitchen peering anxiously through the curtains. I didn't know where Mandy was, but I assumed she was making a call to her mother or taking refuge somewhere in the house.

"Mama, where's Uncle George?" I asked in bewilderment.

Mama flicked the curtains shut and turned to me. "He's gone to get help. He told me he'll be back as soon as he can."

Kobe howls of "Mandy. MANDEEEE," rattled the glass in our windows.

Mama Adele looked at me with a sad smile. "Boy" she said, "Don't go out there the police have been called."

"I know you're in there you slut! Come out!" Kobe roared. I knew my clever wife would not show herself. Kobe was an enraged buffalo: - Wwunded and dangerous.

I shook my head. "No mama, I'll go out there and talk to him. It should buy us enough time for the police to get here." *Besides* I thought to myself, *what use is a man if he cannot defend his own home?* I had to make it clear to that rich bastard that Mandy was my wife and she was mine to care for. My responsibility. I was the man of the house and this was my duty. The thought of being able to punch his smirk off his face was a great motivator.

"If you come out now, I will forgive you." Kobe howled. We heard him kicking over mama's tomato plants. I winced. Our food bill just went up. Even now, food shortages were rampant.

The morning sun had risen bright and beautiful, promising a good start to the day. Kobe stood between the sun and all of us huddled in our house. The shadow he casted on Mama's kitchen curtains felt like a blot on reality.

Mama remarked, "Boy, that Kobe. He out for blood." She harrumphed and began packing away her knives. "Be careful." She gave me a Look. I knew what it meant. *Don't kill the bastard.* We couldn't afford neither the trouble, nor the expense needed to clear my name should that happen. I nodded.

Mandy crept into the kitchen and stood by the hallway entrance. I was distracted by her. Her mouth was drawn into line and her complexion wan. My heart went out to her.

"I called my Mama. She'll deal with Kobe and his mama" she announced. Mama Adel and I heaved a sigh of relief. My wife seemed rather tense and antsy. I uncurled her tender palms where her nails dug into her flesh. We shared a quick kiss and Mama pretended not to see to give us privacy.

"Go hide yourself love" She looked sad as she cupped my cheek.

We could smell the stench of gasoline even from inside the kitchen. It had permeated throughout the whole house. A susurration of metal scraping against metal, echoed from the garden.

POVERTY OF THE MIND

The count of "NINE" was followed by a rock through the window. Mandy and I shrieked in tandem, as glass shrapnel sprayed all over the kitchen. Mama began praying audibly.

Between all three of us, we managed to get the doors and windows damped down, and all the entrances barricaded with kitchen furniture. Thankfully, nobody was hurt. My wife pulled me into the hallway as she tied something to my arm.

"Wear this, it will protect you". It was a fetish but it could not hurt to use it. She smelled like ash and blood, but then the entire kitchen did.

"FIVE" Kobe's wrath had silenced the street: no birds sang. No dogs barked. The phone in our house rang. We ignored it.

"Come out! Show yourself, you witch!"

I gave my Mandy a push to send her back into the hallway, back upstairs and, safely out of his reach. "Stay upstairs and out of sight," I called after her retreating back.

"WITCHES WILL BURN IN FIRE!" Kobe cackled. The crackle and pop of the bonfire increased as it roared along with him. smoke drifted in through the cracks. Our garden was burning.

My hands felt ice cold. I reached for a kitchen cleaver lying on the chopping board but Mama Adel stopped me by placing her hand over mine. Mama Adel handed me her rolling pin instead. She grinned at me, with a wicked twinkle in her eye.

"This won't kill him, but it'll make him wish he was dead."

I accepted and we shared a conspiratorial smile. I got my grit and toughness from my mother. No question about it.

MY HUMBLE BEGINNINGS

"THREE!" Another rock bounced off a barricaded window with a thud and the crash of broken glass. I heard Janet swear from the living room. Mama pretended not to hear. I chalked up one to Janet. My sister was tough for a girl.

"Mama, are you alright?" Janet called out.

"We are" I answered. Janet did not reply. My sister was still angry. She would have many words for me later.

"TWO!" gasoline splashed against the windows. Fire bloomed along the wooden lintels, despite the damping down. We frantically poured pitchers of water over the fire. It was a tricky beast to contain and delighted in eating all the flourishes and carvings Janet and Uncle George had put into the lintels.

Mama Adel pressed her thumb to my forehead. "God go with you." Ever practical, she remained calm. "Try to stall for time and talk him down. Your father should be back within twenty minutes."

Nodding, I shifted the table away and prepared to step out. Before I did I pleaded, "Help me protect Mandy."

Mama Adel frowned and after a long moment nodded. "God go with you."

I grunted an assent as I stepped out.

Like a ghoul, Kobe stood over the bonfire. It was fueled with plants from Mama's garden - our food supply. Gasoline made the flames leap and prance according to the wind. I prayed to an uncaring God that it would rain heavily.

Something slimy and blackened splattered across my face. I wiped it off to free up my vision. It tasted like garden eggs. My stomach rumbled. Prison had treated Kobe well. He had bulked up and looked like he had spent the last two years in a spa resort instead of prison. Even now, it paid to have family connections. The slimy bastard hurled another garden egg in my direction. He was so rich that he thought nothing about wasting food. If I squeezed him, I wondered if rancid oil would ooze out of his pores.

I tucked Mama's rolling pin into my back pocket and stepped towards him holding my hands up to show that I was unarmed.

"Morning." I greeted him with false cheer. The bastard's malice fuelled the bonfire, for it spluttered and sparked despite the damp morning dew. An idle corner of my brain noted that the ground was unusually rusty and to put away the garden tools when we were done to prevent them from getting worse.

I was close enough now to see that he was drunk. It wasn't just gasoline we had smelt but expensive brandy mixed with cheap toddy. I kicked dirt over the bonfire to put it out. Kobe snarled and spat at me.

"You turned her into a slut." He flung away the empty can into mama's plantain grove. They were the only plants left standing in the garden. His tone turned pious and mournful when he murmured "I can forgive her." He seemed to be talking more to himself than to me. His attention switched back to me. "Bring her out or I'll send you and your worthless family to hell." He jerked his head towards the gasoline drenched kitchen door.

Shit. Mandy. My family. Panic bloomed in my belly. Worms fought to crawl up my chest and out my throat. I needed to lure his attention away from the house and my family.

"You'll scare her like this. I can't bring her out if you will scare her." I avoided making direct eye contact with him. "You want her back don't you?" I pleaded in a soothing tone.

MY HUMBLE BEGINNINGS

Kobe shrugged nonchalantly "It doesn't matter if she's scared. She was promised to me. She's mine. Bring her out you cowardly thief" Rage invaded my brain. I remembered all the beatings, along with the wanton destruction of our house and our shop. All because I had the audacity to succeed where he had failed. He had everything served up on a platter to him, yet he had failed. I won.

He would do as he liked and get no punishment for it. As usual. Not today. Rage smouldered in my belly. I could not plead anymore. Not today, not ever.

I blurted out "I married Mandy. I'm her husband in the eyes of the law and our elders." I bared my teeth at him and snarled "You will never get her back you insane piece of shit. Never. Over my dead body."

"YOU!" Kobe bellowed and charged. I had to lure him away from the house. I gritted my teeth and ran out to meet him. I caught the bastard in a headlock as he head butted me in the stomach. Mama's rolling pin was forgotten in my blind rage. I felt it fall out and I tripped over it. We went down in a tangle of wrath and limbs. The heavens opened up on us and it started raining, snuffing out the last of the bonfire - now nothing would burn. I knew God was watching. There was a curious tingling at the back of my head, as reality became optional.

My grip on his head was loosened when Kobe wrenched his head away. I moved to catch his throat with my arm to choke him when Kobe punched me in the ribs again, causing me to screech in pain and let him go. Seizing his chance, Kobe wrenched himself free and lunged for my throat. I slipped on something fleshy and we went down.

Roaring with laughter, Kobe locked his hands around my throat. I scrabbled at his fingers, frantic with the need to pry them away to no avail. Kobe used his body weight to keep me pinned to the ground and I couldn't use my legs to kick him off. Desperate for air, I clawed at his face. The bastard kept grinning and laughing, never once letting go. I managed to jam a finger into his eye. SQUELCH. It popped like a fat grub. The bastard was devil touched. He merely laughed louder and shoved his face closer to mine, giving me a scarlet grin stained with blood from his eye. "See you in hell," he whispered.

I gave up on prying his fingers away and reached out with my free hand, even as I tried to jam my finger in deeper to reach his brain. I failed because Kobe moved his head out of my reach. I had God's protection, the Devil could not touch me. The rain was a sign that he was watching but he only helped those that helped themselves. I had only a few seconds left of air, my strength was draining away. Something fleshy and cold met my fingers. Good enough. I brought it up and across the side of his head, putting the force of my desperation behind it. It worked. He panicked and let me go to rear back and paw at his eyes. It turned out to be his sacrifice: a black cockerel. Using my legs for leverage I bucked him off and rolled to my feet.

I had only a few seconds to catch my breath. Kobe had Satan riding his soul when he came for me. I threw the filthy thing at him to distract him. He dodged and kept coming. I ran away from the house out into the garden wall closer to the road to lead his possessed body away from the house, Mandy, Mama, and Janet. I had to lure him away, to keep his attention on me until help arrived. I knew I would survive this, like I had survived everything else. When I reached our garden wall that met the road, I dug my heels in and turned to face him. I caught him with a kick before he could reach me, sending him arse over heels. Lunging forward, I stomped hard on his crotch, and followed up with several kicks to his kidney. It was right and justified that I should do this. He had plagued us for more than half my life just because he could! God was good for he gave me my vengeance.

Curled into a ball of shivering pain at my feet, Kobe managed a hoarse whisper between groans.

"...and your worthless grave digger family disappear. ...Mandy ...be mine." He chuckled at me, secure in the knowledge that his privilege would protect him. I lost track of my surroundings. I had him by the throat and had been throttling him for some time. I learned that he in fact did not ooze rancid oil, but smelly shit. The bastard shat himself. *HA!* I thought with detached satisfaction. Even the devil could not save him from me. I let go of his throat and decided to pulverise his face. I settled into a soothing rhythm, watching with vicious euphoria as his nose broke, and his teeth came loose.

Oddly, I sensed a low chant and an irritating person trying to hold me back. I turned my head to snarl, only to catch a whiff of her. I knew that scent. It was Mandy and she was telling me to stop. *Why?* I stared at her in puzzlement. A shadow fell over Kobe's bloody body.

"You can't kill him!" Janet growled. She slapped me in the face and tackled me into submission. She had me in an arm lock as she hissed, "The police!" I blinked and came back to myself. I looked at Kobe. There were no regrets. One eye was gone and his face was a pulverized mess. I flung bloody fluid off my fingers. She was right, the bastard could not die because he was too well connected to die. We would catch hell for this because I had nearly beaten him to death. Even now, I had to hope that he would not die. I spat at him and hoped he lost that eye. That was the least of what he deserved.

I ceased struggling and chose to hug Mandy instead. she stopped chanting, cut away the fetish tied to my arm and pushed me away. Slipping the fetish into Kobe's pocket, Mandy knelt to check his pulse. Janet told me later I was growling and laughing at the same time. Mandy closed her eyes with relief and announced.

"He's alive. I'll dial the ambulance" My clever wife used Kobe's flip phone to dial.

Janet shook me to get my attention and yelled "Jolie! Tell me what happened!"

POVERTY OF THE MIND

I stumbled backwards as my sister dragged me away from Kobe's foul carcass. I checked myself for injuries as I croaked "Talk... Kobe... mama said no knife... He... He attacked." I pointed to the bruises congealing on my throat. "I protected the ..... Mm.. Mandy" I pointed to the scorched earth "...Kobe...burnt the garden.... burn ...h...house."

Mandy was burying something with an expression of loathing. Janet let me go then, allowing me to sit down and rub my throat. "If not him...then me. Better HIM than me." Janet nodded at me, then strode off.

The bastard was groaning weakly and twitching. I must have lost some time, because the next thing I saw was Janet hog tying Kobe with relish. Mandy held me upright and as adrenaline drained from my body, it took all my strength not to close my eyes and black out. I was afraid that I would never wake up again. Uncle George appeared leading a procession of policemen who swarmed our compound, like maggots on a corpse to catalogue every shred of evidence. Several clustered around me, blocking my Uncle George from sight.

"What happened hear na?" A deep bass voice spoke and I could see a pair of shiny black boots.

Mandy spoke for me. "That man invaded my compound, burned my garden down and attacked my husband." She waved at the garden, then pointed to Kobe who was trussed up like a pig, and to the bruises on my neck. The inspector said something, I didn't understand. It blended into a pleasant rumble. It was peaceful, lying here in her arms, looking at the sky. The rain had tapered off giving way to a beautiful blue. *Those are good boots*, I thought. They looked very well kept. I wondered if I could get the name and address of his cobbler. Uncle George and I would appreciate such a fine pair of boots.

"My name is (Mandy's full name) Komtar."

The inspector did a subtle double take. "I will need your…" he looked at me for the first time.

"Husband" Mandy replied curtly. I knew even passed out cold, the Satan who rode Kobe soul kept him aware. It was a heavy thing to feel its regard. I felt the devil leave Kobe's carcass, as the greasy feeling in the air cleared up. At that moment, I knew what made "Kobe" himself was broken. The Devil always took his due. He would never trouble us again. As a man, he was finished.

My home and hearth were defended. There was no more to do. I closed my eyes for a second, and that was the last thing I remembered for a good long while.

FAMILY CONFERENCE

My tailored slacks were going to get rumpled. They hung off my waist, with one leg in and the other out, as I wobbled around our bedroom trying not to fall over. The damn brace around my neck felt like an iron collar. I sank into my bed butt first and managed to finish dressing without mishap. Mandy strolled out of our bathroom to sit down at her dressing table. She giggled as I caught her eye. Standing like a ruler, I swiped the towel from her hands and helped her dry her hair. She handed me her hairbrush and we both shared a smile as I helped her brush and dress her hair. *Wife, wife, wife.* My heart sang.

"Husband" Mandy announced. "Mama Adel needs to see us all in the kitchen." She turned back to the mirror to finish dressing.

It was getting extremely difficult to resist the urge to scratch under the neck brace. Our Ghanaian summers meant the temperature was scorching, even in the shade. "Hmm I hope Mama will be quick. The hotel won't hold our lunch reservations for long." I stood up "I'll go see what she wants. Meet me in the car."

Mandy replied, "I called the hotel to reschedule to dinner. My mama called while you were in the shower. She wants to see me. I need to go visit her. She'll send a car to our house." She turned to me with a serious expression "Don't meddle in this Jolie. Promise me."

Shrugging internally, I nodded. "Alright, I won't Mandy, but I'm confident that we'll nail the bastard in court. He won't bother us again."

She stamped her foot and scowled at me with her hands on her hips. "Jolie!" My heart melted because she looked so adorable. I knew better than to show anything but attentiveness. I sat up straight to attention spreading my palms in surrender.

"I'll try not to wife" I reached out, pulling her down into a hug. It felt good to hold her like that.

Mandy yelped. "Shoo! Shoo!" she swatted my arm with her comb and all but shoved me out the bedroom door. "I'm going to be late!" she yelped in mock anger. I stalked out, as dignified as a man should be but left my cackle behind as the door swung shut.

Janet had no remark for my grand entrance or attire as I swept into the kitchen. I grabbed the mug and poured myself a cup of coffee. That was odd. The kitchen clock ticked and tocked as it strained to fill the silence. Ah, the family conference. Everyone huddled over their cups of coffee and waited for someone to speak. Looking around the kitchen, my sisters had done a good job of cleaning up the broken glass and furniture. Uncle George worked fast to replace the gasoline-soaked window frames and door. The scraps sat outside, waiting to be chopped up into logs to be used as fuel for cooking.

My father spoke first. "Jolie, Mr Frank Kwambe tells us that this could get very expensive." Uncle George explained "He's our lawyer. The nephew of my friend Uncle John."

MY HUMBLE BEGINNINGS

I vaguely remembered seeing a boy in short pants and chubby cheeks running around the neighbourhood. Huh, time flies. Uncle George continued "Kobe's family will sue us and press charges for aggravated assault." I took a sip of coffee and made a face. Gina must have made this.

"Alright, Uncle George. How much?" I ran the numbers through my head, I had a few investments I could sacrifice, if we needed to, but for once money wasn't an issue, I thought with pride.

Wearing an ugly expression, Janet growled at me "They mean to bankrupt us and drive us back into poverty." She slammed her coffee mug down upon the table, cracking it. "I've had incidents happen at my shop earlier today. My assistant phoned in just now."

Gina was praying softly with Mama and the clicking of the rosary beads were in dissonant counterpoint to the kitchen clock. "I can't afford to take more days off or close down the shop. If this goes on, I'll start losing customers." I fought to keep my back straight and my shoulders unbowed as the weight of Janet's disgust settled on me.

Uncle George spoke softly but we all heard him, "They're asking for more than what we have. They want our house and half a million in cash or assets."

I snorted in disgust. Uncle George sounded defeated as he told us "I found out the presiding Judge in charge of our case is a relative of <Kobe's family >" He held a hand up to indicate that he wasn't finished "Our lawyer has advised us to press charges, as we have a good chance of winning." He sighed, looking defeated as he continued. "Kobe's family is being... difficult over the amount of injuries he sustained."

I poured myself another cup of coffee and I considered the situation. Before I could speak, Gina's quiet voice interrupted us all.

"We need to replant Mama's garden as soon as possible."

Mama had taken to praying silently, murmuring the words under her breath but she nodded at Gina who continued "I've been talking to the traders at the market. They say it's getting harder to bring food in or sell. Too many regulations." As one, we looked out our empty windows to the neatly raked patch of scorched earth. No plants were left standing, except a few vines that Mama had staked to the garden wall. I swore softly. Mama and Uncle George pretended not to hear.

The front door opened and shut, and we all heard a car driving off. Janet's scowl singed the skin on my forehead.

Uncle George continued. "This means that we can't buy the farm like we planned to." He sighed, rising to put his coffee mug in the sink.

Gina continued "A few of our neighbours are willing to donate cuttings and seedlings to get our garden started. It'll be a year until we can depend on it."

I sipped my coffee and munched on a biscuit. Gingersnaps. Gina must have made them. "Okay, I can send more, more …" I ducked instinctively, having seen the expression on Janet's face and the way her hand tightened on her cracked coffee mug.

Mama Adel laid her hand on Janet's arm and shook her head. Janet stood up, threw the mug in the bin with a crash of pottery, and stormed off, shutting the door behind her gently. The kitchen clock marched on. Tick. Tock.

Grief dragged Mama Adel face downwards and for once, she looked her age. I felt her grief seep into my body to settle in my stomach and my heart. Uncle George squeezed her hand and my parents exchanged a look of mutual support and love.

MY HUMBLE BEGINNINGS

Awkwardly clearing my throat I said "...more money back. I've got enough cash on hand to cover the Lawyer fees. I can get more but that will take time." I turned to my father to avoid looking at Gina and Mama Adel. "Uncle George, I need to leave again soon, to keep my business from falling apart." I heard the unspoken accusation, though my family was kind enough to not voice it out aloud.

Uncle George relaxed as he told me, "Thank you Jollie. That will be helpful." I had hoped for pride but I would settle for seeing less stress.

Mama Adel stood up and followed my father out of the kitchen. She paused in the doorway to announce "The priest is coming today. Jolie, can you stay home and wait for him? Your father needs to go visiting and I will be taking a rest upstairs."

I nodded, as a million possible plans raced through my head. My father put on his hat and stepped out the kitchen door while Gina, playing the dutiful daughter, tidied the kitchen. I could only sit mute and motionless as one by one, my family exited the kitchen. TICK TOCK. The kitchen clock marched on.

LEAVE TAKING Taking Leave?

Between the lawyer's fees, the court settlements, my medical bills, and the cost of repairing the garden, I could no longer afford to give Mandy the honeymoon she wanted. In fact, I needed to head back as soon as possible. My business was holding on, but I would lose customers if I took more time off. I had been away for three going on four months, most of which I spent lying in a hospital bed, convalescing.

I rarely saw my wife during this period. When I did see her, she seemed tense and on edge most of the time. Janet told me she always showed up on time to take her shift at my bedside and cared for me well. Except for Mama Adel, everyone avoided Mandy. They were courteous but never more than that. Mandy paid them no mind.

Only Mama Adel tried to include her in our family life as much as possible, but Mandy preferred to stay shut up in the spare room she claimed for her studies. No one knew what she meant exactly. We often smelled smoke and heard odd noises when she was in there. That circle of avoidance extended to me as well.

Months passed as I lay around the house slowly recovering. I tried to help as much around the house as I could but there was little I could do as bending, lifting, and walking required assistance. As a result, I spent most of the time in the kitchen, helping Mama and Janet by doing the food prep for our meals. I could sit and chop vegetables, stir a pot, or grind spices. The forced inactivity drove me crazy. I ran my business as best as I could through the telephone and hoped that when I got back, it was still standing.

It was raining outside: A Ghanaian drizzle. The rain fell steadily on Mama's thirsty plants. After Kobe's rampage, we moved the garden to the back of the house behind the kitchen. To cover the scar the bonfire left, Uncle George put in a carp pond, so we would at least have fish to eat. It was something he saw in a magazine. Gina transplanted Mama's plantain trees to the back of the house and replanted them, so we would have a vegetable garden again. Luck favoured us, and it was doing well. We were looking forward to a good harvest come autumn.

I was working in the kitchen shelling peanuts alongside Janet one dreary afternoon. The monsoon season had started and the weatherman predicted floods. We sat side by side, working in cozy silence. Mama had gone upstairs to take her nap. I these loved moments of peace and warmth. They came at went at their own will. You could not force them nor hold on to them. That made me appreciate these fleeting times. The radio was tuned to the BBC channel. A Dr who radioplay was running. Janet had odd taste and loved Dr who plays to bits. Me? I preferred rap. It was a legacy of my sojourn in America.

MY HUMBLE BEGINNINGS

"Where's Gina?" I asked. I had not seen my sister at home for... I counted off and realised that the last time I had seen Gina in the house was last month. She went to Church with us and came back home for lunch before going off again. The oddest thing was that neither Uncle George nor Mama Adel were concerned over Gina's disappearance. Come to think of it, my father was rarely home, and spent most of his days and nights at the shop.

Janet grunted. "Busy working."

I frowned while expertly cracking and shelling groundnuts for soup. "So busy she doesn't come back home? I didn't think she was that kind of girl." Janet's bowl of shelled nuts fell to the floor with a clang. Nuts scattered and rolled all over the kitchen floor. "Janet!" I protested "Careful!" I hated food waste.

Janet said nothing, she had gripped the metal bow hard enough to deform it. I looked at Janet much more closely. In high choler, and a strangled voice. "Gina moved out. She's living in one of her houses in Accra."

"Our parents agree? What if someone tries to take advantage of her, you know how Gina is." I was concerned. My baby sister was a gazelle and in my experience, people often took advantage of people with her personality type.

"Gina can take care of herself," Janet announced. "She's no longer that weak delicate creature you remember from our childhood." Janet's lip curled in disgust hurled at me "Only you Jolie, would be the cow that rejoices at being taken into a beautiful abattoir."

I was beginning to get irritated, I knew who she referenced with that comment. "Janet! Give that a rest? You've made your views very clear." Janet stooped to pick up the nuts. One by one they went into the bowl. I wanted to help. I puffed my cheeks out and sighed. "I know you don't like Mandy. Can you at least tolerate her?" I pleaded.

"She's trying her best. At the engagement, no one but her mother spoke for her. Not her aunts, nor her cousins. Her father has all but disowned her. She is his daughter in name only, and that is due to Madam Komtar."

Janet stood up clutching her bowl shelled nuts and set it down carefully on the table. I grabbed both her hands and begged "Please Janet, she has no one but us. She's my wife." I had to try.

Janet flung my grip off to pace around the kitchen. The clock in the parlour struck six. "Did you know that your beloved 'wife'" Janet told me with eerie serenity "Is a witch? Why else would she spend so much time up there, in that room. We've all heard the chanting and the noises. Every day there's smoke. All of the brandy in the house has disappeared." She radiated disgust.

I had enough of Janet's disgust. "She's helping! She told me that she would take care of Kobe and his family! Whatever she's doing up there, it's for our good. For US!" I thumped my chest. "I trust her, and I've never been wrong about people before"

Janet spat back, "Otoolege !" That wasn't true! Janet said, "You see how beautiful she is and you're fooled. You think beauty means character." She took in my beaten and battered state. "Tell me ONE good thing that has happened to us since she came." Janet jabbed my chest. I had to sit on my hands to prevent myself from grabbing her wrist and breaking it. I knew I could do it. It wasn't Mandy's fault that Kobe showed up. "Everything that has happened is directly linked to HER" Janet bellowed.

"Kobe is insane. He would come around to make trouble for us even if Mandy wasn't in the picture," I shot back.

"You attracted his attention by stealing his bride. No good comes of being a thief" Janet replied in agitation. Upstairs, we both heard the scrape and shuffle of a chair. Mama Adel had woken from her nap.

MY HUMBLE BEGINNINGS

"So far, our garden has burnt down. We're dangerously close to being bankrupt from all the bills we had to pay." She ticked off each point on her finger "My shop has been targeted. Finished commissions have been smashed. My customers are coming after me. Even if I work around the clock, there is no way I can complete the orders in time."

Janet was shaking from anger and fear. I looked at my sister properly. She looked terrible: too much stress and too little sleep. She was running on pure adrenaline. "Uncle George has to spend most of his nights there to make sure no one breaks in. I'm terrified that he'll get killed stopping Kobe's goons."

I had no idea that it was *THIS* terrible.

"We can't trust anyone I hired, and all my trustworthy workers have been run off, or lured away with better pay and opportunities." Janet poured herself cold coffee from the canister we kept in the fridge.

She sank heavily into a chair. Scowling she stated, "I have worked as hard as you, if not harder for my entire life." Janet added some cooking sherry Mama kept into her coffee and two tablespoons full of sugar. "Now everything is about to come crashing down because of YOUR MESS!" She leaned forward and shoved her finger into my face. "I will not let your damn messes drag me down again." Glowering at me, she sat down, slammed her coffee down and scowled. She looked so much like Uncle George that my heart skipped a beat. Any minute now, she would explode and my buttocks would get a tanning.

I stifled a smile. Janet took after our father. My sister looked ready to cry as she hid her face in her hands. Raising her head up with our father's stare she continued, "You swagger back home after years away. You buy this land and pay for this house to be built. You think you run everything." Janet drained her coffee and moved on to straight sherry. "Let me ask: Who kept us afloat when you weren't here? Who paid off all the debts *YOU* incurred? Who cleans up your messes?"

"I did," I tried to say in a voice that would not come out. I could not speak: speech curdled in my throat. "Not you, you selfish bastard! Not you. You were too busy chasing your dream to take notice of us at home" she said. "ME and GINA!"

"I sent money back," I said in a tiny voice.

Janet scoffed. "Too little, too late by then." She slammed back a shot of sherry. This had been building up for several years now as she explained, "If you never had gone to America, if you never had incurred that debt. Gina would not have nightmares every night that keep her awake for weeks." The sherry bottle was emptying at a rapid pace. "These days, it's Gina who keeps the house running, *AND* runs her chop bar, which *SHE* built WITHOUT your help. Mama is getting on in her years and cannot manage as well. She needs her family around her. It is GINA who keeps Mama company during the day. Our parents are getting older Jolie, they need care and attention. Not all this..." She waved her hand at me and the kitchen garden. "Drama. Think a little! Why did you have to bring such a girl home? Our parents can't take the stress anymore. You were the only son that stayed, so they're very proud of you and love you the most." Here Janet paused in her tirade.

"That's...that--" I began weakly.

Janet cut me off. "If it were me all those years ago, who fell for some rich boy, Mama would have locked me up in the house and never let me out of sight. Think Jolie think! What did Mama do for you? Who begged Madam Komtar to give you a chance? Mama did, when the sane and logical thing to do was to lock you up and bring a priest to say prayers over you until you came to your senses" Janet emptied the sherry bottle and deflated from weariness. I could only stare at my sister in mute astonishment.

"She's no good for you," Janet sighed. "I could have built up my shop and customer base quicker if it weren't for having to pay off all those debts." Regret was written across her face. "I'm on the verge of expanding my business, but now I can't with all that's happened. It'll take me years to recover, and I don't know if I can this time around!" She scowled at me. "You selfish bastard, you think that we need you and your money. That's all you care about. That and your precious Mandy." Janet un-crossed her legs and sat up straight. "Let me tell you. With what me and Gina make now, we don't need your money. We could support this house with no problems." Over the years, I had forgotten how tough my sister was - both my sisters.

I opened my mouth to protest. Janet cut me off with an upraised hand. "Don't get me wrong brother, we all appreciate the luxuries and breathing room your money has brought us. The price paid for them is too high." She pointed to the brace on my neck. "How many years of your life will this witch cost you?" She demanded.

I had no answer for that save "I love Mandy, we will be together til death do us part."

Janet scoffed "HA!" and waggled a finger in my face. "Let me tell you, without that witch weighing us down all these years, we all could have been so much better."

That was it. My hand came up of its own accord and slapped right Janet across the face. It was an out of body experience as I watched my hand connect in slow motion, and her head rocking back with the force I put being my swing. Janet did not hit back. To her I was too far gone. Gingerly working her jaw, she got up to retrieve some ice for her swelling cheek.

"Do not insult Mandy. She is my wife." I stated with dignity. "Whether you like it or not, she is now family."

Janet spat, "She barren. What family?" That stung more than anyone would know. I desperately wanted children that came from me and Mandy. It was that bastard's Kobe's fault. Our children would have been beautiful and intelligent but the devil had decided otherwise. Holding a handful of ice cubes up to her face, Janet threw the ultimatum at me. "Either she leaves, or we all do. Don't think I can't persuade Mama to leave too. We don't need your money to live well." This time, I left with as much dignity as I could muster. After all that had been said, what was left between us?

By the time I was well enough to move around unaided and without the support of the neck brace, I had spent half a year away from my business. My business partners in Indonesia told me to take it easy and rest well. I was worried I would come back and find that everything had imploded.

Janet was true to her word. She moved out, and only came back on Sundays to attend Church and do lunch with the rest of the family. Mandy was included with grudging forbearance. Uncle George disapproved. He rarely whistled and spent most of his time at Janet's shop. When he was home, he took to brooding on the verandah by the kitchen.

Mama called it his thinking space and told me to let him be.

I begged Mandy to make more of an effort and to stop spending so much time in that room. She agreed. When I went in there afterwards, everything was as it should be. Only Mama Adel seemed willing to make an effort. They spent many hours in the kitchen cooking together. I didn't see who was there to cook for, as there were only the four of us. Janet and Gina had moved out but they both enjoyed female bonding.

In the last month before I had to leave to go back to Indonesia, Mandy was a balm to my soul. She was attentive and caring. She was the best wife and daughter-in-law anyone could ask for. Mandy and I spent many hours together, cuddling and talking of the future. She made me promise to be faithful to her and promised the same to me too. I fell in love with her all over again. It was like we were teenagers cuddling on that secret path under the Wawa tree. This time, nobody could stop us, and that made it all the sweeter.

We both knew that the time I had at home was limited. I had to get back to Indonesia: I had been away too long. I wanted to take her with me, but she refused. She was too scared of her mother, who had not given her permission. She didn't want to anger her mother even further, as she had disobeyed her parents will to marry me. She confessed in tremulous voice that her Mama was a vodou priestess, and she was afraid of her. My heart melted. My poor sweet wife. I understood everything then. It wasn't her fault, her Mama forced her. No wonder Mandy had to break away from her family. Now she had no one to rely on, except me. I set up a bank account and a credit card for her so that she wasn't reliant on anyone for spending money. Mandy squealed and gave me a night to remember.

To give us the life we deserved, I needed to focus on my business. Mandy was welcome to join me as soon as she squared things up with her mother. By the time my plane taxied off the runway, if my wife wanted a solid gold toilet to shit in I would have gotten it for her, no questions asked, along with a white servant to help her clean off. Nothing was too good for my Mandy.

I didn't see the warning signs then, as I was too focused on chasing the next dollar.

AUTUMN 2009

ALL THE COWS COME HOME

A LETTER FROM HOME

To my son

Whom I'm very proud of.

I've watched you grow up, first with bemusement, then with pride. You were a handful and I'm sure your mother would agree too. Remember when you were seven, you asked if you could go to school? I didn't think much of it then, I thought you would get tired of it and give up after one semester. Imagine my surprise when not only did you get an education, you did well. I brag to all my friends that I have an educated son, the first in the family. Mama was always telling me about your Mr Tano who spoke well of you every time he saw her at the market.

When I was a teenager, I was like you. I thought life was easy. Tough, but as long as you put in the work, you would succeed. When the time came to put everything into practice, the pieces I held did not fit the puzzle. Life muted me and robbed me of my identity. The only thing I've achieved in my life was to raise a beautiful, strong, hardworking family. I've never regretted marrying your Mother or having you as children. I still miss your brothers who left and think of them often.

I've seen you fight against the current with all your might. I've seen you take rejection, fear, hurt, pain, and turn it upside down even when everyone was against you. What hardships life threw at you, you emerged victorious. I'm proud of you, more than words can describe.

When I meet God, I'll tell him about you.

My life was ruled by fear. I wished I had started my own business earlier, maybe I could have given you a better life. I started too late, just as the economy crashed. I was too bold, too brash, and burned all my bridges behind me.

Learn from my mistakes son. Fear is false evidence. Fear is a barrier to your true potential. Listen to it, but don't let it rule you. Learn to live your dream, not your fear. Once Mohammed Ali was asked, "How many push up does it take?" and this is what he said: "I only count when it hurts." Life mutes you, robs you of your identity, then shapes you into a person that you do not recognise - if you let it.

MY HUMBLE BEGINNINGS

Fight for what you want. I won't be around to support you any longer. You are lucky son, to have found success at such a young age. Keep pushing, find the next mountain to conquer, or you will grow stale and forget yourself. Family and work give meaning to life, don't lose sight of either of them. Find balance and always leave yourself an escape route.

I regret not being able to spend more time with you all. Family is all I have left in this world. I carry many regrets that only you, my children can resolve for me. In the end, the most valuable thing you possess is time. God has given you a finite amount of time, use it wisely.

Wealth does not determine happiness. Treasure your family, for they are the ones who will carry you with them after you are gone.

I'll be watching from Heaven. I pray, when we meet again, it is as two old men. We'll sit out on the verandah, share a drink, and I'll listen to your adventures in life. I'm looking forward to it, it would be quite the tale. From the slums of Ashaiman, to the tops of the world.

Keep on living. Take care of your sisters, and your mother most of all. She is my heart. It's time for me to go, I have to get off this bus now. I'm sorry son. God calls me home.

Your loving father (Uncle) George Adamah

LUCKY NUMBER SEVEN

Janet picked me up at the Accra International Airport. We drove straight to the cemetery where my father was laid to rest. My flight had been delayed, and I was late. I was supposed to fly out a week earlier, but the client would have called off the deal if I would have left.

When we arrived, the grave was bare of mourners save for my mother. "Mama!" I ran to her. She hugged me back, just like when I was a boy. Only this time, I was the one offering comfort. Grief had hollowed her out and shrunk her down to her bones: it felt like the wind would blow her away. When we broke apart, she was dry eyed but I was ready to bawl my eyes out. Janet's calligraphy chiselled into the marble headstone summed up his life.

George Adamah,
Beloved Father, and Husband of Adele
<fullname> BORN <> DIED <>

The spot where he was laid to rest was a beautiful one. It was situated at the crest of a small hill, overlooking a sloping valley. There was a stone bench set up nearby. I think he would have liked it. Janet handed me a perfume bottle.

"Spray it over his grave," she instructed.

Puzzled, I looked to Mama Adel for an explanation.

"This was your father's favourite perfume. He was a sharp dresser and wore this scent together with the watches you gifted him." Mama Adel chuckled, amusement tinged with nostalgia "Ooo! I got so many compliments from all my friends every Sunday."

Hesitantly, I stepped up to do as instructed. I don't know if God was watching or if it was a coincidence. The scented mist, and the setting sun collided in such a way that it created a rainbow.

Grief hit me in the chest. My father was gone. I wished I had more time with him. I wished I had flown back home as soon as Mama told me he was sick. I stayed to close the deal I was working on. It would have allowed me to set my parents up for the rest of their life, and it would be one less worry off my mind. It didn't matter anymore.

Uncle George was right. Time was valuable. It didn't matter anymore. Not the money nor the house. It hit me then. I didn't need the multi-million dollar mansion or the private jet. It was worthless.

MY HUMBLE BEGINNINGS

It did not bring me happiness. It was clich, but I wanted my father back. I didn't get to spend enough time with him. In this life, my father quietly supported me. My mother encouraged me. My sisters protected me. Family.

God wasn't enough for Mama. I knew that. Her heart lay under our feet, buried with my father, her husband. My parents were a unit similar to how water was wet. To conceive of a world without Uncle George was disorientating. My parents were my greatest asset. I had to do something to keep Mama on this side of the earth. I wouldn't be a useless son.

Mama Adel was leaning on Janet for support. Janet, who was closest to my father, out of all of us, was impassive.

"Well, we better get going. Gina's got dinner on the stove. You know how she gets if you disrespect her food," Janet commented acerbically. Mama and I shared a look of fond exasperation.

<Sharing stories about Uncle George>

It was late when we got back, almost 8 pm. Gina met us at the door, with a worried smile.

"I thought something had happened!" Between the three of us, we got Mama settled in her room. I offered to make up a tray for her and take it upstairs, but Mama Adel refused. She wasn't hungry.

The three of us sat down to dinner. Gina, as usual, had put on a homecoming feast fit for a king. The head of the table felt empty, and the house felt too silent. We heard the kitchen clock count the minutes away. Tick-tock. Tick-Tock. Uncle George was a taciturn fellow, who preferred to ration his words. We never noticed, but he was always part of our conversation. His silence was expressive. There was a tear in our family, one which time could never heal.

POVERTY OF THE MIND

"Is Mandy coming along?" Gina asked after we said grace. I had no appetite but I forced myself to eat anyway.

"Mandy?" Janet replied. "Yes, I left her with Mama Adel at the gravesite." Gina treated us to an Uncle Georgish frown.

"I wouldn't have left Mama alone. Mandy promised to watch her," said Gina. Unease had ants crawling up my arms again. I shook my head.

"I didn't know that. When we got there, Mama Adel was alone." I scraped plate clean out of habit.

"Surely Mandy wouldn't do that. She loves Mama." Janet stood up abruptly. "I'm done. I'll go take some food to mama, then I'm heading off to bed," she announced.

I turned to Gina for support, "She told me herself!" I protested. I was talking to the empty air. Gina had walked into the kitchen to do the washing up. My sisters were magicians. Always pulling a disappearing act.

I packed the uneaten food away and found the fridge full of leftovers. We would be eating these for a week. Maybe the church would take some. I spotted a dish of eggplants and stole it to empty it out into the compost pile later. I could never stand the slimy things. Disgusting. I was still recycling so it wasn't waste. Gina shooed me away before I could do more.

"Go to bed Jolie, You look terrible." Gina shoved me out the kitchen door. *When had she become so bossy?*

The Cuckoo clock from the parlour, chimed nine. My wife hadn't returned and I was beginning to get worried. *Maybe she's at her parents' house.* I decided to take a shower first. Ghana had come a long way, but our water supply was as uncertain as ever. We had to order

MY HUMBLE BEGINNINGS

it every month from the city. It came in huge tankers that filled up the water tank.

I was getting seriously worried. It wasn't safe to be out at night.

There was a phone in our room. Mandy had asked for it to be installed so that she could talk to her girlfriends without disturbing Mama. I tried her parents' house. No one picked up. An irate Madam Komtar, told me to look after my wife better before hanging up. I tried her cellphone. No answer, it went straight to voicemail. I tried her emergency phone and heard the faintest of buzzing. I tracked it down to her closet and found it buried in a box of sex toys. My wife was planning a good night for me. She was a sweet girl We haven't seen each other for a while. The toys looked very well used. The phone was almost dead but I still flicked on. What I saw disturbed me. On the screen was a grainy photo, a selfie of her posing with an unfamiliar man. I replaced everything as I found it in the closet. Everything would be okay. It had to be.

I was a fool.

<Family interaction>

Mandy came back the next day, just in time for lunch. I had my suspicions. There were too many red flags to ignore. She was as sweet and as caring to me as a man could want, and I couldn't accuse her willy nilly. I couldn't blame her if she acted up. We had spent most of our marriage in a long-distance relationship. I was confident that we could work this out. She was my heart, and I was hers.

My sisters made no comment on her disappearance and breezy reappearance. Mama Adel was lost in her own world, spending almost her entire day in the parlour. She liked to listen to <old time city band> Ron the radio, and sew on the settee. When the weather permitted, Mama sat out by the carp pond Uncle George put in all those years ago. We had stopped raising fish though. It was too much work, and none of us had the time.

Our workload increased with Uncle George gone because he was the one who managed the family' finances. We discovered that Uncle George was the one who had kept us afloat through a delicate network of favours. Much of which were the debts I incurred before I married Mandy. I thought I had paid it all off. Our bank statements and loan agreement papers said otherwise. Uncle George paid it off in full a few years ago. I think that was around the time my father started dressing up.

I was insanely busy. Despite being in Ghana, work followed me. Half my time was spent on my Blackberry answering emails from my team or taking calls from clients. We had survived the Asian financial crisis, but we were not out of the woods yet.

Uncle George's papers took up the rest of my time. My father died without leaving a legal will. I think he assumed that everything would automatically go to me upon his death but the courts dictated that his property was to be divided up as per custom. It was a mess. I had to hire lawyers to contest this, as well as show the courts that I was making an effort to locate my brothers. I barely had any time for myself.

I found my father's death certificates. He had died at the military hospital, number 37 . The same one where I was born. Time of death was dated: August 17th. 7.07. Mama had hidden it under a pile of recipe notes and account ledgers.

The school we had built for our community was doing well. Attendance was near perfect and so were exam scores. Ninety-seven percent of our students graduated and went on to University. Take THAT Mr Rex.

MY HUMBLE BEGINNINGS

The annual school fundraiser was coming up. I made a mental note to write another check. We didn't make any money from the school. All the money was re-invested and we were doing well enough to have almost 30% of our student body attend on scholarship. The only discrepancy I discovered was that it was built on a plot of land I deeded to Mandy as a wedding gift. She owned the land, and not the school. We paid her rent every year. I frowned. I would need to iron it out later. It wasn't a problem right now.

Around the time we bought the farm it supplied most of our food. Mandy had given us a small loan to help us get started. My wife was a sweet, and caring person. Uncle George had not paid it off yet. I thought that Gina should have it since she was the one who managed it along with our kitchen.

The woodworking workshop was Janet's free and clear. She had bought Uncle George out five years ago.

I was surprised to find that our house was in Mama's name. Uncle George had given it to her a few years ago, along with several small investments that would allow her to live a comfortable life. Uncle George had settled everything nicely.

We needed someone to help us look after Mama Adel. My sisters did what they could, but with our father gone, we found life had gotten a little bit harder. All the goodwill we enjoyed from our suppliers was due in part to him. My sisters were busy reassuring our network of friends and relatives that all was the same. Aunt Grace and Uncle Danso sent their condolences and largely faded out of our lives.

TRUE COLOURS

In our day-to-day life, Mandy and I were sweet lovebirds. My sisters understood and put up with it. They only asked that I talk Mandy into behaving better. I didn't understand. Mandy was not like they said she was. We needed someone to look after Mama Adel and my wife was the best candidate. To her credit, she volunteered for it. She took it upon herself to organise shifts for us. I had weekend duty, as I was not working, while Gina had afternoons and Janet the nights.

Gina's restaurant catered to the afternoon and dinner crowd so her days started later than usual. Janet's hours were more reasonable, closer to office hours, but they started very early. For a while, this schedule worked but as time went by, we needed to rely more heavily on Mandy. We could not leave Mama Adel alone. She had stopped eating and taking care of herself. Mandy protested that she could keep Mama Adel company and do all the house chores but we still hired a house girl to do some of the work.

As the months went by, Mandy would make sure Mama Adel, ate and drank her breakfast, then disappeared for the rest of the day after instructing the house girl to care for Mama. This wasn't right. Mama needed family around her. Not the hired help.

Mandy protested that she didn't have the training to look after Mama Adel properly and bring her out from her shell. So, I hired a nurse and a companion, one that Mandy recommended, over my sister's protestations. I had to stay and manage Uncle George affairs, and my business. I had no time for either of their complaints.

Janet told me in colourful language to, "Stop thinking with the wrong head." Gina spent thirty minutes delivering a lecture of filial piety and respect for our elders.

Gina had been threatening to go on strike for years and made good on her promises. She banned us from the kitchen. The house girl feared Gina more than me and refused to step foot in there.

She told me she had been hired to clean, not to cook. I fired her on the spot. Gina hired her to work in the Accra restaurant instead. My sister spread the word, making me out to be difficult to work for. No one reputable would work for us, no matter how much money

MY HUMBLE BEGINNINGS

I offered. Mandy tried to do housework, but she wasn't raised to do it. She had never so much as swept the floor, much less done the laundry by hand. She always had a washing machine in her house, which was operated by her maid. I tried to be patient with her, but there was only so much dirt I could tolerate around the house. Gina wasn't a monster, she kept the areas Mama Adel used clean, and banned us from it too.

When I tried sneaking in at night to steal some coffee and gingersnaps and reheat some jollof rice for Mandy, Gina put a lock on the fridge and the kitchen door that same night. Mandy discovered this the next day when she tried to make breakfast for the two of us. I lost my temper. I got a carpenter to remove the kitchen door, and a locksmith to dismantle all the locks in the house, save for our room. Uncle George had carved that door, so I had it stacked up in the shed.

When Gina discovered this, we had a screaming match out in the vegetable garden. All the neighbours came out to watch the show. I was so angry that I ran them off with the garden rake. Nosy fuckers. Gina accused me of being a 'fool' and a useless money-hungry person. She told me that I had forgotten my roots, all for the sake of a harlot.

She brought Mama Adel out and showed me her arms which were covered in bruises. "Your wife did this she said." I shook my head. Mama fell down the stairs. My mother nodded her head slowly. I told Gina she was an idiot. These accusations were baseless. What evidence was there?

Gina lost it, she punched me in the face sending sprawling backwards. You stupid, God-cursed Fool! If it wasn't for you... if wasn't for HER... I would have had the family I wanted."

She was sprouting nonsense! We fell to fighting like we were children again, scrapping in the dirt. Gina was out for blood, and strong from years of pounding fufu and stirring large vats of curry. Mama Adel didn't stop us. She stood there and watched us, with her arms curled inward, clutching herself, with her gaze fixed firmly on the ground. From nowhere, Mandy was there, pulling me off Gina. I had won, but only by a slight margin. I had it. I gave Gina a choice, either she could stop this nonsense and pull her weight or she could leave. I could look after Mama on my own.

My baby sister spat on me. She informed me in no uncertain terms that for one, *SHE* was taking Mama away to look after her properly and that all of Mama Adel's things were coming with her. Two, she did not need my help in paying the bills, she let me do it because she knew that it gave me a sense of accomplishment and grounded me.

She gave me an ultimatum of her own: Cast Mandy off or we were no longer related. Janet had agreed to this and was supposed to tell me this week. I pointed them to the front gate.

My family left. Janet had a small workshop attached to the back of the house. It took them both a week, but they hired movers to move everything out. They didn't tell me where they were staying or when they would be back.

Mandy was standing beside me all that time. My rock. My heart. When it was all said and done, and the house empty of my mother, my father, and my sisters, Mandy told me that it was a relief to know that Mama was being properly taken care of. I just felt... empty. She told me that now, we could start our own life together, one without their meddling influence. I believed her, and we spent a happy week shopping for new decorations and new furniture to fill the house. I had to import furniture from my own factory in Indonesia. No carpenter in the Greater Accra region would work for me. Janet had put the word out. In this, my sisters were united.

I was content to go along with what my sweet, kind, and caring wife said and did. What struck me as odd, was the little smile she wore all the time and, she was more cheerful than usual. Still, everything *seemed* normal. That smile haunted me.

A PRUDENT WIFE IS A GIFT FROM THE LORD

Things started to go wrong. Looking back, I wondered why I had been so blind. My wife spent most of her time out of the house. I became suspicious so I hired a private investigator and found that she spent most of her time visiting friends and shopping. She hid her purchases at her parents' house. I wondered where the hell she got all that ready money. The amount of money that flowed through her hands, exceeded what I gave her. She received nothing from her parents after our marriage and her disinheritance. I knew that she had reconciled with them, a few years back when her father was ill but I didn't think they had lawyers revoke the document. A daughter was like spilled milk after all. She belonged to her husband's family.

Her closet was full of outfits that would have set up our entire neighbourhood for generations to come. I had never noticed and simply took pride in my stylish and elegant wife. A closer look at the labels revealed that they came from exclusive Paris ateliers and fashion houses that I could not afford. *Just where was she getting the money from?* No matter how hard I tried, I could not escape these questions. Our marriage had been a long-distance relationship since its inception. How could it not have problems?

It all came crashing down when the P.I. delivered his report. There were pages and pages of financial statements detailing the payments made to Mandy from a company called <escort services> . Deposits of cash, and payments dated back years. There was an office building located in the notorious red-light district listed in Mandy's name. The detective had helpfully included pictures of the building in question. My wife owned several brothels in Ghana, *and* there was one in Morocco. The money she generated from her brothels paid for her extensive shoe collection.. She had an international escort agency which she ran from the internet. It catered to clients all around the globe. The size and scope of her operations was mind boggling.

All this information barely scratched the surface. The notes attached explained that it was dangerous to investigate further and explained that there were possibly several offshore Swiss bank accounts. Mandy was wealthier than I was, by a staggering degree. *When did she build all this? How?* It turned out that her parents had settled property on her at birth. She was independently wealthy before she met me. She didn't need me to provide for her, then and now. Her disinheritance meant she wouldn't get any of the family wealth when her father passed, it would all go to her brothers. However, what was already bestowed to her, she got to keep.

They had managed to get ahold of photographic evidence. There was a CD for me containing hours of porn with my wife as the star. I could not stop watching. It was horrifying. I needed to get myself tested for HIV.

I checked into a hotel that night. I could not bear to stay under the same roof as Mandy. I had married a harlot. She enjoyed being a sex toy for men and made good money from it.

I was so stupid! Janet was right. How many years had I wasted on her? Our marriage was a sham and we spent most of our time apart. Mandy had never wanted to move to Indonesia to be with me. She had her own life away from me and my family. She told us she was studying for her business degree. She attended and graduated in three years instead of the usual four. Where had she spent the last year?

My parents were right. They had tried to warn me over and over. I had failed to look pass my feelings and her beauty. Time had proven that Mandy was never interested in children.In fact, she didn't like them. I had failed to ask the most basic questions any sane person would when bringing home a prospect to meet the family. The truth was, Mandy would not have made a good wife or mother. She was

MY HUMBLE BEGINNINGS

girlfriend material. A good time girl. We were all wrong for each other. They were right. I should have listened.

I knew why I married her, I loved her. I did not know why she married me. She used me, but for what? What did she want from me? She never needed me to start with.

I was trapped in a marriage with a woman who had used me for her own ends, whom I now hated. Divorce did not exist in Ghana. My family had left me at my instigation. I was alone. I had no support.

WINTER 2009

INTERNATIONAL RELATIONS

TABLOIDS

SHOCKING SEX SCANDAL!

"Today in court, popular socialite, Mandy Adamah, nee Komtar, daughter of that famous General Komtar, has filed for divorce. Mandy reveals to us the sordid sexual abuse that took place nightly at the Mansion on Ashaiman road," the smartly dressed woman, announced. "Here live on channel 3, we are proud to present you with the inside scoop! Please give a round of applause for the lady of the hour, Mandy Komtar!"

The television lights brightened, and the spotlight swiveled to focus follow a heavily bruised woman, making her careful way down to the presenter's couch.

Interviewer: Welcome! Please, I hear you're starting a new shelter for women who were victims of domestic abuse.

M: Yes, I don't want anyone else to go through what I've been through. I am fortunate to have a supportive family, and the funds to hire good lawyers. Not many share the same fortune as I.

Interviewer; That is very generous of you. Domestic abuse is an epidemic that is hidden in homes across Ghana. We are proud to have on our set Mandy Adamah. She is a brave woman who does not fear the shame and censure of what we Ghanaians term as a "failed marriage." Thank you for stepping forth with our story.

M: How would you describe Jolie Adamah?

M: As a boy and a man. He was relentless. He never took no for an answer. He would tell me sweet things to make my girlish heart beat faster. He would show up after work and we would meet by the path between our neighbourhoods. He made me feel special. Friends and family told me later that he hung around waiting to see me. My parents separated us and sent me to South Africa to study. When I came back, he proposed. He's chased me for a decade. He would show up at places I frequented with my friends. He bombarded me with gifts, and affection until I felt that I had to say yes. He always found a way to touch my heart.

Interview: So, it sounds like he didn't know when to stop. Would you say that he was a stalker?

M: You have to understand, I was a young sheltered girl. I had no notion of the world beyond my home, my schooling, and the church. It all seemed so romantic at first. He swept me off my feet and made me believe that I was his girl. The love of his life. Looking back now, I would have to agree that he was a stalker.

Interview: It was a whirlwind romance. Where did it all go wrong?

M: It is hard to tell. We had a good healthy relationship at the start. I married Jolie because I thought he was a kind and caring man. Over

MY HUMBLE BEGINNINGS

time, I found that he was anything but. He's very controlling and he presents his requests in such a reasonable manner that it was hard for me to say no. It started out as minor things, "Have a drink ready when I come home," and moved on graphic sex acts he wanted me to perform for him on camera. We had a long-distance relationship, at that time, because I was studying at Africa University. I trusted him, and he abused that trust. I didn't feel comfortable at first, but over time I ignored the feeling and told myself that this is what a good wife does for her husband, to keep him interested.

Interviewer: (Sympathetic noises.)

M: One day, about two years into our relationship. I was doing sexy things for my husband in our private chat room where we were video calling each other. Long-distance make intimacy hard. Then out of the blue, a stranger said "Nice tits." I looked at the list of active members. There had been eight to ten men watching me do all these things for my husband. I shocked and humiliated that I pulled the plug on the computer and ran out of the room.

Interviewer: That's where it all started? Did you ever say no to him?

M: I did. I told him many times no. Jolie is very persuasive. He convinced me that I was imagining things, that it was just what any other normal couple would do for each other. He would buy me gifts and make me feel special all over again. It's very hard to break out of that cycle.

Interview: Obviously you did! How did you do it?

M: We had a long-distance relationship. He would come back to Indonesia for Christmas, and New Year's. I hated the month of December, when he returned to Ghana. I would have to perform for him in bed like a dog. He liked my mouth on him, he spat on me, and kicked me. I think he needed to beat and humiliate me to gain any enjoyment out of the act.

POVERTY OF THE MIND

When his father died, I was so scared. I respected Uncle George, he was a kind man. I knew that if it weren't for Uncle George, my life ... my life *sob* ... would have been worse. I was in danger. I don't know where I would have ended up.

Interviewer: It took great courage for you to speak up. How did you manage it?

M: It was him or me. I did want to die. My family told me to go to the police. I got in touch with the family lawyer, and together we went to the police station to file a report against my ... hu.. ex-husb...

Interviewer: Please, take your time. It must be very distressing for you. We understand.

M: My ex-husband was away on the weekends often. He told me he was having lunch with his clients and the estate lawyers. My friends told me that he was seeing other women. I took the chance, because I didn't want to live like this anymore. If he caught me and beat me to death, at least I wouldn't suffer anymore.

Interviewer: Oh my! If you could go back in time and warn your young self, what would you say?

Mandy Adamah turned to the camera with a brave smile and a grief laden stare.

M: RUN.

Interview: Indeed!

That's all we have time for today, everyone. Please give a round of applause for our brave Mandy. If you want to help, call the hotline now. The Mercy hope charity is accepting donations for a women's shelter to be built next year.

MY HUMBLE BEGINNINGS

LIGHTHOUSE

I clicked off the TV in disgust. My wife, that harlot, was a scheming jezebel. She had used me well for her own ends. I rolled over and pull the pillow over my head. Living in a five-star hotel meant that I didn't have to worry about anything. I just had to bring my credit cards.

The doorbell rang indicating room service arrived.

"Bring it in na!" I shouted in a desultory fashion. The service staff wheeled the cart in and began quietly removing all the empty whiskey bottles. I drained the one I had in my hand, and tossed it to the nattily dressed waiter "Oy! boy. Bring me another two. Put it on my tab. If you bring up in fifteen minutes, there's ten dollars in it for you." I tossed him a tenner, which he pocketed with practised ease.

Shambling over to my food, I lifted the cover. My favourite, fish head curry. We had that at our wedding. I threw the silver serving lid at the mirror, shattering it.

Why? How? How as I so stupid? How long was she lying? Did I marry and fall in love with someone that never existed? I trod on glass shard and cursed myself for being a fool. I knew I was racking up a huge bill but I couldn't bring myself to give a damn.

After that shocking "expose" I couldn't show my face out on the streets. The interview was on every channel. Pack of lies!

Where was that boy with my whiskey! No one would have anything to do with me. I couldn't go home, Mandy lived there. She had sold everything my Uncle George and Janet made, all of Janet's handiwork, and Uncle George's carvings. Gone. The house was a hollow shell. To my wife, I was nothing more than a steppingstone. *I could stay here.*

Someone knocked at the door. Finally! My whiskey. "I'll be right there!" I straightened my bathrobe.

I opened the door to a suit, and promptly slammed the door in their faces. Leaning against it, I slid down to the ground. Not today!

"Mr Jolie!" I didn't answer. "I've a package for you" someone called through the door. Likely a man from the Ga tribe. He sounded like a gorilla goon.

"GO AWAY" I croaked. I sat there until was silence from the other side.

"Mr Jolie! your whiskey is here!" A soft voice called. I cracked open the door, only to have a suit shove his way inside.

He outweighed me by two stone, which meant he came from a comfortable, if not well off background. His suit was Ralph Lauren, and his shoes were custom-made. I didn't recognise him. He had my bottle of whiskey in one hand, and an envelope in the other hand.

"How did you find me here?" I demanded.

He shrugged and politely said "It wasn't easy but this is what I would do if I were in your shoes." Holding my whiskey just out of reach he asked, "Are you Mr Jolie <fullname> Adamah?" Remaining out of reach seemed prudent.

"Yes." I grumpily replied. "I am!" I caught the bottle before I fell and shattered. Taking a drink straight from the bottle, I sat down heavily on the bed and re-adjusted my bathrobe. I should really take a shower. The suit served me my papers.

"This is a notice of summons, for one Jolie <full name> Adamah to appear in court on <date> " It was a week from now. The suit turned to look at me. "I'm sorry brother, I knew your father."

MY HUMBLE BEGINNINGS

Once he left, I read it over. Mandy was suing me for emotional damages. She wanted everything. She was going to take me to the cleaners, and I believed she would win. None of the lawyers in town were hired by Mandy. I was going to lose the house. I checked the blackout curtains, making sure no light leaked through, then stretch out on the bed. Almost all the TV channels were carrying the "shocking sex scandal" story.

"Housekeeping!" I savoured the burn that slid down my throat.

"Come on right in." Someone pushed a cart into the room. An older lady stood guard over the young house keepers, who scurried around, staying well out of reach. I had the strangest urge to say "BOO!"

Giggling, I downed the last of my whiskey. That's odd, I just cracked this one open! The Aunt's lip curled in disgust at me. She shooed everyone out and finished up the room herself before leaving. Ignoring her, I shambled over to the bathroom to wash my face.

My cellphone rang, I had left it on the sink. In foul humor "WHAT!" I yelled into it.

"Hello Jolie. It's me, Dane"

"Sorry, I thou…Well, what do you want?" I groused.

"I'm here to help you thick-headed bastard. If you prefer to stay in that bottle of Jack, you've crawled into until you die, I'm going to hang up." I wasn't an alcoholic. This…was pain medication to numb the dissociation I felt. Nothing made sense anymore.

Defeated I asked, "…Please don't hang up."

"Well, the good news is that we were able to prove our identity with the burnt remains of your passport."

POVERTY OF THE MIND

Sighing into the pregnant pause, "What's the bad news?"

I heard the shuffle of papers and children laughing in the background as the heavyset man replied "The bad news is that you can't leave the country until the immigration officials clear you."

"I know. I can't get a Ghanaian passport for love or money. My parents didn't file for a birth certificate when I was born."

Where was the other bottle of whiskey? I needed it.

"Look Jolie, I know you're hurting. Put down that bottle. It doesn't help," Dane my best and only friend in the world said. "Focus. Bring your brilliant brain into this picture. Right now, it's just your heart that's hurting."

He was right. "Look, you can head over to Hong Kong. Border controls over there are loosening. If you get your passport, you can get into China at least, and from there, fly back to Indonesia. We've survived the Asian financial crisis."

"Dane, I think I can get a Nigerian passport," I said.

"Good, do it. You need to come back before the year is out."

"Dane, I can't."

"What do you mean you can't?" He spluttered.

"Mandy will get everything. I think she's going to get the business and she will dismantle it and squeeze every last cent out of it."

"What? Mandy? She doesn't know jack!"

"This is serious. She's General Komtar's daughter. Her family has the clout and the connections." With the story Mandy spun, there was

MY HUMBLE BEGINNINGS

no court that would rule in my favour. "Get out while you can, she's come after everyone connected to me."

"She's a crazy bitch." Dane said.

"Yes she is." I agreed "Too bad I found out too late. She was good at pretending."

"I've got to go."

Dane hung up. He was right, I couldn't sit here any longer I had to do something. The rumour mill was effective and Mandy had been planting evidence for as long as we were married together.

The hotel delivered the newspapers every day. I knew I was running up a huge bill, but I couldn't care less. I saved and scrimped my entire life, only to have a Jezebel of a wife snatch it all away. Shaking the newspaper open, I checked the date. It had been three weeks since I checked in. Rooms here weren't cheap.

"Hope mercy charity opens its doors today in the former mansion that once saw decadent drug-fuelled orgies. Mandy believes in turning bad into good and has opened the doors of her home to the poor unfortunate souls..." read an article on the front page, right under the date. I chucked it aside.

So, she was running a trafficking ring out of the house my father built. Ha, every single word out of her mouth was a lie. I rolled over and pulled the pillow over my head. Tomorrow... no. I had to do something now. If I pushed it off to tomorrow, it would be an endless series of tomorrows.

Getting up, I headed to the bathroom to clean myself up. I hadn't showered for a week. I looked as terrible as expected. A three-week drunken bender would deplete anyone's bodily health. I stared at myself in the mirror.

POVERTY OF THE MIND

Look Jolie, you need to leave. Men do not run. They stay and fight. *She'll get everything*, I told myself." I need to stop her but how?

I went back and forth in my mind: *You can build yourself up again.*

No I can't. I'm too tired. I hurt.

I can build myself up again.

No I can't.

I must.

You've got friends.

Most of them left or were chased off by Mandy.

She's not my Mandy. Never has been

That was true. Learn from it.

ARREST

I checked out of the hotel as soon as I finished my shower. I didn't dare stay there for yet another day. I was afraid I would indeed drink myself to death like Dane said.

The late afternoon sun felt like a warm blanket on my skin. *Welcome back to reality*, I told myself sourly. I needed to fight this. There was no point in cowering and waiting for the lion to eat me. I hadn't had lunch yet. I had no appetite for the fish head curry I ordered earlier and left it congealing in its silver serving dish back at the hotel. It would probably go to the cleaners. Since I was in the neighbourhood, I stopped by Gina's chop bar to grab a bite.

MY HUMBLE BEGINNINGS

It was as Janet had said. There was a queue of people waiting outside to eat Gina's cooking. I half expected to be shown the door, but no one recognised me. I didn't see my sister or anyone I knew for that matter. I ordered goat pepeh soup and fufu. The crowd was a mix of businessmen and working-class families who came here on their day off. All the plates were scraped clean: the customers loved her food. This chop bar was a local lunch and dinner joint. I knew Gina had a proper sit-down restaurant but I didn't know where it was.

Tucking into my food with renewed gusto, I felt my resolve firm up.

Halfway through my meal, Gina interrupted.

"Hello brother." She greeted me quietly. The chop bar was noisy enough to mask our conversation.

I sighed, "I'm sorry" I said. "You were right"

Gina folded her arms and asked. "What's going to happen to Mama's house?" I mopped up the last of the soup.

Frowning and swallowing, I answered, "I don't know. I'm preparing for the worst. I'm going to fight this." Gina rubbed her eyes and sighed.

"You know, I've often thought that our lives would be a lot better, had you been born a girl. Mama, and Uncle George would have married you off early to keep you out of trouble."

I gaped at Gina. A girl? Really? "Close your mouth Jolie. You really do look like a fish. Janet was right."

Some clumsy oaf stumbled against me, shoving me against the table. Gina flicked a finger, and there was a helpful waiter ushering the fumble-footed man out.

"My court date is set for next week. She's coming after everyone I know. You better get what you can from the house," I said.

"Too late, your beloved has stripped out anything Janet or Uncle George made and sold it at the market." That was a puzzler, I blinked at Gina in stupefaction.

"Really? that was quick! Janet's work is in great demand? It's worth a lot of money."

"Brother..." She said slowly, "How can someone so smart be so stupid. "Listen, you need to go check on the house. She's blocked me from entering and claimed it. . Mama's not doing so well. She needs familiar surroundings. Can you get the cuckoo clock that Uncle George made? Mama's been asking for it. There are a couple of commissions that Janet left in the shop you need to retrieve." The buzz of conversation dimmed as lunch hour drew to a close.

"I'm headed back today. I need to stop by the lawyer's offices." I wiped my hands off as I continued, "The one good omen is that Mandy can't touch Janet's business. Janet bought out Uncle George many years ago, so it's hers, down to the last speck of sawdust." Gina nodded.

"She told me to pay you off. I'm glad I did. She saw this coming." I agreed with Gina wholeheartedly. A waiter set down a plate of fresh fruits and lemon water. Gina thanked her and waved her away.

"How's Mama?" I asked. I ate a piece of watermelon. These were a truce offering. Gina never fed anyone, not family, for free.

"Mama's recovering. The doctors say that she hasn't been eating for a month or more. A few more days and she would have died. I suspect Mandy and that friend of hers were starving Mama."

MY HUMBLE BEGINNINGS

Guilt crawled up my ass into my spine, shrinking me down to the size of a rotten tomato.

"Oh" I managed.

"Mama is beginning to forget that Uncle George has been called to the Lord. She keeps asking when he will be home."

"Can I come see her?" I asked.

Gina shrugged "I'll have to ask Janet, and right now. She'll rip you apart on sight."

Deserving of that as I was, I wanted to see Janet try.

"Right now, the only way you'll get to see Mama, is if she asks for you."

Puffing my cheeks out in a sigh, I polished off the plate of fruits.

"There's another piece of good news. I'm getting access to Uncle George's bank account today. The lawyers tell me that it is likely that everything will go to me."

"I'm worried Jolie. I can take care of Mama, but I don't have as much of a cushion as I'd like."

I nodded. "I'm worried too." I pushed away my plate. "Thanks for the food sister. We'll get through this" Gina waved me off, and trundled back into work.

When I got back to the house, there was a party in full swing. All the lights were blazing - the electric bill would be enormous. Music spilled out of the windows and, young well-dressed people strolled in and out like they owned the place. From a far, it made for a pretty tableau. I pretended to be one of the wait staff and let myself in through the pantry door. Gina's kitchen had been replaced by an industrial one of steel and chrome. All of the homely touches Janet had carved into it were gone. I slipped into the dining room, behind a waiter. Nobody noticed. Someone had rolled out a piano into the dining room. Mandy was sitting in the lap of a young male pianist, fondling him like one would fondle a dog. Thank god she didn't see me, she was too intent on her fun. The house was packed enough that people saw the uniform, and not the face. Uncle George's clock was nowhere to be found.

I managed to sneak upstairs without being noticed. There were couples everywhere in various states of undress. There was a full blown orgy going on in what used to be my parents' room. All the service staff looked underage and some were still children. My wife had turned my home into a brothel. It was as Gina said: the house had been hollowed out. Everywhere I looked there was something new and fancy. Nothing of my family remained.

I wondered where sh-- Oh. my face drained. The credit cards I gave her. I needed to cut her off before she ruined me utterly. How much had she spent already? Pushing that worry to the back of my mind, I made my way downstairs to find Mandy. I checked the parlour. It was a heaving mass of writhing bodies, and the funk of sex hung heavily in the air. *Just who the hell is the depraved sex maniac here?* I thought sourly.

I found Mandy in the dining room, making a different kind of music with the young pianist she was touching earlier. Disgusted, I pulled her off the boy. He was young enough to be my nephew. Neatly avoiding her wild swings, I announced to the room at large, "Party is over. I'm calling the police!" She was high as a kite. I dumped her in the bathroom and turned the shower on to sober her up.

Drunk and stoned revellers caught wind of the word "police" and repeated it throughout the house in a panic. There was a mad stampede for the exit. They trod on each other in their haste to escape.

MY HUMBLE BEGINNINGS

The car after expensive car peeled away. I said a prayer for our vegetable garden.

The rent boy, if he was a rent boy, had his pants buttoned up when I came back down. I could see that he was shaking with terror. I threw a Benjamin at him and told him to call a cab.

There was drug paraphernalia and cocaine stacked in neat little bags on the dining table. There was a buffet laid out for hungry guests. It looked fresh and was still steaming hot. The party had just gotten into full swing. Several young girls and boys huddled in Mama's room. I would never tell my family what the hell happened here. They told me that "Madam" would come to take them home. I debated calling the cops, but first I needed to dispose of the drugs. I used a pair of kitchen tongues to pick it all up and dump it in an oil barrel we used for burning rubbish. That's how the police found me. Standing over a burning barrel of drugs.

They arrested me and sent Mandy to the hospital. I was charged with possession of drugs, attempting to destroy evidence, solicitation, sex with a minor, running a brothel... and any other charges they could come up with. They were relentless. Thank God for my lawyer, John Kwambe. Uncle George and him had built up a good relationship. He agreed to represent me, for my father's sake.

They held me for a month before I was released on bail. I had a solid alibi. The hotel receipts proved I had been staying there for three weeks. Gina and her staff testified that they had seen me at lunch. The drug charges stuck. I found out that Mandy had been using my credit cards to pay someone to buy drugs. When they released me, my family refused to talk to me. They refused to listen when I pled ignorance. Everyone knew how smitten I was with my wife. How I could not refuse her the slightest thing. She could not have done it without my willing consent.

POVERTY OF THE MIND

My inbox was full of frantic emails from Dane and my team. The last email was dated the day prior. Dane had met with a horrific accident. A truck had careened off the road and hit him. Dane was in the ICU, and they don't know if he would survive. I went home to the house and found it deserted. The post box had a stack of credit card bills. I owed close to 50,000 US dollars this month. Paying them off took everything I had left on me. I called the credit card company and had them all cancelled.

When I arrived back at the house, I found the garden half destroyed. We were expecting a bumper crop of tomatoes. Everything had been harvested. Plants were missing. My neighbours told me that there had been some workers in a week ago taking away plants. Apparently, there had been a scruffle and the police were called. My sisters had come back to save the garden.

The place was deserted, save for a team of staff who were in charge of keeping the house and grounds pristine. They told me that Mandy had gone to stay with her parents. My life was in shambles. The nail in the coffin was my wife strolling back into my house with a pleased look on her face and a new man on her arm.

I stared at this man, he was wearing *MY* clothes and shoes! He had ruined my custommade <fancy shoes > by kicking something and stepping in sewage. The exchange went as expected. I was escorted off the property before I had a chance to retrieve any of my possessions. I only had a suitcase of clothing I packed for my three week drunken bender.

While I was locked up, I had missed the date for the court appointment mediation. My lawyers tried to fight, but Mandy got the house and the farm. I knew my sisters would fight

this. I had the family lawyer send them a notice.

MY HUMBLE BEGINNINGS

She also came after Janet's workshop, and Gina's restaurants. When I asked her why she was doing this she just smiled at me. I should have left her to Kobe Biabako. They were a pair of devils - the both of them.

The court acquitted me of any wrongdoing, thanks to the efforts of my lawyer, and fined me for causing a "public disturbance to the peace." I don't know if anyone was charged. I couldn't care anymore.

I crossed over to Nigeria to look for a job. I was too recognisable in Ghana. Still, No one would hire me. The government had frozen all my bank accounts, and I was still suspected of drug trafficking and money laundering.

I finally found work as a clerk in some shipping office, doing international export and import to earn the money I needed for my daily food costs and my flight ticket out. I sold my share of the business to Dane's family for a reasonable sum. That way, at least Mandy could not dismantle that too.

The Nigerian immigration granted me a valid passport, wiping out all my savings. Hong Kong was the only country that would grant me a visa.

From start to finish the dismantling of my life took six months.

HONG KONG

I landed in Hong Kong, amidst a miserable drizzle. The airport was a haven where I sat and scanned the classified ads for a suitable place to stay. I needed to conserve funds. I wasn't sure if I could find work quickly.

Half a morning and most of an afternoon later of browsing through the classifies and the internet yielded frustration. Ten obscenity-filled calls and a depletion of all the ready money I had on me. No one wanted to rent to an African. We were seen as dirty, smelly barbarians.

To my everlasting relief, the last call connected, with the last of my credit.

"Hello!" a rough voice answered. "Who's this?" it asked.

"I'm Jolie remember? I'm calling about the room," I said.

"Oh yes, it's available. Rent is due on the first and the fifteen. No deposit needed. If you're late on rent or turn out to be a little fucker, you're evicted. Ask for Bonnie when you arrive at the address," the rough voice answered.

The address was across the bay, near the harbour. The building in question was old and run down. There were no working lifts. On the outside, the flat was grey and dingy while the inside was decorated with cast-off furniture painted in mismatched swatches of paint. It should have been hideous to the eye, but it worked, reminding me of Janet's colourful paintings.

It had the basics, tv, couch, table, and roach infestation. Bonnie turned out to be a fellow Ghanaian. He told me they came from outside - garbage collection in the building was terrible. I was instructed to take out the garbage every day and throw it into the street bins, else we would attract more roaches.

My room was the tiny pantry/storeroom turned bedroom just off the kitchen, next to the bathroom. It had one window which opened out to a view of dirty grey buildings. There was a mattress and a bed. It was clean, had running water, and electricity. It was tiny, just big enough for a bed and small cabinet that doubled as a cupboard and a desk. It was better than some of the places I had lived in. It was comfortable as far as the dismal surroundings, and roach infestation would allow.

MY HUMBLE BEGINNINGS

I liked Bonnie. He was well spoken, if brash and reminded me of an American friend. We went out for a quick dinner at a char chan teng once I got settled in. When we got to talking, we discovered that we had been on the periphery of each other's network. We both hailed from Ashaiman, and went to the same primary school. He graduated and went on to study economics at the university on a scholarship. It was a damn small world.

Bonnie was handsome if you discounted the disfiguring scar that stretched across his face. As it was Hong Kong and the humidity and heat were a killer, he had his shirt off. The ladies would love him. Of that I was sure.

Bonnie connected me with a friend of his who was looking for a clerk and general worker. I took the job. It paid enough to cover rent, and utilities, with some left over for food. I wagered I would be eating egg, fried rice for the duration of my stay.

I discovered later, that while Bonnie was a friendly gregarious sort, he always looked out for himself first. I was a long-term investment. I would learn that in time.

I would start the new job the next day. In the meantime, we spent the rest of the day playing tourists and counting off all the streets that appeared in Jackie Chan movies.

I counted my first day in Hong Kong a resounding success.

My second day started at the crack of dawn. I woke up out of habit to take a run and put in a work out. I met Bonnie's girlfriend in the kitchen when I ventured out to make coffee. Her name was "Lilu" and she spoke limited English in a heavy accent. I realized that I had forgotten to buy groceries as I was having too much fun the day before. She kindly offered me coffee and toast to tide me over.

POVERTY OF THE MIND

The work address I was given was in a tiny office not far from the flat. I had gotten there early so I decided to treat myself to breakfast. However, the waiters refused me service and the shop owner came out to shoo me off, while yelling obscenities in Cantonese. I had to settle for a bun bought from the 7/11.

Bonnie's friend was a lady who owned a secondhand goods store. My job was to be her assistant. I was hired on the spot after I demonstrated I knew how to work with wood. At the end of the day, when I was picking up groceries for myself, I reflected that the more things change, the more things stay the same. I should have listened to Uncle George by saving more and staying home to become a carpenter.

The casual racism was hard to adapt to. I wasn't seen as human, but subhuman. It was something I was used to, having faced it all my life from my childhood to facing off my soon-to-be ex-wife's parents. At the end of the day, I was exhausted and fell asleep as soon as my eyes shut.

I lived from day-to-day. I didn't have anything to strive for. All my life's work had been destroyed by my ex-wife. She was my goal, and she turned out to be false.

Janet contacted me once a month to keep me updated. It was cheaper than getting the lawyers to do it. My divorce was almost finalised. Mandy was suing Janet for ownership of the cars we used and everything she could possibly lay claim to. Mama had made a full recovery and was still coming to the terms with Uncle George's death.

I had too much free time and for once, I filled it with doing nothing. I spent my time in bars and at the houses of adventurous women. Beer and sex made up most of my free time. I knew in the back of my head this couldn't last and it only takes one slip for this holiday to turn into self-destruction. It was a dangerous tightrope to walk. I knew from second-hand experience, that it was better to never to regret and repent after.

MY HUMBLE BEGINNINGS

I did eventually discover how Bonnie supported himself. He was a rent boy and a highly paid one at that. He travelled regularly around southeast Asia, going to Singapore, Thailand, Dubai, and China on a regular basis. I had caught him on his month off, and in between it all, he worked for a man named Peter, who was listed as our landlord.

I knew I couldn't stay in Hong Kong in the long term, there was no future for me. I did have my sights set on China and Guangzhou. I would be reaching my forties soon; I lived like a college student. As my friend Dane would say. "This shit ain't going to fly." Took me a while to understand, but it meant intolerable.

Bonnie was another character. He was polite and gregarious, but had a temper on him, getting into frequent brawls when he got drunk. He only stopped if he or his opponent went down. He kept it under control for the most part and I learned to watch out for the warning signs. Mama would have said, "He was devil touched." I hoped he did not like men too, for he was always looking at me and weighing me up.

As time went on, I found that it was harder and harder to pay the rent. Somehow, there was always this new event to go to or utilities to be paid. No matter how careful I was, there was never enough for rent. I couldn't quite account for it. There was always some emergency that popped up. I scraped by usually, by hook or by crook but was late on the rent. Bonnie blew up at me and I had to sit on my hands to prevent it from turning into an all-out brawl. I couldn't afford the doctor's fees. Even with the credit card, it wasn't a wise financial choice.

One day, when I had just arrived back from work, Bonnie told me, "Get dressed and showered. Put on your fancy brand new suit. We've got an appointment in an hour. You have twenty minutes."

He was dressed to kill and had his hair artfully dishevelled. That bloody explained why several of my pocket squares were missing. I needed to put a lock on my suitcase. My suits were the only assets I had left with me. My heart sank.

"Do this and I'll call this week's rent and next week's rent even. You owe me. Don't fuck this up, or you'll be out before you can say Uncle." I did as I was told. Going along with what Bonnie wanted and not having to worry about next week's rent would be a relief.

Our "appointment" turned out to be a private dinner hosted by an elegant couple in a penthouse suite of an upscale area. The penthouse was your standard showroom piece. It was exquisitely decorated with a great view of Hong Kong's skyline. . There was a St Andrew's cross mounted on the wall, disguised as a piece of avant garde art. I had to smother a smirk and send up a silent prayer to God. I did not want to get sucked into sex work. Never again.

The dinner was pleasant and polite. I unwound enough to enjoy myself and got caught up in the conversation. Peter seemed interested in me and so did the woman, Angie. She was in her fifties but looked twenty. After dinner, we retired to the living room to admire the view and drink coffee. Bonnie and Peter started canoodling. I was left alone with Angie. I was exhausted and most certainly didn't feel like talking to her.

Desperate for a distraction, I started talking to Angie, trying to make her laugh as if she were Mandy. It worked. I was the perfect gentleman: I listened and she soon saw me as a human. When Bonnie and Peter emerged, both with satisfied grins, Angie was laughing and smiling. A complete change from the silent woman she was when we came in.

Back home, Bonnie congratulated me. "Jolie boy-o! You did good! Angie's asking for you again. You should go into business for yourself!" He flashed a card at me. "We've got an invitation to the biggest swingers' party. They hold it annually and I've been hoping to score an invite." Bonnie back slapped me. "You've got to come with me, we'll make a matched set." He eyed me critically. "If you do, your rent for the next two months is forgiven." I brighten up at that. It meant more money for the things that mattered.

The party was a midlife crisis. Most couples were over thirty and very well-preserved. There were go-go boys and girls dancing on the poles. It was a wild event, with booze and drugs flowing through. I saw bouncers and medical staff on hand. I tipped my hat to the organisers. They did a good job, from the food to the aftercare. I don't remember much of it but recall spending most of the evening talking to an older lady named Emily. I escaped the party with a name card and a new friend without having to do the horizontal tango.

In retrospect, Bonnie dragging me to his work date and that party was one of the better things to happen to me. This was how I got to know Emily and her circle.

THE GOOD WIFE

Emily eventually became my mentor. In hours, we were simply good friends, even if she did pay me for my time. After she heard my story, she got me a good job working as her personal assistant in one of her companies. I didn't just make lattes and run dry cleaning. I also helped her manage her businesses. She also moved me into one of her flats and only charged me enough rent to cover the taxes and utilities. Everything else was taken care of. She told me she didn't like her boys to become lazy and depend on her for everything. She was wise. I was of the same mind too. I relished the chance to get back to doing work I understood and loved. She even paid for me to attend university too. I had managed to get my GED but never finished my degree. She told me I could never have too much education.

I was grateful for everything and worked hard both in the office and at pleasing her. I understood how Mandy felt. It wasn't as easy as it looked but it was no different from reading a difficult client and giving them what they wanted.

I got good at both my jobs. It helped that I found Emily and her friends attractive. They were elegant ladies if a tad snobbish at times. As long as you knew your place and stayed loyal, they would look after you well.

Emily did. Whatever I wanted, I got. I only had to pay for food and rent. I saved half my pay after expenses and spent the rest. I had a car and accompanied her on trips overseas.

She was a fan of mahjong and taught me how to play. I was such a terrible player that she didn't speak to me for a week.

I knew it couldn't last though I was hooked on this life. None of this was mine, and I got into the habit of spending money as fast as I could make it. Only my ingrained habit and a fear of being destitute kept my savings account from being totally drained. I spent the allowance she gave me on myself and keeping Emily happy.

After a year or two, it did not bring me as much pleasure as before. I was living the life I wanted and dreamed about since I was a child, before I saw Mandy. Still, there was a hollow feeling at the back of my heart. As I was enjoying the money and the luxury, it bothered me that this was not mine. That I had not earned it with my own two hands. Emily took me under her wing and taught me the art of managing my finances. In hindsight, she did it to prepare me for when she would let me fend for myself.

SAKURA

I met Sakura just as Emily was beginning to tire of me. I had taken her advice on investing and saving, but perhaps not as well as I should have. It wasn't personal, Emily was getting older and had moved on from the death of her husband. I heard from her that she had met someone new.

MY HUMBLE BEGINNINGS

Emily still kept me on her payroll because I was just that good. She "lent" my time out to her friends who were in need of comforting after their husbands cheated on them, or ran away with the maid, or died. The first two happened more often than the public faces of these ladies would suggest. Wealth, education, and taste were not something to aspire to, they were part of how things were.

Sakura was a lovely Japanese woman. I didn't know her real name, nor did she know mine. In this world, in this time, my name was Wine.

AMERICA LOST

My divorce with Mandy was ongoing and my accounts had long been drained. Mandy got everything I owned but we narrowly avoided losing Janet's shop and Gina's restaurants. Needless to say, my sisters were livid and had long stopped talking to me, save for the monthly emails updating me on what was going on at home. I had to fly back a few times to attend court dates. I was not found guilty but was fined for <x offence>. The judge called me <proverb for stupid unwary idiot> for not noticing what was under my nose. I agreed. Janet warned, "*I was the cow who got slaughter and eaten.*" Mandy was enjoying her just harvest.

Sakura was five foot two, and full of pain. Her husband had been cheating on her for the past five years. They had no children, not by choice, because they had trouble conceiving. I learned all of this from Emily.

When I set eyes on Sakura, it was love at first sight. The first time I felt this way was when I set eyes on Mandy nearly two and a half decades ago. She had an ethereal beauty, such that stylish maidens of the Tolkien persuasion would kill for.

She wore minimal makeup and was dressed in a simple sheathe dress. I didn't understand the man who came home to this and then cheated on her with another woman. This was what excess on a daily basis did to you. You just started taking it for granted.

A few months after this, I decided I was quitting, or rather the decision had been made for me. Emily's boyfriend turned fiancée had found out about me so the rug was being abruptly pulled out from under me. Good, lavish living had made me soft. I did have a savings account, a healthy wage from working as an escort, and my day job. Still, it wasn't as much as it should have been.

I was politely evicted from Emily's flat and my credit card and expense accounts were cut off. Emily's lawyer had me sign an NDA in exchange for a hefty severance package.

Emily left me with a parting gift. She arranged for my PR status in China and gave me enough for a plane ticket to Guangzhou. We had talked about this over the course of the year as we both knew that the relationship would come to a close. I did not know rent boys could get severance packages. I didn't walk away empty handed though. I learned much from Emily, especially finesse and class.

Emily had financed a lavish lifestyle for nearly half a decade and I had the wardrobe to match. She got me a job that would boost my CV and paid for my education. I would be forever grateful to this woman.

I didn't want to waste money, so I booked a flight from Shenzen airport to Guangzhou and walked into China. I was confident I would survive and thrive.

BLUE

PHOENIX

I held a handkerchief up to my mouth to catch all the snot and spit that was leaking out of me. "Please, God put me out of my misery,"

MY HUMBLE BEGINNINGS

I moaned. The waiters at this cafe were watching me like a hawk for signs of mental instability. "Hallo! Please bring me…" *cough* "…more coffee…" Cough. Hack. Cough. "…and a honey lemon tea."

As the waiter strode away to punch in my order, a gun cracking noise broke the quiet, cutting through the background music. Coughing, I grabbed for more tissue and made it just in time to catch the volcano of snot.

"Hello" she said. I wiped my crusty face, squinting blearily at the petite beauty standing before me. She slammed a business card on the table between us. "Go see a doctor, you're disturbing the peace." I was going to die anyway, why waste money. She talked in disgust. "Call the number on the card." It said *Hospital*. I tried to thank her, but she had already left in a huff.

I knew I was being dramatic, but I thought the situation warranted it. I was glad it was my day off. I was too sick to work. Mandy had tracked me down the month prior. Her lawyers demanded alimony. She sent me death threat too. I had gotten into a car accident twice and had been mugged. I was feeling run down in general and started to think I was cursed. It had been a decade but that damned woman needed her pound of blood.

I got up, paid, and left. Doctors were a waste of money. I strode past snack stalls selling hot tea and tea eggs. There was a chill wind blowing, cutting straight through my bones. I tossed my scarf ends over my shoulder as a shield against the wind. Janet had called earlier to demand help with this month's bills. I was looking at escort work if I things did not work out this month. The latest round of lawyers' fees had almost wiped us all out.

We didn't understand why she was still coming after us. We had treated Mandy well when she was my wife and I had given her whatever she wanted to the best of my ability.

POVERTY OF THE MIND

A child scampered into my field of vision. "Hei ren! Hei ren!" This declaration meant "*Black person! Black person!*" I scowled at the little scamp and removed myself from its presence. It never paid to be confrontational in China. I didn't know who's this kid was but the clothing indicated rich parents. It is better to back down. I had friends of friends, who ran afoul of these people. They made Mandy look sane. When in doubt de-escalate. Pride is a luxury only the powerful can afford.

The metro station was a haven of warmth generated by the volume of bodies transiting through its bowels each day. I was on my way back to my apartment near <X district> . I looked forward to taking a warm shower and crashing straight into bed.

The door of my apartment was open. My roommate, Chin chin, had returned from the Dongzhi Festival.

"Wine-ah! You're back, come, eat. Eat!" He beckoned me inside, to the dining table where a bowl of brightly coloured tang yuan sat.

"Thanks!" I said with enthusiasm. "I better not eat these. I've got a terrible cold and a sore throat."

I put on a mournful look. I did like the tang yuan. The glutinous rice balls were tasty. I needed honey lemon tea.

Lee bounced into the kitchen. She was his chipper girlfriend. I liked them both, even if they got sickeningly cute.

My phone rang. I squinted at the number. It was Ghana, from Mama Adel. I didn't know why the hell she was calling. International calls were expensive. Couldn't she have waited until next week for our monthly check ins?

I waited till I was inside my own bedroom before picking up.

MY HUMBLE BEGINNINGS

"Mama!" I answered in Ewe "How are you?"

Mama Adel launched straight into her lecture "Boy. Your devil wife has just gotten our cars impounded. Gina needs the Range Rover to head out to her farm. You need to do something about this!" Mama Adel groused. "I should have beat you when you said you were in love with Mandy. We spoiled you. That's why this happened!"

Stifling a sigh I replied, "I'm sorry Mama," for what felt like the hundredth time. This was a familiar conversation, repeated at least once every other month. Gina had stopped talking to me entirely. Janet pretended we were not related and kept things impersonal.

I had no idea how I could make it better. My days with Emily seemed like a dream. I was tempted to try and call her up, but part of the severance package included a no contact clause. I missed Emily and hoped she was doing well. Her marriage came up in the social section of the paper. I was happy for her.

I had a client meeting in an hour and a half. I needed to get dressed.

Work was good. I invested my severance package from Emily's financing scheme. It had done well. I had a tidy sum to use as capital for a new business but I didn't know what I would do. At the moment, I was working in an English tuition center part-time and taking on students. I had also recently picked up a sales job. One of my boss's relatives owned a factory that was not doing so well. I needed the extra money, so I offered to help them gain more orders. The commission was decent and allowed me to put aside more money for my savings account. It was a good deal that benefited both of us.

I was considering opening my own company if business was good. I needed someone to tour the factories and vet them for quality. I couldn't be everywhere at once. <lee lee> and <chin chin> were busy canoodling outside. I promised myself if I scored this deal and hit my savings target, I could move out and into my own place. I even had it picked out already.

An hour later, saw me near <Y district> at <x building> . I met with my clients Mr and Mrs Wong, who owned a phone manufacturing company and needed parts to package the finished products. I was in the process of reconnecting with my old friends and colleagues because I needed a network to help my clients. Dane's family was doing well despite his passing a year after the accident. It was then I thought that there might have been something to Black Magic. I got the deal.

The next week I moved out into a new flat that was closer to the metro station. I saw the girl again, several times as the cafe was also close to the metro. I liked her on sight, she gave me the same feeling Sakura and Mandy did. I spent hours wrestling with myself before I gave in, and spent more time at the cafe, just hoping to see her.

I wasn't successful. In the meantime, my cold had gotten worse. I got winded just walking up the stairs. Talking to clients or students became impossible. I gave in and called the number on the card.

The doctor who saw me was a middle-aged man who spoke English with the lilt of the well-educated. The doctor told me I had a severe case of pneumonia.

A week later I went to the cafe again, hoping to catch a glimpse of her. I was in luck. I thanked her for the card and told her the doctor was a good one.

"Of course, he is my father" she snapped back.

I brought her a gift of "fancy coffee" and asked if she would like to go see <A event > with me. She accepted the coffee but refused the invite. Over the next month, I kept running into her at the cafe or the hospital where I had to go back to get my check-ups.

MY HUMBLE BEGINNINGS

She intrigued me, with her serious air and her pixie-ish charm. I wore her down eventually, and she agreed to go on a date with me. I took her to a coffee tasting event and we had McDonalds after. On the day she agreed to be my girlfriend, she gave me blue shirt and a pair of blue Toms. Life was good. We were married not long after.

I quit my teaching job and opened my own company after Blues agreed to go on a date with me. When I married her my company was big enough to for me to hire my own personal assistant. Life was good. With Blues, married life was sweet. She didn't want to have children yet, she wanted to focus on her career first. I agreed.

Mama and Janet sent their congratulations. They didn't fly to China to meet Blues, but we set up a Skype video conference.

Mandy married Kobe around the same time I started dating Blues. The long, drawn-out suit ended when the courts ruled in Mandy's favour. Janet and Gina kept their businesses, and personal property. We lost everything else . From the investment account we started to help pay the lawyers with the proceeds from the sale of my business, to the produce business we set up to sell the excess from the farm we started before I got married to Mandy. Everything that I was connected to or had my name on it. Mandy got in lieu of Alimony. In exchange Mandy had to stop spread the slander. She had to recant her story. She agreed. Integrity meant nothing to a woman like her.

I was just relieved. My family started talking to me again. We could all move on with our lives.

RECONCILIATION

CALL

Dr Blues picked up her phone but after rethinking it, she put it face down again. Sighing, she turned the modern, black leather chair around to face the window view. She loved the fact she could swivel around with the new chair. When it first arrived, the delivery men took their time putting it together while she waited impatiently. Finally left alone with the chair, she sat in it and spun herself around a few times before resuming normal adult behaviour. Smiling at the thought of it, Dr Blues stood up and walked over to the tea table, pouring hot water into a cup and teapot to clean them. As she set about cleaning other utensils used in the process of making tea, Dr Wong, walked in without knocking.

"Nu er, there is a patient in the ER needing a doctor who can speak English," said Dr Wong to his daughter, who was spooning out some dried tea leaves into a turquoise green teapot.

"Baba, there is a team of doctors undergoing English training to handle patients who speak English," she replied while setting the temperature on the sophisticated water kettle. Eighty degree celcius, the perfect temperature for green tea.

"Yes, dear but two of them are assisting another doctor in an operation theatre, two are with in-house patients, and the remaining one is on a personal day."

"Nu er, we still need someone to attend to this patient."

Pressing on the on/off button of the electric kettle, Dr Blues turned to the ex-director and nodded. Walking towards him, she reached to grab her white doctor's coat hanging on the clothes rack by the door. Dr Blues pulled the door close behind her as her father called the elevator.

"Baba, have you spoken to her?" Dr Blues inquired as she buttoned up her doctor's coat, patting her hidden pocket, making sure her phone is there.

"Yes, dear. She insisted on a female doctor, though."

MY HUMBLE BEGINNINGS

"The problem is our English team consists of too many male doctors. We need to hire a few more female doctors who at least have some command of spoken English."

"We can choose to train some female doctors."

"When I started the programme Baba, they were unwilling to participate. I have tried offering monetary rewards for their time and effort but to no avail."

"I see. Well, let's deal with this patient first and then hold a meeting with the board to discuss this matter. Remember, even though you are a director, you will still need the majority of the board to back you up on your decision."

Smiling up to the grey-haired man beside her, Dr Blues said, "Baba, I am glad you stayed on as a doctor. If I were to run this place myself, I think I would do it the American way and irk the board."

"Well, that's what fathers are for, nu er, to watch over their children no matter how old they are."

The elevator dinged and the doors opened to the ER department.

"Doctor, after you." ushered Dr Wong. Nodding and smiling at her father's work façade, Dr Blues stepped out ahead of her father, greeting the head nurse who was waiting for her, chart in hand. As they conversed, Dr Blues discovered the patient repudiated being touched by male doctors. As they approached the drawn curtains, Dr Blues heard an undertone of words in a strange language. She motioning for her father to stay back just as she ventured closer to the curtain and called out.

"Hello, Miss. Are you comfortable for me to come in and examine you?"

POVERTY OF THE MIND

"Are you a doctor?"

"Yes, I am."

"Please come in."

Pushing the curtains aside, Dr Blues came to face an apprehensive woman covered from head to toe in a modern abaya. A black hijab adorned with rose patterns covered her hair, falling past her chest.

"Will you be comfortable with me touching you? I will need to do some basic checks."

"As long as it's no male doctor or nurse, I am okay." Respecting her wishes, I called out to a female orderly I remember trailing the head nurse when she greeted me. Together, they helped Nur, the patient, to sit up in bed.

After doing the routine check, Dr Blues inquired why she checked herself into the ER while Nur adjusted her hijab.

Her worry lines deepened. "Doctor, I have been bleeding for nearly two weeks. The flow is constantly heavy and today, I fainted while working."

"Has this happened before?"

"No, doctor. I am prone to getting cramps when it's that time, but the bleeding never goes more than six days. This time its too long."

"I would like to do a scan, Nur. Have a better look at what's going on inside, is that okay? Listening to her explain more about her menstruation cycle, Dr Blues asked the nurse to prepare the ultrasound machine and made a call to Doctor Li, the resident gynaecologist.

MY HUMBLE BEGINNINGS

Dr Li, a senior doctor, arrived just as Nur was wheeled out of her room for her scan. Dr Blues conversed softly with Dr Li about the patient's situation and inability to speak Chinese, adding that once the ultrasound is done, Dr Li should inform her.

Dr Li, nodded, "Wǒ hěn yíhàn yǒu shíhòu bù huì shuō yīngyǔ."

Dr Blues touched Dr Li's elbow slightly, "Dàjiě, méiguānxì. Wǒ kěyǐ bāngmáng. Big sister, don't worry. I will do my best to help. Also, this is no longer my job scope. I look forward to your observations."

"Doctor, you are a trained gynecologist. You can order a test anytime for any patient. I am at your back and call."

"No, dàjiě. This is your department. I have overstepped and I apologize. I do hope you can continue to guide me as I am still new."

"Always modest! I am still amazed how you handle patients like her. Maybe I am old fashioned, but I can't help entertaining mixed feelings about treating her."

"Dàjiě, we are doctors."

"You are right. My bad. Okay, let me go ahead and handle the patient."

"Xie xie ni, dàjiě."

Dr Wong stood at the nurses' counter, his gaze following the new director from the moment she stepped out of the patient's room with Dr Li. He noted how his once tactless protégé known for treading on toes was now able to deal with the patients' complaints while defusing potential strife. Seeing how she handled today's challenge without overstepping Dr Li's authority filled him with pride. He struggled to contain himself as she thanked Dr Li and made her way over to him.

POVERTY OF THE MIND

Noticing a strange look on her father's face, Dr Blues tilted her head questioningly. Smiling, Dr Wong shook his head from side to side and beckoned her over. He turned as she approached him and took his elbow, guiding him back to the elevator.

"Baba, why are you smiling?"

"Well, I am pleased."

"At my work?"

"More so at the way you handled the situation. Having a young director overstep a doctor's seniority is considered an offence in our culture, even when the director has the right to do so. But you showed sufficient respect without you exceeding your boundaries as a director" He praised.

"Well, I have a good teacher," she complimented, giving his arm a slight squeeze.

"Now, let's go back and have that tea." Dr. Wong suggested.

Thirty minutes later, seated around the tea table, Dr Wong picked up the porcelain teacup with a plum blossom, hand-painted image and took a whiff of the tea.

"Hm, wūlóngchá." Another whiff was followed by a sip. "From Wu Yi Mountain?" he asked looking at Dr Blues. She smiled.

"As always, Baba. You know your tea," she said with a smile, pouring herself a cup.

Dr Wong drained his cup and placed it on the rosewood table top.

"Nu er, the good tea requires a good discussion topic."

MY HUMBLE BEGINNINGS

Nodding, Dr Blues picked up her narcissus, hand-painted cup and sipped.

'How about you and Mama?'

"Well, we are working on it but I will be honest. I am more concerned about you."

"'Baba…" came a tired voice from Dr Blues, knowing well where this was heading."

"I know you don't want me pushing it, but we are worried."

"Worried enough to take matters into your own hands and invite him to the Crown Plaza."

"Nu er, tell me you do not miss him. Tell me you aren't misleading Dr Chen."

A stubborn look took over Dr Blues face as she gritted her teeth, thinning her lips.

"Don't be so hard on yourself." Her father warned.

"Baba, you didn't like him and even attempted to stop me from marrying him by trying to send me back to America!" burst Dr Blues.

"You told me you would disown your only daughter should she choose to go down that path. To make matters worse, he has a daughter with some other woman! How can I be with a man like that? I want kids of my own, not raising another woman's child."

Sighing, "Yes, I did say that and I understand, he has baggage now. Daughter, when you brought him home, I hated him on sight. I even arranged a private meeting with Wine weeks after meeting him and ask him to leave you, telling him I would give him enough money to buy properties in Ghana."

Stunned at this sudden revelation, Dr Blues stared at her father as he continued, "I even offered to set him up as a shareholder for life, if he would leave you.

"And you guessed right. He turned me down. He turned it all down, saying he would do his best to make you a happy woman and would achieve success through his own sweat and blood. That day, dear, despite my intense dislike for Wine, I couldn't help but see a younger version of myself in him and I grew to respect him."

"Baba…" she said softly as tears began to pool in her eyes.

Dr Wong went on, "I knew then he loved you. He still does, and so do you. But you are stubborn daughter. Stubbornness you inherited from me. I wish I had passed on a better gene, like my handsome looks." He joked, drawing a laugh from Dr Blues.

"You are right, Baba. I am trying to forget him. And I do still want to be with him. Why am I so torn up inside?"

"Because loving someone is never meant to be easy, baobei," replied Dr Wong as he pulled his daughter into his arms, letting her cry quietly into his shoulder. After some time, as her sobbing died down, he asked, "Are you going to try mending the fences?"

"Would you be okay if I did that?"

"Well, in all honesty, it will be hard to uphold your current position. But if the heart wants what it wants, the brain can't stop it."

Laughing, Dr Blues asked if he used this line on her romantic mother.

Winking, Dr Wong replied, "And she loved it."

"I think I will make that call now, Baba," Dr Blues said as she stood up, walked over to her coat and pulled out her phone.

NEW DIRECTOR

Doctor Blues looked around the room she would soon acquire. The rectangular-shaped room located on the corner of the 17th floor faced one of the noisiest highways in Guangzhou. The newly constructed highways and walkways were part of the rapid development programme the Chinese government had pledged to undergo that year.

Standing up, she walked over to one of the many floor-length windows and looked out to the quiet day. At 4 pm, barely any cars were on the road. Dark clouds drew closer to town as sunlight strained to shine through them. *Calm before the storm*, thought Dr Blues as she followed one of the sun's glints off the opposite building. A muted cough sounded from behind a closed door leading to the director's bedroom drawing her attention. Returning to her seat at one of the four rosewood inlaid mother of pearl stools, she waited patiently for the director to emerge.

Director Wong came out of his private quarters to see one of his best doctors seated at the rosewood tea table. He stood for a minute admiring the young lady dressed in a haute culture, white, sleeveless knee-length dress, paired with Louis Vuitton open-toed, black suede heels. Her long, powder blue coat was casually thrown over the black sofa at the opposite end of the room. A wisp of hair straying from the clip holding them in place framed her heart-shaped face, giving her an air of innocence. Clearly caught up in her thoughts, he snuck up behind her, and stood quietly watching her. She pondered a trick she used to play on him as a child every time she visited him in this very hospital.

After some time, Dr Shi Wei turned around, drawn by the silence, and nearly jumped out of her seat to when she discovered a grinning man behind her.

"Baba! Xia le wo!" Exclaimed Shi Wei, lovingly smacking her father on his arm as he burst out in a roaring laughter.

"Nu er! Zhe shi ni ying de de!"

Pretending to pout at her father, Shi Wei crossed her arms, "Zhe yang, wo bu xing he ni yi qi he cha !"

"Now, now, you know I was just kidding, Shi Wei."

"'Baba, my heart leapt so high it nearly hit the ceiling!"

"Ahhh… Exactly like how you used to scare me! Hiding behind the door, under my desk, behind the examination curtain. Daughter, you were a naughty little one! I miss my cheeky one."

"Baba, I can't be doing that anymore. Especially now."

"Wo zhi dao. Dan shi. I can't help it but miss my little one. Sending you away to America was wrong on my part."

"Please don't say that baba. Had I stayed, I may not have pursued medicine and studied at your alma mater."

"Dui dui. But I lost out on your childhood. Sending you over at that age was a huge sacrifice though you have turned into a gorgeous woman and competent physician."

"Baba, you and Mama have raised me well. Your sacrifices are worth it. We still have time to make up for our relationship especially now. I'm home for good."

MY HUMBLE BEGINNINGS

"And take over as director of (hospital name)."

Ushering her toward the director's chair, Shi Wei walked over and placed her hand on the armrest of the majestic oriental chair. *Fit for a King or leader*, she thought, *and hopefully me.* Trailing her fingers over the intricate, dragon-carved, lacquer-covered rosewood chair, inlaid with mother of pearl and flecks of gold motive on the seat and back, Shi Wei couldn't help but admire her father's determination in acquiring the chair. Originating from the Song Dynasty, the chair was said to belong to a valued advisor close to the king.

Looking over to Baba for approval, Shi Wei eased into the chair, noting its broad seat fixed with a cushion-like covering. Baba sat down in one of the two modern chairs opposite the large work desk.

"Shi Wei, I have told you how this chair came to be mine. Now, I am happy to give it to my only child."

"Baba. I am honoured but this is yours."

Holding up a hand to silence her protest he said, "Daughter, for you are precious. This is a gift you can't say no to."

With a twinkle in her eyes she replied, "Just like the new car you bought for me when I was elected last week?"

He Smiled at the thought of delight on her face when she saw the yellow Volkswagen, "Yes, just like that."

Shi Wei walked over to her father and hugged him from the back.

"Baba, there is no luckier daughter than me."

Kissing him on his head, Shi Wei suggested lunch at one of his favourite Hakka restaurants.

POVERTY OF THE MIND

As they disembarked the metro at Gangding, Shi Wei linked arm with her father's and walked into the adjoining mall. He spotted a beautiful lily-shaped broach in muted tones. Showing it to Shi Wei, he wondered if his wife would like it.

Shi Wei smiled. Strained from living apart for nearly 20 years, her parents were trying to mend things.

Being traditional, they did not believe in divorce. They were surprised and disappointed when she filed for a divorce.

Director Wong, an immigrant from Fujian, had a strong love for Kejia, or Hakka cuisine. Hakka cuisine originated from southeast China and the demand for perfection in the food texture made it popular in a Cantonese foodie city. Unlike Cantonese cooking, incorporating almost all edible meats, concentrate on steaming and stir frying. The food is spiced sufficiently without overwhelming the flavour of the primary ingredients. Hakka cooking is heavily influenced by the use of preserved meats. Often served as stewed, braised, and roasted meats, Hakka cuisine is best described as a simple but tasty dish. The skills in cooking Hakka dishes lies in the ability to cook the meat thoroughly without hardening it, bringing out the umami taste of the meat. Preserved vegetables are often used in Hakka dishes when steaming minced pork and salted vegetables in braised pork dishes. Besides meat, Hakka dishes are known for their Yong Tau Foo, which is flavoured ground pork or fish paste stuffed in vegetables like ladies' fingers, aubergines, green chillies, mushrooms, fried tofu, and more. Yong Tau Foo is eaten in numerous ways, most popularly, served dry with a sauce or served as a soup dish.

"Baba, Mummy will be waiting for us at the restaurant."

"Since she returned from her girls-only trip to Cambodia three days ago, I haven't seen her."

"Have you been staying in the office, Baba?"

MY HUMBLE BEGINNINGS

"Yes. Late nights. Need to arrange a smooth transition. Then I can go to the Maldives with Mummy."

"Second honeymoon?" I teased.

"Don't be naughty. It's just a holiday" chastised Director Wong.

Laughing at his reddening cheeks she acquiesced.

"Okay, Baba. Calm down. It's the American in me."

"Haiya, You must remember, the American way won't work with the doctors. It is a culture too open. You have to relearn the tricks of the Chinese trade daughter. We never speak directly on matters. Learn to play the game well and you will go climb up fast.'

"Yes, Baba. I know I lack the skills. I am working on it. That's why I need to spend more time with you. Learning this and being your daughter again," she said, squeezing her father's hand as they approached the restaurant. "Let's concentrate on lunch and us."

"Tonight we talk about your speech, key i ma ?"

"Okay, Baba," she agreed as a waitress walked up to them.

The speaker on the elevated stage of the conference centre in the Crown Plaza spoke of Shi Wei's credentials. Her nerves gave way to pacing backstage.

Shi Wei went through the speech she had penned with her father then typed up late last night again. For one, the whole speech will be in Chinese, a language that still seemed foreign to her.

Outgoing Director Wong walked up to her.

"Are you ready, daughter?"

"Baba, what if I mispronounce a work?"

"Don't worry, daughter. We all face this. Just give it your best."

Pushing her hair off her shoulder, Shi Wei turned to face the stairs leading up to the podium just as the speaker announced her name. A thunderous applause followed. She saw Director Wong raising a fist into the air, saying "Jia You!" – Good Luck – as she climbed the stairs.

"… I pledge to give my best and more just like the director before me. Together, hand in hand, we shall propel the hospital greater heights!"

Bowing to the crowd, Shi Wei straighten her back as another thunderous applause broke through the banquet. At the end of the red carpeted staircase, Shi Wei was guided by one of the emcees to the entrance of the hall.

There, a reporter and cameraman bearing the CCTV work tags approached Shi Wei as the camera focused on her.

"Director Shi Wei, congratulations on your new post."

"Thank you, Miss Tan. I honestly did nothing to deserve this promotion."

"You are too modest! Since your return five years ago, the medical community has closely followed your research in the field of ovarian cancer, making startling discoveries."

"Which are still being tested, Miss Tan."

"True, yet the breakthrough, if successful, will save millions of women around the world."

"Therefore, patience is of essence here."

MY HUMBLE BEGINNINGS

"Director, in your speech you mentioned establishing an English speaking team of experts to assist the increasing number of wai guo ren influxing Guangzhou. What influenced your decision?

"Guangzhou is the heart of production in China, with over seventy percent of factories churning out goods which are then bought by foreigners and sent back home. Some of these foreigners, drawn by the advantages China has to offer, have decided to set up shop here."

"True."

"And as we all realize, people get sick over time. I once walked into the examination room and gathered through a conversation with a foreigner, the difficulty of finding a doctor who understood enough English for her to explain her ailments. This led to the establishment of a team of medical experts with sufficient English to assist the ever-growing foreign population."

"In addition, we also heard of your intent to set up a section of the hospital dedicated to foreign mothers."

"Yes. Our gynaecologists tend to mix Traditional Chinese Medicine, or TCM, with Western Medication, WM. Our local Chinese doctors have wondrously combined both medications, coming up with a wide range of remedies. However, foreigners new to our TCM, find it difficult to embrace any prescription with this mix. Therefore, a department set up with English-speaking staff can help overcome foreigners' anxiety. We can better meet their demands as well, providing them with the medical care that meets their standards.

"Statistics have shown an increased number of foreign women needing natal care but the lack of access to good pre and postnatal care. This has deterred foreign mothers from giving birth in China."

The giggling of a child behind her drew her attention away from the recorder angled in front of her. Turning around, she saw her father carrying a young, dark curly-haired girl in his arms. A wave of emotion hit Dr Blues when she chanced upon the tall, bald man standing next to her father.

"I see. And you are needed again. Xie Xie ni, Director Shi Wei and congratulations again!" While the reporter wrapped up the interview, walking towards the elevator with her cameraman, Shi Wei stood rooted to the ground, daring not to face the trio behind her. She gulped a few times before turning to face them, taking in the encouraging smile from her father.

"Wine," she whispered.

I smiled.

CAN IT WORK

The three of us sat at a table in the Crown Plaza's restaurant. Sasha, wearing a pink cheongsam, stood on the red cushioned chair next to me, playing with the yellow sash tied to the back of the chair which she pulled towards her. I kept a watchful eye on her and another on Shi Wei who sat opposite us, twirling a toothpick, with a blank look in her eyes.

'Dr Blues?' I ventured gently using a nickname I gave her.

Shi Wei refused to respond to this. Determined not to look at me, she asked, "Why are you here, Wine?"

"Believe it or not, I got a call from your old man late last night. During our catch-up, he learned about Sasha. He mentioned your investiture and insisted I bring her along."

Sipping from her glass, Shi Wei watched Sasha. Silence descended between us. With only the bustle of the busy restaurant to fill the silence and Sasha singing a song only she knew the words to, Shi

Wei questioned, "Why did my father invite you?" I heard her say in a soft voice.

I did not venture an answer immediately, knowing when she uses that tone, she was thinking aloud. She gave herself a small shake and raised her hand to massage one temple, "Maybe he knew something you didn't dare to dwell on, Dr Blues."

Her agitation was apparent when the toothpick she was twirling snapped. Picking up on my voice, Sasha turned to face me.

"Blue?" she questioned me. "Abeoji, I like blue! Blueberries!"

Smiling at my little cherub of joy, I opened my mouth to respond when Shi Wei's asked, "She is already speaking English?" A look of surprise and disbelief was apparent on her face as she stared at Sasha who was pointing and identifying the colours she saw on her bowl and plate.

"Yes. She learns very fast." I said, looking down at Sasha who was tugging on my sleeve. "Purple, dear."

"Pulple!" she repeated, still having problems pronouncing 'r.'

"Sasha, come look at the menu with abeoji."

Sasha stood up and climbed onto my lap from her chair. She sat down comfortably on one thigh as I turned the menu to the children's section. "Abeoji, can I have blueberries?"

"I don't think they have those on the menu, baby girl."

"Blue cake, please?" said Sasha, looking up pleadingly at me.

I chortled down at her huge brown eyes. "Maybe next time, dear."

POVERTY OF THE MIND

I kissed her on the back of her head as she pouted at my response. Dumping the huge menu on the table, Sasha ran a finger down the list.

"She is mimicking her father, I see," said Shi Wei, now tapping the edge of her menu with the broken toothpick.

"She even likes the same food as I do." I said as I waved a passing waitress over and ordered my favourite plate of steamed broccoli with soy sauce and sliced chilli on the side.

"I want chao fan!" announced Sasha pointing at a picture of fried noodles.

"Like how abeoji likes them?"

"Yes, please!" Shi Wei, smiled at Sasha's boundless enthusiasm as she bounced up and down on my lap while I placed a few more orders.

"She is really adorable, Wine."

"She is not what I expected in a child and to know she is mine, fills me up with joy."

Taking a closer look at Wine, Shi Wei noted the subtle changes in the man she once loved. He used to be awkward among children even when he came to the hospital looking for her. Some children he approached would cry. *But that could be because of a preordained fear towards people of different skin colour,* she thought. Yet now he handles his 4-year-old daughter by himself.

"Does she have an ayi?"

"More like a nanny and she lives in the next building block to us."

"She must be from quite a wealthy family."

MY HUMBLE BEGINNINGS

Her comment was expected as the area I lived in was virtually dominated by high-income earners. This being my first property, I made sure I found the perfect abode to suit my lifestyle and to bring a wife home, a wife who unfortunately left me.

"Wine, what happened to us?"

"Do you really want me to answer that dear?"

Sighing, Shi Wei reached for the cup of red date tea and took a sip.

"I really miss us, Wine."

"And I have missed you, Dr Blues. My life is filled with work and now Sasha, but the part where I need a companion, my life partner, is like a black hole, sucking away at life, leaving me feeling hollow."

As I said this, I saw tears pool in her eyes, looking away as she collected her composure. I gave Sasha a tweak on her button nose and played, Itsy bitsy spider with my fingers running up and down her arms drawing laughter.

"Wine, what you hope to gain from meeting me today?" questioned Shi Wei just as the waitress came to our table and laid it with Sasha's orders. In addition to her orders, three more dishes graced our table: dried chilli cabbage drenched with vinegar, braised meat stewed in rice wine, and dark soy sauce paired with steamed buns that Shi Wei loved.

She stared at the order, "You still remember. Oh, Wine." She burst into tears, scrunching the napkin to her face.

Sasha was reaching for the fried rice when Shi Wei started crying. She climbed down her chair, ran halfway round the table, and gave Dr Blues a hug which she returned albeit to her surprise. Gobsmacked to see the two women closest to my heart together, I smiled knowing the love was still there and perhaps that love could venture onto a path I had been praying for.

I stood up, walked over to the duo as I heard Sasha telling Dr Blues how I would comfort her with her favourite teddy bear and a good cuddle in bed when she cries at night for her mother.

Wiping her tears on the napkin, Dr Blues inquired, "Do you still miss your mother?"

"I miss eomma. But abeoji and Anne take good care of me. I am happy," said the apple of my eye.

I gave Dr Blues's shoulders a gentle squeeze and turned to pick up my little angel. Carrying her back to her chair, Dr Blues sniffed discretely and asked me, "What is life like for you now that you are raising Sasha?"

I settled Sasha down into her chair, placing some fried rice and broccoli onto her bowl to which Sasha tutted out "No no no. Plate abeoji." In southern Chinese culture, it is considered rude to eat from the plate because is generally used to keep unwanted leftovers. Sasha's Korean mother taught her to eat from one, hoping to integrate her into the western culture. To date, Sasha was still uncomfortable with using chopsticks, though she doesn't mind being fed with them.

"It is an uphill battle" I said, as I wiped a grain of rice lingering on Sasha's chin.

"Abeoji? Water, please." said Sasha, pointing at the white plastic cup I had placed out of her reach.

"There is only tea here, baby girl."

"Okay," she said as I pass on the glass of lukewarm tea to her.

MY HUMBLE BEGINNINGS

"Why does she call you abo… errr… that?"

"Abeoji "means father in Korean."

"Does she still speak Korean?"

"Yes, she does when she speaks to her mother on the phone. And she is learning Putong Hua in Kindie.'

"Incredible. She managed to pick up this much English in less than a year. I must say it's because she has no other means to communicate with me as my Korean is atrocious. So, English it is, for us."

For the next few minutes, we sat in silence as we enjoyed our meal. Sharing Sasha's fried rice, a hand suddenly emerged into my line of sight, placing two slices of braised meat on my pile of fried rice. I looked up to Dr Blues' shy smile. I bit into the tender meat, graciously accepting this as an opportunity to rekindle our once torrid love affair.

AUTUMN 2010

SASHA

REUNION

Sakura flicked her hair back, and I had to swallow down my thirst. She was delicious. Motherhood had not changed her figure one bit. I looked at Sasha and saw nothing of myself or my family in her.

"Sasha is a quiet, well-behaved kid. As long as you stick to her routine, she can be managed," Sakura instructed.

"I keep things neat at home. She's Montessori trained as a result. It would be best if you stuck to it."

Sasha was shy and hung back behind Sakura. There was no Nanny with them, as was the usual custom with families of her calibre. I nodded gravely at Sakura, to show that I was listening. She was an old hookup, part of my past life, and nothing more though I still felt the chemistry between us.

"Wine, Sasha is easy to look after."

She slid a folder across the kitchen countertop to me. "This contains everything you need to know."

I nodded again and flicked through it. It contained schedules, likes and dislikes, as well as a list of recommended reading. It was a comprehensive manual for raising Sasha.

"I've taken the liberty of emailing a soft copy to your personal email and your assistant Nalia, who arranged for the paternity test."

Sasha was attracted by a plate of practice cookies I had made while waiting for them. She took a step forward and asked for one in Korean. I looked to Sakura for confirmation, and she nodded.

She spoke to Sasha lovingly in Korean, rubbing the child's back in affection. They were chocolate. Sasha took a bite and was occupied with chewing thoughtfully. There was flour and mixing bowls scattered across the counter. They had arrived before I could clean up. Long years in the service industry meant I made a habit of neatness even when slacking off on cleaning up immediately. The usual rule was to clean as you go.

What Sakura had not told me, but I had picked up on, was that Sasha, whom I mentally dubbed "The Pixie" was as picky as an aunt with ten rmb to spend at the market about the people she kept company with.

I think I had won her over with chocolate chip cookies.

"Wine, please remember that she'll need her shots, the vaccination schedule is right here. Don't forget! I'll be back for her, do look after her for me until I can" she told me.

I nodded absently, feeling like one of those bobble-headed dolls. My attention instead was on the child.

Sasha declared "Good, not strawberry!"

Sakura and I beamed at Sasha.

"I think I can handle it Sakura," I told her.

She nodded and said, "It shouldn't be too hard. My lawyers' number is included in the email, and if you need anything, you can call them. I've got a childcare expert on hand."

She slid a couple more business cards to me and tucked them into the folder. "Every possible contingency has been planned for and taken care of." She straightened and picked up her Birkin bag. "I've got an appointment for a wedding dress fitting in an hour, I'll be back in the evening to collect her." As she was leaving she said, "Please don't encourage her to make a mess. I've worked too hard to instill neat habits and tidiness into my daughter."

The child in question was sitting daintily on a barstool, slowly working her way through the plate of chocolate chip cookies as the front door shut behind Sakura, leaving us both alone.

CUPCAKES AND CHERRY BLOSSOMS

Disheartened, I made my way to my friend Bill's bar, thinking to drink away my worry. Sitting on the barstool of his bar, I recalled Bill sharing bonding ideas with me after hearing my distressing tale. I looked at him in a new light.

POVERTY OF THE MIND

"You do know how to win a girl's heart, mate?" I joked. Truth be told, there was some truth to what Bill said. I decided to observe Sasha for a few days before trying some ideas I once used when I was forced to teach in China.

The next day, I noticed Sasha loveed tinkering in the kitchen. Sakura disliked being hampered in the kitchen, often shooing Sasha off to play in her room with her huge dollhouse. Thankful for the years living abroad and fending for myself, I knew I find my way well enough in the kitchen without creating a disaster.

As I walked to the door, I called out to my ladies about my trip to the mall after putting together a list to make banana cakes, an act that required little thinking on my part, having baked it often enough. Bubbling with excitement, I hopped in a local green and yellow cab to the nearest mall to do something I usually detested: shopping.

Stepping back from the kitchen counter to look at my amateurish display of ingredients, I nearly lost my balance at the step stool I kept behind me. Setting the stool back up, I looked again at the array, making sure nothing was amiss. Then, I walked into the sitting room, sat opposite Sasha, and asked her if she'd like to eat cake.

Turning her head in my direction, the little one nodded.

"How about we bake that cake?" I asked. Uncertainty crossed her face, clearly not quite comprehending. I called out to Sakura, hoping for her assistance but I could get the message across. Coming out of the room she shared with Sasha, which would later become Sasha's room, Sakura looked at me with raised eyebrows. As I quickly explained my plan to win Sasha's trust, Sakura's eyebrows raised higher until they merged with her fringe. A smile slowly lit up her face.

"I am impressed, Wine. It seems like you are really making an effort here."

MY HUMBLE BEGINNINGS

"I want to be closer to my child, and am willing to go the extra mile for that," I said quietly. I may not have been in her life for the past four years, but I intend to be there for her from now on."

Absorbing everything I said, Sakura slowly nodded, 'I'm glad to hear that, Wine. She needs a father figure and who better to be that if not you?" With that, she turned to Sasha, excitedly conversing with her. I could see her eyes fill with joy mixed with a kind of cautiousness.

My heart rate elevated. I quenched my nerves by following Sakura who was now leading Sasha into the kitchen. Excitement again took over her little body. Testing the waters, I tentatively extended my hand out for hers to guide her to the mini apron I bought just for her.

Allowing me to put the apron over her head and tie it up, was like a victory lap! I took her over to the stool I bought for her. Stepping up, she began to inspect the contents on the counter before her, querying her mother over them.

Stepping away from us, Sakura explained to Sasha and I that she would not be assisting in the cooking. With slightly trembling hands, I took Sasha's small hand in mine. When she didn't pull away I felt another leap of faith.

I taught her how to measure out the flour and allowed her to have a hand with the sugar. Breaking a banana into pieces, I showed her how to mash the overripe bananas. In a separate bowl, we added baking soda, brown sugar, and just the perfect amount of cinnamon powder to enhance the flavour of the cake. Sasha helped me break two eggs and pour the banana into the mixing bowl. With a spatula in each of our hands, we mixed the batter until we decided it was perfect, giggling at the splattered batter. We laughed even louder when we heard Sakura tutting at the mess we were making. Finally, we poured the batter into the heart-shaped baking tray and into the oven.

POVERTY OF THE MIND

Staring at the once spotless kitchen, now in disarray, Sakura began to tidy up. Little Sasha ran over to her mother, rapidly asserting her desire to help clean. She urged Sakura to relax in the living room, before tugging at my arm. In awe at her changes in demure, I worked together with this petite princess of mine to slowly return the kitchen to its former glory.

As we took nearly all evening to bake, the little one was famished. Gobbling her dinner, Sasha insisted that tthe three of us have the banana cake for dessert. Laughing, I agreed.

After clearing the table, I laid out the plates for desserts, setting the cake in the middle of our four-seater dinner table.

"Sasha, would you like to cut the cake for eomma and abeoji?" I asked Sasha who was standing on her chair, staring intently at the cake.

"Yes!"

After placing her hands over the plastic knife, I wrapped one hand over hers and assisted in cutting and serving the cake first to her mother, then me, and finally her.

"Eomma feels special today, Sasha."

"Why Eomma?" asked Sasha.

"Because Eomma got the chance to eat a cake made by Sasha and her father. Do you think this cake will taste good?"

"Yes!" shrieked little Sasha excitedly.

"Do you know what's even better, Sasha?" I asked as she began to dig into her cake.

MY HUMBLE BEGINNINGS

"What, abeoji?" asked Sasha.

"Having some ice cream with the cake,: I said.

Ice cream was her favourite dessert.

"Looking at me Sasha asked, "Ice cream and cake for Sasha? Can I?"

I looked towards Sakura who nodded her consent to have the ice cream added. With that, I put a generous dollop of chocolate chip ice cream on our cakes.

Unable to contain her curiosity, Sasha dug her spoon into the cake, dipping it into the quickly melting ice cream and into her mouth. I watched a look of surprise and pleasure wash over her face. Looking to her mother, Sasha urged her to do the same.

Sakura took a similar generous bite and the surprise in her eyes told me enough. Together, the three of us did away with the whole banana cake.

As she licked her spoon clean, Sasha turned to ask me if we could bake another cake tomorrow. Delighted, I suggested that we make something every weekend.

Ever since the first baking session, Sasha began to look forward to our weekend cooking sessions and over time, my presence. We made little trips out together without Sakura, going to the playground and sometimes for our secret ice cream moments. The clincher was when Sasha one day asked for me to read her a bedtime story from the book we purchased earlier that day. This routine, usually carried out by her mother, slowly became my routine. I often found myself wishing for the day to end, just to spend time with Sasha. Bonding with her, became my number one priority.

DESPERATION

POVERTY OF THE MIND

I dialled Sakura's number and prayed that she would pick up.

"Wine, this isn't a good time," Sakura hissed. I could hear the chatter and buzz of a crowd.

"She needs her mother! Not me!" I burst out in frustration I scrubbed my hands through my hair. I needed to get a shave yet again.

Silence reigned in the apartment, save for muffled sobs behind a locked door.

"Wine!" Sakura snapped, "Right now, you're all she has!"

"I didn't ask for this!" I snapped right back.

"Did I sleep with a coward, or was the Wine back then just doing a job?"

"Sakura," I hissed. I had to bite back words that no man should say to a lady. "This is not helping. I am neither a coward nor a liar."

"Wine," Sakura said. I could hear the exasperation in her voice. "No parent signs up for this, we're all improvising and hoping our children turn out right."

"I need help now, not vague advice." I bit back "She is your daughter. You should have gotten an abortion. This was a mistake I cannot handle her."

"Wine listen." Sakura sounded concerned. "Look, I know it's hard, but she's your mistake too. If you feel that strongly about it, all you have to do is look after her for a few years until she's of school age. My family has discovered Sasha's existence. I have no choice."

"I don't know what else to do. You need to talk to her."

"Wine I can't. The child psychologist said that the best break is a clean break."

Silence reigned on both ends of the phone. I think she felt defeated too. I can't imagine any mother sending her child away to be raised by strangers, without grief and heartbreak.

"I nearly did have an abortion. Emily helped me."

"Why didn't you?" I felt compelled to ask.

"I couldn't kill any child of mine, even one who should never have existed. I wanted to see what she would be like with my genes and yours. Peter and I never did manage to have children."

I scrubbed my hands through my hair. That was a hell of a backhanded compliment. "I'm not equipped to handle Sasha," I told her flatly, "I'm no parent."

"If you feel that strongly about it, you only have to look after her until she's of boarding school age in a few years. My family has secured a placement in a good school in Britain. She'll be well looked after there."

"I see," was all I could manage. "I still need help now. You know your daughter, so far has managed to chase away every person I've hired to watch her, even with me next door."

Sakura chuckled. "Sasha is usually very well-behaved, until she's not."

"I've never seen her well-behaved," I replied in droll tones.

"There must be something in her environment she doesn't like or something that you're doing. I'll text you a number to an international agency. They are very discreet and cater to families like mine. My lawyers will get in touch with you should you need help."

"With what?" I asked stupidly. I blamed the exhaustion. I needed a week's vacation and a willing partner. I stretched and idly mused when was the last was time that I got any. It was just before Sasha burst into my life.

"Anything Sasha needs, you can send the bill to my lawyers. It'll be taken care of."

"Oh. I do-" I began to demur. I was not one to take a handout.

"Wine, don't turn it down. Emily told me that you've done well for yourself, but you have no idea how expensive raising a child can get."

I shut up. It was true. "Please, just call her. I can't take the temper tantrums anymore. Every doctor I've consulted says that it'll damage her psyche if this continues."

"I can't make promises Wine. I rather that she settle in as soon as possible. You can do it Wine. Emily told me your story. You're an honourable man, that's why I sent her to you. I do not have a choice. We don't make the world we live in."

From halfway across the globe, and through the years, I was strongly reminded of how fragile a creature the confident Sakura was underneath the facade. That still had not changed.

"I understand Sakura" I told her.

"Please don't call me again. Contact my lawyers, you have their number," she told me. "Don't make it harder on me that it already is." With that, Sakura hung up.

I tried calling again, but the number was disconnected.

I sat down on the glitter covered couch. Sasha had no one, only me to look out for her. If I abandoned her, who would she have? Sakura

MY HUMBLE BEGINNINGS

could not care for her, Sasha was her secret shame. She did not tell me this, but I knew from paying attention to the papers. Her divorce from her husband wasn't secret, it was announced in the newspapers. Her impending re-marriage to another equally wealthy and distinguished tycoon garnered attention too. Sakura was reported as "single and childless." Sasha did not exist.

I got up and went to try to pry my daughter out of her room. When I cracked the door open, there was no sign of her. The room was wrecked. It was amazing how much force a grieving toddler was capable of. The pillows were thrown across the room and the heavy chair I kept in there was upended. One leg was chipped and another wrenched loose.

"Sasha" I called out carefully. "I have barley tea and ice cream. Do you want some?"

There was sniffle from under the bed. I peeked down and there she was, having wedged herself up against the wall with some pillows she brought with her. There was a stream of incomprehensible Korean that needed no translation. I got the message and left the room.

I baited the kitchen table with two bowls of ice cream. All children love sweets. I had discovered this early on. Sakura told me that Sasha did not and only ate healthy treats.

I made as much noise as possible when I sat down to eat. I disliked sweets and gained no pleasure from them. Desperate times called for desperate measures.

"Sasha, the ice cream is melting. I'll have to eat it all," I called out theatrically. For good measure, I clinked the spoons on the bowls.

I could feel a wild animal's interest locking in on the ice cream. A small hand tugged at my pants leg. "What kind?" Sasha asked grumpily. She looked like a pixie with her upturned nose and Asian features albeit tear stained and grubby.

"Chocolate." Children love chocolate. Women too judging by the reactions I got in the past. I squinted at the child. Would this work?

"I don't like chocolate. I want strawberry." The imperiousness of women at every age never changed.

"Alright child. Come sit up here." I helped her up into her booster seat, "And wipe your face with this," and handed her a wet wipe.

As soon as I set the strawberry ice cream in front of her, Sasha shovelled it into her mouth like she was starving.

"Sasha," I asked, "What's wrong?"

"I hate you." Sasha declared in clear unaccented English. "Where's Omma?" she asked.

I mentally smacked myself on the forehead. Sasha knew how to speak English, she had been pretending that she only spoke Korean.

"I'm sorry that you hate me Sasha, but I'm here to look after you. Omma is not here."

"You hit me. You are not nice," she stated flatly while pointing the sticky spoon at me. She held out her bowl clearly asking for more.

"No Sasha, you've had enough," I told her firmly. "You weren't listening, so I had to hit you."

The imp glared at me and in that moment she looked so much like Uncle George that it brought back memories. I couldn't help it. I broke out in laughter.

MY HUMBLE BEGINNINGS

"It's not funny Uncle Wine!"

"No, it's not," I agreed. If she could talk, then she could be reasoned with. "Sasha." I looked her in the eyes, as I pushed my bowl of half melted ice cream over. "You can have this instead. Listen to me while I talk."

The imp grimaced, and I could see the gears grinding away in her head. She nodded and accepted the bowl. I felt like we had just declared a truce.

"Sasha, I don't want to hit you. I'm sorry I lost my temper," I apologised sincerely to her. "Eomma told me that you are a good girl, who knows how to behave well."

Sasha bristled, "Uncle Wine you are a very bad man. You sent Eomma away."

I puffed my cheeks out in a sigh. "Omma has to go back to take care of something." I prayed to the heavens that this excuse would work.

Sasha frowned and said carefully "A bee-sin-ness- trip?" she asked.

I nodded firmly. "Yes, she has to take care of work."

"When will she be back?" Sasha asked then returned to licking both bowls free of ice cream.

"I don't know Sasha. We are stuck with each other." I pointed at her ice cream "Do you want more of the good things? Ice cream, toys, and fun?"

Sasha glared at me, apparently too wise and wary to be taken in by gifts.

"You've got a choice Sasha, you can behave well and China will be fun for you, or there will be no ice cream, no treats, no fun," I told her sternly. With children and dogs, you must lay down the law. "What do you want?"

"I want phone," Sasha stated firmly. "I want Mmma."

Good, we were getting somewhere. "I cannot give you Omma, I can get you a phone."

I treated her to a stern glare of my own. "You must behave and be a good girl," I told her. "Right now, it's past your bedtime. Wash your face and go to bed. Tomorrow, if you behave, I'll get you your phone."

I had an old iPhone she could use, but I needed to make it kid-proof. I was told to supervise all phone and internet time.

The imp clambered out of her seat, clutching the bowls. Falling down the last few inches and landing on her rump did not faze her. She politely put her dirty dishes in the sink, using a nearby stool to do so. She washed her face too. When she was done, she climbed down, turned to me an announced "Finished!" in proud tones.

"I go to bed now Uncle Wine." With that, she stalked off to sleep in the wreck of her room. I stared at her in amazement. She was remarkably precocious for a child of her age.

FULL CIRCLE GHANA

HOME AGAIN

"Jolie! Come into the kitchen! We have to talk!"

It was the dry season in Ghana, and the heat had cured us all of any motivation to move. The leather couch sat stuck to my skin despite

MY HUMBLE BEGINNINGS

the fan I had pointing at me. The ice tea next to me was sweating. Mama was still too frugal to allow me to turn on the air-conditioner I had put ineven though it ran off solar energy.

Reality TV and post-lunch programming of reruns provided the perfect cover for my idle brooding.

"Jolie!" My mother's stern tone had me on my feet. Parents install our emotional buttons and despite your best efforts to remove them, they know how to use them.

I dragged myself off the couch and into the kitchen.

"Yes, Mama," I answered politely. I was a grown man, but when my mother called, I came running and sat down like a good boy when she said so. She was my mother and we shared a bond not even God could break. I would not be here on God's green earth without her and her efforts at holding the family together.

Mama Adel was busy chopping peppers and onions for dinner. I suspected this was for the church social tomorrow.

"Go get the coffee brewing on the stove. Use the good China up in the cupboard. There are some leftovers from this morning. Bring them out and reheat them in the microwave. We need to talk." Her knife never stopped moving as she spoke. Mama had taught Gina all that she knew about cooking.

Outside in the courtyard, Sasha and some neighbourhood kids were laughing as they chanted the skipping rope song.

"Yes Mama," I replied as I did as I was told. This kitchen wasn't mine. All the cupboards were painted in bright colours- Janet's work- but not carved. I found a dish of garden eggs in the fridge that was earmarked for dinner that night. I made a mental note to "accidentally" toss it out for the chickens and have it replaced with something much more palatable. The stuff was disgusting. I could never stand to eat the slimy things.

I joined Mama Adel at the kitchen table, to lay out a feast of food. My sisters never stinted me every time I came back. They always laid out a feast. I found that I had been missing the taste and flavours of home when I sat down to eat at their table.

Mama Adel eyed my plating skills critically. "Passable," she grunted. "Good thing that Blues of yours is a better cook. You never did like being in the kitchen child."

I shrugged my shoulders, to declare to her cooking was only a means to an end.

Mama pushed up her eyeglasses with her wrist.

"Son, what are you going to do about Sasha?"

I poured a tall glass of iced coffee.

"I'm thinking of putting her in boarding school," I kept mine plain, and desperately wished for a beer instead. I couldn't take it and got up to get the other chopping board and knife to help her. Mama Adel tipped the neatly sliced onions into a glass mixing bowl next to her.

"Thank you child." She pointed at the onions with the tip of her knife, "Chop length ways."

We worked in tandem, enjoying a companionable silence.

"I never asked for this" I confessed. "You're always saying God has his plans for us. I just wish for once, they included a stretch of peace. It's been one crisis after another." The onions made my eyes sting, and they started watering. I felt so weary.

MY HUMBLE BEGINNINGS

"I don't know what to do with her."

My knife picked up speed as I vented my feelings on the poor innocent onions. "I don't want to, but I cannot refuse to take responsibility."

Mama Adel laid down her knife. I could her the clock tick-tock in the afternoon silence. The girls had gone over to badger the next-door aunty and uncle for treats.

"Son, let me tell you something. Who are you to say that this is not God's design for you?" I put down my knife to take a sip of coffee and waited as Mama Adel continued, "All children are a gift. Don't blame Sakura she had a difficult choice, just like I had." I gaped at her.

"Mama" I asked weakly "Who?"

"Son, when you were conceived, it was unexpected. Gina was still nursing at that time, and it would have been bad luck to have another baby so soon. It would have killed us all. Your father was so angry. We had a big fight, and he did not talk to me until you were born. When he held you in his hands, that's when he forgave me."

I understood the words my mother was speaking but failed to make any sense of it. A tingle started up in the back of my head.

"He took me to the hospital to get an abortion. The same hospital that you were later born in."

Reality seemed optional at that point. Looking upon my mother's face, she did not seem real. Neither were my hands for that matter, forcing me to drop the knife. Mama Adel's speech marched on.

"The nurses told your father to wait outside and they took me to a hospital bed and gave me a pill to swallow. I asked for a glass of water and hid the pill under my tongue." She grinned slyly. "I tricked them. I left the glass on the bedside and then complained of nausea. They let me go outside to vomit. I spat the pill out and hid it under a bush. You wouldn't be here if I had swallowed that pill."

She reached over and patted my hands. "Son, I appreciate everything you've done for me and the family. I know it hasn't been easy." Mama Adel counted off on her fingers, "Out of all your brothers, you are the only one who stayed and supported us. Despite everything, we are still grateful for it."

I tried to say, "But Mandy…"

She shook her head to forestall me. "Your sister, Janet, thinks all men are useless." Picking up her knife she continued chopping onions. I think it must have been the onions that made my eyes water, for tears dripped down my cheeks. "If it weren't for you supporting us, we would not be as well off as we are today." She held up a hand to stall my protests once more. "Oh, Gina would not have gotten her start if you hadn't helped her. Janet would not have been able to expand her workshop or a business if you hadn't invested money into our vegetable garden and helped pay the bills. You put food on the table son and a roof over my head. When you were small," she held her hand up by her knee, "This tall, you were already trying to help. You never asked for lunch but always managed to find it, at least for yourself and your sisters six days out of seven in a week." Mama Adel smiled at me, and that smile brought me back to reality. "Who is to say that you were not a gift then and now?" She asked. I had no answer for that.

She paused deliberately. "Sasha could live with us you know. Your sisters love her and she is happy here. Over here, she'll just be a pretty light-skinned ewe girl."

Right on cue, Janet and Gina clomped into the kitchen from the backdoor, hauling being them was a crestfallen Sasha. They were

MY HUMBLE BEGINNINGS

squabbling in a mix of English and broken ewe on Sasha's part. The Pixie had my gift of languages and absorbed them like a sponge.

Janet marched right up to me and cackled "She's yours alright, she's got the same look you had, when you were caught doing something you shouldn't."

I turned to my sisters and asked with a weary sigh, "What was she doing this time?" I was too emotionally exhausted to deal with this.

The Pixie tugged on my hand. "Uncle Wine, Aunt Janet says that I can't go out with her after dinner."

I Looked over to Janet who replied in Twi, "I'm going to visit a friend." Her arched eyebrow left no uncertain doubt who or what that friend was. "We're going clubbing after," Janet explained.

I patted Sasha's hand. "Yes child, when you are older. After dinner time is grown-up time. We talked about this remember?" I told her sternly in mandarin. Sasha pouted but was too ladylike to stomp her foot in anger.

Mama Adel cackled "Yes, son. You wore the same expression when I told you to go take a shower."

I turned to my daughter and said, "Go wash your face and take a shower. We're going out to dinner." Sasha clenched her fist, stalking out of the kitchen, and muttering to herself in an odd mixture of Korean, English, Mandarin, and broken ewe. Ah, perils of being a polyglot.

Mama Adel shrugged and finished up the last of the onions. "What harm could there be. I was just about to start dinner."

My sisters said in unison, "We have plans." I hated when they did that. It was creepy then, and still was. I had to suppress a shudder.

Mama Adel put away her onions with satisfaction. She was laying out a feast for tomorrow's church social and had just gotten all the prep work done. They looked at each other, then at me.

"It'll be an early dinner. Sasha eats dinner around seven. Any later she can't sleep and her schedule gets all messed up." I sat up straight. "Come on! It'll be good for us. When was the last time all of us got together in public?"

Gina frowned. "I can't remember."

I turned to Gina. "Does your restaurant have a table? Could I book one for all of us?"

The clock chimed five in the evening. I could hear the call to prayer from a mosque nearby. Gina furrowed her lips in an Uncle George-ish manner that gave me a pang of grief. I missed him badly, even after all those years.

Firing off a short message, Gina answered "Yes, my head waiter just informed me we have a spare table."

EPILOGE

I was settled into my bed in the guest room, relaxing into food-induced somnolence while watching the mini-television I bought. It gave my eyes someplace to rest, while I thought. Sasha had her own room and was asleep across the hallway. My phone rang on the other side of the table. It was Blues.

"Hey babes! Late shift at the hospital?" I answered with sympathy. It had to be close to 4 am back in China.

"Have you eaten? Do you want me to order you something to eat?" I could order food for Blues through the internet even halfway around the globe. It was a marvellous thing.

MY HUMBLE BEGINNINGS

"Wine." Blues said abruptly. "What do you think about having a child?" The silence between us seemed strained.

"I would love for you to have our children," I said cautiously. There had to be something I was missing.

I heard her exhale explosively along with the rustle of papers and the clink of a coffee cup. I waited for the other shoe to drop.

"Wine, I'm pregnant."

Milton Keynes UK
Ingram Content Group UK Ltd.
UKHW022341030324
438776UK00013B/2035